Cassie Edwards
THE SAVAGE SERIES

SAVAGE PROMISE

Letitia knew that she should draw away from Kanuga, but
his flesh against hers, where his thumb was now caressing
her beneath her chin, made ecstasy move in with bone-
weakening intensity. With one bold movement he swept her
into his arms. All thoughts of her father were forgotten when
he leaned over her with burning eyes, his mouth too soon
covering hers with a reckless passion.

With a moan of ecstasy, she gave him back his kiss, her
arms twining around his neck. All of her senses were
centered on the pounding of her heart and the need that he
was arousing within her.

D0816275

CASSIE EDWARDS

SAVAGE
Promise

LEISURE BOOKS NEW YORK CITY

A LEISURE BOOK®

February 1992

Published by

Dorchester Publishing Co., Inc.
276 Fifth Avenue
New York, NY 10001

SAVAGE
Promise

With much love I dedicate *Savage Promise* to:
My sister-in-Law Delores Cobb and her family;
My brothers Fred Cline and Joe Decker and their families;
My son Brian, for being himself — sweet and caring;
My friends Steve and Darlene Strupp and their children; and
My husband Charlie, for whom I write all of my books.

Once a proud race,
Is now down on their knees.
What broke their iron-clad will?
The white man's greed.

Once across the plains,
Their homes could be seen.
Life was for the living,
The peaceful, free and serene.

Once upon a time,
That fateful day came,
Carefree lives were taken,
Life was never the same.

Once the white man came,
Not bothering to see.
The Indians tried to be friends,
But that could never be.

Oh, yes, there were the special ones,
They seemed to understand.
But they could not change the mind,
Of God's immortal white man.

So much blood was spilled,
Freedom taken away.
Oh, great American Indian,
It should not have ended this way.

—MISSY GRBOVAC
Romance reader and
devoted fan.

Introduction

The Tlingit Indians are the northernmost Indians of the North Pacific coast of North America, inhabiting the islands and coastal lands of southern Alaska. For the most part, the Tlingit lived peacefully among themselves until the arrival of the white men in the 1700's. In time, the Tlingit, the tribal name meaning 'people', were forced to co-exist peacefully with both the Russians and the Americans, for nothing or no one could stop the flow of traders who sought the gleaming gold pelts of the marten, the shiny pelts of the mink and sea otter, and the thick and silky furs of the silver and blue fox.

Chapter One

Courage consists not in blindly overlooking danger,
But in seeing it, and conquering it.

—RICHTER

ALASKA, THE TLINGIT INDIAN TERRITORY
EARLY SPRING, 1780

The wild wind was whipping snow horizontally before it, the sibilant rush a deafening hiss. Though she was clad in furs, the cold bit into Letitia Wilson like a thousand icy teeth, the wind worse than the low temperatures because it was pulling heat away from her body.

Before leaving her father's brig, the *Stacy*, Letitia's first impulse had been to pile on as many layers of warm clothes as possible, but her father had warned her not to, instructing her that that would lead to perspiration, which then would lead to frost inside her clothing.

Sobbing, and with her rifle aimed straight ahead, Letitia hovered near her father, who lay half-conscious in the snow, in a pool of his own blood. She wanted to see if his wounds were fatal, but she had to keep her eyes alert for the bear. It had only been a few minutes since it retreated. One of the biggest polar bears that she had ever seen—perhaps three quarters of a ton—its threat would remain as long as it was alive.

Letitia's gloved fingers shook violently from fear as she continued to watch through the blinding, swirling gale for the bear to return. After it had attacked and mauled her father she had managed only one shot at the large beast before it bounded away into the unpenetrable sheet of snow.

She wasn't sure if it had fled because it was wounded—or because it was momentarily frightened by the blast of her weapon.

The bear had appeared suddenly out of the blinding tempest. Her father had had no chance to fire his rifle before the bear jumped him. Its claws had quickly penetrated her father's fur garments, more quickly than Letitia could grab her father's rifle and shoot it.

Letitia knew that the bear could appear just as quickly a second time, but should it decide to attack again, she was ready for it!

She winced when her father groaned with pain, but still she did not dare glance his way. The bear could choose that exact moment to attack!

If only her father had been given some warning earlier that the damnable bear was near, she thought woefully. Jerome Wilson was skilled with all firearms. Nothing would ever have had a chance against him under normal circumstances.

Not that these were normal circumstances, Letitia thought, her teeth chattering. Getting lost in the Alaskan wilderness at age eighteen was never part of her plan.

She was afraid of frostbite. Already her face was feeling strangely tight where it was exposed, her fur hood only framing her delicate facial features. The sudden spring storm had separated her and her father from the rest of the American explorers who had come to Alaska from New York to find a location for their trading post and fort.

Letitia tried not to think of what the other explorers' doom might be, although her fiancé, Jonathan Beals, was among them. Right now she had to concentrate on her father's survival and her own. All around them the raging waves of snow swept through the trees. Branches snapped in the wind. Huge fir trees were being uprooted with a sound like gunfire.

Suddenly, a movement and a flash of white fur emerged out of nowhere, as the bear again approached Letitia and her father on its hind legs, its claws distended, its sharp teeth bared.

Though pale and rigid with fright, Letitia put pressure on the trigger of the rifle. She was momentarily thrown off guard when she spied a trickle of blood spoiling the polar bear's magnificent white pelt. Now she knew that she had shot the animal earlier! It had just not been enough to stop the huge creature. The bullet had only stunned the bear for a few minutes; then, surely angrier because of its pain, the bear was making its second attack on its victims!

This time Letitia had to be sure that her aim was more accurate. She would not have time to fire more than once.

If that did not do it ...

Suddenly the sound of gunfire through the hissing of the blizzard made Letitia jump with a start. She watched in amazement as the bear's body jerked several times with the impact of the bullets into it, and blood spattered everywhere. She lowered her rifle slowly to her side as the animal crumpled into a heap of fur and blood onto the white ground.

Then Letitia's eyes widened in wonder as a dogsled pulled by many huskies appeared through the haze of blowing snow. Her fingers tightened about the rifle. Though this man had obviously saved both her and her father's lives, she feared who it might be. If the stranger was a Russian, then her father's plans to foil the Russians would be spoiled.

If it was a Tlingit Indian, she had no idea what to expect. For the most part the Indians were known to be peaceful, yet she had been warned by her father of their growing discontent with the white people who continued to invade their hunting ground, eager for *brown gold*—furs, which the Indians claimed belonged only to them.

Letitia had studied books and newspaper articles about the Tlingit Indians before making this journey to Alaska and had discovered that the Tlingit chief, Kanuga, was friendly with the Russians.

But what of the Americans? As far as she knew, it had been many years since the first American missionary had first approached the Tlingit with their teachings of the Bible.

But at this moment it mattered not to her who had arrived on that dogsled firing his weapon at the horrible bear. Her father could now be taken to warmth and shelter. His wounds could be medicated.

Finally able to check on her father, Letitia dropped her rifle and moved to her knees beside him. She touched his face, relieved when his eyes flickered open and he looked up at her, his lips trembling as he so very softly spoke her name.

"Papa, you're going to be all right," Letitia tried to reassure him. "Help has arrived." She looked at the blood oozing from the wounds on his chest, freezing in jet streams on his shredded fur coat. "We'll get you some place warm. Your wounds will be seen to."

Letitia looked quickly away from him as the long string of huskies pulling the dogsled stopped close beside her. A man clad in a dazzling white coat of polar bear fur stepped down from the sled and came to stand over her. He reached a gloved hand to her. She hesitated, then let him help her up.

When she was standing and close enough to see the stranger's face, the copper color of it contrasting with the white of his fur hood, she found herself staring. It was not so much because he was an Indian. It was his absolute handsomeness! He was tall. His silver eyes were intense, his cheekbones hard. His nose was straight, and his lips were sensitively sculpted.

Kanuga was taken a back by the face that he discovered framed by the fur hood. It was a woman who stared up at him, not a man! In one sweep of his eyes he discovered intriguing blue eyes fringed with heavy golden lashes, a full, ripe mouth, and delicately chiseled features. Though the hood of her fur garment covered most of her hair, some silken fronds had fallen free at her brow and cheeks. Her hair was golden, the color of the sun.

Finding a white woman wandering alongside a man in the Alaskan wilderness was not a usual thing.

Forcing his eyes from this woman of intriguing beauty, he looked down at the wounded man and instantly saw that he was in need of quick medical attention. The bear had inflicted life-threatening wounds.

But Kanuga knew that the man's weakened state from loss of blood and exposure of the wound to the frigid air were more of a threat than the wound itself.

Though it was not something that Kanuga

wanted to do, having grown weary of the white intruders in the Tlingit Territory long ago, he had no choice but to offer help. He was known for his gentle ways and kind heart. It was no different now, no matter the color of the skin. He would not let this man die.

Kanuga looked slowly at Letitia. What was this man to her, he wondered? Was he her husband? Should the man die, what then of her?

But he cast this wonder from his mind. She had to be a Russian, from Fort Anecia. As soon as the storm abated, he would deliver her and her male companion back to the fort. Her fascination would end there!

"*Hade-krigut*," Kanuga said, nodding toward his dogsled. "You will come." He bent to one knee and picked Letitia's father up in his arms and carried him to the sled, a flat-bottomed toboggan of narrow boards curled up in front.

Concluding that this Indian had learned the English language from the American missionaries, Letitia watched him, not knowing whether to be afraid or just grateful that he had happened along in time to rescue her and her father.

After the Indian had covered her father with many furs, her eyes followed him to the bear, then were drawn away when through the swirling snow came the plaintive, drawn-out howls of wolves. She shuddered and clasped her arms about herself, trying not to worry about the threat of the wolves and recalling what her father had said about them—that even a hungry pack rarely attacked a human being. Still, the howling seemed to be drawing closer and closer.

Kanuga stood over the bear, gazing down at it. Reaching inside his fur coat, he withdrew a tiny buckskin pouch. Opening it, he sprinkled sacred eagle down from it over the bear so that the animal would not be offended and its spirit would have no fear of returning to the vicinity of Kanuga's village after its reincarnation. Then he bound the bear with a rope to the back of the sled so that it could be dragged behind it.

Then he took Letitia by one elbow and walked her to the sled, urging her, without troubling himself to speak to her, to sit down beside her father. All the while he frowned down at her, but he offered her several furs and blankets to cover herself.

His aloofness and the quiet anger in his eyes worried Letitia. Though he was generous now, what were his plans for later?

"Are my father and I now your captives?" she asked guardedly. "Where are you taking us? What will you do with us? My father is injured badly. Please help him."

Kanuga's eyes lit up when she revealed that the man was her father.

Yet that should not matter to him, he quickly reminded himself. He would not allow her to be anything to him!

"Do not fear me," Kanuga said, his eyes locked with hers. "Kanuga is a *ach-run*—friend. Your father will be cared for. Then you will be allowed to go."

Letitia's eyebrows arched. She recognized his

name. This Indian was not just any Indian, he was a powerful chief!

She was not sure if it was a blessing or a curse that he, personally, had saved them from the bear. Surely he looked on them with pure contempt as just more intruders on his land.

But that he had bothered to save them gave her reason to hope.

"Thank you so much," Letitia murmured, hoping to win him over with pure kindness. She smiled up at Kanuga as he shook out the bundle of furs that lay on her lap and gently covered her with them. "You speak English quite fluently," she said. "Do all of your people?"

Kanuga gave her a steady, silent stare, not responding to her question nor commenting on *her* ability to speak English, since all of the Russians at Fort Anecia knew the English language as well as they knew Russian, having learned it for trading purposes with occasional traders from America.

Though unnerved by his steady stare and his abrupt silence, Letitia continued to talk to him. "You call yourself Kanuga," she said. "I not only know that you are a chief, but I also know the meaning of your name. Before traveling to Alaska I studied the Tlingit language. Your name fits you well, for I know that Kanuga means 'silver eyes.'"

When he again did not respond in any fashion to what she said, she quickly added, "My name is Letitia. Letitia Wilson." She offered him her gloved hand in friendship and it was also ignored. She slowly eased her hand beneath the thick covering of furs, her smile waning.

Knowing that it was best not to enter into friendly conversation with the woman, for he was already too obsessed by forbidden thoughts about her, Kanuga turned his face away and went to stand at his position at the back of the sled. Grabbing his whip, he snapped it in the air over the backs of the huskies, alerting them to follow his command to move onward. Soon the sled was sliding through deep snow, the dog's breaths like white silver in the wind.

Letitia held her gloves to her face to ward off the freezing cold that was biting into her flesh. She peered anxiously over the gloves when she heard the howls of the wolves again. Her insides quaking, she grabbed for her father so that he would not be thrown from the sled when the huskies were ordered to stop and the sled lurched to a sudden halt.

Kanuga grabbed his rifle and aimed at the many gray shadows that were moving soundlessly into view out of the vast, snowy mist. The shadows took the form of wolves as they moved closer, and Letitia's breath caught in her throat. As a spattering of gunfire filled the air, she flinched. One wolf, then two fell to the ground.

Then everything became a frenzy as several of the surviving wolves pounced on those that had fallen and proceeded to tear them to pieces with their sharp teeth, while others came nearer and nearer, standing in a semicircle around the sled, baring their teeth as they growled.

Kanuga aimed his rifle again and fired right into

the mouth of one of the wolves. While it was being devoured by the pack, he jumped from the sled and loosened the bear and rolled it toward those that had broken away from the frenzy of the others. He regretted losing the pelt to the wolves, but he could tell that it was an old bear, one that was not eatable. Bears of such an age often had parasites deadly to humans.

Now that all of the surviving wolves were busy tearing the dead wolves and the bear apart, leaving none that were interested in anything but the meal at hand, Kanuga jumped back on the sled and snapped his whip until the huskies resumed their journey through the whipping wind and the grinding sheet of white.

Sobbing, her whole body trembling from the ordeal, Letitia snuggled close to her father, relieved when he managed a smile of reassurance for her.

But too quickly doubts assailed her again, leaving her almost limp with grief and fear. "Oh, Papa," she sobbed. "Where are Jonathan and the others? Do you think they are—dead?"

Jerome's face became distorted with pain, and Letitia regretted having voiced her worries. But she could hardly bear to think of her fiancé out there somewhere, possibly alone, dying from exposure or worse—from the attack of bears or wolves. Though she had not loved Jonathan the way a woman should love a man when she accepted his proposal of marriage, she had cared for him immensely. They had been friends since childhood. And at the time it had seemed easier to accept his proposal of marriage than to wait for the right man to come along. Especially since her father had decided to move to what she considered the ends of the earth.

To Alaska!

Letitia would have never guessed that there was a man in Alaska who could stir longings within her.

But of course, she had not known there would be someone as intriguing and handsome as Kanuga!

Her thoughts returned to Jonathan, of the future they had planned together. She had always known that theirs would not be a passionate marriage. It would be one of mutual understanding and caring. If anything had happened to Jonathan now, she would mourn the loss, but she would only miss him as friends miss one another.

Never as a lover.

Soon the dogsled arrived at a village consisting of massive cedar plank houses known as longhouses. A village by a river, it had been established in a sheltered location near a small bay that offered protection from sudden, violent storms.

As though guarding them, masses of totem poles fronted the houses, some of which served as house posts, in that they supported heavy logs which formed the main roof beams over the main log framework of the building. The brilliance of the blacks, reds, and blue-greens used in the painting on the totem poles and in the heraldic designs which gaily decorated some of the larger longhouses, caused Letitia to gasp in admiration, for this lent a majesty to the buildings, which were already impressive because of their size. And to think she had envisioned most Indians living in primitive ice houses!

Letitia gaped openly when Kanuga directed his huskies to stop beside a house that was much larger and more impressive than the others. Its planking seemed to have been whitewashed and covered with magnificent painted symbols in the design of a beaver, most surely to denote Kanuga's lineage.

Kanuga jumped from the sled and hurried to Letitia's father. He lifted him up into his arms and glanced over at Letitia. "*Hande*," he said, walking toward the door of the longhouse, which was framed by a totem pole. "This way. *Jet-a-nelch*, it is warm inside."

Shivering from the intense cold, Letitia cast off the furs and followed Kanuga into the house. Inside, a welcoming fire, its smoke rising through a hole in the roof, provided both heat and light. A seal-oil lamp flickered its golden light on a setting that Letitia felt was mystical, even otherworldly.

A keen fascination swept through her.

The brig *Stacy* lay at anchor in the Taku River. Bundled snugly in warm furs, Kimberly Wilson stood at the ship's rail, looking down at a treacherous, brilliant river of ice that was broken into jumbled ridges and criscrossed by wide breaks.

Then she looked into the distance, realizing

that she was witnessing a *whiteout*. The snow was ever-swirling, the clouds hiding the sun and diffusing the light so evenly that no shadows were cast, white snow and white sky weirdly becoming one.

And then there were the shots that she had heard only moments ago. Everything that she called precious in her life may have been snatched from her because of her husband's eagerness to settle in Alaska and her daughter's adventurous nature, which compelled her to follow along with him everywhere he went, as though she were a man, the son Kimberly and Jerome Wilson had never been able to have.

"Oh, Letitia," Kimberly cried, sniffing back tears. "Where are you? Why didn't you stay on the ship with me?"

"What is it that you are worrying about now?" Barbara asked, moving to her aunt's side. She hugged her fur coat around her, and her nostrils flared in the cold, whipping wind. "Why are you out here? You are going to take a chill."

Kimberly turned and gazed at her niece. Barbara was not at all like her father, God rest his soul, who had been Kimberly's beloved brother. Of late, Kimberly had become uncomfortable in her niece's presence. Somehow she had lost control of her. Barbara's desires were not of the saintly sort.

"I was worrying about Letitia and Jerome," Kimberly murmured, speaking over her shoulder as she turned and walked toward the companionway ladder, which led to the cabins below deck. "Did you hear gunfire, Barbara? I'm sure I did. I am so worried."

Barbara hurried down the steps beside Kimberly, on down a dim corridor, and opened the door for her aunt, then followed her into the master cabin, glad to step inside its toasty warmth. She closed the door and removed her coat and threw herself on the bed. Stretching out on her stomach, she rested her chin in her hands as she looked up at her aunt with an evil sort of glint in her slanted green eyes.

"Auntie, you worry too much," she scolded. "Uncle Jerome and Letitia can take care of themselves. It's ourselves that we should be concerned about. Don't you feel abandoned? Almost every last man on this ship worth anything is among the explorers who left with Uncle Jerome."

Barbara frowned and tossed herself over to lie on her back. "Every last damn man in the world seems lost to me up here in this forsaken, frozen country," she whispered to herself, making sure that her aunt didn't hear. How long had it been since she had been with a man? The need was gnawing at her, twisting as though a hot poker were scorching her. She was hungry for a man, yet not so much that she had slept with the ship's crew. She looked on them as filthy and beneath her. She was used to affluent men and those with status in the community, who paid her well for time spent with her.

"Barbara, I'll be back," Kimberly said, going back to the door and opening it again.

Barbara rose quickly to a sitting position. She

crossed her legs beneath her silk dress, the low neckline of which revealed well-rounded breasts. Her raven black hair hung in a silken sheen across her shoulders and down her back. "Aunt Kimberly, where are you off to now?" she asked, sighing languidly.

"To the chapel," Kimberly said sullenly. "I plan to light three candles—one for Jerome, one for Letitia, and one for Jonathan."

"Why not light candles for the whole missing team of explorers?" Barbara giggled. "That would keep your mind off your worries. Lighting that many candles would busy your hands for hours."

Kimberly pursed her lips together and slouched her thin shoulders, realizing that Barbara was poking fun at her and hurting inside over her niece's incapacity to care as deeply for humanity as she should. Since Barbara's parents' deaths, she had changed into someone Kimberly hardly knew at all.

And, oh, how that saddened her!

Kimberly and her husband had willingly taken Barbara in to raise as their own at the tender age of eleven, but Kimberly could not help feeling now that she had failed her beloved brother terribly.

Balding, with tufts of corn-colored hair collecting about his ears and on his bare chest, Colonel Alexsei Golodoff stood shirtless before his fireplace in his office at Fort Anecia. He was sipping vodka from a long-stemmed glass, alternating drinks with long drags on his cigar.

Frowning, Colonel Golodoff glanced toward the window behind his desk. The snowstorm was still raging. He could hear the whistle of the wind down the chimney and around the corners of this two-storied building which housed his office and living quarters. He forked a heavy, golden eyebrow and stroked his graying beard with his free hand as he pondered the sound of gunfire that he had heard a short while ago. None of his Russian trappers were out in the storm. He had ordered them to stay in their cabins until further word.

So who had fired the gun? There had been more than one blast echoing across the snow-covered plain.

He went to a table where food was piled on a platter. He eyed the *kulich*, a sweet Russian bread decorated with frosting, but chose a *perozhke*, a pastry filled with a meat mixture.

He ate this delicacy in quick bites, then went back to the fireplace and stared into the flames that circled the logs on the grate. Perhaps he had not really heard gunfire. It was probably only more firs being uprooted. He had heard more than one tree snapping from the ground like gunfire beneath the force of the wind since he'd lived in Alaska. He was certainly not going to send any of his men out in this damn weather to investigate. They'd be fair bait for anything that had got stirred from its hibernation sooner than planned. Spring was taking its damn time this year.

He became lost in thought as he tipped the

glass to his lips and let the rest of the vodka slide down his throat. A man of iron determination, his flaring nostrils had caught the heady scent of an empire long ago. The aroma had led him, siren-like, to these lands. Upon his arrival, he had explained to the Tlingit Indians that he was an assistant to the great Russian emperor, the Czar, and that the Czar had sent him to build a fort where the Russians could trade with the Tlingit.

The Tlingit had asked him what he was willing to give them in return for a small portion of their land, and Colonel Golodoff had cleverly produced an assortment of beads, bottles, and iron chisels from which to make their ceremonial paraphernalia in the form of woodcarvings, costumes, masks, and blankets.

The bargain had been quickly sealed.

Thus, for a time, the *promyshlenniki*, Russian fur hunters, had descended on Alaska like a human plague.

Until Kanuga had become chief.

The Colonel plodded heavily to the liquor cabinet and poured himself a more potent drink, a fiery *braga*, a drink fermented from fruits, yeast, and sugar. He drank it quickly and set the empty glass aside.

"No, I'm not going to bother with anything out in that weather today," he said to himself. He went back to his desk and lowered himself tiredly into his chair, propping his bare feet up on his desk. "Nothing or nobody would survive long out there today. I'm glad I'm here and they're there."

His shaggy brows lowered, knotting over his

hawk nose; he laughed throatily as he rested his head against the back of the chair and soon dozed softly, his dreams filled as always with the "brown gold," the furs of Alaska, and how he could trick Kanuga out of more of them.

Chapter Two

Thy words have darted hope into my soul,
And comfort dawns upon me.

— SOUTHERN

The daylight was filtering through the smokehole overhead with a pale blue shimmering light. Letitia looked slowly around the room, observing how the Tlingit chief lived as Kanuga placed her father on a pallet of furs close to the fire.

The caribou-hide floor was sunken to leave benches at ground level for sitting. The large house was divided into three rooms by planked screens with small oval openings cut through their centers and painted images.

A profusion of carved articles littered the outer room, and carved friezes decorated the raised platforms along the outside walls. Straining her neck, Letitia could see beds in the other rooms, covered with blankets and furs.

Strips of cedar bark, lengths of mountain-goat wool and dog hair, and bundles of sea-lion whiskers were piled up beneath the platforms in the outer room, presumably to be used in various crafts.

She looked around the room again and saw carved and painted cedar settees with elaborate forms of backrests and side panels beside the fire and stores of baled-up food on shelves along the outer walls. Bladder bags, packed with fish oil, were suspended from the roof, together with racks on which fish had been left to smoke dry.

A moan of pain drew Letitia out of her fascinated perusal of her surroundings. She looked down at her father; his lips were trembling and his nostrils quivered with each breath. Yet, thankfully, having been placed so close to the warmth of the fire, his face had already lost some of its bluish pallor.

Forgetting everything but her father's welfare, Letitia quickly jerked off her gloves and the coat she wore over her long-sleeved buckskin dress that clung to her, accentuating her supple figure and her well-formed breasts. She knelt and began removing her father's blood-soiled coat.

When it was off and the extent of his wounds was fully revealed to her, she turned her face away, a bitterness rushing into her throat as she fought the urge to retch.

She looked quickly at Kanuga, who was suddenly beside her with a basin of water. They exchanged looks and she felt a blush heat up her cheeks when his gaze lowered and swept over her, keen admiration in his eyes.

In that moment she was also able to assess him, for he had shed his polar-bear garment. Silently she admired his powerful, muscled build beneath his fringed buckskin shirt trimmed with porcupine embroidery. His thigh muscles were flexed tight, straining against his buckskin trousers as he knelt close to her father. His dark hair fell loose to the shoulders; his silver eyes were intense and mesmerizing.

Kanuga looked quickly away from Letitia and busied himself with cutting Jerome's blood-soaked buckskin shirt down the front with a sharp knife, then laying it open so that he would have full access to the terrible gashes made by the bear's sharp and deadly claws.

Slipping his knife back inside the leather sheath at his waist, Kanuga then reached into the basin of water and lifted a cloth from it and wrung it out.

Letitia was just about to ask him to let her be the one to tend to her father's wounds, to cleanse them, when she was surprised by Kanuga's suddenly turning to her and reaching for her face with the damp cloth.

Wondering what his intentions could be, Letitia edged away from him. Her heart started to throb nervously when he followed her. She scarcely breathed when he wove his fingers through her hair and held her face in place and began dabbing her skin with the cloth.

"What . . . are . . . you doing?" she finally gasped, paling.

Kanuga did not answer her, just held the cloth away from her so that she could see tinges of red on it.

She moved a hand to her cheek. "What is that?" she murmured. "What did you wash from my face?"

"*Sche*," Kanuga said, rinsing the cloth. "Blood."

"Blood?" Letitia questioned. "Whose? I wasn't wounded." She glanced down at her father.

"When the bear was shot, it's blood most likely splattered," Kanuga said, smoothing more of the stain from her other cheek, his gaze moving over her again.

"Oh, I see," Letitia said, clearing her throat when again she felt herself being reviewed by his wandering eyes. She had to wonder what he was thinking. He did not smile, and within his eyes she saw a distant coldness, as though she were an enemy.

She quickly turned her attention back to her father. "Let me cleanse my father's wounds myself," she said, yet dreading the chore, afraid of hurting him. Such horrendous wounds must surely already be setting her father's soul afire with scourging pain!

"*Aganreka*," Kanuga said, willingly handing over the cloth to Letitia. "Very good. That will enable me to prepare a medicinal drink for your father. It will relax him. It will lessen the pain. It will help him ease into a peaceful sleep."

Letitia glanced at Kanuga questioningly. "I'm not sure...." she said, doubt thick in her voice.

"What is this drink made of? Are you sure it is safe?"

Kanuga's eyes danced, and his lips lifted into a smile. "No harm will come to your father," he said, standing and reaching for several herbs that hung dried and wrinkled from the rafters of his house. "It is a potion that has been handed down from generations of Tlingit. None have died yet who drank it."

A loose, nervous smile fluttered along Letitia's lips. She watched Kanuga long enough to see him grind the herbs up and sprinkle them into a tin cup of water, setting this into the hot coals of the fire to heat.

Then she looked away from him and began bathing her father's wounds, wincing as he flinched and cried out, his eyes hazed with pain.

Tears began streaming down Letitia's face. The wounds were clean enough now to see how serious they were. If he did not get medical attention soon, the deep gashes would become infected. If they became infected, he would not have a chance of surviving.

"Papa," Letitia said, flipping her hair back as she leaned down close to his face. "I love you, Papa. Oh, I love you so much."

Jerome licked his parched lips as he looked up at her. "Honey, things'll be all right," he tried to reassure her, his voice weak. "After the storm passes, get me back to the ship."

"But, Papa, if you aren't well enough to be moved, I can't take you anywhere," Letitia said, smoothing his thick red hair back from his brow.

"You must be given a chance to heal before you are taken out on a dogsled again."

Jerome glanced over at Kanuga, who was lifting the tin cup from the ashes of the fire, stirring more herbs into the warmed liquid. "He can take me safely back to the ship," he said raspily.

"We'll see," Letitia said, dropping the cloth into the water. She lifted the skirt of her buckskin dress and began tearing away the bottom half of her cotton slip. When she had enough of the white garment, she began wrapping it around her father's chest, securely tying it at the ends once his wound was completely covered.

Kanuga came to kneel beside her. "Give him this potion," he said, handing the cup to Letitia. "Tomorrow I will make an ointment for his wounds. Kanuga knows many secrets of the forest. Medicinal herbs is one of them."

Wondering why he was being so cooperative and friendly, Letitia only momentarily hesitated to take the cup of strange-smelling brew.

"Take it," Kanuga grumbled. "Trust Kanuga. Your father will be better off for it."

Then, seeing no threat in Kanuga, only strength and a great gentleness, Letitia accepted the cup, then knelt over her father. With one hand she held his head up from the pallet of furs. With the other she tilted the cup to his lips.

"Papa, Kanuga has made this for you," she murmured. "It will make you feel better. You will sleep. In sleep you will find release from the pain."

His eyes glassy, his face suddenly flushed with

the first signs of fever, Jerome let Letitia feed him the liquid. He choked and coughed, then emptied the cup and closed his eyes, already feeling a sort of euphoria claiming his senses. He inhaled a shaky breath and let himself float off into a peaceful, lethargic darkness.

Letitia eased her father's head back down and set the cup aside. She turned grateful eyes to Kanuga. "Thank you," she said humbly. "For everything, Kanuga. You are very kind."

Kanuga's insides stirred sensually, this woman's sweetness threatening to cause him to forget all of the reasons why he should not be drawn to her as a man is drawn to a woman. His gaze moved to her hair; its rich, golden tresses fell to her waist in a cascade of curls.

Then he looked at her breasts, stirred to a deep passion when he saw how rounded and mature they were for her seventeen or eighteen winters.

He bolted to his feet and moved to the other side of the fire, again forcing himself to ignore the intriguing white woman. He stared into the flames, determined not to be kind to Letitia anymore. He did not need her gratefulness. Everything that he had done was more for himself than for her. All he wanted was to get her father well enough to return to Fort Anecia so that Kanuga could get the man and his daughter from his mind.

He stared into the flames awhile longer, then could not help but look at Letitia again. She was so close, so lovely, so available. Should he choose to take her to his bed...

Stung by Kanuga's refusal to answer her, Letitia tried to ignore his presence. She pushed the basin of bloody water away from her and reached for a blanket to draw over her father's sleeping form.

She had kicked off her snowshoes when she first entered the house; now Letitia removed her boots and socks and wriggled her toes up close to the fire. Realizing that Kanuga had turned his gaze back to her and was now watching her every movement, her face became hot with a blush. She drew her feet back beneath her and crossed her legs so that she could hide her feet with the skirt of her dress. Still under Kanuga's close scrutiny, she squirmed uneasily.

Finally, unnerved by his silent stare, Letitia glared back at Kanuga and folded her arms angrily across her chest. "You have chosen to ignore what I say, so why do you continue looking at me?" she snapped angrily. "Haven't you ever seen an American woman before?"

Her lips parted and her eyes widened as a sudden thought seized her. "My Lord, you don't think my father and I are Russian, do you?" she gasped.

She moved quickly to her knees and looked across the fire, directly into his eyes. "Of course you wouldn't," she said. "I am not conversing with you in Russian."

Kanuga's heart leapt into his throat. If she was American, that meant that an American ship must have arrived at Alaskan Tlingit territory and that Americans were exploring, possibly to settle there. The Russians had caused him much stress. Must he now have the Americans to deal with? The thought filled him with much frustrated anger.

Knowing that she was not Russian pleased his very soul, yet he knew that it truly should make no difference to him, for he knew that he would have to rid his land of the Americans as well as the Russians. He was the chief of his people, and it was for their best interest that he did everything. And it was imperative that he return their land and pelts to the Tlingit!

"You are American? I thought you had learned the American language well, as most have at Fort Anccia, in order to trade with the Tlingit," he finally said. "The Tlingit learned the American language from American missionaries, who came long ago to teach ways of their gods. We do not waste time learning Russian. It is not necessary. The Russians will be leaving Alaska soon."

Relieved that Kanuga was finally talking with her, Letitia plied him with more questions, hoping to get answers before he decided to quit talking again. "Do you make war with the Russians?" she asked gingerly. "How many Russians are there in Alaska?"

"There are too many," was his brisk answer. His eyes lit with fire. "And, no, we have not made war with the Russians, but perhaps it will be required soon. They have been asked to leave. If they do not, then we shall see." He nodded, his jaw tight. "Yes. Soon we shall see."

"You do not welcome Americans to Alaska,

either, do you?" Letitia asked guardedly. "Would you use force to make us leave?"

"White people are no longer welcome to Tlingit territory," Kanuga said, his voice flat. "Russians or Americans. My father welcomed white people many years ago because they had goods to trade that were much desired by the Tlingit people. Great ships arrived with tools, clothing, firearms, food, and a variety of trinkets. But trouble began when our women were taken as wives without the customary payment for the privilege."

Letitia paled. "Why, how horrible," she gasped.

"Also, white traders accuse the Tlingit of being dishonest due to our practice of dyeing black furs red to increase their value." His eyes took on a far-away look as he stared into the flames of the fire. "It became known to me after my father's death that Broderick Bowman, the evil American trader at the Russian fort, presented my father with a letter of introduction which he was told to show to other traders he came in contact with. In the belief that these were complimentary, and not being able to read them to see how wrong he was to believe this, my father regarded them as personal privileges and displayed them with the other privileges he owned. The letters, of course, contained such compliments as 'This Indian is the biggest liar and cheat in Alaska.'"

"Broderick Bowman must be a most undesirable man," Letitia said. She paused, then added, "You said that he is an American. How is it that he lives with the Russians at Fort Anecia?"

"A few winters ago, this man was the only survivor of a shipwreck close to Alaska's shores," he said. "The Russians took him in. He became the voice of the Russian fort between the Russians and Tlingit. He is a clever, evil man."

Letitia then picked up on Kanuga's mention of his father. "You said that your father is dead," she murmured. "I am sorry, Kanuga."

She glanced around the house, then back at Kanuga. "Your mother," she said with an air of caution. "Is she still living?"

She swallowed uneasily. "Do you—have a wife?" she asked softly.

Kanuga's eyes locked with hers. "There is no wife. *Tu-iisch wuuna de klekak*," he said somberly. "My father died a year ago. So did my mother. They were buried in a snowslide." He held his shoulders proudly squared. "I then took the title of chief and serve my people well in that capacity."

Letitia smiled at him, her thick lashes fluttering nervously. "I am sure that you do, Kanuga," she said softly, feeling strangely thrilled to know that he was not married. "And I am sure that you will find a way to live in harmony with those who continue to come to Alaska, just as you have done thus far with the Russians."

Kanuga's jaw firmed solidly and his lips became tightly pursed. He started to say something, but stopped when Letitia's father emitted a blood-curdling scream and his body began to twitch.

Letitia gasped in alarm when she saw how

much more flushed his face was than before. She reached a hand to his brow and winced when the heat of his flesh seemed to melt into hers.

"Papa, oh Papa," she cried. "You have a raging temperature! What am I to do?"

Kanuga moved to his feet. He grabbed his hooded fur coat and stepped into his snowshoes. "Your father needs more than the medicine that I was going to offer him tomorrow," he said sternly. "My brother has recently been initiated into the society of healers. A shaman, he knows many powers of healing. I shall go for him. He shall perform his first healing ritual. Your father will be blessed to be the recipient of my brother's newly found magic."

Letitia did not have time to respond. Kanuga was already gone. She bit her lower lip in frustration. "Papa, now what am I to do?" she whispered. "Should I allow it? Or should I tell him to take his hocus-pocus elsewhere?"

Wolves were howling in the distance. The storm was still raging. "Papa, I have no choice but to let Kanuga's brother try and help you," she said, caressing his fevered brow. His eyes and mind were closed to all that was happening around him. "We have no choice, Papa. I must try anything and everything to get you well."

Chapter Three

She is a woman, therefore may be woo'd,
She is a woman, therefore may be won.
                              —SHAKESPEARE

Making ready for his shaman brother to arrive
for the curing ceremony, Kanuga spread fresh
shaggy moose and caribou hides on the floor and
placed cushions made of bundles of brushwood
covered with hare skins around the fire. Now he
and Letitia sat there, waiting in silence. Kanuga
tried not to look at Letitia, her loveliness disturbing him in ways he only wanted to feel for
the women of his tribe.

But it was as though she were a spirit beck-
oning to him, causing him to cast another quick
glance at her. The sight of her cascade of gleaming golden hair spilling across her shoulders,
resting on the magnificence of her breasts straining against the buckskin fabric of her dress,

proved just how hard it was for him to concentrate on anything but her.

With her delicate, flawless features, she was like a flower plucked out of the snow, all fresh and pure. When he had been close enough to her to catch her scent, he had thought that she even had the fragrance of the forest roses that bloomed in Alaska's brief summer months.

When she turned her eyes to him, so luminously blue, so trusting, he looked quickly away from her, his heart pounding. It seemed that too much lay in balance here, in the success of his shaman brother in healing this white woman's father. He could not deny how he hungered to have her full trust, just as he would like to trust her and the Americans who had accompanied her to the Alaskan wilderness for the pelts that had lured them there.

He could not deny that his feelings went even farther than merely hungering for shared trusts. He wished to hold Letitia in his arms, to become her sole protector!

Her sole lover!

And he knew that this was foolish.

His devotion was to his people, not to this woman. Feelings this strong for someone of a different skin color would bring nothing but tragedy to his people. He must not allow that to happen!

Forcing his thoughts away from Letitia, Kanuga looked toward the door, wondering what was keeping Atkuk. Perhaps his shaman brother, whose training was complete, his status as a full shaman publicly announced, did not wish to use his powers to heal the white man after all.

Yet it had always been Kanuga's belief that Atkuk's heart was good toward all men, no matter the color of their skin.

Kanuga was proud of his younger brother.

Letitia began to fidget with the ends of the hare skin covering the cushion on which she sat. She glanced from Kanuga to the door, then to her father, her trust in her decision to allow this healing ritual by a Tlingit shaman waning when she saw how her father's face crumpled with weary pain.

Where was Kanuga's brother? Had he become filled with doubts about performing his sacred rituals for an injured white man? Or did he not have enough faith in his powers to come as was requested of him by his chieftain brother?

If he was filled with such doubts, then she should fear even more a ritual that went against everything taught to her about her God all her life. Prayers should be enough at this time—at least until she could get her father to the ship where he could be seen to by a physician!

Yet deep down inside herself, she knew that she had no choice but to agree to this ceremony, since she and her father were far from their ship, at the mercy of the Tlingit people, while her father was too ill to travel.

Again she glanced over at Kanuga, realizing also that she had agreed to what he had advised to please him. Although she knew that to let herself fantasize over him was fruitless, she could not help but be filled with strange yearnings when their eyes made contact, and even at other times, when she was sneaking glances at him when he was not aware that she was.

Oh, but wasn't he so tall and powerfully built, like some golden god?

Mesmerized by him, she could not keep from staring at his bronzed face. It was so finely chiseled, displaying hard cheekbones, a straight nose and finely sculpted lips.

And his eyes! Whenever he looked at her, she could not help but marvel over how intense his eyes were, how silver!

So hypnotic—and dangerous!

A groan behind her drew Letitia quickly around. Guilt spread through her, knowing that her thoughts should be first and foremost about her father!

She bit her lower lip when she saw how his face was still distorted with pain, even though he was in some strange sort of lethargic sleep.

She started to rise, to go to him, but was stopped when she heard a strange sort of thumping noise outside the dwelling.

She leaned forward and looked quickly at Kanuga.

"That is my brother," Kanuga reassured her, seeing the alarm and questioning in her eyes. "He is tapping his staff on a board outside to warn of his approach."

He leaned closer to Letitia and held her arm in an effort to comfort her. "Do not be afraid," he said softly. "A limited number of people are inspired by stronger spirit powers than others.

These are our shamans. My brother is one of the blessed of the three shamans of my village. You will soon see his powers. Your father will feel them."

The weight of his hand on her arm, the warmth reaching through the buckskin fabric of her dress, made Letitia swallow hard. She had to force herself not to become caught up in fantasies again—not at this time. This time was meant to be solely her father's. Perhaps the shaman really could perform a miracle today.

If her own God would allow it.

Letitia's breath caught in her throat when a Tlingit Indian as tall, yet not as powerfully built, as Kanuga entered the dwelling. His blackened face glistened in the flicker of the fire, and his dark hair twisted and coiled into long, matted plaits beneath a headdress of grizzly-bear claws.

Letitia did not think he was as old as Kanuga, who was surely twenty-five years of age, and he had one distinctive difference in features. Contrasting against the blackness of his face, a tooth as white as snow protruded from his others where it had crowded in with another tooth, one atop the other, and pushed out to take on the appearance of a fang.

She wrenched her eyes away from the strange fang and saw that he was wrapped in thick bearskins; and when these fell to the floor at his feet, she saw that he wore a floor-length, painted caribou-skin robe.

Beneath the dancing light of the fire, Letitia could make out the designs on the robe—what the Tlingits called the devilfish, or *octupus*, with its long, sucker-covered tentacles.

She also recognized the *tekijek*, or water spirit, in the shape of a killer whale, featured as the central figure in the robe's design, the devilfish balanced by a painting of the whale on the opposite edge.

Letitia's gaze shifted, wary of what Atkuk had brought with him. In one hand he carried a buckskin bag and in his other what appeared to be some sort of grotesque puppet.

She watched guardedly as he crossed the room and knelt down beside her father, emptying things from his bag haphazardly, but then carefully arranging in order what were perhaps the symbols given to him by his *spirits*—the jointed puppet, a skull, a length of braided cedar bark, and a small box containing what looked like shark's teeth and oddly shaped pebbles.

As though he were in some sort of deep meditation, he placed a beaded necklace around his neck, on which were displayed amulets and charms with magic qualities. These were tufts of feathers and hair, small incised stones, and a bone headscratcher.

Letitia grew tense and started to rise, but was stopped by Kanuga's firm grip on her hand when Atkuk picked up the puppet and held it over her father. With rods, he manipulated its articulated joints into what appeared to be some sort of dance. Decorated with mica flakes, the puppet made a spectacular, dramatic performance as it swept up and around and over Letitia's father, accompanied by a throaty song sung by Atkuk.

When this was over, and the puppet was laid aside, Atkuk lifted two rattles, one for each hand, in the shape of a crane—a human-like figure forming the bird's backbone, with his head doubling as the bird's tail, while a moon-like face represented the wing joint.

Standing over Letitia's father, he began to shake the rattles and hum a slow song. The humming was low, and it was obvious to Letitia that he was having difficulty in contacting his spirit powers.

A tremor coursed through her. She hugged herself with her arms when Atkuk began to sing more loudly, asking his powers for their assistance. The words he sang made Letitia again feel that this was wrong—that her own God might not approve.

Yet she had no choice but to wait for the performance to end.

She jumped with a start when Kanuga curled a hand around one of hers, easing it onto her lap, where he continued to hold it. Blushing, she gave him a guarded smile, then again looked at the shaman, again unnerved by the words of his song.

"I beg you, Supernatural Power, take pity and make well this man," Atkuk sang, his rattles shaking in the rhythm of his song as he hovered over Letitia's father, staring down at him with eyes the same silver color as Kanuga's. "I implore you, Supernatural Power, take pity and take out this sickness from this man. Oh, take pity that I may make well this man, oh Supernatural Power, that I may cure this man, that I may obtain easily this sickness of this man, oh Great, Real Supernatural Power. You Great Life-Bringer, Supernatural Power."

Letitia's eyes widened when Atkuk knelt down beside her father and laid his rattle aside. Alarm filled her when the young shaman began unfolding the pelts away from her father. She brushed Kanuga's hand away and started to rise, to go to the shaman to protest, but a strong grip on her wrist urged her back down beside Kanuga.

"I have told you that your father will come to no harm at the hands of my brother," Kanuga whispered, lightening his hold on her wrist when he felt her becoming less tense. "Let my brother complete his healing ritual. Soon it will be over."

So badly wanting to believe that no harm was going to come to her father and that this would be over soon, Letitia inhaled several nervous breaths and gave Kanuga a quavering smile.

Then, still wary, she focused her full attention on what the shaman was doing. It took all of her willpower not to get up again to protest when Atkuk drew the last protective pelt from her father, revealing his bandaged chest. She eyed Atkuk closely when he reached inside his bag of healing paraphernalia and removed from it some sort of bone in the shape of a tube. She gasped with added alarm when he placed this bone to the flesh of her father's chest, right below the bandages, and began sucking. In the blink of an eye, Atkuk turned to Letitia with a ball of eagle down soaked in blood in his hand, offering it to her.

"And what shall I do with the evil spirit that I have removed from your father?" Atkuk said, proud of his ability to perform this feat so convincingly. It was not considered fraudulent to conceal the bloody down feathers on his person before the extraction. The spirit powers had told him to make it visible to this white woman in this manner, and since it had been done at the spirits' bidding, the trick was, in effect, supernatural.

Every bone in her body tense, Letitia rose to her feet, eyeing the bloody mass in the shaman's hand as a tremor coursed through her. She looked up at Atkuk, past the black paint smeared across a face that was surely as handsome as Kanuga's, and into eyes that were as silver—and as friendly.

"How did you do that?" she finally said, her voice breaking. "Surely that did not come from ...my father."

"Yes, it was extracted from your father. Please understand that evil spirits come in all forms," Atkuk explained. "Your father soon will be well enough for him to return to his people. Your heart should be glad for that, *ssik-gu schau-wof*. Now tell me, beautiful woman, what do I do with the evil spirit that I hold in my hand? Do you wish to take it and bury it yourself? Or shall I do this for you?"

"Atkuk, your performance was grand," Kanuga said, rising to stand beside Letitia. He glanced down at Letitia, then back up at Atkuk. "And appreciated," he quickly added. His gaze went to the bloody down feathers in his brother's hand.

"Perhaps you could bury this deeply in the snow for Letitia and her father." He glanced down at Letitia again, then at his brother. "That, also, would be appreciated."

Letitia saw that Kanuga was doing all of her talking for her and came out of what had seemed a trance caused by the bloody mass in Atkuk's hands. She looked down at her father and saw no bloody wounds on his body which could have been caused by Atkuk while performing his mysterious feat of magic, and she could tell by her father's steady breathing that no harm had been done by the ritual. There seemed to be no further cause for alarm, for surely Atkuk would now leave her to look after her father in her own way.

"You are very kind to offer assistance to me and my father," Letitia finally said, offering Atkuk her handshake, then quickly withdrawing it when she again glanced down at the bloody mess in his hand. "Thank you, Atkuk. Your kindness is appreciated."

"Atkuk is only too pleased that you asked for his healing powers," Atkuk said, smiling proudly down at Letitia. "This was my first healing ritual since I earned the title of shaman."

"You think that I asked...?" Letitia began, then looked over at Kanuga, realizing that he had not told his brother that it was Kanuga's idea.

When Kanuga's lips tugged into a smile, she could not be angry at him. Instead, she was becoming more aware of how he could affect her.

How could she not be affected? Always, his smile and his eyes caused sweet currents of warmth to sweep through her.

She understood very well that she could not leave this place soon enough, for otherwise she would be lost to this handsome, mysterious Tlingit chief.

Perhaps forever!

And there was Jonathan—sweet, trusting Jonathan, to whom she had promised her future.

She turned her eyes back to her father, and her sanity returned. At present, she must devote her every thought—her every action—to getting him well enough to return to the ship. There she would forget Kanuga.

"It is time to return to my brother shaman and tell them of my first healing success," Atkuk said. He knelt and scooped up all of his paraphernalia and placed them in his bag, then rose to his full height again and gave Letitia and Kanuga a last smile and left.

"You see, Letitia?" Kanuga said, placing a hand to her cheek. "It is over. Was not my brother clever in his performance? Do you not feel as though you were foolish to have feared him?"

Letitia knew that she should draw away from Kanuga, but his flesh against hers, where his thumb was now caressing her beneath her chin, made ecstasy move in with bone-weakening intensity. With one bold movement he swept her into his arms. All thoughts of her father were forgotten when he leaned over her with burning eyes, his mouth too soon covering hers with a reckless passion.

With a moan of ecstasy, she gave him back his

kiss, her arms twining around his neck. All of her senses were centered on the pounding of her heart and the need that he was arousing within her.

A groan behind her made Letitia wrench herself with alarm out of Kanuga's arms. She drew a ragged breath as she touched her lips, where they still throbbed from his kiss.

"Letitia..." her father whispered in his lethargic sleep, as though he had sensed her reckless behavior. "Letitia..."

Guilt springing forth, Letitia stifled a sob of regret and rushed to her father's side, kneeling beside him. Her hands trembled as she began covering him again with the warm pelts. Tears streamed down her cheeks as she was torn with feelings—and regrets she did not want to feel. It had been so deliciously sweet and wonderful in Kanuga's arms. How could she deny that she wanted it to happen again?

And she knew that it would, if she stayed another night in the Tlingit village.

"Papa, please wake up," Letitia whispered, close to his ear. "Only moments ago you spoke my name. Aren't you aware that you did? Oh Papa, you have to get well soon. We must return to the ship. If not, oh Papa, I don't know what to expect...."

A firm hand suddenly on her shoulder made Letitia flinch. Had Kanuga heard the desperation she was feeling to leave the village? Did he sense that what she was voicing was a lie—that she could hardly bear the thought of never seeing him again?

"Letitia, the night is yours with your father," Kanuga said, his desire for her a torch burning his insides; yet it was a desire he must feed somewhere else. "Kanuga will sleep elsewhere."

Letitia looked quickly up at him. "You are going away?" she said, panic rising within her. She gazed up at his solemn expression. "You are leaving the village?"

Kanuga moved his hand to touch Letitia's hair, its utter softness sending a raging hunger for her more intensely through him. He turned quickly away from her and slung a beaver cloak around his shoulders. "No, I do not leave my village," he said, his voice low. "I will not be far from you. Sleep well."

Letitia started to rise, to go to him, but thought better of it when he turned back to face her and their eyes made contact. She was acutely aware again of what they had shared in that brief moment only a heartbeat ago, and she could tell that he was as troubled as she. It showed in the silent, troubled shadows of his eyes.

Kanuga swung around and was gone in a blink of an eye. Letitia felt his absence like a heavy weight on her heart, then turned back to her father and gazed down at him. He was no better and no worse since the shaman's healing ritual. He was sleeping soundly now, her name lost to him again somewhere deep inside his unconscious mind.

Seeing that her father was sleeping as peacefully as possible, and weary from the long day's activities and shocks to her own system, Letitia eyed the thick pelts that lay on the floor beside her father. If she could go to sleep, she also could forget her wounds—even those to her heart!

She eyed the fire. It seemed to be burning strongly enough, yet, afraid that it might go out through the night, she yanked on her boots before stretching out on the pelts, snuggling beneath others. She soon closed her eyes, but could not forget the wonders of Kanuga all that simply. In her mind she could still see his eyes. She could still feel the magic of his kiss, the fire in his touch. . . .

Soon weariness won her over and she was fast asleep.

His face cleansed of the black ash, his eyes proudly gleaming, Atkuk entered the lodge belonging to Kosko, an older shaman of fifty winters, with floor-length gray hair. Kosko and Athas, another shaman only slightly older than Atkuk, sat in the darkened house, the fire's glow the only light. In this uncertain light, the shaman awaiting Atkuk seemed distorted and mysterious to him, yet was not he now a part of them—a shaman in his own right?

As Atkuk joined them beside the fire, he stole a glance at Kosko's face and noted again its texture—the deep lines, the florid skin, the saggy lower lids of the dull gray eyes, and the uncompromising mouth. It was this shaman whom Atkuk felt ill at ease with. Though Kosko was his elder, and a man to be admired and looked up to, Atkuk did not wholly trust him. It was the way that Kosko always stared at him. It was in Kosko's eyes that he did not approve of Atkuk's new status of shaman.

"And did you perform well your first healing ritual?" Athas asked, his friendly eyes anxious as he peered across the fire at Atkuk.

Feeling that he had achieved a close bond with Athas, Atkuk was glad that it was this shaman who inquired of his successes today. Kosko just sat there, chewing his pellets of tobacco mixed with a dried fungus, staring.

"I performed well the magic that I took to the ailing white man," Atkuk said, accepting a stone pipe from Athas, smoke curling up from the tobacco. "I went into a trance and could see through him as though he were transparent."

He placed the mouthpiece between his teeth and inhaled a puff of smoke into his lungs. The pipe represented a whale chasing a seal, the creator of the pipe having used a circular composition to create the illusion of motion. The whale's head contained the pipe bowl the mouthpiece was between the seal's head and whale's tail.

"Did you employ much elaborate trickery?" Athas asked, leaning forward for Atkuk's answer.

"Much," Atkuk said proudly.

"It is not good to perform Tlingit magic over white people," Kosko said, spitting a stream of tobacco into a small earthen jar. He wiped the brown spittle from his mouth with the back of his hand and glared over at Atkuk. "It is not good that Kanuga brought the white people to our village. They will expect more than magic from the Tlingit. They will want more of our brown gold!"

"They are only here until the white man's wounds begin healing," Atkuk said. "It is best that I performed magic well so that he and the woman can leave soon."

"You should have used bad charms on them," Kosko said, his mouth twisting in a feral snarl. "You should have worked evil on them, to precipitate a disaster and bring misfortune into their lives."

Atkuk's jaw tightened. "That is not what my brother Kanuga wanted," he said flatly, daring to defy his elder. "Kanuga has the last word." He paused, then added, "His voice is stronger than even yours, Kosko, because he is the chief of our people." He paused again, and handed the pipe back to Athas, yet not taking his eyes off Kosko. "Do you forget that he is also your chief, Kosko?"

Athas stared with slack-jawed disbelief at Atkuk, then looked slowly over at Kosko who said nothing, but let out his breath in a little hiss.

Kanuga trudged across the packed snow which led from house to house and stopped before one that he had become quite familiar with. Inside waited the village prostitute, her time already spoken for by Kanuga earlier in the day, even before he had come across Letitia in danger in the snowstorm with her wounded father.

His blood boiling with the need for a woman, and his need to fight off sensual feelings for Letitia, he went inside, where the soft light from the fire revealed to him a skilled lover awaiting him with pallets of prime pelts spread across the floor beside the fire.

Dark eyes watched Kanuga as he disrobed. Long and lean fingers moved over him as he knelt down over the prostitute whose name had been taken from her when she had chosen the profession that was condemned in so many Tlingit eyes.

But to Kanuga, her purpose in life benefited him well, since he had not, until today, until Letita, found a woman whose heartbeat matched his.

Kanuga clung to the woman and entered her with a sensation of hot relief mingled with regret. His body rose up and down in rhythmic movements, and soon he lost himself in the wonders of the flesh, but all the while pretending it was Letitia in his arms. He was fascinated by everything about her. Her lips and the kiss she had given him! Her eyes, luminously blue! Her slim and sinuous body, which for a moment he had held, close to totally possessing!

As he reached the ultimate of sensations with the prostitute, he cried out Letitia's name, every part of his body tingling with desire for Letitia alone!

And then he drew away from the prostitute, staring into the flames of the fire. It seemed to suddenly take on the shape of a woman dancing, her hair long and flowing, the color of the sun! Even in the fire he was seeing Letitia! He knew that he would not sleep tonight. The prostitute had not been enough to quell his desires.

Chapter Four

If I must die,
I will encounter darkness as a bride,
And hug it in my arms.

—SHAKESPEARE

A noise startled Letitia awake. For a moment she was disoriented and forgot where she was. The fire in the firepit had burned down to soft embers, deepening everything in shadows too dark to make out anything around her.

As she rose to one elbow, peering into the darkness, and then down at herself and how she was dressed, she recalled that before falling to sleep, she had been so cold that she had slipped into her fur coat and snuggled the hood over her head, tying it securely beneath her chin and drawing the fur of the hood closer to her face, to seek warmth from it.

Memories of what had transpired before then came to her in flashes.

The moment that she and her father realized that they had been separated from the others of the expedition.

The moment of the bear attack.

Her father's piercing screams as the bear mauled him.

Her courage to pick up her father's rifle and fire at the bear, causing it to retreat.

And then the ensuing silence and the fear as she had waited for the bear to return to kill her.

Just as Kanuga came to her mind, with the wonder of him and how his kiss had inflamed her very soul, there was a quick movement behind her. Before she could turn and see who it was, a hand was clasped over her mouth, while another hand grabbed her by the wrist and began dragging her across the floor.

Fear piercing her heart, her eyes wide as she realized that the figure looming over her, behind her, was not Kanuga, Letitia tried to jerk her assailant's hand from her mouth so that she could scream, to alert Kanuga or anyone who might be close enough to hear.

But no matter how hard she tried, the grip was too firm on her mouth, and as she was then dragged through the door, her thoughts raced, wondering who her abductor was.

Could it be another Indian, who wanted more from her and her father than peaceful relations?

Yet, if it was another Indian, wanting to see

her and her father dead, why was her father being left behind, undisturbed?

Unless she was being abducted for ransom . . . ?

The night air, in its cold intensity, stung the flesh of Letitia's face as she was taken outside. She again struggled with all of her might, but to no avail as her assailant continued to drag her unmercifully through the snow until the village was left behind. They came to a team of dogs and, in what seemed a flash of time, she found herself gagged, then tied onto the sled beneath a layer of warm pelts.

Desperate, so afraid that her insides quavered, she tried to see the face of her abductor, but all that she could see were shadows where the fur of his hood hung low over his eyes. He wore a scarf tied around the lower half of his face, protecting him well from her searching eyes.

A snap of a whip along the backs of the huskies, and a loud shout from the man, soon sent the sled on its way. Terrified of what the next moments would bring her, and wondering about the welfare of her father now that she was gone, Letitia stifled a sob in the depths of her throat. How could Kanuga have let this happen to her? He had vowed that she was safe! He had promised that her father would be all right! Oh, but where had he been while she was being abducted? He had said that he would be close by!

Knowing that it was best not to dwell on things she had no control over—thoughts that would most surely bring tears that would freeze on her

face—Letitia tried to force her thoughts elsewhere.

The weather.

She would think of the weather!

At least that was in her favor! The storm had
abated. The winds were now only a whisper.

She looked up at the sky. It was deep violet,
the stars shining brilliantly, like gleaming se-
quins flashing in the night. The soft light of the
moon gleamed on the snow, yet gave no clues as
to where she was being taken. All that she could
see on this vast, frostbitten land, were trees all
lace-like with their covers of snow.

She felt at least thankful that the howling of
the wolves had been left behind. Now everything
around her was silent but for the creaking of the
sled and the crunch of the snow as the sled
plowed its way through it, the breath of the dogs
great puffs of silver as it rose into the night air.

But the gray light of night gave no clues as to
where she was being taken, except...except
for...

Letitia's eyes widened when in the distance she
was now able to make out something else on the
horizon. She had heard about the Russian fort,
but she had not seen it. What loomed closer and
closer as the dogsled trudged through the snow
was surely the fort, the wooden palisades rising
into the sky, lit by occasional pine torches that
had been placed at intervals on the high fence,
like beacons in the night.

Now she understood who her abductor was—
a Russian!

But she could not understand why the Russians would be interested in her.

Her heart sank.

The Russians had surely discovered that the Americans had arrived at Alaska's shores, and that she and her father had been taken to the Indian village. The reason for her abduction surely *was* ransom—the terms more than likely that the Russians would agree to return her to the Americans only if the Americans would promise to leave Alaska, leaving the Russians in charge of the *brown gold*, the furs that Chinese merchants would pay small fortunes for.

She was reminded of why her father had come to what most would say were forbidden shores. Alaska's mainland teemed with beaver and silver and red fox, but most of its coast swarmed with sea otter—playful, mink-like creatures, four to six feet long, possessing a luxuriant coat.

The Russian were not expected to want to share these riches with the Americans, but Letitia did not want to even wager a guess as to what length they would go to stop them.

The thought terrified her.

Tears that she could not hold back any longer swam in her eyes as she struggled to get free from her prison of pelts. She must escape and find her way back to the Indian village and plead for Kanuga's help! Surely he had defenses against the Russians. With her father disabled, and the rest of the men of the expedition missing, surely lost somewhere in this vast wilderness of snow, her mother and Barbara and the small crew that remained on the ship were sitting targets for the Russians. Everyone on the ship would be at their mercy!

Her thoughts stilled as the dogsled moved into the shadow of the fort's protective fence. At this range, Letitia could tell that it was unexpectedly vulnerable, giving her a small ray of hope. Its one wide gate was open and unbarred. The moon revealed that one lookout sat on a ledge outside a watchtower with his musket resting across his knees, seemingly more interested in taking long pulls from his pipe than in guard duty. He did not even offer any acknowledgment as Letitia's abductor sent his dogsled on through the gate, cautiously directing his dogs into the dark shadows inside the fence, behind a scattering of log buildings. Soon they stopped at a small, isolated cabin at the far end of the courtyard.

Surprised to have been brought to such a small building instead of what appeared to be the main structure, which was a two-story affair, Letitia eyed her abductor even more warily as he came to her and began untying the ropes that held her in place. There was something about his actions that led her to realize that she had miscalculated his intentions. If he had been bringing her to the fort as part of a plan etched out by the officer in charge here, then why had he brought her here? Why was there any reason to keep her hidden now?

And the way he kept glancing guardedly up at the second story of the main complex, where seal-oil lamps burned brightly in the windows, and the way his hands trembled in his haste to untie her ropes, made Letitia fearful that her abductor might be the only one in on the plan.

As the last rope fell away, Letitia took the opportunity to give her abductor a shove. As he momentarily lost his balance, she was able to see his face for the first time, for the thrust of the shove had caused his hood to fall back from his head and the scarf to fall down from his face. In a brief glance, she could see that he had unpleasant, hawk-like features, with narrow, beady eyes. Bald, and with creases of wrinkles criscrossing his brow, he appeared to be a man of perhaps fifty years of age. And there were deep grooves of wrinkles at the corners of his mouth which gave him the appearance of a man who had frowned so often, his skin had frozen in a brooding, discontented look.

Knocking the rest of the pelts aside, Letitia jumped from the sled, but as her boots made contact with the crushed-down snow, her eyes widened and her heart skipped a beat when she found that she could not keep her footing. As she fell, she looked frantically over at her abductor. He had steadied himself and was glaring down at her.

A sob lodged in her throat when she saw him reach out for her, his hands soon on her waist, stopping her fall.

She tried to jerk herself free again, but the effort was futile. He was holding her in an iron grip and shoving her toward the cabin, where he shook his snowshoes off and kicked the door open with a booted foot.

Pale light from a seal-oil lamp and flames burning low in a stone fireplace revealed to Letitia a drab, one-room dwelling with scant furniture. A small bed covered with filthy blankets was shoved against the far wall. A kitchen table occupied the middle of the room, a bottle of vodka and dishes of half eaten food on it.

Letitia looked guardedly around her. Various pelts and occasional traps that still had smears of blood on their toothy edges hung from the walls. An assortment of weapons stood here and there against the walls, and a litter of yellowed papers and maps were strewn across the wooden floor.

This was obviously not the living quarters of an important Russian leader—or anyone of importance to anyone!

She eyed the man guardedly again, wondering who on earth he was and why he had chosen to abduct her, if not for the whole community of Russians who could benefit from such a kidnapping.

Letitia was ushered to the fireplace, which she at least welcomed. Its heat was already touching her face with a gentle, pleasant warmth.

Hunkering low before the fire and turning her face from her abductor, Letitia could hear him rustling out of his fur coat. She winced when he finally spoke to her, now standing close behind her.

"Turn around," he said, his voice precise and

cold. He placed his fists on his hips. "Let me see how pretty my Tlingit maiden is." He chuckled. "I stole you from right beneath Kanuga's nose, didn't I? Guess I'm lucky as hell that he's a sound sleeper."

He grew even more somber. "Had he not been, I'd have killed him quick with my knife," he grumbled. "He's been too much trouble, anyhow, since he's become chief. He doesn't cooperate with me. That ain't right. I'm Broderick Bowman, the best trader in these parts, ain't I?"

Letitia's eyes widened when she recognized the name Broderick Bowman and realized that her abductor was not a Russian at all, but an American, working with the Russians as a go-between between them and the Tlingit Indians. She knew, from what Kanuga had said about him, that there was no love exchanged between Bowman and Kanuga, and that it would make things much simpler for this trader if he didn't have Kanuga to deal with.

Then another thought struck her. If her father had made any sound at all while Broderick Bowman had been abducting her, the evil agent would have slain him, thinking that he was Kanuga awakening, discovering someone in his tent.

It was apparent to Letitia that thus far, Broderick did not know he had abducted a white woman instead of an Indian!

When he discovered his mistake, he would realize that he had gotten more than he had bargained for—not only a woman to rape but also proof that other Americans besides himself had come to Alaska.

Knowing that she had no way to delay the inevitable revelation of her identity to Broderick, Letitia straightened her back, sucked in a deep, quavering breath, then swung around and faced the trader. Very boldly, she untied her hood, then slipped the hood off her head, so that her hair tumbled free and long down her back. She held her chin high, smiling to herself when she saw him become pale, his beady eyes widening with acute surprise when he saw that she was anything but Indian, with her blue eyes flashing angrily.

"Who the hell are you?" Broderick said, taking a step closer as he looked at her intensely, his eyes raking slowly over her, then stopping again at her face. "I thought I was getting me an Injun squaw for the night. How did you happen to be—?"

"To be in Kanuga's house?" Letitia said, before he had managed to complete the question. "I was there because he was kind enough to ask me."

She placed her hands on her hips and her eyes flashed maliciously. "But you?" she dared. "Do you steal into tents often in the night and abduct ladies? If so, how did you manage to live so long? If Kanuga *had* been in that tent, you would be dead. Because scum like you exist even here in Alaska, I am sure that he sleeps with one eye open."

Broderick took a clumsy step away from her, then felt around behind him until he found the bottle of vodka on his kitchen table. Quickly he uncorked it and took a deep gulp, then set the bottle back on the table as he again went to stand over Letitia, studying her.

"Damn it, tell me why you were in Kanuga's longhouse, and if that wasn't Kanuga, who was that I saw sleeping close to where you were?" Broderick growled out. "I don't remember seeing you here at the fort. Where'd you come from?"

Hoping to keep the trader from finding out the truth for as long as possible, Letitia pursed her lips tightly together and refused to respond to anything else he was saying. Her father and his men were in Alaska, surveying in secret, hoping to build a trading post in direct competition with the Russians. If she could delay the Russians discovering this until her father was well, or until the others of the expedition found their way back to the ship, just perhaps there would be some hope for their plans.

Infuriated, Broderick doubled his fists at his sides, anger building inside him in hot flashes. He wasn't sure what he was going to do with her. Kill her? Or set her free to freeze to death in the snow? He wanted no one to see the mistake that he had made by stealing someone other than an Injun squaw to use, then discard in the snow to die. He was already being called a bungler by the Russians and the Tlingits alike. Tonight he had wanted a woman to prove his manhood—at least to himself.

Most of all, he had wanted a silken body next to him in bed!

An evil glint rose into his eyes as his lips tugged into a slow smile. Yes, he had made a mistake tonight, but what did it truly matter? No one would ever know the difference. He would rape the beautiful woman, then set her free, un-clothed, in the wilds of Alaska. If the cold didn't get her, the wolves would!

"And so you choose not to say anything else, do you?" he said, his teeth clenched. "I'll show you just how much I care."

He gripped her wrists hard and half dragged her close to the bed. "Get undressed, wench," he grumbled. "I had plans for tonight, and you ain't goin' to spoil them."

Letitia snatched her wrists away from him, then fear and revulsion gripped her at the pit of her stomach as she watched him quickly discard his shirt, then place his hands at the waist of his buckskin breeches.

"So you want me to undress you, huh?" Brod-erick said, his eyes dancing as his loins became afire with lusty need. He shrugged. "That's all right with me. It'd be my pleasure."

Filled with panic, Letitia backed away from him, her eyes darting around her for something to protect herself with. Her gaze went from weapon to weapon, realizing that none was close enough to grab and prepare for firing before he could get it from her.

Then her gaze stopped on the bottle of vodka on the table. Her pulse raced. Only a couple of steps and she could have the bottle in her hand.

Yes, she thought anxiously, that would do!

If she hit him hard enough, he could be unconscious for hours!

Scarcely breathing, a cold fear gripping her heart, she watched Broderick start to lower his breeches. Just as they were draped around his ankles, she made her move before he could step out of them. She did not realize that she could move so quickly.

She lunged for the bottle.

She picked it up.

She rushed to Broderick as he looked disbelievingly at her as she raised it over his head.

Then she lowered it toward his head with all of the energy and speed that she could muster.

The noise the bottle made as it made contact with his head, and the shattering of the glass, made a cascade of shivers race up and down Letitia's spine. She watched Broderick crumple in a heap at her feet, groaning, then quickly stepped around him and hurried toward the door.

Before stepping outside she placed the hood on her head, tying it securely beneath her chin. And after she had slipped her feet into Broderick's snowshoes, she thought of one other thing.

A weapon!

She grabbed a rifle and rushed out into the night air—and was stunned to find that the dogs were no longer attached to the sled. Someone had come and seen to their welfare.

Now what was she to do? she wondered frantically. Even if she was able to escape from the Russian fort without being seen, it was quite a distance to the Indian village, and farther still, she was sure, to the ship.

She didn't know which way to travel to get to either!

On the dogsled on her way to the Russian fort, everything had been distorted for her, her fear of where she was being taken blurring her sense of direction!

Swimming with doubt that she was going to survive this night, Letitia shook her head with despair. Then her gaze found something in the snow.

Tracks!

Tracks made from the dogsled that had brought her to this fort!

If she could follow the prints, surely she could find her way back to the village!

Moving stealthily behind the other cabins and buildings, taking the same route that Broderick had taken to hide his evil activities tonight, Letitia got to the tall fortress palisade undetected. She smiled when she discovered that the sentry was still not attending to his duties. This time, instead of enjoying his pipe, he was fast asleep!

She hurried on past him, through the gate and to freedom. She trembled inwardly when she remembered the polar bear that had attacked her father and how he had not been able to fend off the attack. How did she expect to be able to fight off such an attack when she was so much less experienced with a firearm than her father?

She cast all doubts from her mind, knowing that hope was her only companion tonight, and kept her eyes on the tracks in the snow.

For the moment the moon allowed her to follow them easily. But she had seen the clouds building in the west, already erasing some of the stars from the sky, and she knew that soon the moon might fade, too.

Chapter Five

But then her face,
So lovely, yet so arch, so full of mirth,
The overflowings of an innocent heart.
                                    —ROGERS

A sob of fear lodged in Letitia's throat when black clouds moved across the sky and quickly covered the moon, and great sheets of snow began to fall just as quickly. Panic filling her, she watched the last of the tracks in the snow become mashed with white and disappear from her sight behind a veil of spinning snowflakes.

"I'm going to get lost out here again!" she cried in despair, her eyes peering uselessly into the white cloud surrounding her. The urgent snow was everywhere! And she couldn't help recalling how quickly the bear had come out of nowhere the last time she was disoriented by the snow.

Her father hadn't had a chance.

Nor would she.

Forcing back the urge to cry, knowing that the last thing she needed was frozen tears on a face that was already tight from the bitter cold, she trudged on through the snow, unsure of her direction. To keep moving was all that was important now. Should she give in to the cold, she would die much faster from that than from a bear attack.

"I must continue to be brave," she told herself, forcing one snowshoe ahead of the other, finding them to be clumsier with each step taken. Supple willow sticks formed the framework. They were boat-shaped, their wooden frames netted with *babiche*, a rawhide thong.

"Fear is my enemy. Fear is my enemy," she kept whispering to herself, over and over again.

A sudden squally wind came up, worsening the visibility, and gusts of wind repeatedly knocked her to her knees.

But determined not to become a victim of this vast, icy wilderness, she kept pushing herself up from the deepening snow, yet fearing that she could not last long at this rate.

She was tiring.

Oh, Lord, she was tiring. . . .

As she was reaching out, feeling her way through the sheets of snow, she stopped in midstep when her gloved hand came in contact with something. A rock wall!

Relief flooded her when she discovered that this wall had an overhang, under which she could take shelter.

"Thank you, God," she whispered, moving beneath the overhang and huddling close to the wall.

Hugging herself for warmth, she tried to see what was around her, discovering only a broad strip of hemlocks stretched out on the one side of the wall, their spreading branches weighed down with snow.

In the other direction, all that she could see was the continuing, raging snowstorm.

Despair filled her. Would this be where she took her last breath? Was it her destiny to die alone?

And if she did, was her body never to be found, to be given a proper burial?

Shivering, her lips tingling from the bitter cold, Letitia thought it best to go on her way. If she didn't keep her body moving, it would just give up.

Fighting a strange lethargic feeling, fearing that was the first symptom of freezing to death, Letitia forced herself to push the snowshoes on through the snow, an inch at a time. Her heart pounded at the thought of having to go another step.

Yet she had no other choice.

She knew that she must keep going!

Her heart stood still for an instant, and her eyes widened when she heard the crunch of snow and the harsh breathing of huskies. She stopped and swung around, knowing that someone had to be near.

Where there were huskies, there was a sled!

Where there was a sled, there was a driver....

But she had not thought they were so close, for suddenly, without notice, the huskies and sled passed on by her, so close that she felt the warmth of the huskies' breaths on her cold, stiff cheeks!

Panic raged through her, feeling that soon she would be totally alone again, yet afraid to shout, to let the passerby know that she was there. What if it was the evil Broderick Bowman from the Russian fort? What if he had come after her?

But she had no choice but to cry out. She had more of a chance of survival at the Russian fort than in the fury of the snowstorm, already half frozen!

Calling on the last of her energy, she began running through the snow, shouting as loudly as her weak voice would allow.

Desperation seized her when she wasn't immediately heard. Again she shouted. She shouted until she no longer had a voice, nor strength....

Her body became limp as she tumbled to the ground, strangely welcoming the soft layer of snow. Closing her eyes, she could recall how wonderful her feather bed had felt back at her home in New York.

The snow so very much resembled the soft down of those feathers. It would be so easy now to let herself fall to sleep.

She was home.

She was in her bed.

She was ...

Suddenly she felt strong arms around her. Her eyes flew open as she was lifted from the snow.

Suddenly she was catapulted back into the real world, realizing that she had not been in her bed at all. She had been close to letting herself die in the wilderness! Someone had heard her screams and shouts after all!

Knowing that she had been rescued, her heart became filled with a joyous relief.

And then fear replaced this joy. The snow was blowing so hard and it was so impenetrable, she couldn't make out the face of the man in whose arms she was being safely held.

It could be Broderick Bowman!

It could be. . . .

Hope suddenly filled her, for she could feel the muscles of this man's arms even through the thickness of his fur coat. Broderick Bowman had not been as muscled. Nor would he be carrying her as though she were a precious jewel.

Surely she was in the handsome Tlingit's arms!

Surely Kanuga had discovered her gone, and had come searching for her!

She tried to speak Kanuga's name, but the cold had robbed her of her voice. She wished that he would say something, but it was obvious that he was too intent at getting her safely out of the cold. It was with much haste that he had her on his sled and enveloped her in *Chilkat* blankets—magnificent mantles made out of mountain-goat wool and cedar wood fiber. It was with much haste that the huskies were again breathing fire as they rode fearlessly onward through the storm.

Letitia closed her eyes, softly dozing, Kanuga's face swimming around in her mind. Although she hadn't yet seen the face of her rescuer, she did believe with all of her heart that it was Kanuga.

And, oh, how she welcomed the warmth of the blankets that he had wrapped around her! She now knew that she was going to live.

A rush of relief breathed through her, knowing that, yes, she was going to live, despite the terrors of the snowstorm.

Suddenly Letitia felt the jolt of the sled as it was drawn to a halt. Again she felt strong arms lift her from the sled, the blankets still secured snugly around her. Soon she was being carried through a narrow passageway into a dark dwelling, where she was finally away from the gusts of frigid winds.

After being placed on the floor, she huddled there in the dark, becoming alarmed when she no longer heard any sounds around her, as though she had been abandoned.

But soon her building panic was replaced by relief when she heard sounds in the dwelling again and recognized them as the snapping of twigs; soon she could expect the welcome warmth of a fire upon her face.

Letitia watched the fire take hold, the hissing and popping of the wood sending a surge of warm blood coursing through her veins. Then she turned wondering eyes toward the man who had saved her. Her heart lurched with delight when he turned her way and she found herself looking into compelling silver eyes.

Kanuga came to her and took the gloves from her hands and began rubbing her hands together, between his, to warm them. *"Uasse-i-tu-eti?"* he asked, searching her face with his eyes. "How are you? How is it that you left my house? When I came to see if you needed anything before you went to sleep for the night, I found you gone!"

Peering up at Kanuga, her heart soaring with happiness that he should care this much for her, Letitia blinked a tear from her eye. "Again you have saved me," she murmured, sniffling. "Kanuga, that dreadful man from the Russian fort came and abducted me! He took me to his cabin! He—he was going to rape me, then send me out into the snow to die!"

A sudden rage lit Kanuga's eyes with fire. "This man," he snarled. "What was his name?"

"It was Broderick Bowman," Letitia said, shivers of revulsion running up and down her spine at the thought of the vile man. "I—I hit him over the head with a bottle of vodka, then escaped."

She took her hands from Kanuga, then leapt into his arms, hugging him with all of her might. "Oh, thank you, Kanuga, for rescuing me," she cried. "I had lost all hope of ever being discovered alive. Soon I would have frozen to death."

The feel of her in his arms made Kanuga's heart race out of control. His need of her outweighed any reason he may have had for denying himself the wonders of holding her, kissing her, having her!

At this moment there were no *sserkans*, no tomorrows. There was only now.

When he had discovered her gone, he had feared losing her forever. Now that he had found

Cassie Edwards

her, he wanted to make her his for an eternity!

Kanuga bent over and smoothed the hood of the fur coat away from Letitia's head, releasing her hair so that it tumbled down her back. His hands framed her face, and raised her lips to his. He kissed her with a kiss that was all consuming, loving the sweetness of her soft lips and how they responded to his kiss.

He now knew that what he had seen in her eyes earlier, at his dwelling in his village, had not been wrong. It was in her kiss that she cared for him. It was in the way she was touching his face with her hands, so gentle, so sweet, that made him know she was not going to deny her feelings for him any longer.

And, he quickly decided, there was no need to delay any further. The abandoned igloo that he had brought Letitia to until the storm passed over was being heated quickly by the fire. The heat generated by a fire and by living bodies produced an interior shell of frozen condensation in an igloo, causing the temperature to rise high enough to allow its occupants to shed their clothes.

Kanuga leaned away from Letitia, his hands unfolding the blankets from around her. Letitia scarcely breathed, her heartbeats threatening to drown her. In that brief moment within his arms, his lips had been so warm and demanding, so filled with ecstasy. She was no longer cold.

Instead, she felt as if a hundred candles had been lighted inside her. Their flames seemed to burn higher as Kanuga gazed down at her with his wondrous silver eyes, while spreading blankets and robes of black bearskin, sea otter pelts, and marmot skins along the frozen floor of the igloo.

Letitia watched, wide-eyed, as Kanuga removed her snowshoes. She trembled with ecstasy when he clasped his hands to her shoulders and urged her down beside the fire, onto the thick pallet that he had prepared for her.

"You are beautiful," he said huskily, his hands going to her hair, running his fingers through it. He leaned over her, his lips brushing hers with a kiss. "Your lips are soft. Your taste is like the scent of roses."

A thrill of desire coursed through Letitia when he slid his lips down her neck, stopping to kiss the hollow of her throat.

And when his hands moved down her body and slipped up inside her dress so that he was cupping her buttocks in a sensual way, her breath was drawn away with a deep gasp of shock.

It became almost too much for her to bear when his hands crept around and his fingers caressed her. She closed her eyes, awakening to delicious feelings never known before.

Somewhere deep inside her consciousness something was telling her that what she was allowing was wrong.

But nothing seemed wrong with Kanuga.

And didn't she belong to him, she thought, to help lay aside nagging doubts? How could she ever forget that he had saved her life not once, but twice?

But she knew that she was not allowing this intimacy between them because of being grateful. She was being awakened to passion—a shared passion. She would not turn her back on such blissful feelings—nor on him!

Kanuga moved away from her momentarily. Smiling down at her, he began removing his clothes. Something compelled her to follow his lead, and she removed her clothes along with him, piece by piece.

A deep blush suffused her face when he stepped out of his last piece of clothing, which gave her her first true look of what a man looked like. Fully clothed, he had made her heart stop. But seeing him nude made a strange warmth begin to curl up at the pit of her stomach, for never had she thought a man could be as beautiful.

Herself nude, she rose to her knees and began running her hands over the smoothness of his body, from his wide shoulders to his narrowed hips, from his hard, flat stomach to his long, firm legs, and to that part of him that was distended and velvety and seemed to have a life of its own as she grazed the flesh of her hand against it.

When his manhood jumped in response to her touch, she gasped and lunged into his arms, hiding her embarrassed blush against the broad column of his throat.

"Let me hold you for a while," Kanuga said softly, smoothing one of his hands along her liquid curves. "What the fire has not heated, my body will." His thumb lightly caressed her cheek. "Do not be embarrassed or afraid. What we do is right. And soon marriage vows will erase all doubts from yours, or anyone else's mind. What I do tonight is not done lightly. It is done from the bottom of my heart."

Letitia eased from his embrace and gazed intensely into his silver eyes and smiled. "I am warm enough," she murmured. "And what I do tonight is not done lightly. It is my first time with a man. Destiny has led me to you. It is to you that I give not only my heart, but also my virginity."

His mouth came down on hers in a fevered kiss, and she stopped thinking, forgetting everything but the rapture that had seized her. She strained up to him suddenly, her arms insistent, her mouth eagerly opening.

Brokenly, between gasps, he kissed her, stretching her out on her back again, on the thick pallet of blankets and furs.

With the smile of a confident lover, he moved over her with his body, molding himself perfectly to the curved hollow of her hips. His hands moved to her buttocks and forced her hips in at his, crushing her against his manhood until it hurt him.

But still he did not enter her. He had heard her confession that this was the first time for her to be with a man. He did not want her to be afraid of it a second time. He must be gentle. He must make it beautiful, so that perhaps she might even be the one to initiate a second time with him!

Letitia's breasts pressed warmly against Kanuga's chest and her lips sucked at his. Her mouth opened to receive his tongue as he forced it through her lips, then his mouth slipped down and fastened gently on a breast, then kissed the nipple, sucking it.

Letitia drew in her breath sharply and gave a cry of sweet agony as his hand began to stroke her throbbing center between her thighs, ever so softly, ever so lovingly, ever so endearingly.

Willingly and passionately, she followed him into the lovemaking as he sculpted himself to her moist body and began pressing himself gently into her slowly yielding flesh. Their naked bodies seemed to fuse, flesh against flesh, as he pressed endlessly deeper until she strained her hips up at him, surrendering her all to him.

Her cry of pain was brief, for soon she was feeling the ultimate of pleasure and gave herself over to the wild ecstasy that he was evoking within her. Over and over again he surged into her, bringing to her fresh stabs of exquisite agony.

She buried her face in his chest, overcome with emotion as his body shook and trembled, his arms holding her as though in a vise as she, too, cried out at her fulfillment.

Too soon, the moment of wonder was over. Her pulse racing, her body still throbbing with pleasure, Letitia lay beneath Kanuga for some time, his hand stroking her back gently.

And then he rolled away from her and drew a sea-otter pelt over them.

"You are so quiet," Kanuga said, turning her face to his as he snuggled close beside her. "Did my loving you offend you?"

Letitia placed a hand to his copper cheek, the mere touch of him making a great gush of feeling sweep through her. "Offend me?" she said, stunned that he might think that he had. "Oh, my love, how could you ever offend me? What we shared was beautiful. It only seemed natural to be with you in such a way."

"This is the beginning of many such times together," Kanuga said, as he drew her close. "After your father is well enough to travel, I shall return him to his ship. But you will stay with me. You will be my wife."

Letitia grew tense. His plan seemed simple, yet saying goodbye to her parents would not be that simple. She had known only the world that included them. It would be hard to say goodbye.

"It is best not to venture out again tonight," Kanuga said, pulling more pelts around them. "The storm is too deadly. We will spend the night in the igloo, then return to my village at daybreak. Then we can discuss plans for our future."

Not knowing what to say, not even aware of what she would do once they returned to the village, Letitia remained silent, relieved that his mouth sealed her words as he kissed her.

Her hands clung to his sinewed shoulders, not wanting to think about anything tonight but him. As his kiss deepened, an exquisite tenderness enveloped her.

Deliciously warmed by the fire and desire, she looked forward to spending a night in his arms. When wolves howled eerily in the distance, she snuggled even closer, experiencing a momentary feeling of unreality, as if the whole night had never truly happened.

In truth, she was exhausted with emotion.

Iuril Golodoff crept into Broderick Bowman's cabin when Broderick did not respond to a knock on the door. He moved into the room, the seal-oil lamp burning so low he could hardly make out anything around him. Squinting, he searched with his eyes, then focused on something in particular. He laughed beneath his breath. Someone had gotten the best of Broderick, and at a most inopportune time, it seemed. The man's breeches were down and twisted around his ankles.

Stepping closer and bending to one knee, Iuril examined Broderick more closely and discovered a lump on his head, spirals of blood seeping from it. "He sure did get more than he bargained for," he said in Russian, then rose to go to a washbasin full of cold water.

Chuckling low, he went to Broderick and, slowly and deliberately, poured the water over Broderick's head, then more slowly over a vulnerable area where his manhood lay shriveled between his thighs.

Broderick awakened with a start, groaning, his head throbbing. When he saw feet standing beside him, he looked up with a jerk of his head, and anger flooded his senses when he found Colonel Golodoff's son standing over him, his dark eyes filled with humor.

"What are you doing here?" Broderick said in

practiced Russian, pushing himself up from the floor. He was weaving from lightheadedness.

"I might ask you the same," Iuril taunted, his gaze moving up and down Broderick's body. "Or might I ask who was here before me? Whoever it was didn't let you use that scrawny thing hanging like a worm between your legs."

Iuril laughed throatily, then added, "I can see why a lady would have second thoughts after seeing what you had to offer. But to go as far as knocking you in the head? She must have been enraged to see that she had wasted time with you."

Broderick looked quickly down at himself, paling from humiliation. He bent over and grabbed his pants and jerked them up into place, glowering at Iuril.

"You little twirp," he growled, looking at Iuril's small stature and his thinning hair at the age of twenty-five. "I'm sure I have more to offer than you. I don't think I've seen a lady in your company for many months now. Why is that, Iuril? You've got nothin' at all between your legs?"

Broderick started to laugh, then winced when it caused his head to throb more painfully. And he had to think up a fast excuse for his condition tonight. If Colonel Golodoff ever heard that he had abducted a woman from the Indian village and brought her to the fort, no matter that he had mistakenly taken a white woman, the colonel would have his head. Colonel Golodoff had warned everyone not to abduct any more Indian squaws because the relations were already too strained with the Tlingit. He had to find a way to keep the colonel from discovering that he had ignored the direct order.

"It wasn't a woman that did this to me," Broderick blurted. "I was gambling with several men tonight and someone among them was a poor loser."

"Who?" Iuril demanded. "I'll go and talk to him."

Broderick's eyes wavered as he looked away from Iuril. "I don't know which one," he said, his voice shallow. "There was more than one. And whoever did it came upon me behind my back while I was gettin' ready for bed. All I know is that someone hit me over the head. That's the last thing I remember."

Iuril chuckled low as he spun around on a heel and walked toward the door. "If you think I believe that tale, then you must think I'm a fool," he said over his shoulder. He glanced back at Broderick. "You'd best hide your tracks well when you plan to poke another man's wife, especially if she decides it isn't worth it and goes back to her husband's bed the same night."

Laughing, Iuril left the cabin, slamming the door behind him. He drew his fur hood more snugly about his face and looked into the distance, at the swirling snow. From his second-story room at the fort he had seen a woman moving from Broderick's cabin, but too soon she had been lost from his sight in the darkness.

This had drawn Iuril from his cozy room to see what Broderick might have to say for himself. He hated the trader immensely and was glad to see that someone had gotten the best of him—had made him look the weak and foolish man that he was.

But Iuril had to wonder just who the woman was.

Whose wife was she?

Shrugging, he fought the wind and snow until he returned to the large dwelling that housed him and his father. He walked up the stairs to the second floor, past his father's room and into his own. Shedding his fur coat and gloves, he peered out the window. One day he would find a way to rid the fort of Broderick Bowman.

He chuckled to himself, thinking that perhaps tonight was just the beginning of the bungling idiot's demise.

Humiliated by the woman's having overpowered him, and by Iuril's mocking laughter, Broderick tossed his clothes aside and climbed into his bed. Drawing thick blankets over himself, he continued thinking of tonight's events. His thoughts dwelt on his humiliation, but in the end turned to revenge. He would have the woman, or die trying.

Also, he must find out what she was doing at the Indian village. It could boost his standing in the Russian community if he could deliver pertinent information about the American woman to them.

What if some American explorers were near, building a fort? The colonel would be delighted to find out that news. He would be grateful to Broderick forever!

His thoughts went back to Iuril, and what he must be thinking. Perhaps even how he was spreading word around at the fort about having discovered Broderick unconscious, and in such an embarrassing condition.

Sweat pearled upon his brow, humiliated again at the thought of Iuril knowing that beyond a shadow of a doubt he had been overpowered by a woman!

But what troubled him the most was that Iuril's mind never rested. Even now he had to be wondering which lady Broderick had been with.

Broderick knew that should the truth ever be known, ugly things could happen to him. In a sense, he was still at the white woman's mercy. Should she tell anyone the events of the evening, he could have not only the Russians angry at him, but also the Tlingit, and more than likely the Americans!

Broderick rolled over on his stomach, groaning. He covered his head with the blankets. "I'm doomed," he whispered harshly. "Doomed!"

Then he smiled to himself. But not if he could come up with a ploy that will work in his favor....

Chapter Six

Her eyes, her lips, her cheeks, her features,
Seem to be drawn by love's own hand, by love.
                                    —DRYDEN

A bright orange sunglow beaming through a window of ice awakened Letitia with a start. She sat bolt upright. Clasping the blankets and pelts around her, she gazed down at Kanuga, filled with remembrances of what they had shared the previous night, and loving him no less this morning.

But their lovemaking seemed a fantasy now. It was daylight—another day. The world had returned with its suspicions, regrets, heartaches, and worries.

She made a move to rise to her feet, but a hand on her wrist pulled her back.

"No, please . . ." she said, her whisper breathless.

But paying no heed to her pleas, which he knew were false, Kanuga eased her pelts aside, then slid his hands warmly down her body. He turned her to face him, and when he kissed her with a deliberate, savage pressure, her body went slack, his hands again intimate on her, knowing.

Despite herself, Letitia was answering to him again, her body arched to his.

Then faint memory of her father came to her mind's eye again. She shrugged Kanuga away and strove to sit up, but he pulled her back again.

When she turned to him, she found silver eyes gazing lovingly into hers and knew that having to resume life as it had been before finding paradise in his arms was going to be the hardest thing she had ever done. He had spoken of marriage after they had made love. Oh, how wonderful it would be to become his wife and live only for him!

But that wasn't possible. Somehow, through her moments with him, she had forgotten her father. Even now, as she delayed a while longer in this igloo turned an ice love palace, the fate of her father was unknown to her!

"*Ii-dek-rahuha?*" Kanuga asked, brushing a fallen lock of Letitia's hair back from her brow. "Are you hungry? I always carry food with me. It is not unusual to be stranded by a storm for many days."

"Yes, I'm hungry, but I don't want to take the time to eat," Letitia said.

She closed her eyes and sucked in a sharp breath of desire as his hands set her skin afire as they cupped both her breasts. "Please," she whispered, realizing that her voice was strangely husky. "Please . . . don't."

"Last night you allowed it," Kanuga softly argued, shaping his body next to hers. "Today you regret it?"

Letitia was torn with feelings. There was no denying that her life had changed because of her one night with Kanuga.

But it had happened because she had let herself get carried away in the moment. Once he had kissed her with such heated passion, and his hands had wandered where no other hands had been before, there had been no turning back. She had entered a realm of joy and forgotten sorrows.

But this was today!

And her father lay awaiting her arrival, surely frightened over her absence!

She opened her eyes and reached a hand to Kanuga's cheek, smiling softly at him. "No," she murmured. "No regrets. But I have other things on my mind today. My father. I must return to my father. What if he . . . he died during the night? I would never forgive myself for having been with a man, making love, while he struggled with his his last breaths."

She paused, then pleaded with him with her eyes. "Please take me to him, Kanuga," she murmured. "The storm has passed over us. The sun is out. The journey to your village today should be an easy one."

Kanuga slipped his arms around Letitia and drew her close to him, finding it hard to deny his body its need of her now that he had been introduced to the sweet agony of knowing her intimately. His father had taught him restraint as soon as he was old enough to know the meaning of the word 'temptation'.

Today would be a true test of those teachings!

Kanuga's hands went to her face, framing it. "Your father is not alone," he reassured her. "When I found you gone, I immediately ordered one of my Tlingit women to his side, to watch and care for him."

He smiled down at her. "And be assured that he did not die," he said gently. "He had much improved when I last saw him. Soon we shall return him to his ship. You will accompany me there, to say a farewell to your family. Then you will return to my village to live with me, as my wife."

Letitia swallowed hard, so wanting to agree to Kanuga's plan but knowing that it was only another part of the fantasy. Neither her father nor her mother would ever approve of leaving her behind—unless perhaps they remained in Alaska, also.

And she did not see how that was possible. It was apparent that Kanuga was intent on ridding the land of everyone but the Indian inhabitants.

Evading any more talk of marriage, Letitia gave Kanuga a soft kiss on his cheek, then gasped for breath when he grabbed her and covered her lips with his mouth in a fiery, possessive kiss. Suddenly all of her reasons to refuse him this further intimacy were cast to the farthest recesses of her mind. Her body responded to the caress of his hands, her mouth to his kiss.

Right now, in his arms, she felt as though they were the only two people in the universe. This moment with him, when again she was being awakened to such a keen passion, seemed like another incredible, beautiful dream—one from which she did not want to awaken.

She did not even feel wanton when she thrust her tongue into his mouth and flickered it in and out, moving it along his lips. She did not feel brazen at all when her hands moved beneath the blankets that had covered him, familiarly touching his body with her searching fingers.

When she came to that part of him that had sent her mind reeling the previous night, she did not hesitate at circling her fingers around the tight, velvety shaft and caressing him, hearing how this caused a husky groan of pleasure to escape from between his lips.

Feeling his tautness, grown to the bursting point from her caresses, and no longer hearing any of her denials of that which he had wanted since his first awakening this morning, Kanuga eased her hand away from his shaft and placed his hands to her waist, lowering her to her back on the blankets and pelts.

She twined her fingers around his neck and moved toward him as he rose above her, and the flesh of her thighs rippled in sinuous hollows as he entered her in one bold thrust.

Only half aware of making whimpering sounds, desire raged and washed over Letitia as

Cassie Edwards

her hips responded to his strokes within her. She thrust her pelvis toward him, her entire body becoming fluid with fire, all senses yearning for the promise that he was offering her.

While he continued filling her with his powerful manliness, thrusting wildly in and out of her, his hands stroked her breasts, then moved slowly down to her legs, behind her knees, and then her calves. The sureness of his caress was lighting her with an acute, building desire.

Wanting to make him feel as good, Letitia's hands began to roam over him, from the flatness of his tight belly, around to his muscled buttocks, and then on around to where she could touch his manhood as it moved in and out of her.

Her fingernails teased him each time she could touch the slightest bit of his velvet hardness, then when he removed it entirely from her, she gripped it with her fingers again and stroked him until he groaned against her lips with a sweet, lethargic kiss.

But wanting to feel him inside her, so near to the sought-for ecstasy that she recalled from the previous lovemaking, she guided him back inside her and placed her legs around him, locking them together at the ankles.

Again she rocked and swayed with him, her senses reeling. But too soon the spinning sensation rose up and flooded her whole body, pushing at the boundaries of who she was, or with whom....

Feeling release so near, not wanting to postpone the wondrous feelings any longer, Kanuga's hands firmly held Letitia's buttocks as he pressed endlessly into her. He gritted his teeth and threw his head back, the fierce yellow light beaming through the window on his face revealing the tormented pain that was driving him onward to the ultimate of pleasure.

The sensations were searing.

His entire being throbbed with the waves of pleasure that were coursing through him, causing him to cry out as the peak of his passion was reached, then regretably too soon left behind.

Kanuga's exhausted body subsided against Letitia's. Breathing hard, he stroked the curves of her thighs. "Now we will go," he said, chuckling as his eyes met the wonder in hers. "Delayed a bit, but now we will go."

Letitia laughed softly, still tingling all over from the lovemaking, and not ashamed of it. Surely you only loved once in your life, and you were lucky if it was as intense a love as she felt for Kanuga.

And who knew about tomorrow?

Today, as last night, she had her beloved.

And she would cherish the memory, always!

Letitia shivered with delight when Kanuga sank his teeth into one nipple, then lapped it with his tongue, but then she pushed him gently away and rose quickly to her knees and looked around her. When she found her discarded clothes, she reached for them and was soon dressed, not bashful at all as she watched Kanuga step nude from the blankets as he also reached for his buckskin breeches and shirt.

She turned her eyes away from him, wondering about this person she had become. In another time and another place, she would have felt like a whore who lifted her skirts for any man who had the right price for services offered.

But she quickly reminded herself that this was not America. This was a distant land, where a wonderful Tlingit chief ruled, and by whose rules she had lived this past night.

And she was not a whore. She was a woman who loved one man with all of her heart. She was a woman who would never go to bed with any man *but* Kanuga.

Kanuga was the only man she would ever desire!

Soon enveloped in her fur coat, hood, and gloves, and with her boots slipped into the snowshoes, Letitia turned to Kanuga and saw that he was also ready to leave their lovenest. Smiling at one another, they bent low and moved through the small passageway until they stepped blinkingly into the sunlight. The wind had dropped from a near gale to a dead calm.

Letitia covered her eyes as the brilliant sunlight reflecting from the white land overpowered her. Although the sun shone for only a few hours in the day, this sunshine was treacherous, for it reflected off the glittering snow, and was painfully dazzling to the eyes.

Kanuga went to his sled and took two pairs of snow glasses that he had fashioned from small pieces of wood, with tiny carved slits to see through and leather thongs to keep them in place.

He took one pair to Letitia, and slipped the other one on himself, over his own eyes.

"That should make your eyes more comfortable," he said, helping slip the snow glasses over her head. He straightened them on her nose, then smiled down at her as she looked up at him.

"Now you can see the man of your desire without squinting," he said, chuckling.

"And what I see is quite handsome," Letitia said, moving into his arms, hugging him.

She was soon aware of the warmth that had been left behind in the igloo. Although the sun shone, it was colder today, and the snow crackled underfoot as they moved toward the sled and huskies. Not the slightest breath of wind touched her face. The silence was complete.

And then the air was filled with Letitia's gasp of horror when she gazed down at the huskies who were curled up beside the sled, great piles of snow drifted over them. She moved quickly to her knees beside them and began frantically scooping the snow from them.

"They're dead!" she cried. "They must have frozen to death in the night! While we slept beside the fire, they . . . they . . ."

A firm hand on her shoulder drew her eyes around. She peered up at Kanuga, seeing a smile quivering on his lips. "Kanuga, what do you find about this that is so amusing?" she said, her voice slight. "These are your dogs. Don't you care—?"

Kanuga bent to one knee beside her. He cupped her chin in one of his hands and forced her eyes back around to look at the dogs. "Do they look frozen?" he said, his free hand patting one dog after another, as they stood on all fours, shaking the snow from their fur.

"This is their life," he explained. "They are used to the frigid temperatures and the snows. They would not know how to live otherwise. This is why they are so valuable. They are even more dependable than most men."

Relieved, Letitia reached a hand to the closest huskie and patted its cold, stiff fur. "For a moment I did think that they were dead," she said, sighing heavily. "I'm so glad that I was wrong. If they had died, I would have been responsible. You were out in the blizzard last night because of me."

Kanuga placed his hand to her elbow and urged her up and toward the sled. "And you were out in the blizzard because of Broderick Bowman," he said, his silver eyes narrowing. "If anything had happened to you, he would have died a slow, agonizing death. As it is, the whole Russian fort will pay for his ignorance."

Letitia stepped up into the sled, eyeing Kanuga warily. "What do you mean?" she dared to ask. "What do you have planned for those who live at the Russian fort?"

Kanuga busied himself wrapping her warmly in blankets and pelts. "This is not the time to tell you," he said. "After we get to my village and get things settled there, then I will tell you."

Letitia opened her mouth to question him again, but he had slipped away from her, positioning himself on the sled behind her.

Soon the whip snapped in the air over the huskies, and they were leaping and bounding through the thick snow, yelping, their breaths like white puffs of clouds rising into the air.

Letitia snuggled down as low as she could beneath the blankets. Her gaze went to the sky. It had cleared, the streaks of black clouds that she had seen earlier trailing back from the southeast having disappeared.

Her thoughts returned to the previous night, when she had felt trapped by the storm. She had never felt so alone, and she hoped that such an experience would never be repeated.

She closed her eyes and let the sled rock her to sleep, and when she awakened she found herself at Kanuga's village, the dogs just now pulling up before Kanuga's longhouse.

Even before Kanuga could get to her to assist her in removing the thick layering of blankets and pelts, she had them thrown aside.

Breathlessly, she kicked the snowshoes off and hurried inside Kanuga's house, her gaze locking on her father the moment he was in sight. Hurrying to him, she fell to her knees beside him, devouring him with her eyes. He seemed no worse, and perhaps somewhat better. She eyed the soft-eyed woman who sat at her father's other side, intent on smoothing a dampened cloth over his brow.

"Papa," Letitia said, looking back down at her father. She yanked her gloves off so that she could take his hand and hold it. "I'm back. Papa, I'm all right."

Jerome opened his eyes and in them Letitia saw a sudden spark of relief. He clasped his fingers around her hands. "Letitia, where have you been?" he asked, his voice raspy.

Letitia was overjoyed that he was well enough to question her. He even looked less feverish. "Papa, I—I was abducted by a man from the Russian fort," she said, hating to reveal even the slightest information about the abduction, not wanting to worry him about it. "But I escaped."

She glanced over her shoulder as Kanuga came into the house, quickly discarding his fur coat. "Because of Kanuga, I am alive," she murmured.

She swallowed hard as she turned her eyes back to her father. "That makes twice that he has saved me, Papa," she said softly. "Twice."

She slipped her hands away from her father's when Kanuga came to her and helped her remove her coat.

"Because of my carelessness, she was abducted," Kanuga said in a growl. "Because I did not sleep in the same house as she. But starting tonight, the mistake will not be repeated. I sleep close at your daughter's side. No harm will come to her, or to you."

A blush swept over Letitia's face, afraid that her father would be able to guess that more than a rescue in the snow had transpired between his daughter and the powerful Tlingit chief. She smiled awkwardly down at her father, realizing that what Kanuga had said had not been interpreted as anything but kindness. Her shoulders relaxed with her relief.

"Tonight she sleeps on my ship," Jerome said, looking past Letitia at Kanuga. He tried to rise on an elbow, then fell back to the pallet of furs, groaning. "Letitia, tell Kanuga that we...we must return to the ship today. Your mother... I'm so worried about...about your mother."

Kanuga's shadow fell over Jerome and Letitia as he came and stood over them. He placed a hand on Letitia's shoulder, showing possession. "Letitia sleeps in my house tonight," he said firmly.

Letitia looked desperately up at him, fearing that the moment of truth was near. In a matter of moments he could tell her father his intentions toward her, and her father would have more than a wife to worry about!

Jerome's eyes narrowed. "You will return me and my daughter to my ship today," he said, again trying to rise, yet again crumpling back down. He closed his eyes, breathing hard.

"You are not well enough to travel," Kanuga said, kneeling down beside Jerome. "You will remain here with me until you are."

Letitia sucked in a wild breath of air, relieved to know that Kanuga was not ready to tell her father about his plans of marriage.

She had to surmise that Kanuga, being the astute man that he was, would not break any news to such an ailing man, not wanting to cause him further distress.

Yet she knew that the time would come, and when it did, whether her father was well or still ill, his reaction would be the same.

He would absolutely forbid such a marriage!
Would Kanuga then force her to stay behind?
Kanuga rose to his full height. He went and
stood beside the Tlingit maiden, who had stood
aside, obediently quiet, since Kanuga and Letitia
had returned to the longhouse. "This is Sweetwater," he said, placing a hand at Sweetwater's
waist, drawing her next to him. "She will see to
your father until he leaves for his ship."

"I am glad to make your acquaintance, Sweetwater," Letitia said, smiling at the lovely, timid
woman attired in a long, clinging buckskin robe
that was adorned with colorful beads. Letitia
concluded that Sweetwater must be in her early
thirties, with only a trace of wrinkles on her
brow.

Sweetwater smiled at Letitia, her straight,
white teeth contrasting with her copper com-
plexion. "Sweetwater make your father comfortable," she said in fluent English. "I nurse him
well."

"That is very kind of you," Letitia said, smiling
back at her. "But don't you have your own family
to tend to?"

A wounded look flashed in Sweetwater's eyes,
then she cast her eyes humbly to the floor.

"She is now a widow and childless," Kanuga
said, stroking Sweetwater's waist-length hair affectionately. "Both her husband and son died in
the river two winters ago when their canoe cap-
sized. She now passes her time helping others."

"I'm so very sorry about your family," Letitia
said, her heart going out to the lovely woman,

hardly able to envision how devastatingly lonely she must be without her loved ones.

"We will transfer your father to another room, to a bed," Kanuga said, bending to scoop Jerome up into his arms. He glanced at Sweetwater. "Kindle the fire in the room that is presently not occupied."

Sweetwater nodded and hurried ahead of Kanuga, and was already fanning the flames in the firepit in the smaller room when Letitia followed Kanuga there. She glanced around the room, which was steeped in shadows, able to make out only walls covered with pelts.

She looked back at her father and Kanuga, holding her breath as Kanuga placed her father on a small bed of furs. She breathed much more easily when Sweetwater was suddenly there, smoothing soft blankets over him.

"I will be fine," Jerome said, his eyelids heavy in his weakness.

Sweetwater settled on the floor beside the bed, looking with concern at Jerome.

"*Hade-krigut,*" Kanuga said, offering Letitia a hand. "You will come with me. It is time for a nourishing meal."

"My wife . . ." Jerome said, pleading up at Kanuga with his bloodshot eyes. "Can you send a messenger to her, saying that Letitia and I are safe? Will you see that she is faring well? Hardly any men were left on the ship to look after her. Please, Kanuga. Send someone to see after her and give her the news that Letitia and I will return to the ship soon?"

Kanuga gazed down at Jerome, his lips tightly pursed. Then without further thought, he nodded. "Word will be sent soon," he said, the lie so easy as it breathed across his lips. He had no intentions of going to the American ship for anything. He had only agreed to do so to ease both Letitia's and her father's minds.

He knew that if he sent word to the American ship and let them know where Letitia and her father were, other Americans could soon arrive at his village for them. There were dangers in that. Thus far, the Americans did not know just how close they were to a Tlingit village. It was to the Tlingits' advantage that only the Tlingit knew.

And it was best to have more time with Letitia, to give his people more time to understand and love her, as he did.

She would soon become Tlingit, and his people would accept her as the bride of their chief.

"Thank you," Letitia said, so touched by this handsome chief's continuing generosity and compassion.

In a lighthearted mood, she went back to the outer room with him and sat down beside him before the raging fire in the firepit. Her stomach growled as she peered into a black pot of food cooking over the coals.

But all desire to eat vanished when Kanuga offered her an oil dish carved in the form of a canoe, the salmon spread out in the dish reeking of fish oil. She shoved the dish away, her nose curling from the stench.

"You must eat to survive the cold weather," Kanuga said, forcing the dish back in her hands.

"But the fish oil ... stinks," Letitia said, wincing again at the foul odor.

Then she was taken aback by how her statement had offended Kanuga. He looked down at her with a tight expression, his eyes gleaming from the insult.

"Fish oil is the Tlingits' universal condiment, and a bowl of grease accompanies every meal," he said, now dipping some of the other boiled foods from the pot into another dish for Letitia. "It is a valuable trade commodity and an indicator of wealth."

Letitia accepted the second dish with a quavering smile, glad that Kanuga took the first one and set it aside.

"*At-i-cha,*" he said stoutly. "You eat!"

"Thank you," she murmured, her fingers already dipping into the rabbit stew, since no utensils for eating were offered her.

She ate ravenously, but began to feel queasy at her stomach as Kanuga talked as he ate, explaining what he planned for this evening.

"Tonight you will accompany me to the Russian fort to see what the Tlingit do to those who abduct women from their village," he said, his eyes dancing. "Even though you are safely with me again, I am going to take payment for you. The Russians must always make payment for their evil deeds done to my people."

He wiped his greasy mouth with the back of

his hand. "Especially Kanuga," he said flatly. "The Tlingit chief!"

Words would not come for Letitia, who was appalled by the thought of what he was expecting of her.

Then she spoke to him, the words spilling from her lips in a rush. "Surely you jest," she said, her eyes wide. "I can't go with you. You shouldn't even want me to!"

"It is imperative that you learn all the ways of the Tlingit," he said matter-of-factly. "Even how vengeance is carried out."

"But, Kanuga, I don't want to," Letitia said, glad that her father was in the other room, perhaps even asleep by now, so that he would not hear Kanuga's plans. "Please. Please don't force me to."

"*Hade-krigut*," he insisted, his face solemn. "You will come. I have spoken. Now do not say any more about it."

Letitia's appetite was suddenly gone, and with it all hope of ever seeing her mother again, or of getting her father safely to the ship. She feared much bloodshed tonight.

Atkuk was just awakening after a night of fitful dreams about his chieftain brother. In this nightmare, Kanuga had been slain, by not only the Russians, but also the Americans.

Laughing, the Russians and Americans had trapped Kanuga and were taking turns shooting him until he fell into a pool of his life's blood, dead.

The American woman soon followed, collapsing over Kanuga's body, her own silken flesh riddled with bullet holes.

His brow pearled with sweat, Atkuk jerked himself completely awake, panting, his eyes filled with despair at the thought of losing his beloved brother. He and Kanuga were all that was left of their family. Without Kanuga, Atkuk would only be half a man.

Wiping the sweat from his brow, Atkuk turned to push himself up from his bed, then stopped with a start when he discovered a long pole with cedar bark wrapped around the end lying through a hole in his wall where several boards had been removed while he had slept.

Fear grabbed him at the pit of his stomach, knowing very well the meaning of such an action. It revealed that another shaman was jealous of him and was treating him as though he was one whose power was too great!

He knew that the pole was a warning—that his life would soon be snuffed from him!

His first thoughts went to Kosko. Atkuk was well aware of having defied the elder shaman, perhaps having even shamed him in front of Athas.

But would Kosko go this far in his anger over such a trivial thing? Atkuk had always suspected that Kosko was capable of anything, even at times taking on the appearance of one who was bewitched.

He shrugged these troubling thoughts aside, not wanting to believe that a shaman so revered by the Tlingit could be evil, in any way.

A brave and holy man, Atkuk shoved the pole from inside his tent, then slung heavy robes around his shoulders and went to kneel beside the low embers of his lodge fire.

His thoughts returned to Kanuga, knowing that if he confided in his brother about this threat to his life, Kanuga would find the jealous shaman, even if it was the great and powerful Kosko, and banish him from the tribe.

But Atkuk could not find it in his heart to trouble his brother with this problem that was Atkuk's alone. His brother already carried the weight of his people on his shoulders.

And there was this new threat, he thought wearily.

The arrival of Americans!

No, he decided. He would not tell Kanuga.

Instead, he lifted his eyes upward and began to pray, sharing his fears only with the Chief Above, who lived in a house in the sky, and who exercised control over man's destiny.

Chapter Seven

*Nature often enshrines gallant and noble
hearts in weak bosoms—oftenest, God
bless her! in female breast.*

—DICKENS

The sky was dark, the moon hidden beneath a
gloom of clouds. Letitia sat angrily in Kanuga's
sled as it slid over the frozen tundra away from
his village. She had fussed with Kanuga until she
was hoarse about being forced to accompany him
and his warriors against the Russians. He had
even gone as far as making her dress the same
as the many Tlingit warriors who were accompanying their chief on this vendetta against the
Russians.

The full-length, hooded fur robe warded off the
frozen temperatures of the night, but the fact that
he would place her in danger, alongside his men,
was almost too much for her to comprehend.

She thought that he cared for her!

How could he, she wondered angrily, if he placed her so willingly in the face of danger?

And Kanuga had not only made her dress the part of a warrior, he had given her a weapon to carry into battle!

Although he had not actually mentioned the word 'battle', Letitia did not expect anything less than being a part of much bloodshed and horror.

She glanced down at the rifle at her side, shivering at the thought of being forced to actually fire it against another human being. She had no personal grudge against the Russians. As far as she knew, they had not even had a part in her abduction.

It had been one man's vile, dirty deed!

And now to go against a whole body of Russians for this one man's misdeeds?

It did not seem a fair thing to do, unless the Russians and the Tlingit had made it a habit to act on any excuse to have battle long before she arrived, and Kanuga had purposely hidden this fact from her!

She could not help but recall Kanuga saying that he did not make war with the Russians, that thus far theirs had been a peaceful co-existence.

She hovered beneath a thick layer of pelts, watching the other sleds and huskies racing through the night on both sides of her. It was like watching a horse race back home.

As one sled was overtaken by another, those dogs would be urged to go faster, overtaking the other one again. It seemed a night of games, instead of warring, as the Tlingit warriors laughed and shouted challenges at one another through the dark.

Even Kanuga joined in, urging his huskies to overtake all of the others.

Even Kanuga turned to his warriors, laughing and urging them to challenge him again.

Shocked and puzzled, Letitia turned with a start and gazed up at Kanuga. His eyes met hers momentarily and held, then looked beyond her into the crystal cold of night, as though she were not even there.

She turned her eyes away from him, wondering if he no longer saw her as a challenge, treating her as though she were just one of the warriors instead of a woman. Had she, she wondered, given herself to him too easily? Did he truly no longer care?

Perhaps, even, he hoped that she would be shot tonight, to rid himself of this white foreign intruder!

Shaking her head to clear her mind of such doubts and frustrations, Letitia focused her eyes straight ahead.

Then her insides quivered with fear when, in the distance, she could see the flickering torches that she remembered having been placed at strategic places outside the fort, on its palisade. They would soon be there!

Oh, thank the Lord that her father had been asleep when she said a quiet goodbye to him. Had he been aware of what she was being forced to be a part of, the shock alone could have killed him.

Letitia became quickly aware of how the mood of the Tlingit warriors had changed. They were no longer laughing and playing games. Silence washed over the warriors, as though waves of an ocean had overtaken them, sucking their breaths away.

She scarcely breathed herself as she watched the walls of the fort coming closer and closer. Fearing the worst, she slipped her gloves off and picked up the rifle, even though she was not at all skilled at using firearms. Until recently she had always had her father for protection. Kanuga had saved her twice, but was it to be for naught? Had he saved her to send her to death at the hands of the Russians?

Bitterness grabbed at Letitia's heart. She set her jaw and clasped hard to the rifle, refusing to look Kanuga's way again. If she must defend herself, she would do so with all of her energies! She would show Kanuga! She would show him that she didn't need him at all.

As the fort was almost reached, Letitia expected a volley of gunfire from the Russians, but then she recalled how lax they were about defending themselves. On this moonless night, the same lazy sentry that she had slipped past was surely asleep again. She could not believe it when the Tlingit sleds came close to the great palisade walls and still had not been detected! The Russians would be easy prey. Even their gate was still wide open, as it had been the other time she was there—an invitation, it seemed, for anyone who might want to enter!

Letitia could not help but glance back at Kanuga, expecting him to give the orders to his warriors to enter the gate, to begin the slaughter of the unsuspecting Russians!

He gave Letitia a smile of confidence, then guided his huskies in a half circle, which sent them traveling to the back of the fort.

Amazed at this strategy, Letitia turned her eyes back around, wondering about the Tlingit who had already stopped their dog teams and were busy loading their sleds with armloads of fire wood!

Stunned, Letitia glanced over her shoulder at Kanuga again just as he drew his dogs to a halt beside the huge piles of firewood.

"What are you doing?" she asked, keeping her voice at a whisper as he came to her. "What are your warriors doing with the firewood? Kanuga, I thought you came to fight the Russians."

Kanuga's eyes were dancing as he took the rifle from Letitia. "You won't be needing this after all," he said, placing the rifle in the sled. He grabbed up her gloves and slipped them on her hands. "At least not yet. As always before, we were able to get past the sentries without any mishap. We must load the wood quickly. Some of the lazy Russians might be awakened by the commotion."

Letitia stepped from the sled, Kanuga helping her as he gripped her waist with both hands. "But Kanuga, I expected something much different than this," she said, marveling at the complexities of this man to whom her heart had been given, and feeling better about him, since he had not deliberately placed her in danger after all.

Everything seemed so innocent.

Yet, strange...

"The Russians will know why the firewood is missing once they discover their loss," Kanuga said, guiding her to the stacks of firewood, padding along like a soundless shadow. "As I told you before, ever since the Russians came to this land of plenty, they have taken our women as wives without the customary payment for the privilege. In retaliation, the Tlingit always help themselves to the Russians' firewood. For your abduction, this is the only payment that Kanuga seeks today."

Letitia gazed up at him, stunned, yet realizing that there were many customs and beliefs of the Tlingit that would surely be strange to her. "But, Kanuga, I am not Tlingit," she murmured. "And I am not your wife."

"Soon you will be both," Kanuga said matter-of-factly. "When you become my wife, you will become Tlingit."

Letitia's eyes brightened, knowing that he did still love her, yet wary because of it. He was as determined for her to become his wife as her father would be determined that she would not be. Then would come the time to choose between two men she loved, even adored, with all of her heart.

Kanuga picked up several split logs and offered them to Letitia. "You are a part of this vengeance," he said. "You will help load the firewood."

Letitia said nothing. She was just anxious to get the sleds loaded and out of there. Feverishly, she helped Kanuga fill his sled.

Soon everyone was pleased enough with their bounty and boarded their sleds again.

After Letitia climbed into Kanuga's sled, he took much care in wrapping her snugly in the pelts again, then stepped to the back of the sled and snapped his whip over the heads of the waiting huskies.

Letitia sighed with much relief when the huskies made a wide half circle, taking her away from the Russian fort. She watched as the other huskies with their sleds raced away into the dark night. Now that she felt safe and was relaxed enough to see the humor of the situation, that stealing the firewood was such an innocent vengeance compared to killing and maiming people, Letitia was able to laugh about it. She was even feeling giddy. Soon she would be back at her father's side. Soon she would be in Kanuga's arms....

Sudden gunfire rang out from the direction of the fort, creating much confusion where only moments ago, there had been a jubilant camaraderie among the victorious Tlingit warriors.

Another shot rang out, and Letitia looked in horror at a young Tlingit Indian on his sled beside Kanuga's, as his body lurched with the impact of the bullet, penetrating his thick fur coat and entering his back.

Kanuga emitted a cry of remorse, drawing his

team of huskies to a sudden halt, along with others who stopped to help the injured warrior. Kanuga saw to the lad's welfare, covering him with warm pelts, then ordered one of his warriors who had been riding two to a sled to leave his sled to the lone driver and drive Kanuga's dog team, while Kanuga took over the reins of the injured warrior's.

Soon the gunfire was left behind, and the sleds were sliding like silent ghosts onward through a soft snowfall that was just beginning to fall from the sky. Tears came to Letitia's eyes; she should not have felt so confident, so soon.

She would be to blame should the young warrior die.

Grabbing a shirt, Colonel Golodoff growled obscenities to himself. He had been awakened by the gunfire. There hadn't been any attacks by the Tlingit since Fort Anecia was built, so the gunfire must have been from one of his men misfiring. He was out for the responsible person's hide, for no one spoiled Colonel Golodoff's sleep!

His shirt buttoned, the suspenders in place over his shoulders, he stomped across the room and just as he circled his fingers around the doorknob, someone knocked on the door.

Now angrier than before at someone else having the nerve to disturb him at this ungodly hour, Colonel Golodoff jerked the door open and found himself staring down into the cool, dark eyes of his son, who also seemed to have dressed in a rush. His shirt was unbuttoned and wasn't tucked into his breeches, which hugged his thick hips tightly.

"Well, Iuril? What brings you to my door this time of night?" Colonel Golodoff growled in Russian. "And, damn it, who misfired the gun? And who is so unskilled with a gun, he misfired not only once, but twice?"

"It wasn't a misfire, Father," Iuril said, smoothing his hands over his balding head. "One of our sentries fired at some Indians."

Colonel Golodoff took a surprised step away from his son, for a moment speechless. Then he said, glaring down at Iuril, "What Indians? We've never fired on the Tlingit since Fort Anecia became established in Alaska. Why would we now?"

"Always before they came like thieves in the night and stole piles of our firewood," Iuril said, circling a hand into a tight fist at his side. "But tonight, they slipped up. They got caught as they were leaving with the firewood. The thieving bastards."

Colonel Golodoff kneaded his chin, a thick eyebrow forked in wonder. "There had to be a reason," he said, nodding. "Iuril, get the men together. Investigate. See why the Indians stole from us tonight."

Iuril laughed throatily. "Father, you know that isn't necessary," he scoffed. "Everyone knows that the Indians are thieves, too lazy to find and cut firewood for themselves. They will use any excuse to steal the wood."

Colonel Golodoff placed a firm hand on Iuril's

shoulder, glaring down at him. "Must I remind you, Iuril, that Kanuga is known to be a man of pride," he said flatly. "He would never steal unless he had cause to. Kanuga is not a thief. He is most definitely not lazy."

"Your defense of the Indian seems genuine enough," Iuril said, stepping away from his father. "I fear that some day your trust in that man will backfire on you."

"Time will prove you wrong about that, my son," Colonel Golodoff said, taking another cigar from his shirt pocket and lighting it. He puffed on the cigar for a moment, then looked at Iuril with a steady gaze. "I forgot to ask. Was anyone injured? Did any of the Indians get shot? Did any of our men?"

"It was too dark to tell where the bullets went," Iuril said. Then he smiled smugly. "But it wasn't too dark to hear a cry of pain. Yes, Father, I believe one of the Indians was shot." He turned to leave, then turned and smiled crookedly at his father. "My, but wouldn't it be interesting if it was Kanuga?"

Laughing boisterously, as if he had forgotten the innocent times when he had played ball with Kanuga on warmer summer days, Iuril left, leaving Colonel Golodoff filled with a sudden cold fear.

Colonel Golodoff began pacing the floor, knowing that if Kanuga was among those shot, and if he died, his bargaining days with the Tlingit were over. Even if any of Kanuga's prized warriors died, there would be more than firewood taken from Fort Anecia!

He wished that the one who had shot the Indian had not acted so carelessly. He knew that Chief Kanuga would have no choice but to retaliate.

And what *had* prompted the Indians to steal the wood, he wondered? They usually did that only after one of their women had been abducted.

Colonel Golodoff went to his window and stared down at the men grouping together in the courtyard, Iuril standing among them. "Damn it, I gave orders to everyone to leave the Indians alone!" he whispered to himself. "If the Russians and Tlingit are to live peacefully together, nothing must be done to antagonize the Indians!"

Though the colonel respected, even admired Kanuga, he realized that the Indian chief was not as easy-going as his predecessor, his chieftain father. It was common knowledge that Kanuga had never liked the interference of the Russians. Since he had gained the title of chief, he had only tolerated the Russians because of the friendship that had existed between his father and the colonel—and the long-ago brief friendship between Kanuga and Iuril.

"But it seems that time is running out for us," Colonel Golodoff said aloud, his words echoing back at him with a tone of gloom. Kanuga would take only so much, he knew, and then everyone at the fort would know what to expect.

Knowing that he should be the one to warn his men of a possible full attack from the Indians, should the injured warrior die, he grabbed a coat, rushed from the room and down the stairs, then out to the courtyard. He shoved Iuril aside and took charge.

"As you all know, there has been an unfortunate firing at the Indians tonight," Colonel Golodoff shouted, his voice silencing the men as they gazed at him with devoted admiration. "As you know, they were here stealing firewood. And you all know what causes them to do this." He frowned as he looked from man to man. "Who among you has an Injun squaw at his cabin?"

There was no response, just a hushed sort of silence. "Well, I take that to mean that none of you has been foolish enough to bring a squaw to the fort," Colonel Golodoff continued. "So, then, where did you poke her? Did you steal her, poke her, then leave her to die in the snow?"

There was still no response. Broderick Bowman looked on, his heart hammering against his chest. He had not yet ventured from the fort to spy on the Tlingit to see if the American woman had returned there safely, and if so, if she was the only American there, and why. He had been too afraid of being caught by not only the Tlingit, but also by the Russians. Neither cared whether he lived or died.

Dead, he would be more valuable, it seemed. His use seemed to have run out long ago after he had started bungling matters between the Tlingit and Russians.

They now all called him a god-damned bungler!

Somehow he hoped to prove them wrong.

The American lady. She was the key to his future, to new beginnings with the Russians!

But until he found the courage to investigate at the Tlingit village, he had to lie low. A warrior being shot tonight made his investigations twice as risky.

"Well, it seems that no one is brave enough to admit their wrongdoing, so all I can do is warn you to be on the lookout for a Tlingit attack," Colonel Golodoff said, turning to walk away.

He stopped and looked from man to man, his eyes narrowing. "Whenever the guilty party wishes to confess," he said, "just make sure I've had a full night's sleep. You'll be better off for it."

Broderick cowered beneath Colonel Golodoff's stare, then felt another pair of eyes on him. Slowly, he turned and faced Iuril. Iuril looked at him with a silent accusation, then smiled at Broderick smugly before turning away from him and falling in step beside his father.

Although it was an intensely cold night, Broderick wiped a bead of sweat from his brow with the sleeve of his fur coat.

The Tlingit procession of dogsleds arrived at the village in a flurry of activity. Letitia climbed from her sled, stumbling through the heavy snow toward Kanuga's longhouse, then stopped and watched as the injured lad was taken quickly to Kanuga's shaman brother's dwelling, as had been instructed by Kanuga.

Soon the air was rent with the cries of those

Cassie Edwards

acquainted with the young warrior, as his mother and sisters raced toward the shaman's longhouse.

Letitia went to the house and moved cautiously and soundlessly through the door and stood in the shadows, away from the others, again spellbound by the performance of Atkuk as he chanted and danced over the injured warrior's quiet body. The Tlingits' close relationship between man and animal was made unusually explicit in the Tlingit salmon rattle that Atkuk was shaking, which contained an effigy of a salmon. Letitia saw the performance as magical and beautiful.

Yet Letitia could not help but question the worth of the shaman's healing practices. Her father was better, but this Indian had been *shot*. A bullet was still lodged in his body! Could he possibly live?

If not, what sort of reprisal would Kanuga make against the Russians then?

Surely not as peaceful a demonstration as stealing firewood!

After the healing ritual was over, someone among the women having even removed the bullet while Atkuk sang over the unconscious lad, Kanuga came to Letitia and led her from his brother's longhouse, and then to his. Inside, away from wondering eyes, he embraced her.

"Is he going to be all right, Kanuga?" Letitia murmured, clinging to him.

"Atkuk has done his best," he said solemnly.

He paused, then said, "Tonight you saw more

than I intended," he said, holding her close. "For that I am sorry."

She leaned away from him, so that their eyes could meet and hold. "And I am sorry, Kanuga," she said, blinking a rush of tears from her eyes. "If not for me..."

He placed a finger to her lips, silencing her. "Never blame yourself," he said thickly. "Never."

He helped her off with her long fur robe, then watched her with a tender heart as she went to the room where her father lay and knelt down beside him, across from where Sweetwater was still sitting vigil, her eyes warming when Letitia smiled at her.

When Jerome opened his eyes and gave Letitia a slow wink of assurance, so much of what had happened tonight faded away into nothingness.

Letitia felt so lucky.

The two men she loved were still alive.

Chapter Eight

How blessings brighten as they take their flight.
                                        —YOUNG

Letitia sat on the floor beside her sleeping father, two empty bowls beside her—her own and her father's. She lifted one of her father's hands to her lips and kissed its palm, then placed it beneath the blankets again.

She smiled at his peaceful sleeping form, so proud that he had eaten his whole bowl of broth. He so needed the nourishment to build his strength back to normal.

And that he was sleeping so soundly, as though he trusted that everything would soon be all right in his world, made Letitia speak a silent word of thanks to the Lord, and then to Kanuga, who continued to make everything possible for her and her father.

Soon she would have to make a decision, a

choice between two men—and two futures.

And the decision had nothing to do with dear, sweet Jonathan. If she chose another man over him, because she had found love within this man's arms, Jonathan would be the first to understand. Theirs was to have been just an arranged marriage—one of a mutual respect and admiration.

As sincere and dear as Jonathan was, Letitia was certain he could find another woman who could give him much more of herself than she could.

Letitia had not offered Jonathan her heart because she loved him, but only out of the devotion of friends.

A firm hand suddenly on her shoulder gave Letitia a start. She turned her eyes quickly up, then smiled.

"Kanuga," she said, placing her hand over his. "I did not hear you come up behind me. I thought that you were still at your brother's lodge, seeing to that young warrior's condition."

"I was there, but I am not needed any longer," Kanuga said, taking Letitia's hand and urging her to her feet. He drew her close and spoke down into her face. "There is nothing for me to do there. Everything is being done that can be. My brother continues to perform his magic over the fallen one."

He looked past Letitia at her father, then back into Letitia's eyes. "Your father?" he said softly. "How does he fare today?"

He spied the empty bowl. "You do not have to

answer me," he said, smiling. "I see that he has eaten. That is proof enough to me that he is much better."

"Yes, and thanks to you," Letitia said, then gazed over at Sweetwater. "And also Sweetwater. No one could be as devoted a nurse."

She then turned her eyes back to Kanuga. "Kanuga, your kindness will always be remembered by my father," she murmured. "I will also remember it. You not only rescued me and my father, you even took us into your dwelling. You have given up your privacy so that my father could be given the best of treatment. No one could ever be as generous as you, Kanuga. No one."

"You and your father would have done the same had it been I who was found stranded in the snow, felled by the attack of a bear," Kanuga said, nodding. "I know this, Letitia. So do not make so much over my having done it. Your heart—your father's heart—matches the goodness of mine."

He drew away from her and led her to the outer room. He bent and scooped up her coat and placed it around her shoulders. "Dress warmly," he said, his tone more a command than a request. "Put on all of your warm garments for outside. You will accompany me on another mission this morning."

Letitia took a quick step away from him, a familiar cold fear catching at her heart when he spoke of another mission. "What sort of mission?" she asked, her voice thin with wariness.

"Please don't tell me that I must accompany you and your warriors again against the Russians. That is the mission you speak of, isn't it, Kanuga? That of avenging the young warrior today?"

She straightened her back and firmed her jaw. "I absolutely refuse to go," she said, her flashing eyes concealing the true fear that she was feeling.

It was not so much that she feared that she would be forced to do what he said—but she feared being so bold as to stand up to him!

Yes, he had vowed to love her, but would such a love wane under the bold face of her defiance?

"Nothing you say or do will make me become a part of your sort of battles again," she reaffirmed. "Nothing!"

Surprising Letitia, a slow smile tugged at the corners of Kanuga's lips. Puzzled, she looked at him, wondering what he was finding so amusing. She had expected him to be angry. Now she had no idea what to expect and braced herself for whatever it might be. This Tlingit Indian was a most complex man, with a most complex personality!

All of which she could not help but admire.

"*Hade-krigut,*" Kanuga said, forcing her gloves into her hands. "Dress warmly. Now. I will be waiting outside."

Letitia watched, her lips parted in surprise that he was still so determined to get his way. She watched Kanuga leave the house, then shook her head as though to clear her thoughts of him. Shaken by his out-and-out stubbornness about making her go with him, Letitia knew that she had no choice but to comply with his wishes. No matter how she looked at it, she and her father were at Kanuga's mercy.

And to make sure things remained peaceful between them all, until her father was well enough to be transported to safety on the ship, she would do as Kanuga asked, no matter if it took her into the face of danger.

Mumbling to herself, Letitia threw the gloves to the floor and shrugged into her coat. Plopping down on the floor, she fit the snowshoes on, then grabbed the gloves again and pulled them on.

After going to take a lingering look at her father, who still slept peacefully, as though not even a part of this world anymore, with Sweetwater keeping vigil at his bedside, Letitia left the house in a huff and stared icily into Kanuga's eyes as he turned and looked at her, again with an amused smile on his lips.

"I don't know what you are finding so amusing about all of this," Letitia fussed, stamping to the sled and climbing on. She peered at the huskies, as peacefully asleep as her father, all rolled up into tight balls, with their backs to the wind.

She then looked farther still, puzzled when she saw no more huskies attached to sleds, nor any warriors ready to guide them away from the village, Lord knew not where.

An eyebrow arched, Letitia looked up at Kanuga as he came to her and fitted warm pelts around her. "Kanuga, I don't understand any of this," she said. "You said that I was to accompany you on a mission. What sort? And are we going to go alone?"

"The mission I speak of?" he said, chuckling low. "It is for food, *ssik-gu schau-wot*. After so much seriousness, you should enjoy a more light-hearted day."

Letitia stared blankly up at him, then began laughing, causing him to look at her with wonder in his silver eyes.

Then her laughter died and anger replaced her feelings of relief. "Why didn't you tell me that in the first place?" she complained, frowning at him as he placed another warm pelt around her legs. "Why did you let me think that we were going to fight the Russians? Do you enjoy teasing me? Do you?"

Kanuga reached a gloved hand to Letitia's face. "It is not so much the teasing that I enjoy," he said, his eyes dancing. "It is the flash of your eyes when you are angry. They are even more intriguing."

"That's a very poor excuse for teasing me about things such as—such as missions," Letitia said, sighing discontentedly. "You had to know that I would be upset if I thought I was going to be forced to ride with you again to the Russian fort. It was only natural that I *would* think that you would plan to do that today. The young warrior would be the cause."

"Perhaps later, but not today," Kanuga said, moving to the rear of the sled as Letitia's eyes followed him. "I will not give the order to seek vengeance until I see what sort is required. If our young warrior dies, we shall have no more patience with the Russians. We will seek war with them. If he should live, perhaps I will give the Russians one more chance to leave Alaska on their own, without any blood being spilled in the white snows of our land."

Slipping her snow glasses over her eyes, Letitia became quiet, again reminded of why her father had come to Alaska. It was becoming more and more evident that once he was well enough to return to his ship, he would be asked to return to America, perhaps in exchange for Kanuga's kindnesses to him for having rescued him from the bear.

As the whip snapped overhead, Letitia snuggled down among the warm pelts, yet not feeling so warm inside. Coming to Alaska had caused many tumultuous feelings within her, none of which she felt capable of dealing with. It seemed to her that she would not be the one to find answers for herself. Her fate seemed to lie in Kanuga's hands.

And even though she loved him, she did not enjoy realizing that he held her destiny within his hands—and heart.

The huskies yelped as they drew the sled through the white wilderness. Today the temperatures were almost a promise of what lay ahead—spring!

While she had the chance, Letitia found herself enjoying the breathtaking view—or what she could see of it through the tiny portals of the snow glasses. Her father had warned her that the winter light was oblique, the winter sun a sorcerer.

He had been right on both counts.

If she looked hard enough, she could see the snow-dappled mountains in the distance, their craggy peaks piercing through the cottony clouds, their lower elevations thickly carpeted in forests whose limbs were weighed down with snow.

Letitia's gaze captured movement ahead and leaned up to take a better look, then smiled to herself when she saw a ground squirrel scurrying over the snow in a brief foray from its hibernation. She knew enough of this land from her studies to know that mice and shrews scurried through passageways under the snow, and that if one looked close enough one could see how frost formed icy tufts around the breathing holes near the burrow entrances of other hibernating animals. If one caught sight of a puff of what looked like snow in the distance, it might be the breath of a bear as it slept soundly until the icebound lakes began to crack and moan in early spring.

Ah, yes, it was a beautiful day. She caught her breath when they came across snowy fields full of arctic hares—very large rabbits, entirely white except for the black tips of their ears. They were pawing through the snow cover for the sparse brown grass below and seemed to be communicating with one another by shadowboxing, each flurry of boxing followed by a few hops in search of better feeding grounds.

And then these were also left behind.

Suddenly the huskies brought the sled to a shuddering halt beside an icebound river. Letitia swept her covering of pelts aside and left the sled, watching with interest as Kanuga unfastened two of the dogs and turned them loose on the snow-covered ice of the river.

Not wanting to be left behind, alone, Letitia rushed along the land beside Kanuga. She eyed the large harpoon he carried, and then an innocent-looking sealskin bag he had placed over his shoulder.

Then her attention was drawn from Kanuga, and she hesitated to follow him any longer when he joined the dogs onto the ice-filled river. She looked at the ice warily, knowing that death would be instant if she fell through to the current below.

"This way," Kanuga encouraged her with the wave of his hand toward Letitia. "The dogs have found breathing holes in the ice. Soon seals will come up for air. My hunt will be over for the day!"

Trusting his knowledge of the ice and anxious to get the hunt over with, Letitia gave Kanuga a soft, quavering smile and followed him. Soon he stopped and knelt down beside where the dogs now obediently lay, their noses at the break in the ice, eagerly watching.

"Watch how it is done," Kanuga encouraged her, giving Letitia a quick glance, then returning to his task at hand. "First I take a downy feather from my bag. Then I lay the feather on the small circle of water. This will give a warning quiver as the animal approaches."

He took the feather from the bag and lay it

carefully on the circle of water.

"Now we wait," he said, his harpoon poised in his hand.

"How long?" Letitia whispered, her eyes glued to the feather, waiting for it to shimmer.

"They should be coming up for a breath soon," Kanuga said, his voice light and breezy.

Letitia knelt down beside Kanuga, hugging herself as the wind picked up speed, fluttering the fur from her hood around her brow and cheeks.

And then, as though lightning had struck, Kanuga had, in one blind jab, thrust his harpoon into the hole and a seal was brought quickly out of the water.

Letitia was breathless. She hadn't even seen the feather quiver! She had scarcely even seen the harpoon's movements, Kanuga had been so swift! So accurate!

She didn't say anything, just knelt there beside him, watching him performing another Tlingit ritual that was unfamiliar to her. She wasn't sure if she should question Kanuga about it, but could hold back no longer when Kanuga did not immediately take the seal to his sled to return with it to his village. He had cut a small slit on the head of the seal, instead.

"What are you doing?" Letitia asked, puzzled even more when Kanuga took a mitten from his bag, and held it to the dead seal's mouth.

"I have carried fresh drinking water in the mitten for the seal," he said, not looking her way, intent on giving the dead seal a drink. "I first released the seal's spirit through a cut on the head, and now I offer it a drink of fresh water so that the water spirits won't be angry at me and will allow me to come again to these waters for food."

Letitia smiled warmly at Kanuga, thinking his customs so innocent, yet she knew that most of the rituals practiced by him and his people were their only reasons for survival.

Letitia tagged along after Kanuga as he carried the seal to the sled, placing it at the back and covering it with stretched and dried sealskins. Letitia thought that they would then return to the village, but she was surprised when Kanuga proved that he had something more on his mind than that. He was collecting firewood beneath a thicket of willow and dwarf birch. Soon he cleared away the snow in a wide circle with his snowshoes, spread some skins over the frozen ground, and built a fire.

"Let us sit and talk before returning to the worries of both our worlds," Kanuga said, fanning his hands over the crackling twigs.

The fire soon erupted into a toasty blaze that was too tempting for Letitia. She sat down beside Kanuga on the pelts.

"It must take so much time to keep your people in food," she said, snuggling next to Kanuga as he swept an arm around her waist.

"We are no different than the four-legged creatures of the tundra," he said. "We press on daily in search of food. But we have the advantage. We have learned skills handed down through generations of Tlingit that outsmart the tiny creatures who are our prey. Wildfowl are entangled in skillfully thrown *bolas*, which are three cords knotted together with stones on the ends. Fish are caught on bone and ivory hooks through holes in the ice. One day soon I will teach you how the salmon are caught."

He placed a finger to her chin and directed her eyes to his, so that they met and held. "My woman, you too will have to learn all ways of existence once you become as Tlingit."

Not wanting to get involved in talking about marriage again, not sure, yet, what the future truly held for them, Letitia guided their conversation away from it. "Tell me," she urged. "Tell me how you catch the salmon. Is it as uniquely done as the seal was harpooned today?"

"No harpoon is used," Kanuga said, laughing. Then within his eyes there appeared a strange sort of mysterious glow as he explained, "Monkshood root is used. It is poisonous, but very useful. I crush it and throw it in the water. Soon every fish within twenty yards will float up to the surface."

Letitia paled. "Poison?" she gasped. "You poison the fish?"

"The fish feel no ill effects from the poison," Kanuga reassured her.

"But the humans who eat the fish surely have some sort of effect from it," Letitia said, recalling the fish she had eaten at Kanuga's village. Her stomach seemed to be turning inside out at the thought of having placed poisonous substances in her system!

Kanuga turned to her, admiring the fire's glow soft in her even softer eyes. "The poison does no harm to those who eat it," he said. He chuckled low. "If so, there would be no Tlingit left on this land of snow and ice."

Letitia noticed that Kanuga had suddenly grown tense; his smile had faded, and his eyes had filled with a silent, strange sort of excitement. When he stood and offered her a hand, urging her up next to him, she followed his gaze and gasped when she saw the huge antlers of a moose between the branches of the willows beside the river.

"I saw the moose tracks earlier," Kanuga whispered. "I had thought that our presence would have frightened him off. But it didn't. He is an offering to my people, it seems."

Kanuga released Letitia's hand and went to the sled and got his rifle. Making no sound, his feet like those of a panther, he moved stealthily toward the grazing moose. Letitia held her breath when he got just on the other side of where the moose was standing. Her eyes widened when he whistled, then she jolted with alarm when the moose raised its head and received a bullet between the eyes.

After the moose was also tied in place behind the sled, Kanuga went and stamped out the fire, gathered up his dogs, then went to Letitia.

"It has been a good day," he said, pride shining in his silver eyes. "*Now* it is time to return home." Hand in hand, they went to the sled.

Chapter Nine

For thee enchanted dreams she weaves,
of changeful beauty, bright and wild.

—OSGOOD

Exhilarated after her exciting outing with Kanuga, Letitia followed him into his longhouse, feeling a strange sort of camaraderie with him, as never before. Yet she feared this bond that was forming between them—a bond that would make it hard to tell him goodbye.

Just inside the large house, Letitia shook off the snowshoes, then went to her father to see if he was faring better since earlier in the morning when she had watched Sweetwater feed him his broth, and had then left him to his nap.

Her heart lurched when she found that he wasn't on his bed, but collapsed on the floor at the far side of the room. Sweetwater knelt beside him, sobbing.

"I could not stop him," Sweetwater cried. "He was determined to get up."

"Papa!" Letitia gasped, rushing to him.

Kanuga was soon there beside her, lifting Jerome up into his arms and carrying him back to the bed.

Letitia followed Kanuga, then knelt over her father as she placed blankets around him. "Papa, what were you trying to do?" she murmured, glad when his eyes opened.

"I wanted to get dressed," Jerome said, his voice weak and drawn. "Letitia, I want to return to the ship. Today."

"Papa, didn't you just prove to yourself that you are in no shape to go anywhere?" she said, smoothing her palm across his perspiration-laced brow. "You must wait until you are stronger." She smiled down at him. "Papa, more than once, when I was a child, you scolded me for being too stubborn. Well, I think you are proving to be much more stubborn than I."

"It is not for myself that I want to leave," Jerome argued. "Letitia, as each day passes I am more and more concerned about those in our expedition who were separated from us in the storm."

He reached for Letitia's hand and clasped onto it almost frantically. "If they were safe, they would have come for us. Don't you remember? Kanuga sent word to the ship, informing them where we are."

He paused, licking his parched lips. "Also, I'm worried about your mother," he said, stopping to inhale a quavering breath.

Then he said, "Surely *you're* concerned about Jonathan? Good Lord, Letitia, he's your fiance. Don't you feel the same urgency as I to return to the ship to see if he made it back safely?"

The word 'fiance' grabbed Letitia at the heart. She realized, when she glanced quickly up at Kanuga, that he understood the meaning of the word, for within the depths of his silver eyes she saw something she never had before—a keen jealousy!

Kanuga's insides stiffened. Letitia had not told him that she was spoken for by another man. Jealousy shook him to the core of his being, yet there was something in the way that Letitia was gazing up at him that did not seem to speak of a mere apology. He could see that she was troubled by his knowing, and that would only be so if she loved him, and not this man called Jonathan. He did know her well enough to know that she would not be the sort to play betrayal games. She would not love one man, and make love with another!

And he knew this to be so, for she had shared too much with him ever to belong spiritually to another man.

Kanuga stepped closer to Jerome and knelt down beside Letitia. He gave Jerome a set stare. "White man, today has already passed. The sun is lowering in the sky. But tomorrow I will return you to your ship," he said, folding his arms tautly across his chest.

He turned his gaze back to Letitia and looked

at her for a moment, then turned back to her father. "But your daughter will stay behind in the Tlingit village with me," he said flatly. "Soon she will become my bride."

The air was rent with tension, so quickly did it fall quiet, as though no one was there. Letitia's words, almost her breath, were stolen from her in that instant. She recalled those intimate moments between her and Kanuga, hoping that her father would not suspect that these truths were what prompted Kanuga's claim on her! It was certain now that Kanuga felt she belonged to him, even though she had never promised him anything but those reckless moments of loving him.

But because of this alone, in a sense she did belong to him!

Oh, how she adored him.

She loved him with all of her heart—with all of her being!

But her father's feelings were equally important to her. She owed him so much. He had been a doting, loving father—had loved her much longer than Kanuga had loved her.

Should her father lose his respect for her, she would want to die!

Letitia gasped when her father tried to push himself up from the bed, his eyes filled with rage.

"And so this is why you've been so generous to us?" Jerome said, his words coming in short raspy sounds. He hung his head, trying to catch his breath, then peered angrily up at Kanuga again. "All along it was because of my daughter!

You . . . wanted . . . my daughter!"

Kanuga rose to his full height, insulted by Jerome's accusation. "Do you think I needed to be kind to you only because of your daughter?" he growled. He doubled a fist to his side. "White man, all I had to do was leave you to die in the snow and she would have been mine! You are on my land, among my people. I am the law here!"

Jerome slumped down onto the bed, breathing hard. He closed his eyes, bouts of weakness surging through him. "No matter what you say," he said, his voice weak. "My daughter returns with me to the ship." He opened his eyes and looked slowly up at Kanuga. "If you do everything from the kindness of your heart, then you will prove it by letting Letitia go without any more argument about it."

Jerome then gazed wistfully up at Letitia—and his insides splashed cold when he read something in her expression as she looked at Kanuga and slowly stood, holding Kanuga's eyes with her own. He could see that there was more there between them than he wanted to accept. It stabbed at his gut, this knowing that his daughter may have allowed the Indian to have reason to think she would stay with him. Those times that Letitia had spent with the handsome Tlingit warrior had perhaps cast a spell over her. She could never before have been around someone whose charm was so blatant, so contagious.

Kanuga placed his hands to Letitia's shoulders. "Now is the time to tell your father," he said thickly.

Letitia's shoulders tightened beneath his grasp, this moment of truth almost too painful to face. "Tell him what?" she murmured, yet afraid to hear his answer. In a matter of moments, she could lose all of the special closeness that she had ever had with her father. Perhaps he would even hate her forever. She wasn't sure if she could bear to lose him.

"You tell him that you will stay in the village with me," Kanuga said, in his silver eyes a silent plea that only Letitia could see. "Tell him you will be my wife."

Letitia could feel her father's eyes on her back, as though boring holes through it, and shivered because of it, afraid of what was now in his mind's eyes as he thought of what she and Kanuga had shared while he was recovering. Did he even see her in Kanuga's arms, making love . . . ?

"I can't," she blurted out, and the shock in Kanuga's eyes caused her to look quickly away from him.

"What do you mean—you can't?" Kanuga gasped, squeezing her shoulders more tightly, causing her to flinch and emit a soft cry of pain.

With tears of regret misting her eyes, she looked back up at Kanuga. "Kanuga, I can't desert my father," she murmured. "He is not a well man." She swallowed hard, seeing the hurtful anger deepening in Kanuga's eyes. "I fear my mother's reactions even more. She's . . . she's not a strong woman. If I turned my back on her and father, she just might have a heart attack, or . . . or a stroke."

"And what of this man your father called your fiance?" Kanuga said between clenched teeth. "You will leave me and go to him, to live the life of a white woman in a white woman's world? The life I offer you here is not enough?"

Fearing what her father must be thinking, Kanuga's words alone proof that there had been more than mere words shared between Letitia and the handsome chief, Letitia glanced quickly over her shoulder at her father, looking for a way to give him an apology about these revelations.

But her eyes widened and her heart frolicked in her chest when she discovered that his eyes were closed, and his weakened state had taken him back into the realm of semi-consciousness.

Although she felt relieved that some of his feelings had been spared by his drifting off to sleep, she could not help fearing that he might have caused himself harm by trying to move around or by getting himself worked up because of Kanuga's demands on him.

Letitia wrenched herself away from Kanuga and knelt quickly at her father's side, touching his cheek with her hand. "Papa?" she said, leaning closer to his ear to make it easier for him to hear her. "Are you all right?"

He did not respond. His eyes remained closed, yet his easy breathing gave assurance that he was asleep only because he had weakened himself too much.

"Your father will be fine," Kanuga said stiffly. "But what about you, Letitia? What is your heart saying to you? Does it tell you to choose your father and this man named Jonathan over the man you love?"

Tears splashed from Letitia's eyes. She so wanted to rush into Kanuga's arms and vow to him that she would never leave him!

But looking at her weakened father, thinking that she might even be the only link back to his health, made her realize exactly what she had to do at this moment. She had to deny herself everything that she ached for.

"I'm sorry, Kanuga," she said, biting her lower lip.

A firm hand on her wrist, and then a sudden jerk pulling her to her feet, made Letitia's heart skip a beat. She blinked her eyes in fright when she found herself face to face with Kanuga as he drew her body against his.

"Kanuga, please . . ." she murmured, suddenly afraid, for she had never seen such fire—such anger—within anyone's eyes before.

Perhaps he even hated her!

"Then you will be marrying another man?" he growled. "This Jonathan who calls himself your fiance?"

Letitia swallowed a fast-growing lump in her throat, wanting anything but this anger between herself and Kanuga. "No," she murmured. "I will not be marrying Jonathan." Tears spread down her cheeks in silvery streams. "It seems that I . . . I won't be marrying anyone. Ever, Kanuga."

Kanuga searched her eyes for hidden answers that she was not speaking and that he wanted to hear. The tears, and the pain in her voice and eyes, revealed her deception—of herself. She did love him. And she would only for a short while deny herself this love. Then, no matter how strong her loyalties were to her father, her loyalty to Kanuga, the man she truly loved, would win out in her heart. He would just have to give her time to work this out.

Letitia was surprised when Kanuga suddenly released his hold on her and turned and left the dwelling after jerking on his beaver cloak. Stunned by his sudden departure, and that he had no further arguments against her decision, Letitia swayed slightly, then crumpled back to the furs spread on the floor beside her father.

Holding her face in her hands and rocking slowly back and forth, she sobbed, knowing that once she had left Kanuga behind, her heart would be separated from her also. It was hard to imagine a lifetime without Kanuga—without his special ways of loving her.

But she would have to learn! Oh, but she would have to learn, no matter the hurt that each day without him would inflict on her!

A warm hand on her cheek made Letitia look suddenly up, hoping that Kanuga had returned to say that he understood her reasons for having to leave him, but she found Sweetwater there instead.

"Do not cry," Sweetwater murmured. "Kanuga is angry now, but later he will return to you, his eyes filled with regret for having upset you. His love for you is strong." She paused, then added, "Do not do anything in haste. It is clear that your love for Kanuga is as strong as is his love for you. Such a love should be cherished today, for who knows of tomorrow?"

"Thank you for caring," Letitia said, touched deeply by Sweetwater's concern. She gave her a hug, then as Sweetwater took her place beside the bed across from Letitia again, Letitia wiped the tears from her eyes and cheeks and peered wistfully at her father. She ran her fingers through his thinning hair, then across the craggy features of his face. She loved him dearly. Never could there have ever been a kinder father. And that she was showing him her true devotion was only right! He deserved no less from a daughter to whom he had dedicated a lifetime!

Weary of thinking, of trying to figure out the rights and wrongs of her life, Letitia rose slowly to her feet. Without much forethought, she pulled her coat on, tying the hood securely around her face, and then thrust her fingers into her gloves.

"I'll be back soon," she whispered to a father who still slept soundly, peacefully. "I need some fresh air."

Slipping her feet into her snowshoes, Letitia left the house, discovering when she got outside that it was already dark. She sighed and hugged herself for more warmth, thinking that she had not seen such a lovely night for some time now. The sky was lit by the breath of an absent sun, stars twinkling like millions of jewels against a velvet backdrop.

It was so beautiful and serene that she decided to take a walk, to absorb the calm. There had been too many storm-filled nights with blustery winds since she arrived at Alaska's shores. Now, with spring just heartbeats away, there was much promise ahead for everyone.

"If only Jonathan and the rest of the expedition are alive," she whispered, yet fearing the worst. She and her father had been lucky. Kanuga had saved them from a sure death.

Letitia's heart jolted with alarm when the figure of a man suddenly stepped in front of her, then she laughed loosely when she focused her eyes in the darkness and realized that it was Kanuga.

"Kanuga, you frightened me," she said, placing a hand to her throat.

"Do you not know the dangers of going outside alone?" he said, moving to stand over her, his eyes stern as he peered down at her through the darkness.

"Yes, I know, but I . . ." Letitia said, her laughter fading when she turned around and peered toward the Tlingit village, suddenly realizing just how far she had wandered.

She looked quickly back up at Kanuga. "I didn't know that I had walked so far."

"Let me walk you back to the village," Kanuga said, taking her by the elbow. He began ushering her through the snow. "Why did you leave the safety of my house?"

"I needed time alone," she murmured. She glanced up at him. "To think."

"To think about what?" Kanuga said, smiling

down at her. He had known she would change her mind eventually.

Letitia looked quickly away from him. "Many things," she said, not wanting to get into a debate again about her decision.

When they reached the village and Kanuga led her up to the door of his longhouse, she did not go immediately inside. "Kanuga, I'm so restless," she murmured. "I know I won't sleep if I go inside." She glanced over at his huskies all rolled up in balls beside his sled, then up at Kanuga. "Can we go for a ride in your sled? Just this one more time? It would surely relax me."

His response was to walk her to the sled. After she climbed in it, he arranged the warm pelts around her, attached his huskies, then rode off toward a planned destination—one that only he could find. As he drove his huskies across the white landscape of ice and snow, he smiled to himself, already envisioning her in his arms in the abandoned igloo, again sharing paradise with her. It would be a lovemaking she would never forget.

He would make it so that she would not want to leave him after tonight.

Chapter Ten

In simple and pure soul I come to you.
—SHAKESPEARE

The soft light of the moon gleamed on the snow as the sled moved onward through the deep velvet of night. Knowing that this would be her last night with Kanuga, Letitia could not help but be filled with melancholy. The decision to leave him had been the hardest decision in her life, and something deep within her told her that she would live to regret it. You could not love as passionately as she loved Kanuga and live serenely without him. From now on, every breath she took—every task she endeavored—would not be done without Kanuga being there, carried inside her heart.

She stifled a sob behind her gloves, knowing that he was now her very soul.

How could one live without one's soul?

Something up ahead, like a white, round ghost rising out of the snow, made Letitia lean forward and gasp in disbelief as the huskies pulled the sled closer.

"The abandoned igloo!" she whispered to herself, memories of that one night she had shared there with Kanuga returning to her in flashes of hot sensuality.

She looked more intensely at the igloo, seeing soft spirals of smoke rising from the smoke hole at the top of the dwelling. Who could have taken occupancy of it?

She peered at the huskies, hurrying toward the igloo as though it was their destination.

Then she turned her head and lifted wondering eyes to Kanuga, knowing by the set of his jaw and the fire in his eyes that this outing had been planned. Had she not left his house for a breath of fresh air, surely his plans would have been to come to her, suggesting it!

The huskies pulled to a stop in front of the igloo. Letitia was torn with what to do. She hungered to be in Kanuga's arms again, yet wouldn't that just make it harder tomorrow, when she said her final goodbyes to him?

Kanuga came to Letitia and unfolded the soft furs from around her, avoiding her eyes that stared, oh so quietly, up at him. When he grabbed her up into his arms and began carrying her toward the igloo, still he avoided looking at her. What was important to him was that she wasn't complaining. She was allowing what he had planned, in hopes of persuading her this last time to become his wife.

He stiffened inside when she finally began to speak, realizing that he had been wrong to hope that she would go willingly with him again where they had first made maddeningly sweet love.

"Kanuga," Letitia said, finally finding a voice to fight for her last breath of sanity—that which would give her the courage, still, to deny Kanuga an evening of loving as only he had taught her how. "Please. Please return me to your village. This isn't right. I have told you my decision. I cannot stay with you. I must go with my parents. It is the only life that I have ever known. Please try and understand."

Just as they reached the igloo, and Kanuga knew that he must relinquish his hold on her long enough for them to crawl through the small entranceway, he looked down at her with eyes dark with feeling.

"Your words do not match those written within the spaces of your heart," he softly argued. "Stay with me for a short while tonight, then I will return you to your father's side. Give me these final moments with you, Letitia. How can you deny that you want this, as badly as I?"

Letitia's pulse raced, his lips only a feather's touch from hers, so close that his breath mingled with hers. When his mouth seized hers in a fiery kiss, she could not help but again abandon herself to the torrent of feelings that were rushing through her.

Twining her arms around his neck, she returned the kiss with a wildness she did not know herself capable of. Her lips quivered against his, low moans of pleasure that she knew were hers filling the night air.

Kanuga's heart thundered wildly inside his chest. His loins were on fire. He realized that he was close to going over the edge into ecstasy, and he had yet to see or touch her slender white body tonight.

And that he must!

He yearned for the feel of her, for the taste of her.

And he would have it all tonight!

And for all tomorrows, he thought angrily to himself, for he would not allow it not to be so!

He eased his mouth from her lips. "*Jet-a-nelch*," he said, smiling down at her. "It is warm inside. Also, I have prepared lovely pelts for us to lie upon." He brushed her lips with his mouth again. "My *schau-wot*, Kanuga will love you as never before."

Letitia nodded silently, knowing that she was too far gone to quarrel with him any longer about what she must do tomorrow. This was tonight. She had him, at least, for one more night....

Her gaze swept over his finely chiseled face, wanting to memorize everything about it—his bold nose, his strong chin, the slope of his hard jaw.

And, ah, those silver eyes, she marveled again to herself. They were so mesmerizingly haunting!

"You are such a beautiful man," she finally

said, leaning a soft kiss to his lips. "Such a dear, beautiful man."

Then her attention was drawn elsewhere, causing her to gasp and her eyes to widen. A curtain of the brightest silver had appeared overhead, covering the entire expanse of the violet sky. The bright tapestry hung down in delicate folds which slowly swayed and changed their form.

And then there was a great explosion of light, as bands of white, green, and violet settled over the land like a shimmering necklace.

"I've never seen anything like it," Letitia said, her voice lilting. "It must be the northern lights I have heard people talk about. But never would I have believed it would be so—so breathtakingly lovely!"

Kanuga drew her next to him, his arm around her waist. "The Tlingit call it the Dawn of the North," he told her. "Seeing it tonight means much to Kanuga. It is a good omen!"

The white bands of energy soared across the night sky, changing shape, disappearing altogether, then lighting up the darkness again.

"It has been said that if you raise your arms and wave at the Dawn of the North, they will come down and carry you away," Kanuga said, smiling down at Letitia as she quickly looked up at him.

"They?" she murmured. She looked at the sky again. "Do you mean angels? That is what the light resembles, Kanuga."

"Whatever you see is how it is within your heart," Kanuga said, nodding.

The lights disappeared again, but did not return this time. When Kanuga saw Letitia shiver, he took her hand and led her toward the entranceway of the igloo. "Let us go inside now," he urged. "But I am glad that you were able to witness one more marvel of the north. That is another reason you should want to stay. Have you ever seen anything to compare in your land called America?"

"There are many things of America that I know would fascinate you," Letitia said, crawling ahead of Kanuga into the igloo. "But, no. Nothing is as beautiful as your northern lights."

Inside, beside a welcoming fire, its smoke rising through a crack in the roof, Letitia's breathing became labored when she looked up at Kanuga as he knelt before her, pulling her gloves off, and then removed her coat and tossed it aside.

When Kanuga's hands went to her hair and he smoothed his powerful hands through its silken tresses, lifting it from her shoulders so that it could lie in a silken, golden mass down her back, Letitia closed her eyes and melted inside from the promise of what they were again going to share.

Even though she knew that she mustn't, her heart had a will of its own, and it was calling out for the rapture that she always found within Kanuga's powerful embrace.

A surge of warmth flooded through Letitia's body when Kanuga's lips began kissing their way down the slender column of her throat, while he busied his fingers with slipping her dress down from her shoulders, and then farther still, away from her breasts.

She sucked in a wild breath when she felt his lips now covering a nipple of one of her breasts, sucking it tautly erect.

Her ragged breathing slowed as he kneaded her breasts, his hands soothingly warm against them.

Then, when he pulled away from her and she opened her eyes, she allowed him to remove the rest of her clothes, then watched as he disrobed, mesmerized anew by his muscled body.

For a moment they lay beside the fire, saying nothing, only looking adoringly into one another's eyes; then they flung themselves together, their lips kissing deliriously, their hands searching each other's bodies.

Then Kanuga tore himself away from Letitia and rose above her, bracing himself on his arms. When he fully mounted her, her back pressed hard into the pelts. His lips silenced her cry of joy as he entered her with one mighty plunge, sinking deeply within her.

Straining her body upward, she moved with him, her hips meeting his as his thrusts came maddeningly quicker. She clasped her fingers to his buttocks, guiding him harder against her throbbing center.

Tremors cascaded down her back as once again his lips paid homage to her breasts, lapping his tongue around first one nipple, and then the other, making her delirious with sensations!

And then he leaned away from her, but only for a moment. His tongue and lips were soon traversing her body, sending her into whirlpools of ecstasy as she discovered there were secret, sensual hideaways on her body that had never been explored until tonight.

Letitia gasped for air, her heart pounding so hard she felt as though she were being swallowed whole by it, when Kanuga's mouth slithered wetly downward, across her stomach, stopping where she so unmercifully throbbed between her thighs.

His tongue soon elicited new rushes of desire inside her. Loving her in this way, so caring, so devotedly, he made her mindless with the pleasure.

Afraid that she would cross that brink of total bliss too soon, she gently lifted his face away.

"Please," she whispered, smiling druggedly down at him. "I want you, Kanuga. Oh, how I want you. I want you now."

Kanuga kissed his way up her glossy textured skin then molded his body against hers, thrusting himself into her moist channel again. Engulfing her within his arms, he pressed into her, their bodies jolting and quivering with their matching passions.

Letitia's gasps became long, soft whimpers, silenced quickly by the demands of Kanuga's mouth as he kissed her, his fingers tracing maddening circles around her belly, up to her breasts, just missing the nipples each time so that they strained with added anticipation.

Kanuga could feel the heat rising in his loins, as if many raging fires had been kindled within them. Sweat pearled his brow, and his body began to stiffen with the building passion.

Emitting a thick, husky groan, he plunged himself more deeply, more heatedly, within her, as he reached the ultimate peak of bliss, smiling to himself when he felt Letitia's response in kind as her body trembled against his at the moment of his release....

Afterwards, fully spent, Kanuga clung to Letitia, his face pressed against her bosom. "Do you not feel the heat of my burning sigh?" he whispered against her flesh, his body still pulsating from the lovemaking. "You do this to me, Letitia. Only you."

He leaned away from her, his fingers smoothing some damp locks back from her eyes, and smiled down at her. "Did I not say that seeing the Dawn of the North tonight was a good omen?" he murmured. "My woman, it proves what I have been saying all along. That you belong to me. The Dawn of the North gave you to me tonight. And so shall you stay with me forever."

Letitia felt the pain of regret at the very pit of her stomach, ashamed that she had been intimate with Kanuga again tonight, when all along she knew that she would be leaving him tomorrow, no matter how much he tried to convince himself that she wouldn't. Now he would most definitely hate her! He might even call her a teasing whore!

She turned her eyes from him, feeling that perhaps she *was* a whore. She had hungers of the flesh that surely women of the night felt, which made them search for men who could quell their hungers, until the next time it came upon them like a damnable curse!

Was this truly what was wrong with her? Letitia wondered frantically. Perhaps she didn't love Kanuga at all! Perhaps she was born to be a loose woman! Perhaps, even, when she returned to America, she would be forced to search forever for a man who could please her as much as Kanuga!

Suddenly the silence of the night was broken by a wailing far in the distance. Letitia sat quickly up and turned to Kanuga, who had already jumped to his feet, hurrying into his clothes.

"Who is that?" Letitia asked, moving to her feet and grabbing up her clothes. "Why are they making such a terrible noise?"

Kanuga jerked on his beaver cloak. Before he had a chance to respond to Letitia's question, there was another wailing voice, and another, and another, until the night reverberated with the swelling chorus. Slow, mournful, and as black as the night that enveloped it, the deathlike dirge set Letitia's nerves on edge with the utter despair of its sounds.

"Perhaps the omens tonight were not all that good after all," Kanuga grumbled, turning to help Letitia into her clothes.

"Why? What's happened?" Letitia asked, letting Kanuga tie her hood in place around her face.

"Someone in my village has died," Kanuga said flatly. "My people are mourning. That is the sound that you hear. Many cries of my people."

"I'm so sorry, Kanuga," Letitia said, watching him stamp out the fire. Then her eyebrows quirked. "But how could we be hearing sounds from your village? Didn't we travel too far away to hear them?"

"At night in Alaska, the sounds travel as though shot by guns, over the open, frozen tundra," Kanuga explained. He took her by the elbow and guided her down to the crawlspace. "Let us go. Quickly."

After they were outside, and Letitia was on the sled, Kanuga hurriedly placed the pelts around her.

"Who do you think it is, Kanuga?" Letitia murmured, yet afraid that she already knew the answer. The young warrior! Oh, God, the young warrior! "Who do you think died?"

"There is only one Tlingit whose life was in question tonight," Kanuga said in a low growl. "And if he has died, those at Fort Anecia will pay, and will pay dearly."

He rose to his full height, looking into the distance, where in the heavens he could see the reflections of great outdoor fires that were now being built in his village, a part of the mourning that had already begun for the dead Tlingit.

"And even before the burial of our fallen comrade, my warriors, under my command, will go to Fort Anecia to seek vengeance," he growled, as he raised a doubled fist into the air.

Great tremors of dread raced up and down Letitia's spine. She now knew that the Tlingits' vengeance would come before her and her father's return to the ship.

She gave Kanuga a troubled glance. Would he expect her to ride with him again to Fort Anecia, to be a part, again, of a sought-for vengeance?

Fear grabbed her at the pit of her stomach at the thought, for it was in Kanuga's eyes that this time the vengeance would not be a simple, bloodless one.

Chapter Eleven

When we cannot act as we wish,
We must act as we can.

—TERRENCE

As Kanuga drove his sled into the village, Letitia looked on with horror at the great bonfires that had been set, causing a great roaring as the flames leapt skyward. Around the fires were a host of Tlingit warriors in full battle array. Many wore body armor—painted moose hides with designs representing animals—and wooden helmets that covered their heads as completely as the head-gear of the medieval knights that Letitia had seen pictured in books. The helmets were animal-shaped, with protruding beaks and gaping jaws, clearly designed to strike fear into the hearts of their opponents.

Kanuga's entrance into the village was met by an onrush of the warriors. Some carrying sinew-backed bows, others rifles, they ran alongside Kanuga's huskie-drawn sled, shouting at him, telling him that the young warrior had died.

They declared loudly that Tlingit law called for exchanging one life for another, an eye for an eye! They called for the death of Iuril, the Russian commandant's son.

After Kanuga drew his sled to a stop in front of his house, Letitia quickly left it and stood stiffly at Kanuga's side as he faced his warriors.

"Valiant warriors, I understand your need to seek another life in exchange for the Tlingit life so tragically lost," he said, his voice carrying into the night like molten steel, his anger was so intense. "I, too, wish for the same vengeance. But I wish to use a different tactic. Let us use this opportunity for bartering with the Russians, instead, to finally force them from our land! They will comply with our demand, or we *will* seek bloodier revenge. We have been patient until now with the Russians only because of the guns and gunpowder they have supplied us with. But the Russians have been holding out on us lately. The Tlingit gunpowder supply is almost gone! When the Russians leave, they will be forced to leave behind all of their supplies which will benefit us!"

Great shouts of approval filled the night air, and once again there was silence.

"My people, I have also been patient with the Russians because of my dead chieftain father's friendship with the Russian colonel," Kanuga said, his voice filled with melancholy at the memory of his father, a man of strength and courage. "But time has run out for such patience. I now see the Russians as an interference!"

"And how shall this bartering be done?" shouted a warrior with headgear in the shape of a raven, stepping forward.

"We shall abduct the Russian colonel's son and bring him back to the village with us," Kanuga said. "We shall hold him here as a hostage until the bartering is over. His fate will rest in the hands of his father!"

Another warrior stepped forward, his headgear hideously shaped like several birds mingled as one. "If the bargaining fails, let me shoot my arrow into the heart of the small Russian!" he shouted, waving his mighty bow in the air. "He has never had a kind word to say to our people! He has even mocked our people! He deserves to die!"

"How he dies, *should* he, will be decided by a council of many," Kanuga said, finding it hard to recall when he and Iuril had ever been friends. Iuril had changed; his heart was no longer a gentle one. "Give me time now to dress in my war gear, and then we shall go like thieves in the night to get Iuril. By morning, his father will realize that his son has been taken, and by whom. And then the waiting begins." He laughed throatily. "I assure you that the waiting will be much harder on Iuril than on any of us!"

Kanuga turned to Letitia and placed an arm around her waist, guiding her to his longhouse. Inside, he gently helped her off with her wraps, then drew her into his arms, but only for a moment. They were interrupted by angry, trembling words behind them.

"Did you think that I was still asleep?" Jerome said from the bedroom, leaning weakly on one elbow and peering through the door. "Did you not know that all of the noise your people made could wake the dead?" He cast Letitia an accusing, frowning look. "Letitia, had I not spoken up, would you have even let this Indian kiss you?"

Letitia felt the blood rush to her cheeks. Her knees grew weak, recalling in flashes what she had actually shared with Kanuga, and not all that long ago.

It had been more than a kiss!

"Papa," she murmured. She went to him and fell to her knees beside his bed. "Kanuga was only giving me comfort. So much is happening that is frightening."

The funeral chant outside was accompanied by a drum, its throbbing beats underscoring the sadness of the assembled voices.

"Papa, don't you hear?" she said quietly. "The people are in mourning for a young warrior who was shot by the Russians."

She swallowed hard as she glanced at Kanuga over her shoulder, then looked back down at her father. "Kanuga and many of his warriors are leaving soon to abduct the Russian colonel's son," she said, taking her father's hand. "Papa, a battle between the Tlingit and the Russians could ensue. We—we could be right in the middle of the confrontation. Don't you think that I have reason to be afraid?''

Jerome searched Letitia's face for the truth and was able to identify a true, wrenching fear at the depths of her eyes.

Then he looked past her, at Kanuga. "If there is a battle, this will delay you taking us to my ship," he said, his voice drawn. "You said that you would take us tomorrow, Kanuga. I had planned on it."

"No plans have changed," Kanuga reassured him. "There will be no battle. Iuril will be brought back to our village and held as a captive. His father will not choose to fight. My warriors outnumber his. He will bargain peacefully for his son."

Kanuga frowned down at Letitia, then looked at her father again. "As I said, no plans have changed," he grumbled. "Letitia stays with me."

Letitia felt her father's eyes on her again, filled with accusations. She rose to her feet and faced Kanuga, her heart pounding, her whole future bleak because of what she was about to say.

But she knew that she had no other choice.

Her father's well-being was all that was important now!

"Kanuga, I must leave with my father," she said, her voice quavering. "Please try and understand. It is for his health that I must accompany him to the ship and stay with him."

A sudden anger flared in Kanuga's eyes. He stepped past Letitia and glared down at Jerome. "So be it, white man," he said, his teeth clenched.

"If Letitia leaves my village and returns to your ship, then you Americans must make haste to leave Alaska. If she should decide to stay with me, perhaps we could work something out that would benefit us all."

"Nothing you say will make me give up my daughter to the sort of life that you will offer her," Jerome said, stopping to inhale a nervous breath. "She goes with me. That . . . is final."

"Then you will all leave Alaska," Kanuga said with keenest regret. "It is best not to permit Americans to establish any trading posts upriver, where they will be in a position to cut off Tlingit trade with the interior. It is enough that the Tlingit have had the Russians to contend with for so long. The Tlingit do not need the Americans added to the battle!"

He turned to Letitia. "Prepare yourself to leave my village at the break of dawn," he said, still so controlled, still so mannered. "And then you will make haste to see that the ship leaves Alaska—soon!"

Regret and hurt feelings were making an empty feeling gnaw at the pit of Letitia's stomach. She had to will herself not to cry, nor to throw herself into the arms of her beloved.

"But the waters are frozen," she uttered softly. "We can't move the ship all that quickly."

"The ice will be breaking up soon," Kanuga said, walking quickly away from her and reaching for his armor. "I will give you until then to leave. But no longer."

"Thank you," Letitia said meekly, then sat beside her father, her shoulders slumped as Kanuga transformed himself into some sort of grotesque giant bird, then left with a massive sinew-backed bow draped over his shoulder, a rifle clutched in his hand.

Letitia felt eyes on her and turned her gaze back to her father. "I'm sorry, Papa," she murmured, wiping tears from her eyes, knowing that he did not realize the truth of her feelings for Kanuga. "But I can't help loving him. I shall love him forever, even while I am in America, going from day to day, doing my chores. He will always be with me, Papa. Always."

Shame engulfed her when her father turned his eyes from her and blatantly ignored her as he began talking in soft tones to Sweetwater after she entered the room and knelt on the floor beside him.

Then, just as quickly, Letitia brushed the shame away and let herself remember that her and Kanuga's feelings had been honest, sincere, and enduring.

She firmed her jaw.

She would never allow herself to feel ashamed again over loving someone so fearlessly, so totally! One day her father would understand, for what she was going to do tomorrow was *for* her father!

Surely he would repay her one day, by forgiving her for having loved Kanuga.

The ceremony before setting out to abduct Iuril had taken the Tlingit through the night. With the sun now rising like a brilliant copper disc on the horizon, the helmeted warriors snapped their whips over their huskies' heads, sending them into a steady frenzy across the dazzling white tundra.

Kanuga was trying to focus his thoughts on what he might gain by taking Iuril for bartering.

But it was his losses that kept coming to mind.

Letitia!

He had lost his Letitia!

Soon he would be taking her to a ship that would take her far away from him. She would then only be an aching memory inside his heart.

His very soul was wounded by her rejection!

A movement in the snow up ahead, far beyond those Tlingit whose eagerness had driven them ahead of Kanuga and his dog team, was another sled with a lone driver. It did not take long for Kanuga to identify the man in charge of the dog team. Short of stature and stout, Iuril Golodoff was easy to recognize, even from behind!

"It is Iuril!" Kanuga shouted to his men. "He is an easy conquest for us today!"

The warriors emitted unearthly growls and high-pitched screams as their dogs bounded closer to Iuril, who frantically tried to make his dogs outrun them once he discovered that he was the object of their chase.

Kanuga was the first to reach Iuril. He pulled his huskies alongside Iuril's, their sleds now side by side. Looking at Iuril with eyes of fire, Kanuga raised his whip in warning. "Stop!" he shouted. "Now! Or your skin will become familiar with the sting of my whip!" He glanced over his shoulder at his advancing warriors, then glowered at Iuril. "Or perhaps you would prefer an arrow through your heart?"

Panic-laden, Iuril didn't heed the warning. "What have I done?" he shouted to Kanuga in English. "Or what am I accused of? Whatever it is, I am innocent! Innocent!"

"In my people's eyes, all Russians on Alaska's soil are guilty of the death of one of our young warriors!" Kanuga shouted back. He jerked his whip back, then snapped it only inches away from Iuril's face. "But we have chosen you to make payment! Only you!"

"My father will come and kill you all for this!" Iuril said, his voice quavering as he drew his dogs to a stop, while all around him circled the helmeted Tlingit warriors. He swallowed hard as he looked from helmet to helmet, seeing the fierceness of each; then as he lowered his eyes, his shoulders sagged in defeat.

"Take him!" Kanuga shouted, watching as two of his warriors who shared a sled jumped from their sled and went to Iuril, jerking him roughly from his.

"Tie him to your sled. Then we shall return to our village," Kanuga ordered.

He then turned his gaze to one of his most trusted warriors. "Remove your warring gear," he said flatly. "See that word is taken to Colonel Golodoff of his son's capture. Tell him what is expected of him, or his son will never be seen alive again."

The warrior quickly shed his warring gear, replacing it with a long, hooded fur robe. Then he rode away.

Kanuga removed his helmet and laid it aside. He stared down at Iuril as the sled that bore him passed by, Iuril cowering beneath a thick layer of pelts. A momentary pang of regret seized Kanuga, now so vividly remembering the times when Iuril and he had talked in a friendly manner, had even exchanged occasional games of handball as children.

Now they were enemies.

And Kanuga would not hesitate to do whatever he must to achieve his goal of vengeance!

He sent his huskies back in the direction of his village, having a matter there that still needed tending to, which had nothing to do with the Russians.

It was a matter of the heart.

A cigar hanging tightly at the corner of his mouth, Colonel Golodoff paced back and forth in his office. Glowering, his brow furrowed into a frown, he was trying to comprehend what the Tlingit messenger had just announced to him. His son! His very own son! His only son! Now held captive?

"How can Kanuga do this to me?" he whispered harshly, yanking the cigar from his mouth. He dropped it to the wooden floor and squashed it out with the heel of his boot, then crumpled into a chair behind his desk.

Nervously, his fingers rifled through a stack of

papers on his desk. "Doesn't Kanuga remember his father's friendship with me?" he asked himself. "His father would never have done anything as despicable as this! Never!"

Hunching over his desk, he ignored the footsteps entering his office. Then he looked slowly up, flinging a suspicious look at Broderick Bowman. "It took you long enough to get here," he shouted, his voice shrill. He pounded his fist on his desktop. "Goddamn it, when I summon you, you're supposed to run. Do you hear?"

Broderick nodded his head anxiously, his eyes wide with a building fear.

"You've heard about Iuril?" Colonel Golodoff said, rising slowly from his chair. He went and stared directly into Broderick's eyes.

"I can't believe Kanuga would do that," Broderick said, shifting his feet nervously.

"Well, damn it, he did," Colonel Golodoff spat. "And we've got to get Iuril back. Do you hear? And it has to be done peacefully. This fort is a valuable trading post. We've got to be allowed to keep it." He leaned closer to Broderick. "Do you understand?"

"Yes, sir," Broderick stammered, swallowing hard. "But what do you expect me to do about it?"

"You are to go to Kanuga and negotiate with him," the Colonel said, stabbing a forefinger against Broderick's chest. "I can't go this time, to bargain for myself, because of the tensions that have been mounting between me and Kanuga. If I faced Kanuga over this, I know I wouldn't be able to keep a civil tongue. I might even be forced to draw a pistol and kill him for what he is forcing my son to endure!"

"Whatever you say," Broderick said, seeing perhaps more value to himself in his going than to the colonel's. This would give him a good reason to see the American lady again, and to discover why she was at the Indian village. It was certain that Iuril had not done any investigating that had uncovered her presence there.

He puffed out his chest, realizing that no one at Fort Anecia but himself knew about the American lady's presence in Alaska!

"We'll give Kanuga at least another full day and night to change his mind about his irrational act," Colonel Golodoff said, easing back down in his chair again. "Anyhow, I mustn't act too eager, or our cause is lost." He placed his fingertips together, nodding his head slowly up and down. "The fort is as valuable as my son's life."

Broderick gasped at this comment, yet knew that he shouldn't be too surprised. There had never been any show of love between the colonel and his son, only a tendency to tolerate one another in the presence of others.

Casting that thought aside, Broderick smiled to himself. He was anxious to see the white woman once more, yet he feared meeting Kanuga face to face again. They hated each other with a vengeance. More than once Kanuga had humiliated Broderick in front of others, realizing that Broderick's vulnerable point was his ability, of late, to bungle most everything he got involved with.

He gazed down at Colonel Golodoff and kneaded his chin thoughtfully, suspecting that the colonel was having him go to Kanuga because he truly didn't think that Broderick was capable of getting anything positive from the Tlingit chief. If the colonel's son was killed, Broderick could be blamed, not the colonel. In a sadistic sort of way, the colonel could claim a clear conscious.

Chapter Twelve

O you much partial gods!
Why gave me ye men affections, and not power
To govern them?

—BARY

Although the sun was brilliant overhead, Letitia had to hug herself to draw more warmth from the fur coat as she watched Kanuga and his warriors returning to the village, the air ringing with their songs of victory.

Placing a hand over her eyes to shield them from the dazzle of the snow and sun, she saw them take a man roughly from one of the sleds and shove him toward one of the smaller houses.

When Kanuga saw her standing there, he grabbed her by a wrist and took her to the small house where the captive was being tied to stakes on the floor.

When Iuril looked up and saw her, his eyes widened with surprise.

"This is Colonel Golodoff's son, Iuril," Kanuga said, releasing his hold on Letitia's wrist. He bent beside Iuril and checked the tightness of the bonds at his wrists. "His father will determine how long he will remain with us."

Letitia inched closer to Kanuga. "Kanuga, do you have to—to treat him so inhumanely?" she murmured. "Can't you just lock him in the house without tying him to the floor?" She glanced over at the smouldering ashes in the firepit, then back at Iuril. "At least add wood to the fire so that he can stay warm."

"He is not your prisoner," Kanuga said, giving her an icy stare. "Should you decide to stay with my people, then you will have a say in the matter. But since you are waiting, even now, for me to take you to the American ship, your word holds no value to me."

"American ship?" Iuril said in Russian, his eyes widening. "What ship, Kanuga?" He paused, closely studying Letitia, then said in fluent English, "Who are you? What are you doing in Alaska?"

"That is the least of your worries, Iuril," Kanuga said, taking Letitia by the elbow and guiding her toward the door. "Your father's reaction to your abduction should be your only concern— and how long he will allow you to take the punishment for what someone at your fort did to our fallen warrior!"

Iuril struggled with his bonds, his face becoming red with the effort. "Kanuga!" he screamed. "Let me go! Would I do this to you? No! You know that I wouldn't!"

Kanuga cast Iuril a glance over his shoulder. "Under the same circumstances, I have no doubt that you would," he said calmly. "So take the punishment for your people like a man, Iuril. It shouldn't be for long." He looked at the warrior who was standing guard over Iuril. "Build up the fire. We won't be accused of letting our prisoner freeze to death."

Letitia smiled softly up at Kanuga, relieved that at least in that respect, he was being kind to Iuril. She wouldn't want to think that Kanuga was capable of any coldheartedness, for in him she had always seen only kindness.

Stepping out into the sunshine again, Letitia flinched when it flashed brightly into her eyes.

Then she gasped slightly when Kanuga drew her back into the shadows of the house, away from anyone's view.

Leaning over Letitia, framing her face between his gloved hands, Kanuga gazed with emotion into her eyes.

"And so you still plan to leave me?" he asked sadly.

"I must," she murmured, casting her eyes downward. "My father and mother need me."

"Do you not understand my need for you?" Kanuga growled, jerking her face so that her eyes were forced to look into his. "What am I to do when this need burns like fire within me? What are you to do when the same fire invades your senses? We are meant to be together, as one being!"

"Kanuga, please don't," Letitia sobbed, tears rushing down her cheeks.

"Forever you will be a part of me," Kanuga continued. "You are in my blood. And you will come back to me, for I know that you feel the same about me. It is in your kiss. It is in your eyes!"

Not giving her a chance to say anything else, Kanuga yanked her into his embrace. Clutching her body against his, he kissed her passionately, then released her so abruptly that she almost slipped in the snow.

Stumbling along after him out from the protective shadows of the house, she went to the sled in front of Kanuga's house, into which he was already placing her father. Sweetwater stood nearby her eyes heavy with sadness.

A sob lodged in Letitia's throat as Kanuga so very kindly positioned warm furs around her father's slight form.

And when she got into the sled beside her father, her eyes wavered as Kanuga was as kind to her, as though there had been no quarrel between them.

Her heart ached to declare her love for him, when he positioned himself behind her and snapped the whip over the huskies' heads, sending the sled hissing across the snow.

But she had made her choice, chartering her own course in life—one that did not include him.

She cuddled beneath the furs, smiling wistfully at her father when she felt his eyes on her, watching her.

"It's going to be all right, Letitia," he offered, reaching to cover her hand with one of his. "Jonathan, should he still be alive, will make you a good and caring husband. In time, you will learn to care as much for him."

Letitia bit her lower lip with frustration and turned away from her father, not wanting to tell him at this time, when he was still so weak, that she would not be marrying Jonathan.

Ever!

Kanuga had changed all of that for her. Kanuga had changed everything.

A forest jay flew suddenly into sight, screeching loudly, and another jay followed in pursuit. With spring so near, these birds would be mating. It would be a time for all hearts to sing; all hearts to share!

Bitterly, Letitia folded her arms across her chest, thinking that life somehow did not know how to treat her fairly. She had given up long ago finding a man who was special. That had been her reason for accepting Jonathan's proposal of marriage.

And now that she had found that impossible dream in Kanuga, she was leaving him behind!

She gave him a slight glance over her shoulder, knowing that it would be so easy to change her mind.

And then the ship came into view, drawing her attention back around to the women standing on the deck waving desperately at those arriving in the sled. "Mother!" Letitia shouted, her voice echoing across the snow and the frozen river. "Oh, mother, it's so good to see you!"

She gazed over at Barbara, not so pleased to see her cousin. Orphaned at age eleven, she had become a part of Letitia's family—and had quickly begun acting as though she were Letitia's sister instead of her cousin.

And she had been treated like a daughter by Letitia's parents!

Yet how could they not have treated her as special? She was beautiful, with intriguing green eyes that were slightly slanted, long and flowing raven-black hair, and the shape of a seductress at her nineteen years of age.

But these better qualities about Barbara had not fooled Letitia one iota. She saw Barbara as a rebellious conniver, full of all sorts of jealousies. And she had bragged often to Letitia of her experiences with men, claiming to be able to get any man that she wanted with just one blink of her eyes.

The crew members who had been left aboard the brig *Stacy* before the expedition had set out to explore the Alaskan wilderness became active. The gangplank was lowered. Two of the sailors came hurriedly from the ship in snowshoes, traipsed across the frozen waters of the river, and met the dog sled.

Soon Jerome was anchored between the two men, being carried toward the ship. Letitia was left behind with Kanuga. She turned to him and reached a hand to his smooth, copper cheek.

"I can't deny that I shall always love you," she murmured, then turned and fled from him, relieved when she was finally standing on the solid flooring of the ship.

When she turned for a last glimpse of Kanuga, her heart fell when she discovered that he had already left, and all she could see of him was a tiny speck on the horizon as his sled moved smoothly along the frozen tundra, and then out of sight.

Then Letitia was able to put Kanuga from her mind for a while. She was welcomed with strong, fitful hugs from her mother, and a soft, quick hug from Barbara. They went to the master cabin of the ship, where Jerome was soon placed comfortably on his massive bed, with many patchwork quilts made by the deft fingers of his wife spread over him.

"It's good to be in my own bed," he said, sighing heavily.

Kimberly sat down beside the bed and reached for his hand, patting it.

"Jonathan?" Jerome asked, hope filling his eyes. "Tell me that he's here. And everyone else. Have they all arrived safely back to the ship?"

Kimberly's tiny facial features became creased in a frown. "No," she murmured. "No one else is here." She stifled a sob behind her hand. "And until now, I thought that you and Letitia had also perished in the terrible storm. I could hardly believe my eyes, Jerome, when I saw you arriving on that sled." She turned to Letitia and reached her free hand out to her. "Letitia, darling. Come here. Let me touch you and know that you are truly here with me."

Letitia moved to her mother and kissed her brow, then knelt down beside her, placing a cheek on her mother's lap. But then she rose again, her eyes wide. "Did you say that you didn't know that we were safe?" she gasped, her spine stiffening. "Kanuga said that he had sent word that we were at his village."

"We received no word from anyone," Kimberly said somberly. "I've cried my eyes out these past several nights. I just knew that I'd never see you again."

Letitia was taken aback by this, having never doubted for a minute that Kanuga had kept his word and had sent someone to the ship to inform her mother that her daughter and husband were safe.

But of course, should she be surprised that he hadn't wanted anyone to interfere in his plans to persuade her to stay with him? He had needed as much time as possible, for these persuasions.

Jerome tried to get up, but fell back down, winded. "I've got to go and find Jonathan," he said, wheezing. He gave Letitia a set stare. "For many reasons, I've got to find him."

"You're going nowhere," Kimberly said, smoothing the quilts up to Jerome's chin. "Nor is anyone else. We can't chance turning what crew is left out into the wilds of Alaska. Should anything happen to them, it would render us helpless."

She leaned a kiss to Jerome's brow. "Now tell me, Jerome," she murmured. "Tell me how you were injured. Tell me how you happened to be with the Indian."

Letitia slipped from the cabin, out into the frosty air on deck. She walked listlessly to the ship's rail and peered into the distance where she had last seen Kanuga. Tears warmed her cheeks as she let herself get caught up in remembrances of being with him. Those moments were precious, to be lived over and over again in her mind's eye. Her loneliness for him was already almost beyond bearing.

Already hardly able to bear Letitia's absence from his life, Kanuga entered his village on his dog sled, determined to make the changes necessary so that she would return to him. He would go to Kosko, one of the shamans of his village. Kosko knew how to use love charms and potions to make a girl fall in love with the man who idolized her. Kosko knew secret formulas for putting names on a girl's ear, eyes, hands, and head, even without her having to be present, making it impossible for her to hear, see, touch, or think without being reminded of him.

This he would ask of Kosko—to make Letitia's mind burn with thoughts of Kanuga!

She would return to him!

She would become his wife!

Not wanting his shaman brother to perform this service for him, for it was an embarrassing request to ask of someone of his blood kin, Kanuga rode on past Atkuk's house.

When he got to Kosko's longhouse, he cleverly hid his dog team and sled behind the house, away from the view of the rest of the villagers, especially Atkuk.

Kanuga then went to Kosko's door and knocked.

When the shaman opened the door and saw that it was Kanuga, he ushered him inside, into a dwelling lighted only by the blaze of the fire in the firepit in the center of the floor.

"Why have you come?" Kosko asked, gesturing to Kanuga to sit on soft mats before the fire. "What service can I perform for you?"

Kanuga gazed across the fire at Kosko, seeing a distinct difference between him and his shaman brother. A man of fifty winters, there was something strangely remote in Kosko's faded gray eyes, but it was not the look of serenity characteristic of most shaman.

And when Kosko smiled, Kanuga noted to himself, it seemed a sinister smile, not one of gentleness.

Kanuga's gaze swept over Kosko's long gray hair circling around thin shoulders, and down the front of a loose buckskin robe, decorated with all sorts of porcupine quills and beads in the shapes of the moon, the sun, the lightning, and the stars. If one didn't know better, Kanuga pondered, Kosko could have been taken for a sorcerer.

"Why have I come?" Kanuga blurted out, not liking where his thoughts had taken him. If Kosko was a sorcerer, then the other shaman would have recognized it and would have seen that his death would have come swiftly. "To ask you to perform a service that will bring my woman back to me."

"And you chose not to ask your brother to do this service for you?" Kosko said, folding his arms across his chest as his lips lifted into a smug smile.

"It is not the sort of thing a brother wants to ask of a brother," Kanuga said, his voice solemn. "It is too personal. And you are never to disclose my coming here to anyone, especially not my brother."

"That is understood," Kosko said, nodding. "Now tell me. The woman you speak of. Who is she?"

"The white woman," Kanuga admitted reluctantly. "The one who is named Letitia."

"But you took her away today, to board her ship to leave Alaska," Kosko said, frowning darkly. "Why did you do that, if you wished for her to stay? You are the chief. All you would have had to do was order her to stay. She would have stayed."

"It was not my wish to force her to do anything against her will," Kanuga said.

"If she does not want you, the chief of our people, why do you want her?" Kosko said, his eyes squinting at Kanuga. "You have many beautiful Tlingit women to choose from who would make your bed warm at night."

Kanuga leaned closer to Kosko. "It is not for

you to question my decision to do anything," he warned. "Now perform your services. Nothing more!"

Kosko reached for his hawk spirit mask, a down-turned beak which touched the upper lip. Brass washers had been used for the irises of the eyes; brightly dyed chicken feathers, human hair, a clump of bark and twigs nailed on top of the head, and eagle feathers decorated the mask.

After placing the mask on, Kosko reached a hand out to Kanuga. "I will need a lock of the woman's hair and a piece of her clothing," he said, smiling devilishly at Kanuga. He did not expect Kanuga to have brought the necessary items, since he surely did not know the requirements of the ritual.

And this was good. Kosko didn't want to do anything to bring the white woman back to his village. He saw her as only an interference—someone who would bring harm to his people by flooding Kanuga's thoughts with her, instead of his duties of chief.

Kanuga reached inside the pocket of his fur coat and brought out a tiny lock of Letitia's hair and a piece of her dress, which he had snipped from Letitia during her sleep.

"I have heard of your requirements from others who have used your services," Kanuga said, handing the hair and piece of cloth over to Kosko. "Now work your magic, Kosko. Prove your worth to your chief."

Out-foxed by Kanuga, Kosko took the items, then smiled to himself as he realized that he would not have to perform the ritual exactly asked of him. Without Kanuga even being aware of it, Kosko was going to actually be casting a spell on *Kanuga*. Kanuga would be walking around in a trance without even realizing it.

Kosko knew that this power was what separated him from the other shaman, but only he was aware of this difference. Kosko knew that most would look to him as evil, should they be able to see inside his darkened heart. From birth, he had been possessed by an evil force that he had been unable to control. He had been very careful to hide his identity, or he would have been killed immediately by the members of his clan. There was no logic in what he did. It just happened that an unseen force was suddenly there, making him do evil instead of good.

He had been clever to direct suspicions about there being an evil shaman among this clan's three healers to Atkuk. Kosko had cast the third shaman under his spell, so that he could not see the wrong that he did.

"Give me one strand of your hair," Kosko said, stretching out a hand to Kanuga.

"That is not normally a part of the ritual," Kanuga said suspiciously.

"It will hasten the process," Kosko lied. "It will bring this woman to your bed much more quickly."

Kanuga inhaled a nervous breath, then plucked a strand of hair from his head and handed it to Kosko. "Now let us get this behind us," he said irritably. "If I am here much longer, surely someone will see my dog team."

Kosko nodded. He placed Kanuga's strand of hair with Letitia's hair and clothing on a broad rock beside the roaring fire, then began chanting to himself, performing this incantation over the personal objects, while sprinkling some magic herbs over them.

Beneath his breath, so that Kanuga could not hear him, Kosko placed a spell on Kanuga which would make him irresistibly attracted to the next woman he would look at. She would be the one he would sleep with. His heart would be lost to her!

Kosko smiled to himself, having no doubt that that woman would be of Tlingit descent!

Kosko then stood suddenly, nodding down at Kanuga. "You may now go," he said. "The performance is over. Soon you will hold your intended in your arms. You will experience lovemaking as never before. From that moment on, she will never love anyone but you."

Strangely lightheaded, Kanuga slowly pushed himself up from the floor. Staggering, he left Kosko's house and climbed aboard his sled and, as though he were doing everything at half of a normal speed, snapped the whip over his dog's heads and rode away toward his own house.

His heart was pounding.

His brow was pearled with sweat.

Somehow he felt that Kosko's performance had gone beyond that of normal magical powers, yet ...yet his thoughts were so muddled that he could not think further on it.

He was even finding it hard to remember why he had gone to Kosko.

What he needed was sleep.

Never had he . . . been so sleepy. . . .

Smiling devilishly, Kosko scooped up the items that he had sprinkled magic herbs over and dumped them into the flames of the fire. He removed all signs of the herbs from the rock and placed it in a dark corner of his house.

Then he returned to the fire and settled back down onto a thick bear pelt, watching his door as Athas came in and sat down beside the fire. Kosko had purposely excluded Atkuk from this private meeting.

"And so, Athas, what shall we do about Atkuk?" Kosko said, his voice a rumble submerging from that unseen evil force deep within him.

Kosko's eyes gleamed with satisfaction that his magical powers had worked so well on Athas and had finally succeeded in turning him against Atkuk. He listened as Athas spoke his thoughts about Kanuga's shaman brother.

"He is a sorcerer, one who is possessed by an evil force," Athas softly mumbled. "He is bewitched."

"You are right. And the proof is in the fact that the young Tlingit warrior died after Atkuk's powers failed him," Kosko chimed in. "Atkuk is evil."

"It is not right for a chief's brother to be a shaman," Athas boldly announced. "There is too much power in one family!"

"Atkuk must die!" Kosko said, thrusting a fist

into the air. "He must die soon!"

"Yes!" Athas cried. "Soon!"

Kosko's shoulders relaxed, proud of the deeds that he managed to accomplish today. Thus far, everything was going as planned. Soon he would be the most admired of all the shaman in all of Alaska!

He poured some elixir from a flask into a wooden cup and gave it to Athas. He watched him drink it, realizing by the glassiness of his eyes that it was indeed potent enough, as it had been the other times he had offered it to him, and he had drunk it.

Kosko's eyes gleamed with pleasure as Athas moved to his feet and walked drunkenly from the house.

Chapter Thirteen

Our acts our angels are, or good or ill,
Our fatal shadows that walk by us still
—FLETCHER

Feeling forlorn, missing Kanuga so much that the
pit of her stomach felt empty, Letitia tossed and
turned in her bed, unable to sleep. She couldn't
erase the memory of being in Kanuga's arms so
easily from her mind.

She could still feel his kiss....

She could still taste his lips....

"Letitia?"

The voice in the dark made Letitia's thoughts
return to the present and her insides tighten up;
she had never liked being forced to share the
small ship's cabin with her cousin Barbara. The
one thing that she would look forward to once
she was back in America, if she could ever look
forward to anything again, was the privacy of

her bedroom. Within those walls she was always in her own private world, able to think of whomever she wanted to think about whenever she wanted to, without interruptions.

Now she expected a barrage of questions from Barbara—questions she wasn't sure she was prepared to answer.

She preferred to keep her precious secrets.

"What do you want, Barbara?" Letitia said, sighing heavily as she turned to face her cousin, whose bed was much too close to hers because of the cramped space. However, her only choice had been to have her bed that close to her cousin or—heaven forbid!—to share a single bed with her. She had already been forced to share her life with her cousin.

Must it be that way forever? she wondered gloomily.

Guilt washed through her over such selfish thoughts. She had always accused Barbara of being the selfish, jealous one, when more often than not, Letitia was proving to herself that Barbara was more the victim of such feelings than the perpetrator.

"Tell me about him," Barbara said in a purr. The wick of the lone candle in the room now swimming around in a melted puddle of wax in the wall sconce revealed the malicious curiosity in Barbara's slanted green eyes. "Letitia, tell me about that handsome Indian chief. Is he married?"

Letitia's jaw tightened, and her own eyes flashed angrily. "No, he's not married," she said, in a much too snappish tone. "Why would you even want to know?"

Barbara flopped over on her stomach, supporting her chin in her hands, the lace of her gown hugging her slender throat. "Why, Letitia, I had always envisioned the Indians of Alaska as being anything but handsome," she murmured. "But Kanuga is tall and statuesque." She emitted a long, quavering sigh. "And he has such intriguing silver eyes! They made me melt inside, Letitia! Actually melt!"

Letitia blanched as she stared disbelievingly at her cousin. She knew that Barbara was much more well-versed on the subject of men than herself, but to be speaking about Kanuga in such a way, as she had spoken so often of men in America just before they had fallen victim to her wiles, made her grow wary. She could not help but say a silent prayer that the ice should melt soon so their ship could be on its way. She feared that perhaps Barbara would somehow find her way to Kanuga's bed. Letitia couldn't allow that.

Yet, suddenly something seemed to compel Letitia into talking about Kanuga *to* Barbara. It was as though some unseen force was urging her into a conversation about the man she loved that otherwise she would have avoided at all cost! The words just suddenly seemed there on her lips, as though she were under some strange sort of spell.

"Kanuga?" she said, looking dreamily over at Barbara. "Yes, he is a handsome man. And, Barbara, he asked me to marry him."

"He did?" Barbara said, scrambling to a sitting

position. "And you returned to the ship? How could you have? The savage in him would make him a masterful lover!"

Letitia was feeling torn, a part of her wanting to lash out at Barbara for calling Kanuga a savage, and for talking about him being a masterful lover when this was something that she felt should be hers, alone, to talk and dream about.

But another part of her made her want to continue talking about Kanuga to her cousin—an open conversation about things that Letitia would have never shared with anyone, especially Barbara!

"He *was* a masterful lover," Letitia said, sitting up. She drew the blankets up just beneath her chin, hugging them to her bosom. She glanced over at Barbara. "It was my first time with a man, you know. And it was wonderful!"

The heat of lust coiled into a throbbing knot between Barbara's thighs. "Letitia, you actually let him make love to you?" she said, smiling devilishly over at Letitia. "My, oh, my, what would your mother say? Her little angel girl with white wings now a tarnished lady."

Something seemed to snap inside Letitia's mind, as if she had just awakened from a trance. She stared, wide-eyed, at Barbara. "What did you say?" she gasped. "What about me being—being a tarnished lady?"

"You had sex with the Indian," Barbara said, shrugging. "You aren't married to him. In your mother's eyes, you would be a tarnished lady."

"Did I actually tell you that?" Letitia gasped,

not able to recall the moment she had let her closely guarded secret breathe across her lips.

"Now what is this?" Barbara said, arching a carefully plucked eyebrow. "What kind of game are you trying to play? Did you or did you not sleep with the Indian?"

Letitia turned her back to Barbara, unable to comprehend what had prompted her to be so open with her cousin, especially about something as personal as having lain with a man for the first time in her life.

Never had she been so open—so foolish!

It had been as though someone else was in her body at that moment, making her say the things that could condemn her!

As though she had been cast beneath some evil spell!

She closed her eyes and held them together tightly, hoping that by doing so the evil spell would disappear, and Barbara would too. She just wanted to be left alone in her disgrace and despair.

Oh, Kanuga, she thought wistfully. Oh, how she missed him! She was beginning to regret her decision to not stay with him.

But now it was too late—too late!

"Letitia, the Indian village can't be far from our ship," Barbara said, leaving her bed to go and look out the small porthole at the side of the cabin. "Last night I watched the reflections of fire in the sky. Were those set in the village? If so, you were almost within shouting distance from the ship. Pity you hadn't realized that. You could have stolen one of the Indian's dogteams and sled and brought your daddy onto the ship without the assistance of the Indians."

Barbara spun around and sat down on the edge of Letitia's bed. She smoothed her hands over Letitia's golden hair, feeling Letitia flinch with the gesture. "But if you had brought Jerome to the ship, you wouldn't have had another night in your savage's arms," she purred. "Letitia, tell me about the way he makes love. Was he passionate?"

Letitia was slowly filling with rage. Her heart pounded from the building anger. Suddenly she tossed her blankets away from herself and turned to Barbara, knocking her hand away. "Barbara, I've had enough," she said, giving her cousin a shove so that she almost fell from the bed. "I don't want to hear any more talk about Kanuga, nor of the lovemaking we shared. It was a beautiful, even a sacred thing. I will not let you poke fun at it and make it dirty."

She jumped from the bed, grabbed on a robe, and slipped her feet into some soft slippers, then stamped to the door. "I plan to sleep elsewhere," she said from between clenched lips. "I'll sleep in Jonathan's bunk. Now and every night until he returns to the ship. Never do I want to share anything with you again."

She took a step closer to Barbara. "And if you tell mother about—about me and Kanuga, I'll tear your hair out," she warned.

Barbara tossed her head back, laughing throatily, her hair rippling in raven-black streamers down her back.

Then she leveled angry eyes at Letitia. "I shall tell Kimberly anything, whenever I please," she warned back. "And just come near me and I'll shove you overboard on the packed ice and snow, food for wolves or bears." Again she laughed. "Bye, bye, sweet cousin. Sweet dreams."

Fuming, Letitia left the cabin and slammed the door with a bang, then felt her way through the darkness, shivering from the cold, until she reached the cabin that had been appointed to Jonathan.

Hurrying inside, she felt around until she found some matches, then lit a candle and the wood in a small stove that Jonathan had prepared for his planned return from the expedition.

Standing over the stove until the fire took hold, Letitia gazed slowly around the room, seeing so many things familiar to her.

Jonathan's maps spread neatly across a desk.

Jonathan's pipe resting on an ashtray.

Turning from these things, a sob catching in Letitia's throat, she suddenly did not think this a wise decision, sleeping with memories of Jonathan, when she did not know if he was even alive. If he was, she dreaded having to tell him that she would not marry him after all.

Feeling weary, Letitia went to the bunk and eased down onto it, pulling some heavy blankets atop her. Closing her eyes, she shut out the world and all of its problems, soon drifting off into sleep.

But that wasn't even a reprieve. First she dreamed of Kanuga, and then Jonathan.

And then she was standing between them both, pleading for them to put away their dueling pistols. When they refused and both shot at each other at the same instant, Letitia grabbed at her chest, the recipient of both of their bullets....

She awakened in a sweat and screaming, then when she realized that it had only been a dream, again fell into a drugged sort of sleep, which was at least dreamless this time.

She welcomed the black void of nothingness.

Like a caged tigress, Barbara paced the cabin, hungering to meet the man who had the skills to lure her cold fish of a cousin into his bed. She knew that Kanuga must be quite a man, and it had been some time now since Barbara had been with a man. It was eating away at her, this hunger to be held and loved. If she could just find a way to get to Kanuga....

Her heart pounding from a building excitement, an idea forming inside her restless brain, Barbara went to the porthole and gazed out at the white stretch of snow and the reflection of fires in the sky, realizing again that the Indian village was not all that far away. In fact, if she walked fast enough, she could get there before frostbite set in!

"I'll do it!" she said, her eyes dancing, the thought of the danger of actually going out alone in the wilderness in the middle of the night giving her a thrill nearly as wonderful as being with a man. "I'll go to Kanuga. He won't turn me away. Being a man who always thinks of himself as the protector of women, he wouldn't turn me away in the cold and make me return to the ship.

"He'll take me in for warmth. Then I'll draw him into making love to me. When I go after a man, I always get him!"

Tingling all over from the anticipation, Barbara drew a buckskin dress over her lacy silk gown, then put on warm socks and boots and grabbed her thick fur parka and gloves and snowshoes, and stepped lightly out into the corridor.

Making sure no one was in sight, and glad that the crew had forgotten to draw in the gangplank, she slipped on the snowshoes and fled into the night.

The stars were blinking overhead. The moon was full, casting weird shadows across the snow where the trees on all sides of her whispered in the wind. Just as her face was growing tight and cold, she spied the fires up ahead.

Smiling, she hurried along, then jumped with alarm when the huskies in the village were awakened as she entered, barking and growling at her presence.

Not sure which way to turn in the village, and frightened of the hideous totem poles all around her that looked alive with the strange creatures carved in them, Barbara stopped beside a house. She jumped with alarm when someone stepped suddenly outside, facing her with the most brilliant silver eyes she could ever imagine.

"Kanuga?" she said, finding it hard to believe

that it had been this simple to find him. All along, while she had been traipsing through the snow, she had not felt alone, as though someone had been there, guiding her.

And to find Kanuga's house so quickly!

"Who are you?" Kanuga growled. "Why are you here?" He looked into Barbara's strangely slanted green eyes, and at the lovely lines of her youthful face.

Although Letitia was still fresh in his heart, this white woman was stirring his insides into a flaming inferno! He did not even know her, yet he wanted her!

How could that be, he wondered?

His brow was even perspiring, his need for this woman was so intense!

"My name is Barbara," Barbara said, seeing his reaction to her, feeling smug and victorious because of it. He was proving that he had not loved Letitia at all. He had only used her, as most men used women! "I have come from the American ship. I have come to be with you, Kanuga. Only you."

Kanuga took her by the elbow and ushered her into his house, then, while staring into her eyes, began disrobing her. "I want you," he said huskily. "I want you now."

Barbara smiled wickedly up at him, lifting her arms as he slipped her dress over her head, leaving on her enticingly thin, silken finerie that she knew revealed her large swell of breasts, her flat tummy, and her muff of black hair between her thighs. She could see his eyes feasting on her. She reveled in it!

But even when her gown was removed and she was standing silkenly nude before Kanuga, she took her turn at disrobing him. Barbara wet her lips slowly with the tip of her tongue as first his powerful, hairless chest was revealed to her. She ran her hands over the muscles, and then finished disrobing him, revealing his risen manhood, silkeny smooth in its firm tautness.

"Handsome Indian, I'm going to make you feel wonderful tonight," Barbara said, kneeling down before him.

Chapter Fourteen

The heart will break,
Yet broken lives on.

—BYRON

His eyes smoky with passion, Kanuga gritted his teeth as Barbara's mouth and tongue performed what seemed to be magic on his body. As she continued to kneel before him, pleasuring him, he ran his fingers through the soft glimmer of her dark hair.

Then, afraid that he was too near to that plateau of total release, he stepped away from her and offered her a hand, helping her up from the floor.

No words were said as he guided her to his bed. Stretching out on her back, Barbara reached her hands out to Kanuga, smiling seductively.

When he came to her, moving over her with his powerful body, she tremored with ecstasy, yet he did not enter her. His tongue made its way down her body, stopping at her throbbing center, causing her breathing to become ragged with anticipation. She became almost delirious from the pleasure as his tongue stroked her wetly, heatedly, his hands on her breasts, kneading them.

"No more," she finally gasped, sweat pearling her brow. She placed her hands to each side of his head and urged him back up, completely over her.

Running her fingers along his pulsing satin hardness, she led him inside her, opening herself more widely, drawing him deeply into her. Barbara closed her eyes and emitted a strange sort of gurgle from the depths of her throat; she had never before been so magnificently filled.

A faint memory of who had also shared such wonders with Kanuga made Letitia's face flash before Barbara's mind's eye, wondering how her cowardly little cousin could have given up this magnificent specimen of a man.

Yet, Barbara also recalled Letitia saying that Kanuga had been the first man with her. This was the reason why Letitia did not know what uniqueness she had had in this man. Barbara, who had been with many men, knew that none compared with Kanuga's lovemaking. None!

And, she decided she would not let him go. She would marry him. After tonight, he would want her to.

Kanuga's thrusts within Barbara became maddeningly faster, faster—in a frantic sort of lovemaking. He held on to her as though she were in a vise, his lips crushing down upon hers in a savage kiss.

When her tongue parted his lips and entered his mouth, flickering it in and out teasingly, he felt the heat in his loins growing to the bursting point.

As though some force were in his house, urging him onward, Kanuga moved his body even faster, his skin wet with perspiration, his heart thumping wildly within his chest.

And then he felt the great shudder in his loins. He screamed out his ecstasy as the flood of pleasure swept raggedly through him. He placed his hands beneath her buttocks and forced her to strain her hips up at him, and pressed deeper and deeper into her until she cried out at her fulfillment, her body vibrating against his, as does the string on a bow vibrate immediately after the arrow has been shot from it.

Breathing hard, their bodies subsided exhaustedly into each other. Barbara ran her hands down Kanuga's back, circling her fingers around his smooth, muscled buttocks, reveling in his manly strength. When he leaned up away from her, their eyes locked in an unspoken understanding, promising more ecstasy even while the air was heavy with the pleasure already achieved.

Rolling away from her, stretching out on his back, Kanuga lifted Barbara atop him. His manhood revitalized, he slipped it inside her, and let her ride him, as though she were on a magnificent, golden steed. His hands clasped hard onto her breasts, causing her to throw her head back in rapture, her dark hair spilling back away from her, so long it reached his thighs.

Kanuga surged upward, into her, his eyes closed, enjoying her. Yet, deep down inside himself, where his desires were formed, he was troubled. In his mind's eye there were brief flashes of another woman's face. There were brief remembrances of hair the color of the sun shimmering across slim white shoulders. There were eyes the color of a spring morning sky, gazing lovingly at him.

There were lips—oh, so inviting.

Oh, so sweet!

But just as quickly the woman he was making love to captured his undivided attention. He opened his eyes and once again he felt the last vestiges of rational mind floating away when he found green, slanted eyes looking seductively down at him. His hands moved over the glossy textured skin of her breasts, and down over her ribs, and then around to the smooth, hard flesh of her buttocks. He formed his hands around her there and held her to him as he thrust endlessly upward.

And then the whole universe seemed to start spinning around as great rushes of tingling heat flooded Kanuga. Gasps like thunder echoed throughout him as his loins shuddered, his release again sought and found.

Barbara gave herself up to the same wild ecstasy, for sure now that he would be hers forever. Their lovemaking had been like a great fire burning with a fierce heat, surely never to be extinguished! And when he asked her to stay, to be his wife, she would not be like her daft cousin Letitia.

She would cry out to him a loud "Yes!"

She would vow to him that she was willing to give up the life she had always known to live with Kanuga, only for his lovemaking!

She was convinced that ten men would never compare with one Kanuga!

Slithering down, stretching herself out atop Kanuga, Barbara framed his face between her hands and darted her tongue moistly into his mouth. She laughed throatily when he suddenly lifted her from him and placed her beneath him, molding himself perfectly to the curved hollow of her hips.

"Who are you?" he asked, his eyes of heated passion searching her face. "Why have you come to me? Why do you give yourself to me like a wildcat, so free-spirited and wild?"

Kanuga started to draw away from her when she did not respond to his questions, then sucked in a wild breath of air, not making a move, when she reached between their bodies and grabbed his manhood, her fingers so cool against his heat.

To reciprocate the pleasure, he locked his lips around one of her nipples and nipped it with his teeth, drawing from her a long, lazy sigh.

Then Kanuga drew away from her, lying on his side beside her. "You are from the American ship," he said, running his hands slowly, caressingly, across her satiny flesh. "Why did you come to Kanuga?"

"I came to you because I had to have you,"

Barbara said in a purr. She placed a hand to his copper cheek. "And, Kanuga, you had to have me. I felt it in the wildness of your lovemaking that you needed a woman like me to fulfill you."

In the depths of Kanuga's mind, he was trying once again to pull from his memory another woman, another time, yet he could not recollect who, or when. Something was causing his thoughts to be scrambled! It was as though a spell had been cast on him, yet why?

And by whom?

Brushing such foolish thoughts aside, wanting to savor this time when his body was so alive with needs and fulfillments, he drew Barbara into a rough embrace, his mouth devouring her in a frenzied kiss.

This fire!

This need!

It seemed to be consuming him!

He could not help but thrust himself inside her again.

Each stroke within her brought up fresh desire, like white heat traveling throughout Kanuga.

And again, unable to hold this energy back any longer, it exploded through him, reaching every cell in his body with heated jolts of overpowering sensations.

Exhausted, breathing hard, Kanuga rolled away from Barbara and drifted off into a fitful sleep. Barbara smiled wickedly down at him, caressing his sweat-pearled brow. All of her life she had dreamed of such a man, yet had never believed there could be such a lover. Her body still trembled from the ferocity of his lovemaking.

"Letitia, how foolish you were to leave him," she whispered, laughing softly. "Now he's mine." She snuggled down beside him, clinging to him. "And I am his."

Content, she closed her eyes, envisioning the moment when she would proudly announce to her Uncle Jerome that she was no longer his responsibility.

She now belonged to Kanuga!

Only Kanuga. . . .

Letitia tossed fitfully on the small bunk on which she slept. In her dreams she was in a house in Kanuga's village, tied to stakes as Iuril had been. Nude, she cast her eyes away from her cousin when Barbara stood over her again, a whip in her hand. She closed her eyes and willed herself not to cry out when she felt the whip tearing her flesh away, while Barbara laughed in a crazy sort of shriekish way as she cracked the whip over and over again against her.

And then, in her dream, the pain was replaced by a sweet warmth when Kanuga was suddenly there, enfolding her ravaged body within his arms, whispering soft and comforting words to her as Barbara stood close by, screaming at him to let Letitia go.

Letitia cried out in her sleep when, in her nightmare, Kanuga dropped her to the floor and stepped over her and went to Barbara and pulled her into his arms, kissing her passionately.

The nightmare worsened when Letitia was

forced to endure the sight of Kanuga tearing Barbara's clothes off, then falling to the floor atop her in a frenzy of lovemaking.

Sobbing, the pain of seeing Kanuga making love to Barbara like many stab wounds in her heart, Letitia tried to go to them and separate them, but her legs would not move.

And even when she turned her eyes away from Barbara's and Kanuga's entwined bodies, she could not get away from their lovemaking, for their bodies were rubbing noisily together, and they were both gasping with pleasure.

It tore at Letitia's heart when she heard them reach that moment of ultimate pleasure. There was no denying it, when they both screamed out just how wonderful it was. . . .

Letitia was wrenched from her sleep as she emitted a loud scream. Sobbing, drawing the blankets up to her chin, she looked frantically around her, glad to discover that she was in bed on her father's ship, and that what she had just experienced had been a nightmare—a nightmare in which she had lost Kanuga to her cousin!

The door of the cabin was flung suddenly open, startling Letitia. Her eyes widened and she gasped when she discovered her father standing in the doorway with a shotgun.

"Letitia," Jerome said, leaning against the door, weakness almost crumpling his legs beneath him. "My God, Letitia, what are you doing here? When I heard the scream I thought that perhaps someone had forced you to Jonathan's room to rape you."

Letitia left the bed hurriedly and went to her father. "Papa, what are you doing out of bed?" she scolded. She slipped an arm around his waist and led him to a chair, helping him down into it.

"God damn it, Letitia, I can't be an invalid forever," Jerome grumbled, laying the shotgun on the floor beside the chair. "And when it comes to protecting my daughter, well, I...."

"You should know by now, Papa, at most times I can take care of myself," Letitia said, patting him on the knee as she knelt down before him. "I'm sorry I awakened you. And I'm sorry that I frightened you." She cast her eyes downward. "I—I just had a nightmare. That's all."

"After all we've been through these past several days, I can understand why," Jerome said, placing a forefinger to her chin, directing her eyes up to his. "But in time those nightmares—*and* the remembrances of times experienced while away from the ship—will be forgotten. When Jonathan returns, he'll help you forget."

"*If* Jonathan returns," Letitia said, rising away from her father. She went to Jonathan's desk and smoothed her hand over his carefully drawn maps. "Papa, I have lost hope in ever seeing Jonathan alive again. It's been too long. If he was anywhere near, someone would have seen him." She glanced over at her father. "And the rest of the expedition, Papa, I—I'm sure they are all dead."

"Let's not be thinking like that," Jerome scolded, slowly pushing himself up from the chair. He steadied himself, taking several deep breaths. "Why are you sleeping in Jonathan's cabin instead of your own?"

He smiled softly over at her. "It's because you miss him, isn't it?" he said. "It's because being here brings you closer to him. That warms my heart, Letitia, to know that you care at least that much for him. He'd be such a perfect husband for you."

Not wanting to get into dialogue about Jonathan again with her father, and glad to see that her father was improved enough to actually have walked from his cabin to this one without assistance, Letitia went to him and hugged him. "I'm glad you're better, Papa," she murmured, then stepped away from him, tensing when she saw his brow furrowed in a frown.

"You haven't said yet why you left your cabin," he said, placing a hand to her shoulder. "Did you and Barbara quarrel? It seems you've been at each other's throats ever since we left New York."

Letitia turned her eyes from him. She walked to the bunk and toyed with the fringes of a blanket. "Yes, papa, Barbara and I have been having many differences," she said stiffly. "Tonight I just couldn't bear any more of her annoyances."

She swung around and faced him. "Nor shall I again," she stated flatly. "I refuse to share a cabin with her any longer, papa."

She paused, then added, "Nor anything else."

She could not block the nightmare from her mind, in which Kanuga and Barbara had been making such frenzied love. It had been so vividly real, as though it had been truly happening at that very moment in time.

"Have I paid too much attention to Barbara, honey?" Jerome said, going to Letitia and drawing her into his gentle embrace. "If I have, I'm sorry. I've just felt so sorry for her, losing both her mother and father so early on in life. I only wanted to help her adjust to their loss. Perhaps I went too far, neglecting you in the process."

Tears swam in Letitia's eyes. "Oh, Papa," she said, her voice a near whisper. "Never could I accuse you of neglecting me. I didn't mean to cause you concern about it."

She slipped from his embrace and placed an arm around his waist. "Now let's get you back to your cabin. Surely mother is worried."

"I refused to let her come with me when I heard you scream," Jerome said, leaning his weight against Letitia's side. "If you were being raped by—"

"By whom, father?" Letitia said, glancing quickly at him.

Jerome's eyes wavered, not wanting to speak the name Kanuga in Letitia's presence again, now that he had achieved the task of getting her away from him.

But it had been Kanuga who had sprung to his mind when he had heard Letitia screaming. He had feared that Kanuga had come into the night to take her away, and had gotten carried away in the process, unable to hold back his desire to claim her as his.

"It could have been anyone," Jerome said somberly. "Anyone."

Letitia could see more in his expression than he was saying aloud, and she knew that he had thought that Kanuga had come aboard the ship for her. She turned her eyes away, not wanting to think any farther on what her father thought Kanuga was capable of, when she knew very well what was in his heart and soul—a genuine caring for her, which never would result in any sort of violence against her person.

Flashes of the nightmare entered her mind again, causing a cold, clammy sweat to creep up her legs.

The nightmare had seemed so real.

Broderick Bowman emptied the bottle of vodka in one deep gulp, then slung the bottle across his cabin, where it shattered into many tiny slivers across the wooden floor. He had awakened from sleep in a nervous sweat, his night having been filled with nightmares of Iuril, and what might be happening to him at the Indian village.

"I can't wait any longer to go and bargain for Iuril," he whispered to himself. "I must get this behind me before Iuril dies, if he isn't dead already! If I don't go and ask for peace talks with Kanuga soon, and Iuril should die, I will be blamed! Then my life won't be worth spit!"

A slow smile flickered on his lips. "And there's the American lady," he whispered to himself. Just thinking of her caused his knees to weaken with desire. "There must be a way to bargain with Kanuga, so that I can also have *her*."

He weaved drunkenly toward the bed and flopped down on it. "Tomorrow," he said, hiccoughing loudly. He wiped his mouth with his hands. "I'll go to the Tlingit village tomorrow. Tonight I . . . I must get some sleep."

Pulling blankets over his fully clothed body, he looked up at the ceiling. "Lord, no more nightmares tonight, please?" he whispered, then smacked his lips thirstily and fluttered his eyes closed. Rumbling snores soon filled the cabin.

Chapter Fifteen

*Advise well before you begin, and when you
have maturely considered, then act
with promptitude.*

—SALLUST

Stretching her arms above her head and yawn-
ing, Letitia looked slowly around her, disoriented
for a moment.

Then she recalled having come to Jonathan's
cabin, and why, and a strange sort of dread
grabbed her at the pit of her stomach. Her nightmares about Barbara and Kanuga together in
passionate embraces were still vivid in her mind,
troubling her anew.

"How could anything seem so real, and not
be?" she said to herself, slipping from the bed.

She glanced down at what she wore and gri-
maced, knowing that she had no choice but to
return to her cabin to get her clothes. She would

have to hold her chin firmly high while Barbara teased and taunted her, but this would be the last time. Once her clothes were removed from her cabin and brought to Jonathan's, she would not have to be alone with Barbara ever again.

"But first I must stoke my fire," she whispered to herself. She knew that she did this only to postpone having to come face to face with Barbara again. She had awakened twice during the night and had placed wood on the fire, so that the cabin was toasty warm.

Nevertheless, she placed several pieces of wood in the stove, and after the fire was curling more earnestly around the wood, the flames golden as they shot up toward the flue of the stove, Letitia sighed resolutely and gazed at the door. There was no getting around it. She had to go to her cabin and get her clothes, yet she still dreaded facing Barbara today. She had revealed too much to her cousin that even now Letitia could not understand what had prompted her to tell her. For a moment it had seemed as though she had become someone else, a person she would even never want to become! She had never wanted to confide in Barbara about anything, especially her intimacies with Kanuga!

But she had, and now Barbara had the power to blackmail her.

"I must get this behind me," she said aloud. She rose to her feet and stamped toward the door. "I shall just go inside my cabin, grab my things, and leave without giving her even that slightest glance. Let her fume over my indifference!"

And let her blackmail me if she must, she thought bitterly to herself. Then at least her parents would finally see just what sort of person Barbara truly was.

When she stepped out into the damp, cold corridor, shivers engulfed Letitia. She stood there for a moment, looking from side to side. Candles were still burning low on the wall sconces. Everything was quiet, except for an occasional popping and cracking from the ship's hull as it tried to move in its grave of ice.

This reminded her that once the ice broke up, Kanuga expected the ship to move away from Alaska's shores.

This reminded her, also, that her father was stubborn, and perhaps would not do as Kanuga had ordered.

It tore at her senses, this fear that before long the two men that she loved most in the world would come face to face, and this time with no intention of being friends. They would become instant enemies once her father told Kanuga that he was in Alaska to build a trading post.

Jerome had never been a man to back away from a challenge—not even if he were surrounded by angry Tlingit.

Not wanting to think further on what the outcome of a confrontation between her father and Kanuga might be, she hurried onward, her eyes on the closed door of her cabin.

Then she glanced over at her parents' closed door, wondering if her father *was* better today. It had been wonderful to see him walking without assistance last evening when he had come to her. It seemed as though being on his ship, with everything familiar to him, and being with his wife again, had given him the strength that he had never had in Kanuga's village.

Just perhaps he was well on the road to complete recovery now.

If nothing else this morning, at least this thought made Letitia happy!

Stepping up to her door, she inhaled a nervous, quavering breath, then placed her hand on the doorknob and determinedly opened it in a quick jerk. Utter silence and a room devoid of candlelight met her as she stepped inside the cabin.

And it was so cold! As though Letitia had stepped into a tomb!

She gazed up at the porthole. There was hardly any daylight filtering through the stained glass.

Then she glanced over at Barbara's bed, seeing not a stirring beneath the pile of blankets. She laughed to herself, thinking that this was going to be easier than she had thought. Barbara was still asleep. Letitia could grab her things and leave without her cousin being aware that she had been there! One of the crew could bring her large trunk that sat at the end of her bed to her later in the day. All that she needed now were the clothes that she could gather up into her arms from the chifferobe.

She tiptoed to her bedside and grabbed her shoes, and before going on to the chifferobe, she stopped and gazed questioningly at Barbara's bed. Something seemed wrong there. The blankets. It was something about the blankets.

She inched closer, and now she could see that there was something wrong in how the blankets should look if someone were there, asleep beneath them.

A warning flashed on in her mind, catapulting her back to last night, and her nightmares. How vividly real they had been! It tore at her being even now recalling how Kanuga and Barbara had so blatantly made love in front of her! It had been so real, as though it could have been happening at that very moment....

Startled by another thought, that perhaps Barbara might have fled in the night and gone to Kanuga, as a wanton and man-starved female such as Barbara might do, Letitia blanched. She dropped her shoes, went shakily to Barbara's bed and grabbed hold of the blankets, then gave a quick jerk.

She gasped from an instant lightheadedness when she discovered that Barbara was not there.

"No!" Letitia wailed, dropping the blankets back in place. "It can't be! She wouldn't!"

Her heart beat with an anxious, fearful thudding as she ran from the cabin and began pounding on her parents' door. She kept saying to herself that she was wrong in her speculations.

Barbara could not be with Kanuga! She was surely somewhere on the ship, philandering with one of the crew members!

"Oh, let that be the answer," she prayed to herself. "Oh, please—please—don't be with Kanuga!"

She could hear a scurrying around in her parents' cabin as someone was coming to the door. As she waited for the door to open, she squeezed her eyes closed, trying not to envision Barbara and Kanuga in a fierce, intimate embrace. This was all in her imagination.

She was wrong!

Wrong!

The door yanked open and Letitia found herself face to face with her father, stunned that he was up again, steady on his feet, when only yesterday morning she had been concerned about whether or not he would ever be well again.

"Papa, you're even stronger than last night?" she murmured, his well-being momentarily crowding out her reason for having come and disturbed him so early in the morning.

"My knees are a bit shaky, but otherwise, I seem to be managing pretty well on my own," he said, stepping aside so that she could come into the cabin.

"And your wounds are healed enough so that it doesn't pain you terribly to be out of bed?" Letitia further questioned, unable to see his bandaged chest beneath his flannel robe.

"I'm fine," Jerome reassured, easing an arm around Kimberly's waist as she came to his side. "But Letitia, *you* don't look so well. You're pale, as though you have just seen a ghost."

"What is it, darling?" Kimberly interjected, her tiny facial features looking even more frail above a high-necked, lacy gown, her gray hair hanging in one long braid down her back. "My word, you pounded on the door as though there were some sort of emergency. What's happened? Why are you so pale? So wide-eyed?"

Letitia clasped her hands behind her, clenching and unclenching them. She gazed from her mother to her father, not sure if she should be feeling foolish for her alarm over Barbara's strange disappearance, when all along she could be just next door, consorting with some sailor!

"It's Barbara," she blurted. "She's not in her cabin."

Kimberly gasped, and looked up at Jerome, then back at Letitia. "Where could she be?" she murmured. "It's . . . it's quite early. Perhaps she's on deck, getting a breath of fresh air?"

"I doubt that," Jerome said, frowning. "It's too cold this time of day to be wandering about outside."

"There is no fire in Barbara's stove," Letitia said. "In fact, it's so cold in the cabin, I doubt if there has been a fire in the stove all night."

"I fear there has been foul play," Jerome said. He looked down at Kimberly. "Help me into my clothes. I've got to take a look around the ship."

"But, Jerome, you're much too weak to go traipsing about the ship," Kimberly fussed, yet helping him to a chair when he frowned down at her.

"I'll be going farther than that if I can't find Barbara on the ship," Jerome grumbled. He started to remove his robe, then looked up at Letitia. "Go get dressed, Letitia. Help look for Barbara. If she isn't here, then I'll be heading out for the Indian village to look for her."

Letitia placed her hands to her throat. "To the Indian village?" she said in a slight gasp. "Why, Papa?"

"Because if she's gone, either the Russians abducted her, or the Indians did," Jerome said grimly. "I plan to check at the Indian village first. If she's not there, I guess I'll have to come face to face with that Colonel Golodoff who runs things at Fort Anecia."

Letitia was rendered silent, deep down inside herself suspecting that Barbara was at the Indian village—and not because she had been abducted. She had been intrigued by Kanuga and had more than likely gone to the village of her own volition in search of him.

Her insides splashed cold at the memory of her recent nightmares. It appeared that perhaps they weren't nightmares at all, but premonitions of what was to be in reality.

"But, Jerome, you can't take out on a dog sled looking for Barbara," Kimberly softly argued. "You will have a relapse. And, darling, I can't bear thinking about you leaving me again."

Jerome looked up at Kimberly. "You won't have to," he said solemnly. "I won't be leaving you *or* Letitia unattended on this ship while I'm away from it. You'll accompany me wherever I go."

"But you'll have a relapse," Kimberly still argued.

"Letitia, go on to your cabin and get dressed," Jerome shouted, gesturing with a hand toward the door. "Your standing there is only delaying things. If you don't leave, I'll be forced to undress in front of you. Do you understand?"

Her face flooding with color, Letitia smiled shakily at her father, turned, and fled from the cabin. She trembled as she hurried back to her cabin and dressed, her thoughts scrambled. She knew that no matter how thoroughly the ship was searched, Barbara would not be found there. They would have to go to Kanuga's village.

Hate for her cousin swelled within her heart. She wasn't sure how to feel about Kanuga, should he have taken Barbara to his bed. And more than likely he would have. He was angry with Letitia for turning her back on him. Having a seductress like Barbara throwing herself at him at his time of anger and rejection would surely be too much of a temptation to turn his back to.

And should she find this to be true, what then? she wondered confusedly.

"Once I am back at that village, I will not leave," she said, firming her chin with a sudden determination, not needing any more time to decide what she must, or must not do. She had made a mistake turning her back on the man she loved. Never would she do it again.

Then her eyes wavered. What if Kanuga no longer wanted her? What if Barbara had pleased him more?

"He said that he would love me forever," Letitia said, recalling the many times he had vowed his love to her. "As I love him."

Dressed warmly in a buckskin dress and her

hooded fur coat, Letitia joined her mother and father out in the corridor. They searched in every nook and cranny, then ordered the dog team set free from the ship, and all three of them boarded the sled.

One of the ship's crew drove the dog team across the wide stretch of snow toward the Indian village, while Letitia sat stiffly beside her father, a shotgun resting on his lap. She feared the confrontation between her father and Kanuga for more than one reason. When her father heard her decision to stay with Kanuga, and that not even he could change her mind again, she had no idea what to expect, especially now that her father was strong enough to fight his own battles—and those of his daughter.

Driving his team hard with fierce snaps of his whip across the huskies' backs, Broderick Bowman was within sight of the Tlingit village. He had been the spokesman for the Russians many times before, but never had it involved bartering for a man's life.

And not only *a* man, the Russian colonel's son! Kanuga would listen to reason, he thought. He didn't want to make war against the Russians, anymore than the Russians wanted to go up against the Tlingit. Too much blood would be spilled in the snow. He smiled smugly. By nightfall he would be returning to Fort Anecia with Iuril, and all will be well again.

As he grew closer to the village and could see beyond the houses into the clearing that the houses were centered around, hope sprang forth. Iuril was not tied to a stake outside in the cold. Kanuga had surely been kindhearted enough to keep Iuril captive in a house. And surely he had been treated with respect. Kanuga and Iuril went back a long way, to the days when they had played handball during the short months of summer.

Kanuga would never let anything happen to Iuril, he told himself. He was sure of that.

He snapped the whip harder against the backs of the huskies and shouted at them, the wind cold against his face, yet invigorating. And as soon as he again came face to face with the lovely American lady he would take her off Kanuga's hands.

He laughed boisterously into the wind.

The fire burned low in the firepit beside Kanuga. He rose onto one elbow and studied Barbara in her sleep. He could not help it when his body began to respond to thoughts of the previous night of lovemaking with this enchantress. She knew so much! She knew how to turn him inside out with lusty desire, and how to make him forget anyone he had ever known before her.

Sweeping the furs aside, away from Barbara, Kanuga's lips began making a heated path down her body, awakening her.

Barbara responded with a giggle and soft purring noises, then turned to him and encircled his manhood with her fingers. She kneaded him for a moment, then kissed the velvet tip, pulling a husky groan from deep within Kanuga.

But her love play drew to a stop when voices outside drew Kanuga away from her.

"Must you leave?" she said, watching Kanuga pull on his fringed breeches.

Kanuga didn't reply. He hurriedly put on the rest of his clothes, and stepped outside the house, stiffening when he found himself face to face with Broderick Bowman.

Chapter Sixteen

There's a divinity that shapes our ends,
Rough-hew them how we will.

—SHAKESPEARE

There was a promise of spring in the air, crisp and pure, the sun warming the earth in its early morning awakening. Kanuga towered over Broderick Bowman outside his house, his eyes glaring down at him.

"Why have you come?" Kanuga said in a low rumble.

Then, suddenly, flashes of memory entered his brain, making him sway and grasp at his head, groaning. Letitia was suddenly back on his mind, as though she had never been erased from it.

He glanced over his shoulder at his house, as something else grabbed him at the pit of his stomach when he also recalled another woman—and what he had foolishly shared with her through the long, lazy night!

How could he have done that?

He loved Letitia! Not the green-eyed seductress!

He turned his eyes back to Broderick, wanting to rid himself of the man so that he could be alone and sort out things inside his mind. "Leave," he growled, pointing to Broderick's dog team. "You are no longer welcome in my village. Do you forget so easily that you stole into my house like a thief in the night and abducted the white woman? It would not take much for me to kill you as you stand there."

Paling, Broderick backed slowly away from Kanuga, then stood his ground. "That is in the past," he said, his voice quavering with a fear that he could not hide. He had never seen Kanuga this angry. And he seemed to be strangely disoriented, making Broderick trust his mood even less!

But, he thought stubbornly to himself, he had come for a purpose. No, he corrected himself— he had come for *dual* purposes, and he would not be forced to leave so easily! "That the woman was white should make all the difference in the world in this matter," he said, straightening his shoulders as he willed himself to face Kanuga's stern stare. "And must I remind you that you came to the Russian fort and stole their wood over this woman? She was not Tlingit, Kanuga. Why would you care what happens to her?"

Kanuga took a quick step forward and grabbed Broderick by the throat, half lifting him from the ground. "She does not have to be Tlingit to be my woman!" he said in a snarl. "Now leave! Mind your business from now on, Broderick, or I won't blink an eye when I kill you. You are worthless— nothing to no one."

Kanuga jerked his hand away from Broderick and walked away from him and the house in which lay a woman he did not know, yet had made love to the entire night. He needed to speak with the Chief Above, to see if he could guide him into understanding what had happened to make him become someone he did not even know. He loved Letitia with all of his heart, yet the first night she was gone, he had taken another woman to his bed!

And this woman was also white!

She was from the American ship!

Surely she knew Letitia well. Had Letitia given the woman her blessing to come to Kanuga to give herself to him?

Had Letitia even prompted her to, because she had never truly wanted him?

He clasped his hands to his brow and groaned, having never before been as confused in his life as now—nor as weary. . . .

Kosko stood in the shadows of the house that held the Russian prisoner, watching with interest all that was transpiring outside Kanuga's house. He had heard all that Kanuga had said, and smiled when he heard the frustration in his voice and saw the confusion in his eyes.

Yet Kosko's smug smile faded when he also

recalled how suddenly Kanuga had seemed to have snapped out of the spell that Kosko had cast over him. Although he had spent a full night with another woman, that had not seemed to affect Kanuga's thinking about Letitia! He still spoke of her as though she were his!

How had his magic gone wrong? Kosko wondered.

Was Kanuga's power even stronger than his?

Was Kanuga, in truth, the true sorcerer in this village?

The barking of dogs drew Kosko's attention elsewhere. He turned and grabbed at his chest, where his heart had momentarily faltered in its beat, when a dog team came bustling into the village, and he recognized one of the women on the sled—Letitia!

The spell he had cast on her had failed also! She had returned to Kanuga, as though Kosko had never said words over her hair and clothing that would make her forget him.

Something had gone awry!

Shivers engulfed Kosko. He was losing his powers of evil!

"I must do something to distract Kanuga's thoughts from this white woman," he whispered to himself. "There has to be a way!"

As though willed to act by an unseen force which seemed always there, guiding Kosko into evil deeds, he left the shadows of the house which housed the prisoner and went to the door, entering without announcing his presence first.

When he came face to face with the warrior

who had been stationed there to look after Iuril's welfare through the night, he smiled, his eyes gleaming. "I have come to see how our prisoner is doing," he said, stepping past the warrior to bend to a knee beside Iuril. "Short Russian, I have come to see if you want to make peace with the Chief Above," he said, touching Iuril's brow with a warm hand.

Iuril wrestled with his bonds, trying to get free again, then relaxed when he realized that the effort was futile. "You are a man of God," he said frantically to Kosko, glancing up at the warrior, then back into Kosko's eyes. "Set me free. Let me return to my people. I shall tell my father that it is best that he leaves Alaska. He will listen."

The warrior knelt down beside Kosko. "I think he speaks the truth," he said, nodding. "I will go and tell Kanuga. He will be glad that the Russian is ready to cooperate with the Tlingit."

"Yes, go and tell him," Kosko said, also nodding. But as the warrior rose to his feet and turned his back to Kosko, Kosko was quickly there behind him, grabbing the warrior's knife from its sheath at his side. Before the warrior could cry out with alarm when Kosko raised the knife for its death plunge, the knife was already in his chest, snuffing his life quickly from him.

Iuril paled and cold sweat rose on his body. "My God," he gasped. "Why . . . did you do that?"

Kosko bent quickly, and before Iuril could cry out, Iuril was also dead with a knife in his chest.

"This is the only way I can draw Kanuga's attention away from the Americans, especially the woman," Kosko mumbled, as if Iuril could hear him. He drew the knife from Iuril's body and positioned it in the warrior's hand to make it look as though the warrior had killed Iuril, then turned the knife back on himself. He laughed throatily. "Now Kanuga will concentrate fully on the Russians."

He left the house, gazing intensely at Kanuga, who had just stopped to look anxiously toward the approaching dog team. Kosko's brow creased into a deep frown. He had never realized how much he hated Kanuga—until now.

Until today he hadn't realized just how strong Kanuga's powers were. This threatened Kosko's entire existence as a shaman in the Tlingit village.

"First I shall kill his brother, then when the opportunity arises, Kanuga," he whispered to himself.

Ducking his head, he hurried away again into the shadows.

Kanuga turned with a start when the approaching dog team caused him to stop and turn, to see who else was disturbing the privacy of his morning and delaying his intention to speak to the Chief Above in private. His heart leapt in his chest when he discovered Letitia among those on the sled, and her eyes met and locked with his in a silent understanding—of mutual love.

With wide strides, he went back to his house and stood before the door and awaited the arrival of the sled. He was anxious to see what had prompted Letitia to return, hoping that he was the reason—only he.

His eyes squinted angrily when he glanced at her father, who seemed well enough now to be taking care of his affairs. The shine of the barrel of a shotgun was quite visible on his lap atop the thick layer of furs.

Kanuga stood tall, straight, and as unbending as a tree as the dog team stopped close to his house. He watched, silent, as Letitia was the first to climb from the sled, her eyes never leaving Kanuga, yet waiting to walk with her father and the frail lady, whose face had enough of Letitia's soft and lovely features to prove that she was Letitia's mother.

Broderick's eyebrows forked as he stepped away from Kanuga when he saw Letitia. Her arrival confused him, for he had thought that she was still at the Indian village.

His gaze shifted, seeing the man and woman with Letitia. It confirmed his belief that Americans had arrived in Alaska. How many were there? he wondered. Colonel Golodoff would be glad to receive this information!

Many things were going in Broderick's favor today. Even if Kanuga had ordered him away, too many things seemed to be surfacing for him to do depart all that quickly.

No matter that Letitia turned her gaze his way and looked at him with utter contempt. He watched the developments unfolding before him, filled with interest and plotting schemes that would benefit him only.

Flanked by her mother and father, Letitia walked up to Kanuga, her heart pounding. She looked past him at his house, wondering if Barbara was there, then up into his eyes, which seemed to be filled with too much apology for Barbara not to have been with him.

"We've come to check on someone who is missing from our ship," Jerome said, resting the barrel of his shotgun on his arm as he held the firearm before him. "We thought we'd check here first, before going on to the Russian fort. This missing person, Kanuga, is my niece. Her name is Barbara. Do you know anyone in your village who might have come in the night and abducted her? If so, go to him. Tell him we want her back. And then, by God, Kanuga, you must make the one responsible for the abduction pay."

Boldly, with her chin lifted and robes of fur draped around her voluptuous curves, Barbara stepped from Kanuga's tent. "No one forced me to come to Kanuga," she announced. "I came on my own." She gave Letitia an icy stare. "And I plan to stay. Kanuga and I are in love. We plan to get married." She laughed throatily. "You were foolish to give him up, Letitia. Foolish!"

Even though she had expected this, Letitia was at first speechless with the shock of actually seeing Barbara there, claiming Kanuga as though he were truly hers.

And then anger flared in her eyes, and she could not help but lunge for Barbara, grabbing her by the hair and wrestling her to the snow-covered ground. "How could you?" she cried, holding Barbara to the ground. Her robes had fallen away from Barbara, revealing her nudity beneath them. "Haven't you taken enough from me in my lifetime? Must you also have the man I love?" She slapped Barbara across the face. "You are nothing but a hussy! A conniving hussy!"

Kanuga stepped forward and took Letitia by the wrist and drew her to her feet, away from Barbara. He clasped his hands to her shoulders, holding her in place. "You are fighting over me," he said, gazing intensely down at her. "Does that mean that you have changed your mind? You have come to be my wife?"

All this time, Jerome had stood as though frozen to the snow beneath his feet, in shock over finding Barbara at Kanuga's house, realizing that she had actually given herself to the Indian, and then watching his very own daughter and niece fighting over the Indian. Then he seemed to snap back to reality when he found his daughter being held immobile by Kanuga.

"Let her go!" Jerome said, aiming the shotgun at Kanuga. "Step aside, Letitia. Let me take care of this Indian once and for all. He's nothing but trouble. Can't you see that?"

A rustling behind him made Jerome turn with a start. He paled when he found a wide circle of Tlingit warriors standing near, rifles aimed at him.

"My warriors protect me well," Kanuga said, his chest swelling proudly. He drew Letitia to his side and stared down at Barbara as she slowly pushed herself up from the ground. "Take this woman who calls herself Barbara back to your ship. She is not welcome in my village any more than you are."

Barbara grabbed the furs around her body and inched toward Kanuga. "You can't mean that," she said, shivering from the cold. "We made passionate love all night. You can't want me to leave. You can't! I want to stay with you! Forever!"

Kimberly gasped and grabbed at her husband's arm for support. "Barbara, what are you saying?" she cried. "Tell me that you didn't— didn't throw yourself at this Indian in such a way. I tried to raise you to be a God-fearing young lady. Where did I go wrong?"

Barbara ignored Kimberly. She went to Kanuga and desperately grabbed him by an arm. "Tell Letitia that you love me!" she wailed. "Tell her!"

Letitia was numb from all that was happening and from what was being revealed to her. Kanuga had been with Barbara all night, making love.

But she could not blame him! She had turned her back on his love! Everything, even her cousin's wanton behavior, was her fault, her fault, alone!

"I never loved you," Kanuga said, his voice drawn. "Nor do I recall making love *to* you. It is as though it never happened." He glowered down at her. "Never could I love anyone but Letitia."

Tears near, Letitia turned her eyes up to him, hating herself for having caused him such pain— so much that he had been driven to take another woman to his bed. "And I love you," she murmured. "I was wrong to leave. But I have returned, to stay. I want to be your wife, Kanuga. I love you very dearly."

She stiffened when she heard her mother and father gasp in unison behind her. She moved to Kanuga's side, where his arm slipped around her waist and held her close. "That is my decision," she said, gazing from her mother to her father. "Please try and understand. Though I feel much loyalty to you, my parents, for all that you have done for me, my loyalty now lies with Kanuga."

"Why?" Kimberly cried, stifling a sob behind a hand. "Oh, why, Letitia?"

Letitia turned scalding eyes to Barbara, who had stepped back to stand, cowering, beside Kimberly. "Because of Barbara and her scheming ways, I have been awakened to what I truly want in life," she said softly. "I know now that I cannot bear to lose Kanuga. I must stay with him. Forever!"

"But he proved his love was not a faithful one," Jerome argued. "He bedded another woman as soon as you left." He frowned over at Barbara. "Another white woman, Letitia. Your very own cousin!"

"I do not blame him for any of this," Letitia said, squaring her shoulders proudly. "It is myself who is at fault. I should have never left Kanuga in the first place. None of this would have happened." She looked pityingly at Barbara. "I'm sorry that you had to find out in such a way the sort of person Barbara is. Had I been able to spare you this, I would have."

"Letitia, please don't ..." Kimberly said, rushing to her daughter and hugging her fitfully.

"Mother, I must," Letitia said, easing away from Kanuga to enwrap her frail mother within her arms. "Don't you see? Nothing will change my mind. Almost losing Kanuga to Barbara was enough of a shock to last me a lifetime." She stepped away from her mother and gazed down at her with deep emotion. "Please try and understand. I love Kanuga, just as you love Papa. Could you have ever lived apart from the man you loved with every fiber of your being?"

Sobbing, Kimberly stared up at Letitia for a moment, then went to the sled and climbed beneath several layers of furs. Barbara climbed in beside her, her face ashen, the life and sparkle erased from her eyes.

"Now, white man, take your two other women and your firearm and return to your ship," Kanuga flatly ordered. "Again I will give you until the ice melts in the river to leave Alaska. But then it must be done swiftly. Do you understand? I will not have you plotting to get Letitia back. She is mine. Mine!"

Letitia looked quickly up at Kanuga. "But Kanuga, you once told my father that perhaps things could be worked out between you should I stay with you," she murmured. "Don't you still feel that you can?"

"Many things have changed my mind," Kanuga said sternly. He eyed Barbara, frowning. "Many things."

Letitia gazed at her father, her heart going out to him as he held himself in check, the pain he was feeling over losing her heavy in his eyes. She wanted to rush into his arms and tell him that she loved him, too, but not in the same way that she loved Kanuga!

But she knew that nothing she could say now would lessen the depths of his feelings. She would only make things worse if she said anything at all. It was hard, nevertheless, to watch him walk away, his shoulders slouched, his head hung, the shotgun held limply in his hand.

An agonizing torment soared through her as he gave her a downcast look over his shoulder, then got on the sled and motioned for the driver to take him away.

Letitia couldn't hold back any longer. Panic grabbed her insides, thinking that she might never see her parents again. Tears streaming down her cheeks, she rushed after the sled as it began sliding along the snow. "Papa!" she cried, waving frantically. "Mother!"

The sled stopped. She ran to it and flung herself into her mother's arms. "Mother, I'll always love you," she sobbed. "Always!"

After sharing clinging hugs with her mother, she went to her father and placed her hands at his cheeks. "Papa, thank you for everything," she murmured, tears cold on her cheeks. "My life. My happinesses. My existence."

She threw herself into his arms and hugged him, then pulled herself away and ran away from the sled, blinded with more rushes of tears.

When strong arms enveloped her, she welcomed Kanuga's embrace. She closed her ears to the barking of the huskies as they drove on away, their barks soon fading in the wind as they moved out of hearing distance.

"Now that that's all over, perhaps we can get our business over with," Broderick said suddenly, jolting Kanuga and Letitia apart. They both turned abruptly to stare at the trader.

"I told you that you were to leave my village," Kanuga said, glaring down at Broderick. "We have nothing to discuss!"

"Colonel Golodoff won't be happy if I go back to Fort Anecia without his son, or with the news that you won't even listen to reason," Broderick growled. "The Colonel told me to barter with you, Kanuga, and damn it, I don't plan to leave until it's done."

The armed warriors crowded in, closer to Broderick, causing him to exhale a frightened breath. He looked anxiously up at Kanuga. "And so you would even hold me prisoner?" he said, folding his arms across his chest. "So be it! Force the Russian's hand!" He leered down at Letitia. "I don't think you're ready to have your lovenest spoiled by spilled blood, are you?"

Although she hated Broderick with a passion quite unlike the passions she shared with Kanuga, Letitia felt compelled to help his cause, mainly to see that some sort of peace was kept between the Russians and the Tlingit.

But not only for them, but also for her beloved parents did she wish this. If a war broke out now, they would become involved, even as innocent bystanders, stranded in the frozen waters of the river! She had to try to stop this from happening, if it even meant begging Kanuga in front of Broderick Bowman. She had let her parents down by parting from them. She could not let them down by not doing everything possible to save them from becoming caught in the middle of a war between the Russians and the Tlingit!

Turning with a jerk, she looked up at Kanuga, placing a gentle hand to his cheek. "Darling, please listen to what Broderick has to say," she said softly. "Perhaps something *can* be worked out. Perhaps Iuril can be set free and returned to his father. He has surely suffered enough for something someone else is guilty of!"

Kanuga saw the silent pleading in the depths of Letitia's eyes, and having already denied her something important today, and because she had gone beyond that which he had expected to please him, he nodded, then eased her hand from his cheek and stepped around her, to stand tall and erect over Broderick.

"Iuril can go free, but only if you have brought word to me that Colonel Golodoff plans to dismantle his fort and return to Russia," Kanuga said flatly.

Broderick nodded his head anxiously. "The colonel wanted me to offer many rations that your people are soon to be without," he said. "He is willing to do anything to keep peace, but he does not want to give up the fort."

He looked slowly around at the warriors, and

the weapons they were carrying, then gazed up at Kanuga again. "You need gunpowder, don't you?" he said warily. "You need traps? Blankets? Cooking utensils? They can all be yours if you will agree to let the Russians stay on Alaskan soil."

"You have heard my terms," Kanuga said, his jaw tight.

Letitia stepped up to Kanuga's side and gazed up at him, then over at the house in which Iuril was held prisoner, and up into Kanuga's eyes again, a silent reminder of that which she had asked of him.

Kanuga stared down at her for a moment longer, then turned once again to Broderick. "Take Iuril back to Fort Anecia along with the news to Colonel Golodoff that if the fort isn't vacated in two days, it will be burned down and everyone in it killed," he said solemnly. Then his lips tugged into a slow smile. "You know that the Tlingit are in number stronger than the Russians. Relay that reminder to Colonel Golodoff also!"

Broderick was frustrated, knowing that he had not gained any footing with Kanuga except to get Iuril freed. "Whatever you say," he finally said. "Take me to Iuril. We'll both go and tell his father what you've said." He pursed his lips tightly together as he glowered up at Kanuga, then said, "But Colonel Golodoff ain't goin' to like it one damn bit."

"I did not expect him to," Kanuga said, turning away from Broderick and walking hand-in-hand with Letitia across the crushed snow of the village. "Come, Broderick. I will take you to Iuril."

When they reached the house and stepped inside, the air was rent with disbelieving gasps. Kanuga was the first to go to Iuril. He knelt to one knee beside him, checking for a pulsebeat at his throat, his eyes locked on the bloody wound on his chest.

"He's dead," he mumbled, going to the warrior, checking for his pulsebeat. He rose slowly to his feet, kneading his brow nervously. "It seems the warrior killed Iuril, then turned the knife on himself."

Puzzled, he shook his head. "But why?" he said, knowing the Tlingit belief was that suicide was unpardonable, and that the one who committed it would be denied entrance into paradise!

"God damn it all to hell," Broderick grumbled, suddenly afraid for his own life.

"I regret this," Kanuga said, turning to Broderick. "But it is still a result of your choice to come into my house to steal my woman away. Everything that has happened since that night has been your fault." He looked down at Iuril once more, regret eating at his heart. "Take him away, Broderick. Take him to Colonel Golodoff and explain who is at fault here. Then tell him that he has two days to vacate the fort. Only two days!"

Broderick looked wildly up at Kanuga, then down at Iuril. Scrambling past Letitia, he lifted Iuril up into his arms and carried him to his sled. But he was not going to take him to Fort Anecia.

Never could he enter Fort Anecia again! Everything was being blamed on him. The only thing that he could do was hide Iuril's body and go into hiding himself until the Russians left!

Broderick snapped his whip against the huskies' backs, not able to get away from the Tlingit village fast enough, and wondered just where he could hide on this vast, white wilderness that soon might become his grave!

"I must find a way," he shouted into the wind. "I've struggled too hard to stay alive for too long, to die now!"

Letitia and Kanuga stepped outside and watched the frenzied flight of Broderick, then went arm and arm into Kanuga's house. They snuggled into a wondrous embrace, their lips meeting in a soft, sweet kiss, for the moment Kanuga's lips stilling Letitia's worries over her parents.

Chapter Seventeen

O thou who dost inhabit in my breast,
Leave not the mansion so long tenantless.
$\qquad\qquad$ —SHAKESPEARE

"*Jet-a-nelch*. Let us go inside where it is warm," Kanuga urged, placing a finger to Letitia's chin and lifting her eyes to meet his hungry gaze. "It is good that you are here again with me. Without you, my heart was heavy with sorrow."

Letitia's thoughts went quickly to Barbara, wondering how much of Kanuga's sorrow had been erased within her arms.

Then she recalled a strange thing that he had said to Barbara—that he did not even recall making love with her.

Had he meant that?

Or had he told Barbara that to show her that having been with her had meant nothing at all to him—a diversion from the torment over having lost the woman he had planned to marry?

Yes, Letitia thought. That would make going into Kanuga's house easier, even if his blankets and furs were still rumpled from his lovemaking with her cousin.

She cringed at the thought of smelling Barbara's perfume lingering in the air or on the blankets. She wanted no reminders of a cousin who had betrayed her in every sense of the word from the moment she had become a part of Letitia's life so long ago.

"Yes, let's go inside," she said, smiling softly up at Kanuga and bracing herself for whatever she would find there.

But she vowed to herself that she was ready to face anything, for she was back with Kanuga. That was all that mattered now. She was back with the man she loved—and he had welcomed her with much love in his heart.

Arm in arm, they went inside his house, where the fire burned bright and warm, reaching to the darkest corners of the dwelling. Tense, her eyes searching around her, Letitia did discover the blankets and furs of his bed in disarray, and yes, she did get a faint whiff of Barbara's cheap perfume.

But soon, Letitia thought victoriously, that would be changed. She was there.

Not Barbara!

And never would Barbara have the chance to interfere in her life again!

Standing beside the fire, Kanuga turned Letitia to face him. Almost meditatingly, he removed her heavy fur garment, his eyes smiling down into hers as he then smoothed his hands down the soft curves of her body that strained suggestively against the buckskin of her dress. The only sounds were those of the crackling fire, and the sudden gasp of Letitia's pleasure as Kanuga curled his fingers around her breasts, cupping them within his powerful hands.

"I was only gone from you a few short hours, yet I missed you so much, Kanuga," Letitia said, reaching to slip his beaver cloak away from his shoulders, letting it fall away from him to the floor. "Nothing could keep me away from you. And oh, Kanuga, I am so happy that you welcomed me back. You could have hated me for having— even momentarily—chosen my parents over you."

"I could never hate you," Kanuga said, sucking in a wild breath as Letitia reached up inside his buckskin shirt and ran her hands over his chest, stopping her hands above where his heart pounded like drums beneath her fingers.

"Your heart pounds so," Letitia said, standing on tiptoe to brush a soft kiss across his lips. "It is wonderful to know that I am the cause, darling."

Kanuga's arms swept around her and drew her roughly against him, his mouth crushing her lips with a fierce kiss as he eased her down on her back onto the furs beside the fire. Tangling together, their lips still locked in a frenzied kiss, they groaned while tearing the clothes from each other.

Once freed of encumbrances, their hands groped and squeezed that which pleasured them, and then both lay quietly within each other's arms, but only for a moment.

Kanuga rose above Letitia, his eyes deep wells of passion, his face a mask of naked desire. His gaze burned upon her bare body, absorbing the sight of her exquisite creamy skin and the wonders of her passion-moist lips. At this moment, with her, there were no sadnesses, no deaths. He would take this moment to forget all uglinesses. While he was with his woman, everything was beautiful.

Again his lips seized Letitia's in a fiery kiss. She abandoned herself to all of the familiar sweet feelings that Kanuga knew how to arouse in her, returning his kiss in kind. She moaned against his lips when he thrust himself inside her. When he began moving in a rhythmic fashion, sparking her desire, her mind soared with bliss.

Locking her legs around him, she drew him more deeply into her and lifted her pelvis to meet each of his heated thrusts, in quick, sure movements. Whenever Barbara and her sensual night with Kanuga would come to mind, Letitia would just as quickly block her out.

She was no longer jealous of her cousin.

In truth, Letitia pitied her. . . .

Barbara lay solemnly on her bed on the ship, her eyes narrowed with hate as she stared up at the ceiling. Suddenly she turned onto her stomach and began wailing, pummeling the mattress with tightened fists. "I hate you!" she cried, pretending the mattress was Letitia. "Never have I hated anyone as much!"

The door opened behind her, and Jerome frowned down at his niece. He was still numb inside over having discovered what sort of a woman she was. At this moment, the loss of his daughter was not as painful as the wound caused by his niece's whoring.

True, he thought to himself, he had always suspected something amiss about her, from the way she would flit from man to man in New York, unable to get serious about any of them, whereas his daughter had been happy to be with only one man—Jonathan.

But he had never thought that Barbara had given herself sexually to any of these men. He had thought that she enjoyed the fun of the balls and theaters, and was simply never able to get enough of the merriment.

All along, he thought angrily to himself, she had gone with them to most surely spend the time with them in bed!

"You *are* a whore, aren't you?" he blurted out, drawing Barbara quickly around to cower beneath his angry stare. "You are nothing but a cheap, whoring bitch."

Barbara flinched at the bitterness in her uncle's voice, and over what he had called her.

Then rage filled her.

"And Letitia is no better?" she dared to say, moving slowly to a sitting position on the bed. "Even now I imagine she is in bed with Kanuga.

Now, uncle dear, what do you think she is doing? Only sucking on a lollipop like the little girl you would like to think she still is?"

Jerome could stand no more of Barbara's insolence, especially when it brought his daughter down to the same level as his niece. Although his legs were still weak, and he experienced occasional lightheadedness, he managed to get over to the bed much more quickly than Barbara could get away from him, and slapped her across her face.

"Never speak of my daughter again in my presence!" he shouted. "You aren't worthy to breathe her name across your lips!"

Barbara's head snapped sideways with the blow, causing her to cry out with pain.

Then, sobbing, she glared up at Jerome. "I hate you," she hissed. "I hate you all!"

Jerome's eyes wavered. He ran the still stinging palm of his hand up and down his leg. "And that is the thanks I get for taking you in?" he said somberly. "That is the thanks I get for allowing you to share everything with my daughter, as though you were her sister? Where did I go wrong, Barbara? Where?"

Barbara turned her eyes away, shame engulfing her. Then she flinched with alarm when Jerome grabbed her chin and forced her eyes around again to look into his.

"As soon as we return to New York, you will be out on your own," he said. "Let's see just how long it is before you come back, crying and begging at my doorstep." He dropped his hand to his side. "I doubt if you will ever get a decent man to give you the time of day."

Turning on a heel, he left the cabin. Kimberly was standing just outside, waiting anxiously, having not had the courage to go with him to talk with Barbara. She gasped when she saw how pale her husband was, seemingly shaken to the core. "My darling," she said, pulling him into her tender embrace. "Did it go all that badly?" But he did not have to answer her. She had heard the outbursts from both her husband and her niece.

"I shall live to regret, always, the day I agreed to take Barbara in, to raise as our own," Jerome said, tears shining in his eyes. "She not only hates Letitia, she hates both you *and* me, Kimberly."

"We've lost much today," Kimberly said, patting Jerome gently on the back. "But, darling, we shall survive it all. You'll see. You and I—we've always been survivors."

"But what of Letitia?" Jerome asked, easing from Kimberly's comforting arms. "Will *she?*"

They flung themselves into each other's arms again, fearfully clinging.

Cuddling close beside the fire, nude beneath a layer of furs, Letitia and Kanuga watched the flames in the firepit stroke the logs in long, slow caresses. Their commitment to one another was now firm, sealed with sweet embraces and kisses.

"I've never been as happy," Letitia murmured, gazing up at Kanuga. "Can it be like this forever, Kanuga? Will you love me this endearingly forever?" She would not think of Barbara, and his reckless night with her. It had had nothing to do with love—only frustration and hurt!

Kanuga took one of her hands and kissed its palm, then swept her into his arms, reveling in the touch of her silken flesh against his body. He moved over her, parting her legs with a knee. He was hard and ready for her again, knowing that he would never get enough of her—and not because of some strange sort of spell such as seemed to have been cast over him while he was with Barbara. But because of his undying love for Letitia.

"Our love will never die," he whispered against her lips, easing his hardness inside her. He watched her eyes take on a dreamy sort of hue, her thick, golden eyelashes fluttering in her ecstasy, as his thrusts became more demanding. "My *schau-wot*, we shall have a lifetime of moments like this. Do you not feel it? The passion is there, always, ready to be unleashed."

He held her closer, breathing hard into the sweet-scented depths of her golden hair. "I give you my heart—my very soul," he whispered huskily into her ear. "We are the wind, the stars, the heavens. We are everything, Letitia, as long as we are together."

"Yes, everything," Letitia said, sighing as the silver flames of desire leapt higher inside her. Her body was turning to liquid fire as his arms held her, oh so close. The blaze of urgency stole her breath away as Kanuga plunged even more deeply and demandingly into her.

And then their worlds fused into one, their

moans of pleasure building to a peak as their bodies quaked in fulfillment against the other.

They then lay clinging in their trembling aftermath of loving. . . .

"I'm so hungry," Letitia whispered, laughing softly as Kanuga gazed down at her unbelievingly.

"Food?" he said, arching an eyebrow. "You think of food when you can have me?"

"Darling, you only quench my thirst for love," Letitia teased back. "But what about my poor stomach? I didn't even have breakfast before coming in search of—"

She looked away from him, not wanting to speak Barbara's name, much less ever think of her again.

Kanuga sensed her hesitation, and the reason for it. He rolled away from her and grabbed up a fur robe from the floor, placing it around her shoulders.

He then slipped into one himself. "Then food it shall be," he said.

He settled on his haunches before the fire, placing a large black pot into the flames. "Before your arrival, Sweetwater brought this pot of stew for my meals today. I hadn't yet had time to place it over the fire to warm it. Soon, beautiful woman, your stomach will be as warm as your heart."

Letitia giggled, snuggling into the fur robe, feeling deliciously content as she gazed with adoration at Kanuga as he began stirring the stew with a long-handled wooden spoon. How could she have ever thought that she could live without him? Seeing him in her dreams would never have been enough.

She wanted to feast upon his lean, bronzed handsome face while always near enough to reach out and touch him.

She wanted to experience his every mood and be there when he needed her to comfort him.

A sudden commotion at the doorway caused Letitia to jump to her feet. Kanuga was soon there beside her, and both were stunned into speechlessness when Atkuk stumbled into the house, a knife protruding from his back.

Kanuga was first to find his voice. "Atkuk!" he shouted, his voice sounding strangled. He rushed to his brother as Atkuk crumpled to the floor on his side, gasping for breath.

Kanuga knelt down beside Atkuk, horror-stricken. His eyes filled with tears as he rested Atkuk's head on his lap, afraid to pull the knife from his back, knowing the damage to his insides that such an effort could cause.

"Who did this to you, Atkuk?" Kanuga cried. "Who?"

Atkuk's eyes were wild, his breathing was shallow. He tried to reach a hand to Kanuga's face and was struggling to speak, but failed at both when his body convulsed and his breathing stopped, his eyes too soon locked in a death's stare.

Letitia stifled a sob behind a hand, then knelt down beside Kanuga. "Darling, I'm so sorry," she said, so badly wanting to draw him into her arms to comfort him. But he still held Atkuk's head on his lap, staring blankly down at him, remorse etched on his face.

Then he finally spoke. "The Russians," he said, his voice drawn. "They are responsible. Broderick Bowman has had time to return Iuril's body to Colonel Golodoff. The colonel sent one of his men to my village to kill my brother as payment for the death of the colonel's son!"

He looked slowly at Letitia, his eyes dark pits of hate. "The Russians will pay," he said, his teeth clenched. "The Tlingit will make war against them. The Russians will lose more than one son! They will lose them all!"

Fear gripped Letitia's heart. She had feared something like this might happen. Her parents. Oh, God, what of her parents? Would she be the one mourning next? If they were drawn into the battle, even as innocent bystanders, their lives could be cut short!

"Please, Kanuga," Letitia pleaded. "Don't do anything in haste."

Kanuga closed Atkuk's eyes, then stretched a blanket over his silent form. He rose to his feet and stood over the fire, his eyes wavering in his sadness. "Nothing will be done in haste," he said softly. "First I must see to my brother's funeral. I must see that my brother enters the Land of the Forever Dead with much dignity."

Letitia sighed with relief, thinking that once Kanuga had time to think about his threat of going to war, and what it eventually might cost his people, he would decide that other means must be found to achieve vengeance against the Russians.

But too soon her hopes were cast to the wind when Kanuga turned to her and revealed to her what her part in the warring would be.

"After my brother's soul is at peace, you will go with me into the battle against the Russians," he said brusquely. "As I have said before, it is best that you learn all ways of the Tlingit, even the warring side. My woman, you will be at my side during the battle. We will fight together as though one heartbeat!"

Letitia stared numbly up at him. When she had made her choices in life, she had never anticipated anything as daring—as dangerous!—as this.

A part of her wanted to run away and hide. Another part of her felt a strange sort of thrill at the prospect of being beside Kanuga at such a challenging time in their lives.

The sun was dipping low in the sky. The wind was sighing around the corners of Colonel Golodoff's house. His shirt gaping open, the buttons open halfway to his waist, he was sitting at his desk, brooding over his journals. His hand trembled as he lifted a glass of vodka to his lips and emptied it in one fast gulp, then rested the empty glass on his leg. What was holding Broderick up?

Broderick had sent word earlier in the day that he was on his way to the Tlingit village. If Kanuga had been receptive to his offer for more supplies in exchange for Iuril, and to letting the Russians stay at the fort, Broderick should have returned by now, Iuril with him.

"He botched it up!" the colonel raved, throwing the glass against the stone facing of the fireplace close to his desk. "And now what can I do? I don't dare go to the village. Broderick and Iuril are both probably dead."

He swallowed back the urge to vomit at the thought of his son possibly being dead, then rose from the chair and went to the window to stare beyond the walls of the fort, at the wide range of wilderness that he had begun to think was no better than a no-man's land!

"If my son and Broderick are dead, then I am next," he whispered harshly to himself, grabbing at the windowsill when waves of lightheadedness swept through him.

Kosko stood in the shadows, watching Kanuga's house, doubts filling him. He had left Atkuk to die alone, but somehow Atkuk had managed to get to Kanuga's house before Kosko could stop him!

After Kosko had plunged the knife into Atkuk's back, he had fled Atkuk's house and was hurrying to his own when a sound behind him had made him turn with a start, gasping for air when he discovered Atkuk only a few footsteps away from Kanuga's house, the knife protruding from his back.

Kosko had been forced to stand numbly by as Atkuk had gone into Kanuga's house, knowing that to go after him and be seen would have been the same as pointing an accusing finger at himself.

Now he had to wait and see if Atkuk had managed to speak Kosko's name before he died! If he did, Kosko would soon know.

Kanuga would come for him!

Kanuga would kill him with his own bare hands!

Sweat formed on Kosko's brow as he waited, his eyes never leaving Kanuga's house.

Chapter Eighteen

The end of man is an action, and not a thought,
Though it were the noblest.

—CARLYLE

The swelling chorus of wailing mourners and the throbbing beats of a drum accompanying the funeral chant doubled Letitia's sadness as she sat on a wide settee, an elaborately carved platform with a backrest and side panels, made comfortable with great piles of otter pelts. Kanuga sat nobly erect beside her, his arms folded stiffly across his chest.

Letitia glanced at Kanuga. She had never seen him look so noble—so handsome. He was wearing a ceremonial robe of white doeskin, on which the figure of a double-headed eagle on the front and back of the garment was outlined in red and trimmed with a double row of white pearl buttons.

Letitia could feel the softness of her own garment against her skin. It was sewn from a doeskin so white that when she drew it over her head, she had felt as though she were slipping into a soft layer of snow instead of a dress. Tiny, pink shells were sewn on the dress in the designs of flowers. Fringe swayed at the hem when she had walked.

If not for the ceremony for which she had been asked to wear it, she could have felt as though she had been transformed into a storybook princess.

Although Kanuga looked so handsome today, it was the remorse in his eyes that made her look away from him, only to look instead upon something even more heart-wrenching.

A sob lodged in her throat when she gazed at Atkuk's wrapped body lying in state on a funeral pyre in the center of the council house. Gifts of food and tobacco were being brought to him by the Tlingit, and also to Kosko, whom Kanuga had assigned to be Atkuk's attendant in charge of his body. The older shaman's duties were not only to look after Atkuk's body while it lay in state, but also to light the funeral pyre and Atkuk's body after it was taken outside, close to his memorial totem pole.

Hardly able to bear the sight of the sad procession of people passing beside Atkuk's body, Letitia drew her eyes away and willed herself to focus her attention and thoughts elsewhere. She gazed around the large dwelling, which was, next to Kanuga's, the largest longhouse in the village.

In the four corners of the longhouse, fires burned in firepits, so high that the flames almost reached up to the smoke hole, sparks showering upward from them.

Kanuga had told her earlier that the house had been made sacred for the funeral ritual. A cedar bark ring, the symbol of supernatural power, had been placed over the doorway, and a rope stretched from the gable to the water's edge outside to prevent anyone from passing in front.

Letitia remembered the massive, elaborately decorated totem pole showing Atkuk's family lineage that had been erected as a memorial to Atkuk, facing the river. Atkuk's ashes would be secreted in a cavity at the top after the ceremony was concluded today.

Letitia was learning quickly the ways of the Tlingit, the strange yet intriguing customs that so differed from anything she had known while living the simple life of white people, in a white people's world. It was all new to her, but a challenge she welcomed, for it symbolized her love of Kanuga and the children they would bear— who in every sense of the world would be raised as Tlingit!

She placed her hand to her abdomen, hoping that soon she would be able to give Kanuga a son.

She glanced over at him, hoping that soon a wedding ceremony would be performed! While she was not married to him, a small voice deep down inside her, where the remnants of the morals she had been taught, cried out to her that in the eyes of the Lord, she was sinning until she took this man to be her husband!

She looked quickly away from Kanuga, casting her eyes downward, realizing that until yesterday she had not been absolutely sure that she wanted such a commitment. Now that she was, the marriage ceremony could not be performed too soon!

But first, she reminded herself, other things were more prominent on Kanuga's mind.

The burial.

And then the attack on the Russians at Fort Anecia!

Her eyes were drawn quickly up again when a lone dancer entered the room, stilling the mournful wails and sending everyone to their feet in a wide circle around the funeral pyre. The dancer was dressed in a garment of many colors, on which were hung deer hoofs and pieces of bone in such a manner as to strike against one another at every motion of the dancer's body.

The man was masked and wore a hat to which rings were attached, concealing the sacred white down of an eagle inside them. As the man started to dance in jerky movements, tossing his head from side to side, good will was ensured at the ceremony as the white eagle down was released from inside the rings and scattered around the room with each jerk of his head.

And then, once good will was assured, other dancers, dressed in garments woven from mountain goat wool, joined in, a drum beating solemnly in the background. The dancers moved their feet in rhythm with the beating of the drum, men and women participating equally in the dance.

Letitia could feel an expectant atmosphere in the longhouse, as though the dancers felt the presence of hovering spirits. All dancers but one of Kanuga's valued warriors stopped and stepped aside. Standing alone, the warrior began to shake, his eyes closed as though he had been taken over by an unseen force. As he lost what seemed almost all conscious control of his actions, he called out to show his inner torment—

"Haiii, hai, o, o, o, o!
Haiii, hai, o, o, o, o!
Hai, ooooh.
Haiii, hai, oh, o, o, o!"

The drummer began to drum very softly, as if to gently coax the spirit of the man into complete possession. The drummer seemed careful not to startle the dancer, since this could perhaps result in his power catching in his chest. As the dancer became more visibly agitated, the drumming grew louder.

Letitia was awe-struck by the continuing performance, as the dancer gasped out a few words of a song in a faltering voice, and then gradually started to sing more confidently. Sometimes he became calmer for a few moments, and the drumming subsided, but finally the dancer leapt into the center of the longhouse, close to the funeral pyre, and danced in a frenzied manner.

Two attendants suddenly appeared and circled the room with the dancer, preventing him from crashing into the crowd of spectators lining the walls and guiding him clear of the central fires. They appeared to have difficulty at times in following some of the more unpredictable dance movements, when the dancer would hold a posture of rigid tension for several minutes and then suddenly rush forward.

Another warrior, who wore a headdress with long streamers of ermine and coiled rings of cedar bark on his head, began dancing, his movements slow and undulating, mimicking the gestures of birds and animals by pausing cautiously, or dropping to the floor and pawing the ground. Violent sobbing accompanied him as he leapt back to his feet in frenzied and exaggerated leaps.

Both of the dancers were so intense in their excited dancing that they soon fell to their knees, exhausted, and had to be helped back to their seats, where they collapsed in tears.

The completion of the funeral ritual was signaled by the approach of other dancers, who knelt silently on the floor for several minutes beside one of the large fires, and then thrust upwards at the smoke-hole with their dance batons, to push away their sorrow. Then they moved back into the crowd.

Everyone's eyes were on Kanuga when he rose to his feet, towering over them all from his platform. Turning to Letitia, he looked down at her with devotion in his eyes and offered her a hand.

Her devotion to him as sincere, she entwined her fingers through his and rose to her feet next to him. Together they left their settee and went to Kosko and nodded at him to step aside, then took his place beside the funeral pyre, standing over Atkuk's body.

Letitia was glad that Atkuk's body was completely enwrapped in the colorful shrouds. It was bad enough that the memory of his frantic last breaths, and the way he had pleaded up at Kanuga with fright-filled eyes as he was dying, was embedded in Letitia's memory like a leaf fossilized in stone.

Seeing Atkuk dead had almost been the same as looking at her beloved Kanuga lying there, his face masked by death. Atkuk and Kanuga had not only been brothers by blood ties, but by resemblances as well. All except for Atkuk's one tooth that had looked so much like a fang.

When the day came that Kanuga should die, she was not sure if she could go on without him. She had already experienced how it felt to be parted from him. With each of her heartbeats, she had so very much missed him!

He *was* her heartbeat, she concluded, the very breath of her life!

Kanuga stared down at his brother's shrouded body for a moment longer. Then, with a flick of a hand, he motioned for several of his warriors to step forward. Solemnly, they positioned themselves around the funeral pyre, then lifted it in unison so as not to disturb Atkuk's body.

Kosko took his place at the head of the procession and led everyone outside to where wood had been placed in a great pile by the river.

Kanuga wove an arm around Letitia's waist and walked with her behind the procession. A brooding sky overhead, the glare reflecting from the snow, imparted an air of mystery to the setting.

When they reached the pile of wood, Letitia's insides tightened as the funeral pyre bearing Atkuk's body was placed in the center. She gasped as a lighted torch was brought to Kosko, and without pause he set the flames of the torch to the wood, igniting it instantaneously in several spots until the fire was roaring, reaching up over the funeral pyre, quickly hiding Atkuk's body behind its thrashing arms of flames, before consuming it.

Unable to bear watching any longer, Letitia looked away and closed her eyes to the horror of the ritual. It was at this moment that she knew that one day, when Kanuga's time had come to die, a shaman would be lighting such a fire beneath his body!

She silently prayed to her Lord that she would not outlast him and have to be witness to such a dreadful sight. She had never believed in cremation. Nor would she ever! She would fight anyone who would demand such an end to the man she loved.

Kanuga turned to her. He drew her into his arms. "It is over," he whispered. "After the ashes cool, Kosko will gather those of my brother and place them in his final resting place in his memorial pole."

He cupped her chin within the palm of his hand and lifted her eyes to meet his. "My brother is now traveling in The Land of the Forever Dead," he said. "But one day he will come to me again in another form when he is reincarnated. There will be a sign shown to me from the Chief Above when my brother returns. And when he does, I know that it will be in the form of something gentle, for Atkuk was the gentlest man I have ever known. Reincarnated, he will be so again."

Letitia's mouth dropped open, stunned by Kanuga's innocence, in that he believed in reincarnation.

Kanuga saw her disbelief in the way she was staring at him, as though seeing him for the first time. And he did not understand. "Why do you look at me in such a way?" he asked, smoothing a thumb over her cheek.

Letitia did not want to tell him that she did not believe in reincarnation, nor in so many other things that she was being faced with. She was too afraid of losing him if he had doubts of her ever fitting into his way of life.

"It's nothing," she murmured, sighing. "Please forgive me if I worried you. I'll be fine."

But she had to wonder if he was going to begin looking at every animal he came face to face with, wondering if it would be his reincarnated brother, afraid to kill even a vicious, life-threatening animal, in case it was Atkuk?

At this moment, she could not help but be uneasy about her future with Kanuga, no matter how much she loved him.

* * *

The fire in the firepit was casting dancing shadows along the curved ceiling and the ice walls of the igloo as Broderick stared across the fire at Iuril's body stretched out on the floor. Iuril's face was a strange purplish hue, and the blood on his shirt sparkled with ice crystals that had not yet melted from the heat of the fire.

Broderick hugged himself, warding off the coldness of his limbs after having driven his dog team in what seemed mindless circles until he had found this igloo a short while ago. When he discovered that it was uninhabited, he had decided that it was at least a temporary hideaway until he decided what his next move might be— where he would go, or how he would survive in this land of ice and snow and many carnivorous animals that soon would roam the land after leaving their hibernation nests.

He continued staring glassily at Iuril. What was he to do with him? he wondered wearily. He had had no choice but to bring Iuril inside with him. He couldn't chance leaving him outside on the sled. If anyone from the Russian community had happened along and seen him, he would be accused of killing him!

"I'm going to die because of it anyway!" he said aloud. "Colonel Golodoff will get much delight in seeing me die at the hands of a firing squad!"

He trembled from head to toe when he heard the distant howling of wolves, realizing his solitude.

* * *

Colonel Golodoff shoved his arms into the sleeves of his fur coat, then lifted the hood over his head. "Make sure you get everything out of that desk!" he ordered, as one of his soldiers continued filling a box with the colonel's belongings. "When you have everything, take it to my ship. Immediately."

Colonel Golodoff had received word by one of his trusted scouts that Iuril was no longer in the Indian village, but with Broderick Bowman. His scout had also told him that Atkuk was dead, and that the Russians were being blamed. He had also learned that immediately after the funeral rites for Atkuk, the Tlingit warriors were going to attack Fort Anecia.

Knowing that he did not have the men to hold up against such an attack, the colonel had decided to vacate the fort. He had never thought it would come to this.

But somehow, things had begun to happen—like dominoes, when one fell, the whole row fell in succession after it.

He knew he had someone to blame, but did not yet know who. The fact that he had lost his son was burden enough now to carry around with him!

And damn that Broderick Bowman, he growled to himself! Why hadn't he brought Iuril to him immediately? Perhaps the Tlingit had gone after him and killed him also!

In time, he vowed to himself, he would know all of the answers, and he would then make someone pay dearly!

Another soldier stood by at attention. "I've sent a scouting party out to look for Broderick and . . . Iuril," he said to the colonel. "I expect him back soon."

"It had better be soon," Colonel Golodoff said, grabbing a fistful of cigars from a box on his desk and thrusting them into the front pocket of his coat. "Or we'll have to leave without them."

"No doubt, sir, that would be the most logical thing to do," the soldier said. "I fear the Tlingit is out for all of our blood this time. And . . . Iuril is already dead, sir."

A commotion outside drew Colonel Golodoff quickly to the window. He grew numb inside when he saw a dog sled arriving with a body stretched out on it beneath a layer of blankets.

"Iuril," he gasped. "My son."

A soldier rushed into his office. "I found Iuril," he said, breathing hard. "But not Broderick Bowman."

"Where did you find Iuril?" the colonel growled, tears of regret filling his eyes as Iuril was carried into his office and placed on the floor at his feet.

"I saw smoke rising from an igloo that is usually abandoned," the soldier commented. "I investigated. I found Iuril there. But he was alone. I—I think Broderick had left to find food. Should I have waited for his return?"

"No," the colonel said, kneeling beside Iuril. "There was no time." He scowled up at the soldier. "My question is, why didn't Broderick bring Iuril to me? What was he doing keeping him—

keeping him to himself in—in a damn igloo?"

The soldier shrugged.

Knowing that he had no time to ponder the reasons Broderick did anything, and glad that he could at least give his son a proper burial, he did not ask any more questions.

"Take Iuril to the ship," Colonel Golodoff said, rising slowly to his full height.

Another soldier came running, breathless, into the office. "Colonel Golodoff, sir," he said, saluting the colonel. "I hate to report to you, sir, that our ship is immobile. It—it is stuck fast in the ice!"

Colonel Golodoff paled, envisioning the Tlingit firing upon his prized ship, its great hull soon enveloped in flames....

His hopes of escaping faded, as did his hopes of ever being a part of Russia's bright future.

Chapter Nineteen

I feel within me a peace above all earthly
*   dignities,*
A still and quiet conscience.

—SHAKESPEARE

There was a strained silence as Kanuga and Letitia lay side by side on their bed. Letitia was dreading what the early morning light would bring—the attack on the Russian fort.

Kanuga's sadnesses were almost overwhelming him. He had no one left of his family since this last vicious murder had snuffed the life out of his beloved brother.

He turned to Letitia, smoothing a fallen lock of her hair back from her brow. She was all that he had that he could truly call his. Although he was the chief of his band of Tlingit, their devotion to him was of another kind, nothing akin to that which family members felt for one another.

In Letitia, he must build a new family. His sons would then carry on his family's lineage, producing great chiefs themselves as their sons would be born to them.

"We must be married soon," Kanuga blurted out, placing a finger to Letitia's chin and drawing her eyes around to meet his. "Tomorrow, Letitia. Tomorrow."

Letitia's heart sang in her happiness, yet something nagged away at this joy, threatening to spoil it. "But, Kanuga, you are in mourning for your brother," she murmured, searching his eyes with her own. "Would a marriage ceremony be appropriate at this time?"

"The ceremony will not be an elaborate one," Kanuga said, pulling her close, her flesh against his warm and soft, awakening passion within him. He stroked her silken back. "But we must be wed, then make plans for children. A son, Letitia. A son must be born to us soon. I am the last of the sons of my family. Our son would carry on the family lineage. He will follow in my footsteps, a chief that my people will accept with much love and devotion in their hearts, as they have accepted me."

"Yes, my love," Letitia whispered, sucking in a wild breath of rapture as he cupped his hand over her womanhood, one of his fingers slipping inside her. She twined her arms around his neck and drew his lips close to hers. "We shall have many sons."

"And also daughters," Kanuga said, moving over her. He placed his hands to her buttocks and arched her body upward, to meet the thrust of his throbbing hardness within her. "And they will be born in your likeness, soft with beauty!"

Letitia threw her head back in ecstasy as he started his movements within her, then sobbed with bliss as his mouth covered her lips in a frenzied kiss. They moved together, their passion building to a boiling point—then were drawn away from each other when a voice spoke outside the house, calling Kanuga's name.

Kanuga gazed with longing into Letitia's eyes, then bolted away from her, to his feet. She watched him, her body like one large pulsebeat, as he stepped quickly into a fringed pair of buckskin breeches, then pulled on a shirt. She sighed and drew a blanket over her as he yanked his beaver cloak around his massive shoulders, then suddenly left her alone as he rushed outside.

She turned on her stomach and rested her chin in her hands, watching the flames caressing the logs in the firepit close beside the bed, so in love it hurt.

She glanced toward the door, wondering what the urgency had been, that Kanuga had to be drawn from his bed in the middle of the night.

She gazed back into the fire, shaking her head in despair. She knew that the news could not be good and wondering what else could happen to postpone hers and Kanuga's total happiness.

Was she dreaming to think that perhaps, one day, they might live a tumult-free life?

* * *

After searching and finally finding the American ship, Broderick Bowman pulled his dogteam to a halt in the shadows of the brig *Stacy*. He had decided to go to the Americans and ask for asylum. He had concluded that he had no other choice. After discovering Iuril's body gone when he returned from searching for food, he had known then the danger to him if he stayed at the igloo—or anywhere that the Russians could find him. The Russians had to be the ones who took Iuril's body away. Who else would want it? And it had probably not taken much thought to realize who else inhabited the igloo with the corpse! He had been assigned to see after Iuril's interests!

Now he would certainly be blamed for Iuril's death. All that he could expect at Fort Anecia was a quick death, or worse yet, a slow, agonizing death laced with tortures that the Russians knew so well.

"And by birthright I am an American," Broderick fussed to himself, stepping from his sled. "How can they refuse me?"

Moving close to the ship, where the gangplank was drawn up, he cupped his hand around his mouth and began shouting at the top of his lungs, hoping that someone would hear him. The longer he was alone, no matter if he was in the shadows of an American ship, he was vulnerable to being found by the Russians.

"Hello!" he shouted again. "I need assistance. Can anyone hear me? Hello!"

Jerome had not been able to sleep, for Letitia's

fate lay heavy on his heart and mind, and he was still fully clothed, alone in his office, poring over the journals to get his mind off Letitia and her decision to marry the Tlingit chief. If his men had not gotten lost in the wilderness, leaving him all but defenseless, he would have used all of his available gunpower to fight for Letitia, even if doing so would make her hate him.

To Jerome, her hate would be better than losing her forever to the savage!

Now his only alternative was to go against Kanuga's orders and find a place to build a fort, so that he could at least be close to his daughter in case she ever needed him or her mother.

In time, he tried to reassure himself, more Americans would come to Alaska, to strengthen his defenses against the Tlingit.

A voice breaking the stillness of the night, a man shouting from somewhere close to the ship, drew Jerome quickly from his chair. The sudden movement caused him to become dizzy, as the weakness from his injury still plagued him.

He steadied himself and yanked on his coat. Grabbing his rifle, he left his office and climbed the companionway ladder to the deck. Cautiously, he went to the ship's rail and peered over the side. The shadows were too deep for him to see the man's face. But it was only one man, lessening the threat. And the person had spoken in the English language, not Russian or Tlingit.

His spine stiffened. He knew of only one American besides himself and those of his expedition who had gotten lost.

Broderick Bowman!

Then hope sprang forth. Perhaps this was not Broderick at all, but one of his lost crew who had found their way back to the ship!

Yet he remained cautious, never trusting anyone but his own family.

"And Jonathan," he whispered to himself. "God bless him. He was a most trustworthy man."

"Who's there?" he shouted back, showing his rifle to the man. "What do you want?"

"Bowman. Broderick Bowman!" he shouted back. "One American to another, I've come to ask for asylum on your ship. The Russians will kill me if they find me. The Tlingit won't allow me in their village! You've got to help me or—I'll die."

His hopes dashed that perhaps one of his men had found his way back to the ship, and none too eager to welcome the man who had abducted Letitia, Jerome almost turned away without acknowledging Bowman's request for asylum.

Then his eyes widened as an idea came suddenly to mind. Broderick had been living with the Russians. That had to mean that he knew many of their secrets—and where their forts were positioned in Alaska. Suddenly the trader was more valuable in his eyes.

"What did you do to anger the Russians?" Jerome asked, still wary of the man and what he was capable of. "Why are you no longer welcome at their fort?"

"I did nothing!" Broderick wailed. "I suspect

they are blaming me for the colonel's son's death! But it was someone else! Not I! Please believe me. I would do you no harm if you take me aboard. I would be grateful! I would do anything for you! Anything!"

A smile touched Jerome's lips. "Then I grant you permission to come aboard," he said, nodding. He glanced over his shoulder and saw the crew members hurrying toward him, armed. His eyes grew into a squint as he caught sight of his wife and niece also approaching him, their eyes wide with fright.

"Who is it?" Kimberly asked, sidling close to her husband as she reached his side.

"It's that damnable Broderick Bowman," Jerome growled, glancing down at Barbara next to him on his other side.

"What does he want?" Barbara interjected, trying to make out Bowman's facial features in the pale light.

Jerome had no doubt why Barbara was interested in this man—she saw all men as potential lovers. He ignored her and began shouting orders to his men to lower the gangplank. Broderick scrambled quickly up the creaking plank and on over to Jerome.

"I'm most grateful, sir," he said, grabbing Jerome's hand and shaking it fitfully. "You've saved my life by allowing me on your ship. I'm damned grateful."

"We'll see," Jerome said, wiping his hand on his coat, as though it had been soiled by the mere touch of Broderick's hand.

Barbara took a step forward, peering into Broderick's face. She didn't see him as handsome, but he did have possibilities. She smiled wickedly up at him, her slanted eyes gleaming into his as he returned the smile.

Broderick felt the heat of desire tightening at his groin as he raked his eyes up and down Barbara, where her curves were not hidden from his view as her coat blew open in the brisk breeze, revealing a lacy chemise clinging to breasts that were well-rounded, their nipples dark and straining against the thin fabric.

"Broderick, you'd best keep your eyes in your head," Jerome warned, giving Barbara a shove toward the companionway ladder. "She's not a part of my generosity."

Broderick shifted his feet nervously on the deck. "You can't blame a man for lookin'," he said, stumbling over his words. "You're a lucky man to have two beautiful daughters."

Jerome leaned into Broderick's face. "She's not my daughter," he snarled. "But that doesn't mean that I don't have complete say over who does or doesn't touch her. Do you understand?"

Broderick smiled awkwardly. "I'm here to please, sir," he said, "Not to cause problems."

"That's more like it," Jerome said, stepping away from Broderick. He turned to his wife and gave her a hug. "Go on back to bed, honey. I've got a few things to talk over with Broderick. Then I'll join you. Soon."

Kimberly nodded, gave Jerome a quick kiss, then walked away, wondering what had happened to Barbara. She wasn't anywhere in sight.

She shrugged, thinking that Barbara had hurried to her cabin, humiliated by Jerome again. Kimberly felt saddened by this. Barbara somehow filled the gap left by Letitia's absence, and she wished her niece and her husband got along better.

"Let's go to my office," Jerome said, taking Broderick by an elbow. "You're going to give me some badly needed information about the Russians."

It was then that Broderick knew why this ship's captain had been so generous. He was not just being kind, he hoped to secure information from him about the Russians. After he got all that he wanted, would he then put him from the ship, of no value again to anyone?

He walked listlessly beside Jerome, then caught a glimpse of Barbara as she hid in the shadows, watching him. He smiled smugly, seeing in her a possibile means of survival.

Letitia moved to a sitting position when Kanuga came into the house in haste. She questioned him with her eyes as he offered her his hand.

"What's the matter?" she murmured. "What did the warrior tell you?"

"*Hade-krigut*," Kanuga insisted, bending to circle his fingers around her wrist and draw her up before him. "You will come. We are going to the Russian fort tonight. Not tomorrow."

Letitia paled and her heart began hammering inside her chest. "What?" she gasped. "Why,

Kanuga? Tell me what's happened."

Kanuga released his hold on her and grabbed her buckskin dress from the floor, thrusting it into her hands. "My scout brought me the news that the Russians have abandoned their fort and are now on their ship that is lodged in the ice," he said. "Now get dressed. We must leave in haste, not even taking time to dress in our warring garments. I do not trust the Russians. I fear they have devised a way of tricking us."

Knowing that she had no choice, Letitia hurried into her dress and then sat down on the floor and yanked first one boot on, and then the other. "Why would they abandon the fort?" she asked, scrambling to her feet and reaching for her coat.

"Because their scout must have heard of our plans to attack them at sun-up," Kanuga said, frowning angrily.

"If they are on their ship, ready to depart when the ice breaks in the river, why do you feel the need to hurry so, to get to their fort?" Letitia said, pulling on her gloves. "Isn't that what you wanted? To see them gone? Lord, Kanuga, I would think you would be glad they left on their own. There won't have to be any bloodshed."

Her lips parted as another thought came to her. She looked up at Kanuga warily. "You don't intend to attack the ship, do you?" she said in almost a whisper.

"That is not my intention," Kanuga said, walking toward the door now that Letitia was dressed warmly enough for travel in the midnight hour.

"I go to the fort to see if they have truly left, or if it is a trick to make us believe they are gone."

"I see," Letitia murmured, stepping outside. She shivered when her face stiffened instantly from the cold. She looked across the vast wilderness, the sky and river merging at the horizon, the ice crystals reflecting the brilliance of the huge, glowing orb of the moon, producing a breathtaking landscape which could have just as well been sprinkled with silver and diamonds.

She then looked around her at the waiting warriors on their sleds, their eyes anxious. Kanuga placed his arm around Letitia's waist and ushered her to the sled, where the dogs were already harnessed, breathing silver smoke from their nostrils into the velvet dark of night. She settled herself beneath the furs and secured herself against the jolt as the dogs made their first yank on the sled, then began pulling it smoothly over the packed-down snow.

Letitia tried not to think about what might lie ahead. If the Russians were setting a trap, the Tlingit could lose many warriors.

But if the Russians had fled a certain massacre, then even Letitia's parents could be spared involvement.

As the sleds moved across the snow-silent slopes, the cracks of the many whips were like shots in a battle, echoing around them like distant thunder. When the fort came into view, and Letitia saw no torches mounted on the high, protective fence, she smiled to herself, glad that the scout had brought accurate news to Kanuga.

She relaxed against the back of the sled, yet watching on all sides of her as Kanuga led his dogs to the outside of the gate. When there was no surprise attack, he led them on inside to the open courtyard, stopping before the large building in the middle of the compound.

"Search everywhere and make sure no Russians are hiding!" Kanuga shouted, stepping from his sled, the moon reflecting in the barrel of his rifle. "Then take what supplies they left behind and load as many as you can on your sleds! We will then burn the fort! That is the only way to be sure that no one will ever use it again!"

Letitia stepped from the sled and went with Kanuga into the main, two-storied structure, gasping when, by the faint glow of a whale-oil lamp, she found herself staring at piles of glossy pelts.

"The Russians weren't finished removing everything to the ship," Kanuga said, his eyes taking in the many piles of otter skins, which surely numbered into the thousands.

Frowning, he went to one of the stacks of pelts and ran his hand over the smooth softness of one of them. "No, they hadn't had the opportunity to get everything to the ship," he grumbled. "They planned to return with their sleds for these pelts. They wouldn't have left them for the Tlingit. They are too valuable a trade product."

Letitia stood back, staring in disbelief at the pelts, shuddering at the thought of how many animals had to have been killed. "There had to be many a slaughter of otters to accumulate these many pelts," she said, moving to Kanuga's side. "It's horrible. How could they kill so many innocent animals?"

"The Tlingit kill the animals, also, but never in such number," Kanuga said, lifting a pelt and running its softness against his cheek. "We kill what we need for survival. But never do we do it in a mass slaughter." He glared at Letitia as he lay the pelt aside. "At this rate, the otter would soon become extinct. Then what of the Tlingit?"

When other warriors came into the room, Kanuga ordered them to remove the pelts to their sleds, and when this was done, and all of the gunpowder and food supplies that had not yet been moved to the ship had been rounded up and loaded on the sleds, Kanuga and his warriors lit torches and placed them at strategic points in the fort.

Letitia went to the dogsled and climbed aboard, her eyes wide, her heart pounding, as the flames of the fort soon leapt high into the sky, emitting a roar across the land.

Suddenly she was afraid.

Should her father decide not to leave Alaska and build a fort, wouldn't Kanuga burn it, also?

And what if her father did not flee as the Russians had? Would Kanuga kill him, to finally rid the land of every nationality but the Tlingit?

Would Kanuga eventually, she wondered, feel that even she was an interference? Wouldn't he perhaps look at her and be reminded of all that the white people had taken from him, and hate her for it, as he had hated those he had driven from the land?

She shuddered at the thought of him ever finding a reason to hate her, when all that she ever wanted was to give her love and loyalty to him solely.

When he came to her smelling of fire and smoke, a glitter of victory in his silver eyes, she left the sled in a bounce and lunged into his arms.

She hugged him to her as though there were no tomorrows.

Chapter Twenty

Lend thy serious hearing to what I shall unfold.
—SHAKESPEARE

The cries of victory as the dog teams drew the warriors' sleds into the village drew the Tlingit from their houses into the cold, pre-dawn air. Kanuga drew his team to a halt and lifted Letitia from the sled. Carrying her, her arm twined about his neck, he went to his people and proudly stood among them.

Letitia scarcely heard what Kanuga was saying when he began shouting to his people. She could still see the fort burning fiercely into the sky and could not help but be frightened for her father. She expected him to build a fort on Alaska's shores: now, surely, he would be even more determined to build it, since he would not readily leave his daughter behind with the Tlingit people.

And what if her father did go against Kanuga's threat? Never had she seen such determination to rid the land of the Russians. One day Kanuga might feel just the same for the Americans!

She did not want to even think about Kanuga attacking her father and burning his fort. Nor did she want to think that her beloved Kanuga might be the one to finally send her father to his death. She could hardly bear to allow herself such thoughts!

Blocking out everything but the present, and that she was in Kanuga's arms, she looked up at him as he stood before his people in the capacity of a great, noble chief having returned home, victorious.

"The Russian fort is gone!" Kanuga shouted. "And soon, as the spring thaw comes to the river, the Russians will flee in their ship."

He glanced down at Letitia and paused for a moment. "And soon also the Americans will be gone from our shores," he boasted loudly, trying not to think about the sadness that he had seen in Letitia's eyes at the mention of her people leaving Alaska, and also trying to ignore the way his declaration had made her grow tense within his arms. She would soon adjust to her losses. To be his wife, she must adapt to many things.

"The land will be ours again," Kanuga continued, again looking at his people. "Do you hear me, my people? The land will be ours! The otter will no longer be slaughtered! They will have a chance to multiply again and be there for many winters to come for our people!"

Great bursts of enthusiasm echoed across the tundra as Kanuga's people began chanting loudly, thrusting their fists into the air over and over again.

"Let us now go to our feast house and celebrate until the sun greets us with its friendly smile," Kanuga interjected. "It, too, will celebrate our new-found freedom from interferences. Now, my people, again even the sun will be solely ours!"

He gazed devotedly down at Letitia, smiling. "And, my people," he said in a gentler tone. "The woman I hold in my arms is the one exception to the white people leaving our land. She will stay. And tomorrow, in a private ceremony, your chief will take a wife." He was glad when the sadness in Letitia's eyes was replaced by happiness as her lips quavered into a wondrous smile.

"And she is going to make me so very happy," Kanuga said, only loud enough for Letitia to hear.

Suddenly sweetly content, her heart warming at the anticipation of actually becoming Kanuga's wife and having the rest of her life to be with him, Letitia lay her cheek against his chest and again tried to block out all of the doubts that had only moments ago been assailing her. This man— this wonderful man—was worth any sorrow she might face. How could she have let herself forget the heartache that she had felt when she left him?

There was no way that she could ever live without him!

The villagers did not show the pleasure Kanuga had expected at his announcement of taking a white woman as his wife, showing only faint signs of approval as he searched their faces.

But he understood. They would have preferred a woman of their own skin coloring, as he would have also, if not for Letitia! To him, the color of the skin no longer mattered, nor that her eyes were the color of the sky on a warm spring day. Even if a son born to them bore the same coloring as Letitia, he would still be a future chief, for he would be the son of a powerful Tlingit chief!

"Let us go to the feast house now and celebrate!" Kanuga said, a sadness suddenly gripping his heart as his eyes moved to the memorial totem pole where his brother's ashes lay. Was the celebration misplaced? he wondered.

Then he decided quickly that it wasn't. Atkuk would be the center of the celebration were he alive! Atkuk's spirit would now be celebrating, for Atkuk had been slain by a Russian! In spirit, Atkuk would be celebrating the revenge his chieftain brother had taken for his death!

Kosko stood beside Athas, glaring at Kanuga, and then Letitia. He had not yet had the chance to plan how Kanuga would die. And tomorrow Kanuga would take the white woman to be his wife?

No, Kosko firmly decided, it could not—it *would* not happen!

A smug smile suddenly touched his lips, as he formulated a plan that would not only claim Kanuga's life, but also the woman's! Although his charms had proven ineffective before when plotting against Kanuga and his woman, what he planned this time needed no special charms. After the celebration, when they would be resting, and before the private marriage ceremony tomorrow, he would put his plan into motion.

"Yes," he whispered to himself. "It is a foolproof plan and no one will ever suspect that I was the cause...."

Jerome awakened with a start, perspiration lacing his brow. Kimberly turned on her side toward him, placing a hand to his cheek. "What's the matter, darling?" she murmured, feeling the clamminess of his face. "What awakened you?"

Jerome leaned up on an elbow. "Damned if I know," he grumbled. "I guess it's my worries about Letitia. There must be a way to get her away from that savage." He sat up and leaned his face into his hands. "When I think of her with him... when I think of never getting to see her again... my gut twists almost in two from the pain!"

Kimberly eased up and sat beside him, cuddling close to him. "The pain is just as unbearable for me," she said, her voice breaking. "What can we do, Jerome? What... can... we do?"

"She has made her choice," Jerome said thickly. "So anything we'd attempt would only make her hate us."

"Jerome, we can't go back to America without her," Kimberly said somberly.

"I don't plan to," Jerome said, patting her hand.

Kimberly gazed quickly up at him. "But you just said that anything we'd attempt would only make her hate us," she said softly.

"I'm not talking about stealing her away from the Tlingit," Jerome said, rising from the bed, pacing. "I plan to build us a fort—a haven for Letitia should she ever come to her senses and leave the savage."

"But, Jerome," Kimberly objected, "Kanuga threatened you—"

"To hell with Kanuga," Jerome said, flinging a hand in the air.

"But there are many Tlingit to our meager crew," Kimberly said in a tiny voice. "It frightens me, Jerome."

"Do you think Kanuga would actually run us off, or attack us, without first thinking what it would mean to Letitia?" Jerome stormed. "No. He wouldn't do anything to jeopardize his relationship with her." He chuckled beneath his breath. "He'll just have to learn to share Alaska with us, that's all."

A knock on the door drew Jerome's eyebrows up with surprise. Slipping into a robe, he went to the door and opened it. He instantly frowned. "What do you want?" he growled, face to face with Broderick.

"Have you seen it yet?" Broderick said, nervously wringing his hands.

"Seen what?" Jerome said, exasperated.

"The reflection of fire in the sky," Broderick said nervously.

"Fire?" Jerome said, looking over his shoulder

at the porthole, then back at Broderick. "What fire?"

"I think you'd best go up top and take a look," Broderick said. "It ain't a pretty sight."

Kimberly rushed from the bed and slipped into a robe. "Does it have anything to do with Letitia?" she asked, her voice rising in pitch, fear grabbing at her heart.

"No, nothing to do with your daughter," Broderick said. "But it has a lot do with what you were planning."

"What I was planning?" Jerome said.

"A fort," Broderick said. "You were planning to build a fort, weren't you? Go up and take a look at what has happened to the Russians' fort," Broderick urged. "Then you might think twice before trying to take what the Tlingits denied the Russians."

"Are you saying the—the Russian fort is burning?" Jerome gasped.

"Exactly," Broderick said, nodding.

Grabbing his coat, Jerome fled past Broderick. His heart sank when he saw the bright reflection of fire in the sky. His eyes wavered, now not sure about a future which included Alaska, no matter that Letitia had chosen it to be her home.

Colonel Golodoff stood at his ship's rail, cursing beneath his breath as he watched the flames eat away at his fort. "The bastard," he grumbled to himself. "The god-damned bastard."

In his mind's eye he was seeing the many otter skins that his men had not had time to remove from the fort. He was remembering the barrel after barrel of gunpowder that they had been forced to abandon, now surely in the hands of the Tlingit. He was remembering the food supply.

"If he thinks that's going to stop me, he's not as smart as he thinks he is," he said to himself. "As soon as this damn ice breaks, more supplies will be brought to us. And then . . ."

The fire was burning high in the feast house. Platters of food were being passed around while dancers performed around the fire. Accepting a platter of an assortment of dried fish, Letitia watched the performance, the laughter and gaiety contagious.

A man completely covered by a bearskin started to dance energetically, using his arms to act out the movements of a bear, gesturing first to one side and then to the other. Although his feet remained motionless, his body moved so violently that it seemed almost as if he were jumping.

An eagle dancer joined the performance next, stretching his arms to the sides and then sweeping the wings of his feathered costume back horizontally. His movements were long and graceful, matching those of an eagle in flight, which made the rapid, jerky gestures of the bear dancer appear even more frenzied.

Other dancers joined in, using certain movements of the head and shoulders which were descriptive of the spirits being represented. One dancer stopped every few steps to pause and turn his head, like a wolf being pursued. The movements of his feet did not vary during the course of the dance, but he held his body tense, giving an effect of jerky motion but conveying an impression of controlled power.

"Is it not beautiful?" Kanuga asked, moving closer to Letitia on the large, fur-covered settee high above the others. "My people should have cause to celebrate more often."

"They do seem so content," Letitia said, setting her empty platter aside. She turned to Kanuga, smiling. "You look content. That makes me happy, Kanuga. So very happy."

"A part of me is sad," Kanuga said, reaching for a red wool blanket that he had brought with him to the celebration. He held the blanket out before him, gazing intensely at it. "Do you see this blanket?"

"Yes, it's quite lovely," Letitia said. "Such a pretty color of red."

"It reminds me of happier days with Colonel Golodoff," Kanuga said, his eyes taking on a faraway look. "He gave me this blanket as a gift when trust was real between us—before it was lost forever."

"I'm sorry things didn't work out for you," Letitia said, reaching to touch the blanket. Although it was wool, it was very soft. "It's too bad everyone couldn't live together in Alaska, sharing."

"My father made the mistake of thinking we could," Kanuga said, laying the blanket aside.

"As did I." He firmed his jaw. "But there will be no more mistakes. The Russians will no longer be here to tempt us with their persuasions."

"Persuasions?" Letitia asked, arching an eyebrow.

"At first, when the Russians first came to Alaska, their business was in fur which they bought, but did not trap," Kanuga explained. "The trapping was up to the Tlingit. In return, the Russians offered knives and kettles, firearms, colored cloth, and woolen blankets of high quality, such as this one that Colonel Golodoff gave me. The comforts were irresistible to a people of a harsh land. Then, the Russians began trapping their own animals, slaughtering them by the hundreds, so that not only did they no longer trade with my people which they had grown used to, but they also took the pelts which belonged *to* my people!"

"I can understand why your admiration for the colonel turned to hate," Letitia said, lowering her eyes, her mind catapulted back to her concerns about her father and what his plans might be. As bitter as Kanuga was about the Russians, there would be no less bitterness for the Americans, even if her father offered Kanuga much better terms than Colonel Golodoff had. At this point, she knew that Kanuga would not listen to any bargaining. His mind was made up that no more forts would be built on Alaska's soil.

"I'm so tired," Letitia said suddenly, rubbing her eyes which unmercifully burned with lack of sleep. "If tomorrow is to be a special day for us,

Kanuga, I should get some rest tonight."

"And so you shall," Kanuga said, rising quickly to his feet. He raised his hands over his head and clapped them loudly together, stopping all the festivities. "The celebration is over, my people. Let us retire to our houses and sleep. Tomorrow is an important day for your chief!"

It did not take long for the villagers to disband. Letitia walked with Kanuga toward their house, then laughed throatily when he suddenly lifted her into his arms and carried her inside. The fire had died to glowing embers, casting a faint, magical glow around the room. Kanuga lowered his mouth to Letitia's lips and kissed her with passion as he carried her to the next room and to their bed. His hands quickly disrobed her, and then he pulled away from her long enough to remove his own clothes.

Leaning down over her, his eyes smiled into hers. Although tired, sleepy, and still worried about her parents, Letitia could never have enough of Kanuga. She beckoned to him with her outstretched arms and welcomed him atop her.

Their mouths met in wild kisses as her hips lifted and met Kanuga's entrance inside her. Rhythmically, they moved together until that peak they both knew so well was finally reached.

Exhausted, pearled with sweat, Kanuga rolled away from her and lay at her side, where she fit her body into his as she yawned lazily.

"Tomorrow," she whispered, loving the feel of his hard body against hers. "My love, I shall become yours for eternity, tomorrow."

* * *

Everything had finally fallen silent in the village. Kosko, bearing a torch, moved stealthily behind the houses until he reached Kanuga's longhouse. His eyes gleaming, his heart pounding greedily, he moved methodically around the building, setting the torch to the wood of the house until fires were taking hold from the front to the back.

Laughing to himself, Kosko watched for a moment, enjoying envisioning Kanuga and Letitia lying there asleep, so trusting, soon to be engulfed in flames.

"His powers shall never outweigh mine again!" he uttered to himself, tossing the torch into the flames. He hunkered over as he fled toward his own house. "He will be dead! Dead!"

He stood in the shadows of his house, watching the flames racing higher on Kanuga's house, popping and crackling as the fire was fed by the dry wood.

Then, content that all was well and that he had achieved his goal, he went inside and stretched out beside his own fire, soon fast asleep.

Letitia tossed and turned in her sleep when something began making her nose twitch. She bolted awake, then screamed when she saw the smoke, and then the flames that were halfway up the walls on all sides of her.

Kanuga awakened with a start, then bolted to his feet. He grabbed on his fringed breeches while Letitia stood frantically beside him, drawing her dress over her head. Kanuga then yanked a bear pelt up from the floor and wrapped it around himself and Letitia, then half dragged her toward the door and outside.

Breathlessly, they watched as the flames quickly engulfed the rest of the house, shooting sparks and rolling smoke high into the heavens.

The villagers came running from their houses, frantic when they saw that it was Kanuga's house that was on fire. When they saw him standing there unharmed, they went to him and surrounded him with loving touches and hugs, sharing these even with Letitia.

Then they all stood by silently watching the inferno until the house was consumed by it.

Kanuga shook his head, not understanding how this could have happened, not wanting to suspect anyone of his people of such a crime. He clenched his teeth angrily, suspecting that it was the Russians. Soon he would pay them a visit. He would show them what a true fire was when he set fire to their prized ship!

But his promises to Letitia came first. He would make her his wife. Then he would make all wrongs right.

Kosko had been awakened by the shouts of the villagers—including shouts of happiness and relief, which had to mean that Kanuga had been rescued.

He now stood among his people, glowering, as Kanuga and Letitia were swept away by the crowd, accompanied to the feast house, which would be their home until another longhouse was built to take the place of the one that was burned.

"Still I shall find a way!" Kosko vowed to himself.

Chapter Twenty-one

O she is all perfection
All that the gaudy heavens could drop down
  glorious.

—LEE

The southerly winds had arrived overnight, changing the land quickly from winter to spring, as though a magic wand had been waved over it. Letitia was bundled up beneath warm pelts beside Kanuga on a sled, snuggling close as a driver took them for a ride through the melting snow.

The wedding ceremony had been a simple one, performed only moments ago. Then Kanuga had asked his new wife to ride with him to see the wonders of spring in Alaska, now her domain as well as his.

Proud and deliriously content, she turned her eyes from her husband back to the scenery unfolding around her, inhaling deeply the smell of spring that filled the air. She marveled at how the willows were quickly showing signs of life along the ravine they were traveling alongside, the snow dripping like falling rain from their boughs.

She marveled and sighed with delight as her eyes turned heavenward, catching the sight of many flocks of wild geese, cranes, and whistling swans flying overhead.

Her gaze traveled downward again, now and then seeing a fox or bear.

And soon everything would be in full bloom, when the short spring turned to summer!

Then, as it seemed to happen every time she found a trace of happiness, her mind was catapulted back to that which filled her with dread. She realized that, along with the melting ice and snows, also came the thawing river, soon to burst its bonds, releasing from within its frozen prison the ships lodged within their icy grip.

She shook her head to clear her thoughts, not wanting to think of what might transpire should her father leave one spot in the river to go to another, to build a fort. She would deal with that, if—and when—it happened. Now was her and Kanuga's special time together. She was going to pretend that they were the only two people on the earth, their future carefree and filled with the happiness they were feeling at this moment.

Oh, but if only today and her happiness could continue on and on!

But she knew that was what dreams were made of, not realities....

Still, she snuggled close to Kanuga, at least for the moment pretending that the day would never end.

Another marvel of the north soon caught Letitia's attention as she again looked heavenward. She gasped, wondering if she were hallucinating! She could swear that she was seeing two—no, three suns at one time!

"How can that be?" she asked anxiously. "Kanuga, do you also see more than one sun in the sky? Or has my failure to wear snow glasses today caused my eyes to become crazed?"

Kanuga gazed at her, his eyes revealing a light amusement. "You are not imagining things, and no, the snow has not harmed your eyes," he said, chuckling. "What you are seeing are *sun dogs*, also called *mock suns*."

He further explained, "In this polar region of Alaska, the low, slanting sunlight and the tiny ice crystals in the air frequently create the illusion of two or even three suns."

He leaned a soft kiss to Letitia's lips, then said, "Such mysteries as those that are appearing in the sky today for us to see are considered good omens. It means, my beautiful wife, that we begin our marriage on good terms with nature."

"That is good to know," Letitia said, giggling. Again she snuggled close to Kanuga's side, again wishing that this contentment could go on and on and hoping that his superstitious belief about the sun's behavior today would be true. They needed a good omen to light the path that lay before them. Indeed, for their marriage to survive, they might need many good omens!

"And up ahead you will see more marvels of spring in Alaska," Kanuga said, gesturing toward many herds of caribou joining up with one another, forming a larger and larger herd. "The caribous' urge to migrate has returned, and with it a longing for the lush green feeding grounds of the unending tundra that shall suddenly appear soon, as the snows turn into small rivulets of water rolling along the land, nourishing the ground, drawing the grass to the surface."

As the south wind rustled through the animals, the caribou set off, thousands of hoofs trampling the melting snow, already baring portions of the damp ground beneath them.

As other herds streamed in from both sides, a forest of antlers surging along, the animals sometimes crowded flank to flank, their antlers clapping together.

"Never have I seen such a sight," Letitia said, as the driver commanded the dog team to turn in another direction with the snap of the whip.

They rode for a while longer, only then to see a herd of musk oxen, which, upon seeing the sled approaching, formed their characteristic circle of defense, old bulls on the outside, shoulder to shoulder, horns lowered, the younger oxen herded into the center, a strategy used as a defense against wolves.

"Will they attack us?" Letitia asked, frantically grasping Kanuga's hand. "They—they are looking us square in the eye, Kanuga!"

"They are more frightened of us than you are

of them," Kanuga quickly reassured her. "Watch. You shall see. Soon they will flee. Some have experienced the slaughter of their kind from the Russians' rifles. They, too, could become extinct, should the Russians have stayed much longer in Alaska."

Letitia sighed with relief when finally the herd broke ranks and stampeded away from them, down a slope, until soon they were out of sight.

When the sled arrived at the spot where the animals had stood, Letitia marveled over how the snow was littered with puffs of soft wool, the *qiviut* that grew under the musk oxen's long, straggling hair, and which they shed in the spring. This was an incredible sight, silken fibers of varying texture and strength lying everywhere.

"And are you impressed by what is now jointly yours, now that you are a part of the Tlingit people?" Kanuga asked, placing a finger to Letitia's chin and directing her eyes into his. "This land. The animals. Everything that is Alaska's is the Tlingits'. Everything that is the Tlingits' is yours."

"Such gifts I never expected when I accepted your proposal of marriage," Letitia said, smiling up at him. "It is better than all the gifts that could have been brought to me at wedding showers given by my friends in New York. Your gifts are much more precious, Kanuga. So very much more precious."

"Wedding showers?" Kanuga said, forking an eyebrow. "You are given gifts while standing in the rain?"

Letitia laughed softly at his beautiful innocence, then placed her hands at his cheeks and brought his mouth to her lips. She kissed him sweetly, then, laughing together, they drew a thick layer of bear pelts over themselves to hide their mischief from the driver's eyes.

Their hands wandered inside each other's coats, farther still inside their clothes, finding each other's pleasure points.

But they were too restricted to do everything they wished, so Kanuga quickly shoved the pelts away from his face so that he could look up at the driver.

"Return us to our village at once!" he shouted, his loins on fire with need. "With haste!"

With the snap of the whip, the huskies made a sharp turn and moved quickly and soundlessly over the feathery snow as Kanuga slipped beneath the bear pelt again, his mouth covering Letitia's with a kiss which gave her the promise of what awaited her back at their house.

Moving stealthily, like a panther stalking its prey, Barbara moved down the candle-lit corridor toward the room that had been assigned to Broderick Bowman. When she finally reached it, she tapped gently on the door, then moved quickly inside as Broderick swung it open.

"Close the door," Barbara whispered, hugging her robe close to her. "Quick now, before someone sees that I'm in here with you."

Broderick scratched his brow idly and closed the door, then turned to Barbara, his eyes almost popping from their sockets when, just as quickly as she had entered the cabin, she let her robe drop from around her, revealing that she wore nothing beneath it.

"What is this?" he said, his pulse suddenly racing out of control, his breathing suddenly shallow as he feasted on her heavy breasts, tiny waist, and tapering ankles. "What...do you think you're doing?"

Flashing her green eyes up at him, Barbara slinked toward him. "What does it look like?" she said in a seductive purr. She reached a hand out to him and ran her fingers down his bare chest furred thickly with ringlets of dark hair, then down to the waistband of his trousers. "You can't deny wanting me since you first saw me, now can you?"

Nervous beads of perspiration rose on his brow and he closed his eyes, hiding a sigh of pleasure behind clenched teeth when she unbuttoned his breeches and slid her hand lower, inside them, soon fondling that which had grown to painful proportions.

"What if...your uncle finds out?" Broderick said in a voice almost choked with passion, his eyes flying open, then closing again, as he was rendered mindless by her skillful hands.

Barbara shrugged, the shrug belied by a gleam in her eyes. "My uncle is too busy going over the plans for his new fort, now that you've assured him there are no Russian outposts left in the area," she said, sounding as if she were straining to keep her patience. "I guess the torching of Fort

Anecia by the Tlingit didn't frighten him enough. Why, he'd not let a little fire scare him away from being close to his daughter."

Her fingers went to the waist of his breeches and began lowering them over his hips, the part of him that was throbbing springing out, more accessible to her.

After she kicked his breeches away from Broderick, Barbara grabbed his hand and yanked him down to the floor. Straddling him, she led his hardness inside her, sucking in a rapturous breath of air as his hands went to her breasts and began squeezing them painfully.

"I knew it was no mistake coming to you," she whispered. She threw her head back in rapture, gasping over and over again as he bucked up into her. "Lord . . . oh, Lord. . . ."

And then their bodies convulsed together in a mutual, frenzied passion, until they were almost drained dry of breath.

Afterwards, Barbara moved away from him. She stretched out on her stomach, leaning her chin in her hands. "I can offer you more of the same if you'll do me a favor," she said, smiling at him devilishly.

"I was afraid this was too good to be true," Broderick said, wiping sweat from his brow. He groaned and stretched out on his back, his toes pointed stiffly to the ceiling as Barbara was quickly there, her mouth on him, causing him to become hard again.

"Anything," he gasped, his heart pounding so

hard he thought he might black out. "I'll do any-thing."

"I thought you might," Barbara said, suddenly sitting up, circling her arms around her knees. She gazed amusedly down at Broderick as he lay there, panting.

"You're a vixen," he said, turning to face her. He began smoothing his hand along her thigh. "Now. Tell me what I've got to do to keep you happy."

"Stop my cousin's marriage to the savage," Barbara said in a sneer. "I promise you even more exciting tricks if you'll persuade Letitia to leave Kanuga. And if you must—kill her."

Broderick suddenly sat up. "Why? So you can have the savage for yourself?" he asked, looking at Barbara warily.

"Something like that," Barbara said, laughing throatily. She shoved Broderick back down on the floor of the cabin. "But don't worry. I have enough for both you and the savage."

"I imagine you do," Broderick said, cold sweat beading his brow again when Barbara's lips slith-ered down his abdomen. He closed his eyes when her mouth closed over him. "I guess I could make some excuse to leave the ship. But . . . how do I lure Letitia away from the village? Kanuga'd have my hide if he caught me anywhere near her."

"You'll think of a solution to both problems," Barbara said, looking up at him wickedly. "I might suggest that you tell my uncle you're going to go and check on the Russians. They are on their ship not far away from us, aren't they?"

"Yes . . . up the river about a mile. . . ."

"Worry my uncle. Tell him you don't trust the Russians. Say that they might come and attack us. Tell him you can go and spy on the Russians for him—all for the benefit of him, his family and crew."

"Yes, that might work," Broderick said, lifting Barbara onto his throbbing member. "But for now, just get busy giving me my first payment for my loyalty to *you*."

Barbara moved on him, laughing throatily at the prospect of Kanuga perhaps losing his beloved Letitia, forever. . . .

Her whole body still throbbing from Kanuga's skilled lovemaking, Letitia lay cuddled next to him. She gazed around her at the feast house in which she and Kanuga still made residence while their new house was being built. She was anxious to have a house of their own again. It gave her a wondrous thrill to be able to share a new house with Kanuga, a house that would be solely theirs. It would be wonderful to share a life with Kanuga!

If only things could be as beautiful as at this moment, this peaceful forever. There would be no tomorrows, only today, only the rapture in being held by him, kissed by him. . . .

"I have a gift for you," Kanuga said, rolling away from her.

"Oh? What?" Letitia said, moving to a sitting position. She drew a blanket around her shoulders as Kanuga went to a trunk and opened it.

Nude, the muscles in his body rippling beneath the slight shadows of the fire, Kanuga went back to Letitia and handed her something quite unfamiliar to her.

"What is this?" she asked.

"It is a mechanical toy—not so much for you as for the child you will soon be carrying," Kanuga said. "My people make these and store them here in the feast house as gifts to the newborn children of neighboring tribes. Today I give one to you, to encourage your body to make a child for us soon."

Letitia giggled when Kanuga showed her how it worked. A piece of fur on an endless thong which was threaded in and out of holes in a board, it made a wooden mouse vanish and reappear when the thong was pulled.

"That is so sweet," she said, now operating the toy herself. Then she held it to her bosom and looked adoringly up at Kangua. "I shall always treasure the gift. And our . . . our son will adore it, also."

"A son?" Kanuga said, his eyes laughing down into hers. "And so you will bear me a son first?"

"Yes," Letitia said, moving into his embrace, hugging him to her. "And then a daughter." She giggled. "And then another son . . . and then another daughter. . . ."

Kanuga threw his head back with laughter, then looked down at her, filled with so many feelings it was hard to describe them. He only knew that he could never love Letitia any more than he did now. She was everything to him. Everything!

He took the toy from her and laid it aside, then entwined his fingers through hers. "It is the belief of the Tlingit that when a woman becomes pregnant, her father loses his power over her, and she becomes a full member of her new family," he said softly. "But you are already my entire family, my *ssik-go schau-wot*, beautiful woman."

Letitia's eyes wavered, the mention of her father bringing back fears and frustrations that she could not let go of.

And then her worries about her father were suddenly multiplied inside her heart when, not far from the village, there came a sound like a thunderclap, announcing the first crack in the ice in the river. As the rents opened, the noise was like the firing of a hundred cannons.

She rushed to her feet, grabbed her fur cloak, slipped her feet into some caribou moccasins, and hurried outside. She covered her mouth with her hand and gasped as she watched water shooting through the widening gaps in the river, great ice floes piling onto each other, forming shining mountains of ice.

Kanuga moved to her side, his cloak thrown around his shoulders. "The bursting and breaking will last two days, then the river will flow freely again," he said. "Soon the ships will be freed and can leave Alaska's shores."

Letitia stiffened, not sure if she could bear the thought of her parents going away to only God knew where.

Chapter Twenty-two

We are ne'er like angels 'till our passion dies.
—DEKKER

Letitia watched Kanuga drape his cloak over his shoulders, his eyes so alive today, his smile reaching clean into Letitia's heart. She sighed, plaiting her hair until it was hanging in one long braid down her back, then turned her back to Kanuga, lifting the braid for him to see. "Do you like it? Do you approve?" she asked anxiously. "Do I look like a Tlingit wife?"

Kanuga went to her and placed his hands on her waist, turning her around to face him. He brushed a soft kiss across her lips. "No matter how you wear your hair, you are now Tlingit, my very perfect wife."

Letitia giggled. She had never thought she could be as happy as she was today! Spring had arrived in Alaska, making everything that had once seemed so bleak now seem filled with promise! Perhaps she might even find the courage to ask Kanuga if he would reconsider ordering her father's ship from Alaska's waters.

Oh, but if that were possible, she marveled to herself, indeed she would be the happiest woman in the world!

"I'm glad you approve," she finally said, leaning into his embrace. She hugged him tightly, then eased away and looked up at him. "You said that you are going to supervise the building of our new house today. I think that's wonderful, darling. Can I come and help?"

"I don't think that would be wise," he said. "Although spring has arrived, the air is still too cold for you to stay out in it for any length of time."

He nodded toward the fire. "You stay here," he said softly. "Keep the fire going."

He circled a hand around one of her wrists and yanked her to him, holding her tightly against him, his eyes two points of fire as he gazed down at her. "Keep the furs spread," he said huskily, his eyes lit with hot passion. "We shall soon be warming them again."

He chuckled low. "I doubt if I can last too long without having you again."

Crushing his mouth to her lips, he kissed her heatedly, then released her and walked away, leaving Letitia shaken with desire.

Letitia placed her fingers to her mouth, touching her lips which were still throbbing from Kanuga's fiery kiss. This passion her husband knew how to awaken in her at the mere touch of his eyes was so intense it frightened her. She felt almost consumed, sometimes, by this need for him.

Being with him had become the most important thing in her life, and she felt selfish because of it. Worry over her parents nagged her at the back of her mind, and she felt guilty for having deserted them—especially if they were forced to return to New York.

Plopping down beside the fire, she toyed with the fringes of her buckskin dress, then slipped her feet into a pair of soft caribou moccasins.

And just as she was about to dip herself another bowl of rabbit stew into the wooden platter that she had emptied while sharing breakfast with Kanuga, she dropped the wooden spoon back into the pot, startled by a sudden presence in the house.

She gasped as she looked up at Kosko, who had come in without knocking and now stood over her unsmilingly.

"Why are you here?" Letitia asked, rising slowly to her feet. She backed away from him when he didn't immediately answer her, alarming her. Although he was a shaman, one of the Tlingit holy men, there was something about him that made shivers ride her spine. She remembered Atkuk's eyes being friendly. Kosko's were cold and penetrating as he continued to stare at her.

"What do you want?" Letitia persisted, firming her chin as a slow irritation began to claim her.

"You should have at least announced your presence before coming into the house. Haven't you ever heard of such a thing as privacy?"

"I have come with a warning," Kosko said, his voice solemn.

A sudden fear gripped Letitia's heart. "Warning?" she said, placing a hand to her throat, her voice quavering. "What sort of a warning?"

"It is about Kanuga," Kosko said somberly.

"What about . . . Kanuga?" Letitia said, taking another step away from him.

She waited a moment longer, then blurted out angrily, "Don't just stand there! Tell me what you have come to say."

She lifted a hand and pointed toward the door. "Or—get out!"

She recoiled beneath his steady stare and his continued silence. He seemed not at all stung by her outburst, or impressed by her courage in ordering him to leave. In her mind's eye she was recalling how he had attended to Atkuk's body at the funeral ceremony. He had surely been chosen by Kanuga because he was the most trusted shaman in the village!

So why couldn't *she* find it in her heart to trust him?

And she had just insulted him!

She feared Kanuga's finding out, yet she knew that if Kosko didn't say something, or leave soon, she would be forced to insult him again. He was invading her privacy. And moment to moment, she was feeling more strongly that something was amiss about him—as though somehow, Kanuga's trust in Kosko had been misplaced!

"I have come to tell you that soon Kanuga will be taking another wife," Kosko finally said, trying another tactic to break Kanuga and Letitia apart, one that was less threatening to his own life. He feared getting caught in his scheming against Kanuga.

The shock of what Kosko had said made a light-headedness sweep over Letitia, causing her to sway and grab at her head.

Then she steadied herself, willing herself to stand up against this latest revelation. It seemed to her that just as everything was going right, something always came along to tear her joy to shreds!

"Another wife?" she said, stiffening her shoulders as she stood firmly beneath Kosko's glittering eyes. "What do you mean, another wife?"

"Tlingit nobles have more than one wife," Kosko said, enjoying toying with Letitia. "It is a prestigious way of displaying their powers. And, ideally, a second wife is the younger sister or a cousin of the first wife, as blood relatives get on better together than those out of the family. It is Kanuga's decision to take your cousin for his second wife. And he shall do it soon. His hunger for her is great."

Letitia gasped. A sick feeling began at the pit of her stomach and worked itself up into her throat, into a cutting bitterness. She swallowed back the urge to vomit, unable to block from her mind's eye the picture of Kanuga and Barbara together in a passionate embrace.

Yet surely what Kosko said wasn't true! Kanuga was content with her!

And never had he mentioned taking another wife—especially not her cousin!

"You're lying," she hissed. "Lying!"

"I am a shaman of my people," Kosko said, the pitch of his voice still and steady. "A shaman does not lie. A shaman tries to better things for his people. Not stir up problems." He frowned at Letitia. "Especially I do what is best to protect my chief."

"Somehow I doubt that," Letitia said, rage filling her. "Now leave. And I will tell Kanuga what you said. As it is untrue, he will surely banish you from the village, a shaman no more!"

"What I said is true," Kosko said, taking a step toward her. "And Kanuga has assigned me to go to the American ship and inform the white woman that he wants her here on the morrow, before the ship is able to float free from the ice. I go soon to carry this message of my chief to the white woman. Prepare yourself for her arrival. Prepare two pallets of furs beside the fire. Kanuga will share these one night with you, and the next night with his new wife."

"No," Letitia said, choking back a sob. "Please tell me that you are lying! I'll even forgive you. I won't even tell Kanuga that you came here like this, stirring up problems between us. Just tell me that you are lying!"

"I cannot tell you something that is not true," Kosko said, turning and walking toward the door.

"Prepare yourself for the second wife," he said over his shoulder. "That is the reason I came to you, to give you a chance to prepare yourself."

Letitia watched him leave. Then, her newly found happiness shattered, she let the tears run freely from her eyes. "I can't stay," she whispered to herself. "I can't bear to be here when Barbara arrives. I'll never share Kanuga with her!"

A sudden hatred for Kanuga swept over her. She doubled a hand into a tight fist at her side.

"He can have her!" she cried, gathering up her outdoor clothes and rushing into them.

Without looking back, she left the feast house. She looked desperately around her for a dog team that was hitched up to a sled. She was frantic to leave before Kanuga returned! How could she face him, when all along he had known that he would be taking a second wife?

He was a liar!

And he was a thief!

He had stolen her heart, as well as her trust.

Spying a team of huskies that were attached to a sled close by, yet resting in curled balls while they waited for their master, Letitia ran and boarded it. Soon, blinded by tears, she had the huskies pulling her in the sled along the melting snow, far from the village.

The morning sunlight softly shattered into uncertain shadows along the ground beside Letitia. No animal tracks crossed her path; no birds flew in the sky; there was not the slightest breath of wind.

Her attention was drawn ahead, to the right of

where she planned to travel, when she saw a small white cloud rising from a snowdrift on the bank. As she came closer to it, she could see that the vapor was coming from a tiny hole around which a crust of ice had formed.

She shuddered, recalling the earlier experience with a bear, when her father had been horribly attacked and wounded by its devastatingly sharp claws. She knew that this vapor was possibly the breath of a bear that was hibernating beneath the snow.

She prayed to herself that the noise from the dog team and sled would not awaken the bear. She had forgotten to bring a firearm with her. She was at the mercy of everything that walked on two and four legs.

Having lost sight of which direction her hasty flight had taken her from the village, she looked from side to side, and up ahead, wondering which way she should go, to get circled around, to find her way to her father's ship.

"I'm so disoriented," she cried aloud. She looked in all directions again. Everything looked the same. "Which way should I go? I can't allow myself to end up back in Kanuga's village. I—I never want to see him again!"

But she also dreaded arriving at the ship. If Kosko got there ahead of her and summoned Barbara to Kanuga's bed, she would want to hide her head and never look anyone in the face again.

Kanuga, Letitia thought woefully to herself, was going to be the cause of her total humiliation.

She directed the huskies into a sharp turn left,

hoping that would take her back in the direction of the river. Traveling in what she hoped was a westerly direction, she found herself suddenly surrounded by great boulders of ice stretching in every direction. She snapped the whip over the huskies' heads when she came to a hill, and the dogs quickly climbed to the plateau beyond.

There the sled ran easily over the snow again, leaving behind the boulders of ice.

Then, to the north, something seemed to loom into the sky. It looked like a huge wall of ice, extending along the entire horizon, and cut evenly on top.

Curious, Letitia sent the huskies toward this wall, soon discovering that it was a titanic pressure ridge, at least forty feet high.

Awed, she could see no end to the massive wall of ice and drew the dogteam to a halt beside it. More impressive still was its symmetry. Its south side was a confused heap of ice blocks, but the north side was cut clearly as if by a knife.

Suddenly her attention was drawn elsewhere. She turned her eyes in the direction of an ominous rumbling. Smiling, she now knew which way to go. The sound she was hearing was coming from the river; it had to be the ice on the move. It was a hissing, clanking, roaring sound, and there was no wind. That had to mean that what sounded like millions of tons of ice grinding together had perhaps been set in motion by a gale blowing hundreds of miles away.

"I must get to the ship," she whispered, relieved to now know how to find it. "My father's ship will soon be set free from its bonds!"

She turned her gaze back at the massive wall of ice. Totally intrigued, having never seen such an incredible sight before, she wanted to take the time to examine it before continuing to the ship.

Her eyes wide with wonder, Letitia left the sled and began walking alongside the wall. As she walked beside it, she slid her hands along the sheet of ice. Then, as if someone had crushed the breath out of her, she gasped, staring at something frozen into the ice.

Horror-stricken, her heart pounding, she stared at the man frozen into the wall in what appeared to be a fetal position, his eyes open in a death stare.

"Jonathan!" Letitia then screamed, her voice echoing back at her in many shrill voices as it reverberated off the ice. "No! Please no! Not dear, sweet Jonathan!"

She touched the ice beneath which Jonathan's face lay, all purple and swollen. "Oh Lord, Jonathan, I'm so sorry," she sobbed.

Her knees grew suddenly weak and her head began spinning. As she crumpled into a heap on the snow at the base of the wall of ice, she welcomed the black void of unconsciousness as it rushed over her.

It had been easy to leave the ship once he had convinced Jerome that he would spy on the Russians for him, and Broderick rode across the land on his sled, laughing boisterously. He snapped the whip across the huskies' backs, having taken a wide turn in the snow that would bring him up behind Kanuga's village instead of directly in front. He had to be careful not to be discovered. He would have to leave his team at least a half mile from Kanuga's village and go the rest of the way by foot, thanking the Lord that the frigid temperatures had changed to more tolerable, even pleasant, weather.

His eyebrows forked when up ahead he saw a great wall of ice that he was not familiar with. "Is that a dog team beside the wall?" he said aloud, idly scratching his brow with his free hand. "What's it doing there? Where's the driver?"

He led his team into a wide turn and headed toward the vacated dog team and sled.

Then his eyes widened and he sucked in a wild breath of air, stunned when he recognized Letitia lying in the snow, unconscious.

As he drew closer, his gaze locked on something else. He paled when he saw the figure of a man frozen into the side of the great ice wall.

The sight of the lifeless, frozen man sent a shiver of doom through him. He crossed himself and looked to the heavens, saying a quiet prayer.

And then his gaze lowered again, to Letitia. As he drew his dogs to a stop beside the other huskies, he welcomed their yelpings as they greeted each other so friskily. It was a welcome sound, making the world seem alive again.

Rushing to Letitia, kneeling down beside her, Broderick placed his cheek to her mouth, to see if she was breathing. When her breath warmed his flesh, he quickly picked her up into his arms and carried her to his sled.

Hurriedly, he covered her with many warm furs, then gazed down at her, remembering what Barbara's intentions were for her, and that he had been willing to go along with her for the payment that she had offered him.

But now that he again gazed on Letitia and her lovely innocence, and saw how vulnerable she was as she lay unconscious, surely from the shock of seeing the man frozen into the ice, he could not find the courage to do her harm.

Instead, he would use having found her to his advantage. He knew of a way to make her father take him totally into his confidence, perhaps even offer him friendship!

"I'll take her to her father," Broderick concluded aloud. "After that, I should be able to get anything I want from him. He'll be forever in my debt."

He frowned darkly when he thought of Barbara, hoping that he wasn't destroying his relationship with her. He had never enjoyed a woman in bed as much as he had her.

Somehow, even, he had to find a way to keep Barbara away from Kanuga.

He suddenly remembered the loud rumblings and roaring sounds that had come from the river only a short while ago.

"That's it!" he said, his eyes wide. "The ship will be able to leave soon. I've got to make sure that Barbara is on it." He chuckled. "As well as myself."

He puffed out his chest, confident that he would now be a welcome traveler on the ship.

He eyed the other sled and huskies. He couldn't leave them behind, abandoned. They were too valuable.

After attaching them to his dogteam, he boarded his sled and rode away in a mad dash, anxious to deliver Letitia to her father. He laughed into the wind, looking forward to Jerome's reaction when he found out how his daughter had been saved—and by whom.

His laughter faded as he wondered about the man frozen in the ice. What had he been to Letitia? It was apparent that he had meant something to her, or why else would she have fainted at the sight?

And, he wondered, what had she been doing out there alone, so far from the Indian village? It was as though she were fleeing from the Tlingit.

He quirked an eyebrow, wondering what would make her leave Kanuga when she had turned her back on her parents to be with the Tlingit chief.

He glanced down at her, intrigued by her. There was no doubt that she had a complicated personality—indeed, she was a woman of mystery....

Chapter Twenty-three

Strong reasons make strong actions.
—SHAKESPEARE

The jostling of the sled awakened Letitia. Blinking her eyes open, she looked quickly around her, gasping when she discovered that she was in a sled, traveling at a high rate of speed across the snow.

Kanuga! she thought frantically. It must be Kanuga! He had searched and found her and was taking her back to his village. Was he going to force her to accept Barbara as his second wife?

"No!" she screamed, tossing the furs away from her. She started to jump from the sled, but stopped when a voice that was not Kanuga's shouted her name.

She turned her head with a start and was stunned to find that the driver of the sled was Broderick Bowman!

In flashes, she recalled the night when he had abducted her. Was he doing so again? If not, why was he driving the sled on which she traveled? Where, even, had he found her?

She looked past him, seeing the other dog team trailing behind. A sick feeling invaded her senses when she was catapulted back to that moment when she found Jonathan in the wall of ice. She must have fainted from the shock!

Tears splashed down her cheeks as she turned her eyes away from Broderick and covered her face with her hands, not even aware now that the dogs were stopping. All that she could think about was Jonathan—dear, sweet Jonathan.

He was dead.

Dead!

When a hand touched her shoulder, she flinched and looked up at Broderick, hate in her eyes. "Keep your hands off me," she said in a low hiss. "Get away from me!"

"I mean you no harm," Broderick said, dropping his hand to his side. "I found you in the snow. You had fainted. I'm taking you to your father's ship."

"And you expect me to believe that?" Letitia snapped, wiping her face clean of tears with the back of a glove. "You're probably taking me back to the Russians. What did you plan to do? Imprison me in the hold of the Russian ship, to use me at your leisure? Or share me with the rest of the crew?"

"I no longer associate myself with the Russians," Broderick said. "I've been taken in by your father. He's given me asylum on his ship. I plan to travel with him to America."

"My father wouldn't waste his time with the likes of you," Letitia said, glaring at him. "So tell me the truth. What are your plans for me?"

"I've already told you," Broderick said, frustration showing in his tone of voice. "I'm taking you to your father's ship."

"Did he tell you to?" Letitia asked, eyeing him warily. "Did he, in fact, tell you to steal me away from Kanuga's village? You have to know that's where I was until... until..."

"Until what?" Broderick said, arching an eyebrow.

Letitia swallowed hard, lowering her eyes when she remembered Kosko's solemn announcement that Kanuga would soon take Barbara for his second wife. Perhaps even now Barbara was with Kanuga, sharing his bed.

"Please take me to my father," she said, sobbing. "Please?"

"Why were you traveling alone, so far from Kanuga's village?" Broderick asked, taking it upon himself to position the furs around Letitia again. "If I hadn't found you, you would have soon frozen to death."

"I don't wish to talk about it," Letitia said, again lowering her eyes. "Just please take me to my father."

Broderick nodded. He went to the back of the sled and took up his reins and whip. Shouting at the huskies, he soon had them moving again at a fast pace across the snow.

The dog team finally stopped close to the ship. Weakly, Letitia let Broderick help her out of the sled, place his arm around her waist, and lead her up the gangplank.

There he relinquished her to her father's care as Jerome was suddenly there, taking her into his arms, looking down into her tear-filled eyes in confusion.

Jerome then looked past Letitia, turning on Broderick a face so impatient, so angry, that Broderick stepped back from it.

"How is it that she is with you?" Jerome demanded. "What's happened to her? Why is she crying?"

"Papa, take me to your cabin," Letitia interjected, for a moment despair and loneliness for Kanuga rushing over her like a nausea. "I'll explain everything to you." Her insides tightened when she looked desperately up at her father. "Is . . . Barbara gone yet?"

"Barbara? Gone?" Jerome said, even more confused. "No. She's here. Why shouldn't she be? Where did you think she had gone?"

Letitia wanted to feel relieved that Barbara was still on the ship, yet she would not allow herself such feelings. Surely Kosko hadn't had a chance to get away yet, to come for Barbara. Perhaps he would come at any moment now. Then Letitia would have to be a witness to Barbara's jubilation for having been chosen as Kanuga's second wife! She wasn't sure if she could bear it!

"It's nothing," she murmured, leaning into her father's embrace as they moved toward the companionway ladder. "Let's not talk about it anymore."

Puzzled by her strange behavior, and filled with many questions about why she had been with Broderick, Jerome led her down the steps and to his cabin, where Kimberly rushed to Letitia, quickly embracing her.

"Darling, you've come back to us," Kimberly said, sobbing as she clung with desperation to Letitia. "I knew that you would! Oh, darling, I knew that you would!"

"Yes, I've come back," Letitia said, her voice lifeless. She slipped away from her mother and removed her coat and gloves, then sat down in front of the stove, holding her hands over it, relishing the warmth against her flesh.

She looked up at her father. "And soon we can return to America?" she said, a silent pleading in her eyes. "I ... I don't ever want to hear the word Alaska again. I hate it. I've had nothing but heartache since we arrived here."

Her eyes pooled with tears. In her mind's eye, she was seeing Jonathan. "I found Jonathan," she said, her voice breaking. She looked from her mother to her father, then down at the floor. "He won't be going back to America with us."

Jerome fell to one knee before Letitia. He took her hands in his, searching her face. "Where did you find him?" he asked. "And why won't he be going back with us to America?"

"He's dead, Papa," Letitia said, bursting into fitful tears as she lunged into his arms. "And he died so horribly!"

Jerome was trembling, tears rolling down his cheeks. "How did he die?" he asked, looking past Letitia, his eyes locked on a map that hung on the wall of his cabin. It was a map that Jonathan had drawn, charting their journey from America to Alaska in minute detail. Jonathan had been skilled in so many ways, a man of much intelligence—and total kindness!

"It was so horrible!" Letitia cried, easing from her father's arms. She ran her fingers over the map that her father's eyes were still concentrating on.

Then she turned and looked wearily at her mother, then her father. "I found him . . ."

She placed a fist to her mouth, finding it hard to say the words.

Then she blurted the rest out. "He was frozen in a wall of ice. I found him like that!" She buried her face in her hands. "I'll never forget the sight! Never!"

Jerome choked back the urge to vomit. "How could that have happened?" he said, shaking his head slowly back and forth.

"We'll never know," Letitia said, going to her father. She hugged him tightly. "But Papa, he's there forever, it seems. The ice was so thick. So very, very thick!"

Kimberly was standing by, listening, horrified. Then, not able to stand thinking about Jonathan and how he had died any longer, she crumpled in a dead faint to the floor.

"Mother!" Letitia cried, rushing to her.

But her father was there before her and had

taken Kimberly up into his arms. He took her to the bed and lay her across it. "Dampen a cloth, Letitia. Place it on her brow!"

Absorbed in caring for her mother's welfare, Letitia forgot her own sorrow for a moment. But she was soon catapulted back to her reason for setting out across the ice when Barbara entered the cabin, her eyes wide with wonder as she looked questioningly at Letitia, then down at her aunt.

"What's going on here?" Barbara demanded, sauntering across the room and staring at Letitia. "Why are you here?" She looked at Jerome and Kimberly. "Why is everyone upset?"

"Jonathan is dead," Jerome said, his voice faltering. "Letitia found his body."

"Oh, so that's why you're here," Barbara said, disappointment thick in her voice. "Just long enough to break the news about Jonathan to everyone." She flipped the hem of her skirt up around her ankles as she eased down into a chair. "I didn't think you'd given up your decision to be Kanuga's wife."

She leaned forward, her green eyes slanting up at Letitia. "And have you married him?" she asked, not seeming to really care. Barbara was wondering about Broderick. Where was he? Why hadn't he done as she had asked? How had he let Letitia slip through his fingers?

But of course she knew why. He was a bungler!

Kimberly awakened, having caught Barbara's indifference about Jonathan; her niece did not seem to care about what should be in all of their hearts.

"Is that all you are concerned about?" she said, stifling a sob. "You shouldn't even be concerning yourself about anything Letitia does. It's Jonathan. You should be sad over Jonathan!"

"I scarcely knew the man," Barbara said, tossing her head to flip her hair back over her shoulders. "He was Letitia's concern. Not mine."

"I can't believe you are so—so heartless," Kimberly said, shaking her head with disgust.

"I see that I'm not wanted here," Barbara said tersely. She rose from the chair and went to the door, yanking it open. "Besides, I've other things to do."

The cabin became strained with silence as she slammed the door behind her. Then Jerome went to Letitia and stood over her. "What about Kanuga?" he said warily. "Why have you decided to leave him?"

"That I have should be all that is important to you," Letitia said, not wanting to talk about Kanuga, ever again. She rose from the chair, running the back of a hand across her brow. "I really am too tired to talk anymore. I'm going to go to my—"

She stopped and chewed on her lower lip nervously, then said, "I'm going to Jonathan's room and lie down."

"But should you?" Kimberly said, reaching a hand out to Letitia. "Will you be all right in Jonathan's room? The memories, Letitia ..."

"I'll be all right there," Letitia said, smiling

weakly at her mother. "Perhaps it is best that I be there. I've much to straighten out in my mind about Jonathan. Somehow, being in his cabin will be like being there with him, talking it all out with him."

"Whatever you think is best," Kimberly said, rising from the bed to give Letitia a soft hug.

A rumbling sound from outside the cabin drew Jerome to the porthole. He peered out, nodding. "It won't be long now," he said, seeing black smoke hanging above the ice. He knew that it was steam, rising from open water. The river was three hundred yards across, covered now only by a floating, half-congealed mush of ice. "Perhaps by this time tomorrow we can be on our way."

Letitia's eyes wavered at the thought.

Jerome saw her uneasiness and suspected why. Kanuga! He was anxious to return to America now that his daughter was back safe and sound on his ship. He cursed to himself this land and its inhabitants. Let the Russians and the Tlingit have it, he thought bitterly. He had discovered what the most important thing in life was to him—the welfare of the ones he loved.

His only regret was leaving Jonathan behind in his grave of ice.

Barbara didn't go directly to her cabin. Instead, she headed for Broderick's. She was determined to stay there until he returned. When he did, she would give him a piece of her mind! Although Letitia was no longer with Kangua at this moment, that did not mean that she would not return to him now that she had brought the news of Jonathan to her parents.

Stamping up to Broderick's door, she opened it with a jerk, startled to find him there, stretched out on the bed, seemingly asleep.

Barbara tore into a fit of rage and went to him. Grabbing hold of his shirt collar, she jerked his head around so that his eyes would be forced to look up at her. "What are you doing here?" she stormed. "Did you know that Letitia is here? No thanks to you! She came on her own, apparently, and brought news of Jonathan. What news do *you* bring, you sonofabitch?"

Broderick cowered beneath Barbara's angry stare, feeling as though he were in the presence of an evil witch. Never had he seen a woman look so wicked. There was more in her green eyes than he wanted to see. He suspected that if she had a weapon, she might even use it on him.

"You don't have to be so upset," he finally said, grabbing her wrist and easing her fingers from his collar. "Letitia didn't come aboard the ship on her own. I brought her."

Barbara stumbled away from him, her eyes wide. Then she scowled, tightening her jaw. "You're lying," she hissed.

"Go and ask her," Broderick said, rising from the bed. "And I didn't have to go into the Indian village to get her, either. I found her lying in the snow, unconscious."

"You what—?" Barbara gasped.

"She had fainted," Broderick said, shrugging. "She had seen Jonathan frozen in a wall of ice.

337

The shock apparently got the best of her."

"And you just had to be the one to rescue her?" Barbara said, placing her hands on her hips. She went to him and spoke up into his face. "Why didn't you just leave her there?"

"I saw more opportunities in rescuing her and bringing her back here to your family," Broderick said, giving her a shove away from him. "You bitch. I don't know why I ever saw any advantage to siding in with your schemes. After your behavior today, I'd say you're crazy."

"How dare you!" Barbara screamed, slapping him across the face.

As Broderick rubbed his burning cheek, his eyes flashed angrily down at Barbara. Then he grabbed her by the wrists and wrestled her to the floor. "I think you owe me something, little lady," he growled, moving over her. His hand reached to yank her dress up above her knees; then he cupped her mound of hair with one hand, thrusting a finger up inside her.

"You didn't steal her away from the Indian village like you were supposed to do," Barbara said, wrestling against his hold, yet becoming inflamed with desire from the sheer brute force of his treatment of her.

"She ain't with Kanuga any longer," Broderick said, brushing her lips with a kiss. "I'd say I had something to do with that. I didn't take her to Kangua when I found her. I brought her here."

"You should have let her die in the snow," Barbara said, her fingers fumbling with his breeches.

"You know she's going back to Kanuga. Then what about me?"

"You've got me, little lady," Broderick said, slipping his free hand down the front of her dress, kneading her breast. "The journey is long to America. Let's you and I take advantage of it. We wouldn't even have to leave the cabin. We could make love all night and all day."

Barbara's eyes rolled back in her head with pleasure as Broderick moved down to position his head between her thighs. She curled her fingers over his bald head and drew him closer, all fight drained from her. All she wanted now was the bliss that this man was promising her.

And then she was drawn quickly away from him when she heard a familiar voice shouting outside the door, in the corridor. Her heart began to pound, her eyes became wild as she scrambled to her feet.

"Kanuga!" she said, quickly straightening her clothes. "Kanuga is on the ship!"

"You stupid woman," Broderick grumbled, buttoning his breeches. "Don't you hear what he's shouting? He's shouting for Letitia! Not you! He's come for her! Not you!"

"I can change his mind," Barbara said, hurrying toward the door.

Broderick reached over to the table beside his bed and picked up an empty vodka bottle and threw it at the door just as Barbara placed her hand at the knob.

When it broke and shattered at her feet, even that did not stop her.

She rushed on out of the cabin, into the corridor, feeling faint with rapture when she found herself eye to eye with Kanuga.

Chapter Twenty-four

When I forget that the stars shine in air,
When I forget that beauty is in stars—
Shall I forget thy beauty.

—THOMSON

Kanuga stopped, stunned by Barbara's sudden appearance. Unaware of other cabin doors opening along the corridor, Kanuga and Barbara silently stared at one another.

Seeing Barbara made Kanuga remember her skills at making love, as though she were possessed by some demon. His gaze raked over her, seeing her still as entrancingly beautiful, yet not moved by her as he had been the other time that he had seen her. Not only had she seemed possessed, he had also, as though the spell that he had asked Kosko to cast over Letitia had been, instead, cast over Kanuga and the white woman with the slanted green eyes. It was as though it had been planned that way by Kosko. But why . . . ?

Barbara was quickly enraptured again by Kanuga's handsomeness, his penetrating silver eyes. They were so mysterious—so beautiful! She could not help herself. She flung herself into his arms, clinging tightly to him. "Take me away with you," she cried. "Before the others discover you here, please take me with you. I love you, Kanuga! I need you."

She placed her hands on each side of his face and drew his lips to hers and kissed him with a fevered passion.

But the kiss was short-lived. Kanuga clasped his fingers to her arms and set her bodily away from him and walked past her when he saw Letitia at the end of the corridor, watching. He ignored the insults Barbara threw at him.

He ignored Letitia's mother as she stood in the doorway of her cabin, seemingly too stunned to move.

He went toward Letitia and grabbed her up into his arms and turned to carry her away, but was stopped when Jerome was suddenly there, blocking the corridor, a shotgun aimed at Kanuga.

"Put her down," Jerome growled. "Do it. Do it now!"

Hardly even aware of her father's threat, thrilling inside over Kanuga's having ignored Barbara and that he was obviously not planning to take her away with him to be his second wife, Letitia gaped openly up at Kanuga. As she had suspected, Kosko had lied to her.

But why?

What would have been his motive?

She cast this wonder from her mind, so glad that Kanuga had come for her, proving once again how much he cared for her.

"My wife belongs with me," Kanuga said stiffly. "I have come to claim her. And as you see, she is not fighting to be released from my arms. She goes with me willingly."

Kimberly grabbed the door facing, the news that Letitia was Kanuga's wife causing a light-headedness to seize her. "No," she gasped. "Dear God no." Her eyes locked with Letitia's. "Tell me it's not true, Letitia. Tell me you didn't marry Kanuga."

Letitia clung around Kanuga's neck, her eyes wavering as she saw the hurt and frustration in her mother's eyes. "Mama, I love him," she murmured. "Please understand. You know what it means to love a man so much. You love father in such a way. Could you live without him, Mama? Could you?"

"Step aside and let us pass," Kanuga said flatly, not disturbed by the continued threat of the shotgun. "Your daughter is no longer your responsibility. She is mine."

Barbara rushed to Kanuga and grabbed his arm. "Kanuga, I can make you a better wife," she pleaded. "Leave Letitia here. Take me with you. Don't you remember the time we spent together? Didn't I show you my skills at making love? They are no less now. Let me show you,

Kanuga. You won't regret it."

Kanuga glowered down at Barbara. "You are a woman of no heart," he said. "Did you not hear that your cousin is now my wife? Do you not care that you are wronging her by asking me to turn my back on her?"

"I just want to be with you," Barbara cried, oblivious of so many eyes on her, staring disbelievingly at her. "I want to be your wife."

"I have a wife," Kanuga said flatly. "She is the only wife I will ever need!"

Tears filled Letitia's eyes, and a wondrous joy filled her heart at his declaration of love for her. Now she was certain Kosko had been lying! He was an evil shaman. She would have to warn Kanuga, soon. There was no telling what Kosko would do next to endanger perhaps both her and Kanuga's lives.

But for now, she was silently thanking God for sending Kanuga for her; she could now salvage her pride!

Barbara backed away from Kanuga and cowered against the wall, enraged by his rejection of her. Then she looked quickly over at Broderick as he cautiously opened the door and stared out. Anger flared in her eyes at the sight of him. He was responsible for bringing Kanuga and Letitia together again!

She lunged toward him and slapped him across the face. "You're a fool!" she screamed. "A blundering idiot! You were supposed to help me win Kanuga back. You were supposed to abduct Letitia—"

She stopped short, her face flooding with color when she realized that she had been saying things in her anger that should have never been revealed to her aunt and uncle.

She turned slowly around, wincing when she found their eyes on her, filled with disbelief that changed slowly to contempt.

Broderick rubbed his scalding cheek and watched Barbara as she fled to her cabin and slammed the door closed behind her.

He turned and looked at Kimberly, and then Jerome, glad that their attention had been drawn back to Kanuga, giving Broderick a reprieve, if only for a moment.

That damned Barbara, he thought angrily to himself, had said far too much. She had revealed that he had been involved in her schemes. He only hoped that in the shock of the moment, their concern would be mainly for their daughter and they would soon forget what Barbara had said about him.

He watched with much apprehension as Kanuga and Jerome stood immobile, staring at one another. He prayed to himself that Letitia would tell Kanuga why he had brought her to the American ship—that, in truth, he had saved her life! At this moment he was glad that he hadn't stolen Letitia from Kanuga's village again, no matter that he had lost Barbara's favor. Kanuga had let him live after the first abduction. If there had been two, and Letitia had lived to tell about it, Kanuga would have stopped at nothing to get Broderick off the ship—to kill him.

"Papa, please put the gun down," Letitia pleaded. "I want to go with Kanuga. Please allow it."

Kanuga gazed down at her, not knowing why she had left him again to return to the American ship. When he had found her gone and had seen no signs of a struggle in the longhouse, which meant that she had not been taken by force, he had known that he would find her with her parents!

He had to wonder if all American brides found it so hard to give up their parents for their husbands?

Perhaps this was one of their customs.

If so, it was a bad one, one that he could never accept.

"I can't let you go with him again," Jerome said, his voice breaking. "Letitia, how can I leave Alaska without you?"

"Papa, I know that it will be hard for you, the same as it will be for me," Letitia pleaded. "But we will just have to adjust to each other's absences. I'm Kanuga's wife. Nothing you do or say will make me change my mind about staying with him."

"But you *had* changed your mind," Kimberly interjected. "You returned to us. Why did you, if you hadn't planned to stay?"

"Mama, it is all because of one man's lie," Letitia said, feeling Kanuga's eyes suddenly on her. She gazed up at him. "It's because of Kosko, Kanuga. He lied to me. He told me that you were going to marry Barbara, because you wanted to have two wives. That is why I left, Kanuga. I couldn't bear the thought of sharing you with ... with anyone."

Kanuga's mouth opened with surprise. Why would Kosko interfere in his life in such a way? What was behind his lie? What other lies had Kosko told *him*? What sort of a man was he, who was revered by all of the Tlingit people, supposedly a man of truth, yet....

Kanuga swore to himself that he would find out all of these answers that were swimming around inside his mind about Kosko.

For now, he had Letitia's welfare in mind—and his own.

Kanuga glared at Jerome and started walking boldly toward him. He didn't look down at the shotgun, just kept his eyes steady with Jerome's.

And when he got within an arm's length of him, even then he did not slow his pace, except to take one wide step around Jerome and head for the companionway ladder.

Letitia held her breath when she heard her father turn and start walking behind her and Kanuga. Only when her mother's voice spoke up close behind her did Letitia look back. Fresh tears spilled from her eyes when she saw her mother hurrying toward her, Letitia's coat in her arms.

"You can't leave the ship without your wrap," Kimberly said, moving to Kanuga's side and keeping pace with him as she handed Letitia the coat. "Darling, I love you. I shall always love you!"

Letitia clasped the coat to her bosom. "As I

will always love you and Papa," she said, then lost sight of them as Kanuga swept her up the steps to the deck. He paused only long enough to place her on her feet, waiting then for her to put her coat on.

Then he grabbed her by the hand and rushed her down the gangplank to his waiting dog team.

Letitia was torn with feelings. A part of her was already missing her parents, and a part of her was blissfully happy to be with Kanuga again!

As she climbed into the sled, Kanuga fitting snug blankets and furs around her, she caught sight of her parents on the deck of the ship. Tears streaming from her eyes, she began waving at them and didn't stop until the sled was too far from the ship for her to see them any longer.

Then she settled into the warm furs, eager to return to the village and begin her life again as Kanuga's wife.

She frowned, wondering what part Kosko would play in their lives now that she had told Kanuga about his lie?

If the shaman was wise, he would already be gone from the Tlingit village—or soon face the wrath of his chief.

His shotgun still clutched in his hand, Jerome went and stood before Broderick, glowering. "I think it's time for you to leave the ship," he said, his voice emotionless. "I don't need you anymore. The ice is breaking up in the river. I plan to leave on the morrow for America. I don't wish to travel with such scum as you on the long voyage across the sea.''

Broderick paled. ''You can't order me from your ship,'' he stammered. ''You promised me asylum. I want to go to America with you. That's my home. I'm anxious to return and see my family.''

''Family?'' Jerome said, almost choking on his sudden laughter. ''You have family? The likes of you was surely born in the gutter.''

''Why have you changed your mind about me?'' Broderick said in a whine. ''Before, you seemed even eager for my friendship. What has changed?''

Jerome lifted the barrel of the shotgun and shoved it against Broderick's chest. ''You weasel, never did I offer you friendship,'' he snarled. ''I was using you only to get information about the Russian forts. And now that I don't plan to stay in Alaska, your usefulness has run out.''

He nudged Broderick harder in the chest with the rifle barrel. ''And do you think I am both blind and deaf?'' he said darkly. ''I heard what Barbara said to you. I saw her slap you. It's plain to see that she had conspired with you about Letitia. I'd hate to ask what she asked you to do. I don't think I'd like to know just exactly what my niece is capable of.''

Kimberly came to Jerome and placed her hand to the barrel of the shotgun and eased it aside, away from Broderick. ''Darling, I don't think he needs any more persuading,'' she murmured.

She cast Broderick a sideways glance, then

looked again at her husband. "He knows to leave now with no more back talk," she said smoothly. "Let him leave."

Broderick stood for a moment longer, staring from Kimberly back to Jerome; then he rushed inside his cabin and grabbed his coat. Without looking back, he fled quickly down the corridor and up the companionway ladder. Knowing that he had nowhere to go filled him with despair and frustration. Should he try to board the Russian ship, they would kill him. And should he try to enter the Tlingit village, they would either kill him or ignore him as though he were a non-person. His survival solely depended on himself and he knew not how he would achieve this.

He knew that being alone in Alaska was sometimes synonomous with death....

His dog team still where he had left it, Broderick quickly boarded the sled. Snapping the whip over the dogs' backs, he sorted through his mind for a way to get back into Kanuga's good graces.

Somehow he would manage it.

Kanuga was his only answer.

Resting the shotgun against the wall, Jerome drew Kimberly into his embrace. He held her tightly while she sobbed against his chest. "It'll be all right, darling," he murmured, himself having to hold back tears, but knowing that his wife needed his strength to lean upon, not his weaknesses.

He patted Kimberly's back. "There, there," he

crooned as she continued crying, her body wracked with the hard sobs. "Please stop. Letitia is happy. That's what you want, isn't it?"

Kimberly crept from his arms and looked pityingly up at her husband. She wiped tears from her eyes with the back of her hand, sniffling. "She did look radiant in her happiness, didn't she?" she said, her voice weak. "To know she is that happy should be my solace while away from her."

Jerome gently gripped her shoulders. "You must realize that we may never see her again," he said sadly. "Are you prepared for that reality, Kimberly?"

"I have no choice, do I?" she said, choking back another sob. "But, darling, must we return to America? Can't we stay in Alaska?"

Jerome's brow knitted into a deep frown. "Let me think about it for a while," he said thoughtfully. "Perhaps we could move up the river. Yes, let me think about it."

Kimberly flung herself back into her husband's arms. "Oh, thank you, darling," she cried. "Thank you so much."

He again held her away from him, looking her squarely in the eye. "I didn't say that we would stay," he said, his voice drawn. "I just said that I'd think about it."

He paused, then added, "Don't count on it, though, darling. Kanuga seems awful determined that no one live here but his people."

Kimberly glanced over at Barbara's closed door, then up at Jerome. "What about Barbara?"

she said, her voice almost failing at the memory of Barbara's performance only moments ago, and what she had revealed while she was so angrily attacking Broderick. It had revealed to Kimberly that Barbara was not deserving of the kindnesses that had been handed to her by her aunt and uncle. It was as though she were a misplaced person—no relation at all to the Wilsons!

"Barbara?" Jerome growled, staring at Barbara's door. He grew cold inside at the mere thought of his niece and the sort of person she had become. "I have to do some thinking on that subject, also. She's a hard one to figure out, that one. It's as though I have never known her."

He looked down at Kimberly, his eyes wavering. "Where did we go wrong?" he asked softly. "We gave her everything. Everything."

"Perhaps too much," Kimberly said. "It came easy—loving her."

"But do you now?" Jerome asked, sighing heavily.

"I've loved her too long not to," Kimberly said, fingering her wedding band. "She was that second child that we could never have."

"She's no longer a child, Kimberly," Jerome grumbled.

Kimberly smiled weakly up at him. "No, I think not," she murmured. She placed a hand at the crook of her back. "I must go and get some rest. I am suddenly very weary."

Jerome picked up his shotgun. "I think I'll join you," he said, his shoulders suddenly not as squared or his stride so steady. "I feel as though

I've been attacked by that bear again. The shocks we've experienced today were as bad as the physical wounds I experienced the day of the attack. God, will life ever be good to us again?''

They leaned into each other's embrace, taking from each other the comfort that was always there between them.

Chapter Twenty-five

The evil that men do live after them;
The good is oft interr'd with their bones.
                              —SHAKESPEARE

Letitia watched, wide-eyed, as Kanuga led the huskies on past their house, stopping instead in front of Kosko's house at the edge of the village. When he left the sled and went inside the house without first announcing himself, she became alarmed for his safety and tossed the furs aside and went after him.

Inside, she stopped and peered into the semi-darkness of the room. The only light in the room filtered down from the smoke-hole in the ceiling. Then she realized, at the same time Kanuga did that Kosko had fled. The house was empty—all of his shaman paraphernalia gone.

She watched as Kanuga knelt on one knee beside the ashes in the firepit, placing a hand over them.

"The ashes are still warm," he said, rising back to his full height. "That means that he has not gotten that far."

He went to Letitia and clasped his fingers gently to her shoulders. "I must go after him," he said quietly. "And you must come with me. I do not want to leave you alone until I know that Kosko is no longer a threat to you."

"Why is he doing these things?" Letitia asked. "I thought he was a holy man for your people. What has changed him?"

She paused, then added, "Or has he been like this all along and kept his true personality hidden?"

"He kept the dark side of himself hidden well," Kanuga agreed. "Next to my brother, I looked to Kosko as the favored of our people's shamans."

He dropped his hands to his sides and went to the door, peering out at the bright sunlight reflecting off the snow. "A demon must have taken possession of his soul," he said, his voice drawn. "But I wonder how long ago? What else has he done that is evil?"

He bowed his head. "I doubt now that I will ever know."

Letitia moved to his side. "Do you truly want to take the time to go after him?" she murmured. "Perhaps it is best to let him go and leave the questions you have about him unanswered. He is gone. Surely he won't return. If he knew that you had gone for me, he would have fled to keep himself free of your scorn—and punishment—for the evil deed. For Kanuga, he knows that I will tell you everything."

"Yes, he knows," Kanuga said, gazing down at Letitia. "And that is why I must find him. He will blame you for having to flee his people. He will hate you. When an evil man—a man who is possessed by demons—hates, there are spells that he can cast on the object of his hatred."

Kanuga's eyes suddenly became two points of fire. His jaw tightened at the memory of how he had taken Barbara to his bed, as though some unseen force had been there, guiding him into doing it. That entire night was a blur to him, as though it had never happened—yet he knew that it had.

Yes, he thought angrily to himself, surely Kosko had cast a spell over him instead of Letitia, as Kanuga had requested. Kosko had caused him to forget about Letitia, and to hunger for another woman.

"Come," he said, between clenched teeth. "It is time to go."

"Where will you look for him?" Letitia asked, cupping a hand over her eyes as the sun momentarily blinded her when she stepped outside.

She followed Kanuga's eyes, seeing them focused on sled and dog marks in the snow, which led away from Kosko's house.

"He is not a clever man as he is *chla-kass*— bad," Kanuga said, helping Letitia into the sled. "The foolish man. He left a trail for me to follow."

Letitia wrapped herself in the furs as Kanuga positioned himself on the sled behind her. She braced herself for the lurch of the sled as Kanuga snapped his whip over the huskies' heads, then watched the tracks in the snow as Kanuga led his dogs beside them.

She then looked into the distance, where the mountains were steeped in beauty and mystery. Soon the forests that surrounded the mountains, and those that lay in their shadow, would lose their shrouds of snow. Everything would be green, welcome after the never-ending white blanket of snow that Letitia had not been able to get used to.

She had to wonder if Kosko had gone to those mountains to hide. If so, it would be virtually impossible to find him.

She glanced over her shoulder at Kanuga, wondering how long he would pursue Kosko.

She hoped not for long.

She didn't see the shaman as worth the trouble!

Yet, she knew that it was for Kanuga's peace of mind that he was driven to find Kosko. And when he found him, she wondered, what then?

Would he kill Kosko with his bare hands?

Or would Kanuga return Kosko to his village and let the people decide his fate?

Letitia's head was jerked around quickly when just up ahead she saw something familiar to her. The abandoned igloo—where she and Kanuga had made love, not only once, but twice! It appeared not to be abandoned any longer. Smoke was spiraling slowly up from the smoke hole. She shifted her eyes and discovered a sled and huskies outside the igloo.

And then she gasped when a man ran from the igloo and boarded the sled. She was close enough now to see who it was as he turned and stared at Kanuga's approaching sled, then turned to his huskies and sent them into a frenzied run as he snapped the whip over their heads.

It was Kosko!

His ground-length gray hair trailing after him, and the long, strangely designed robe that hung beneath the fur coat, proved that it was the evil shaman!

He had apparently taken momentary refuge in the igloo, surely never expecting Kanuga to come after him—at least not this soon.

Letitia grabbed hold of the sides of the sled as Kanuga sent his dogs in a maddening chase after Kosko. The air stung her cheeks as it rushed past her. She felt a sudden sick feeling at the pit of her stomach and covered her mouth with a hand, gulping hard to keep from retching, yet filled with wonder over why she felt so strangely. A sled ride had never bothered her before. Nor had the excitement of danger!

Her hand went to her abdomen and her eyes widened. "Can I be pregnant . . . ?" she whispered to herself, knowing that this month's bleeding had not yet begun.

Her eyes brightened with the thought. She knew how badly Kanuga wanted a child. And they both needed something positive in their lives to outweigh the bad that seemed to be constantly happening to them.

A child, she marveled to herself.

If only it were true!

Her attention was drawn from the wonders of her possible pregnancy, to what Kanuga was getting ready to do. He had grabbed his rifle up from his sled. He was aiming it!

She jumped with alarm as he fired it, watching Kosko to see if Kanuga's aim had been accurate!

Then she realized that Kanuga had not shot directly at Kosko. Instead, he had fired just over his head, a warning to stop.

Letitia scarcely breathed, watching to see if Kosko would stop. When he didn't, Kanuga fired another shot.

Letitia's eyes widened, and she gasped when she saw Kosko's whip snap suddenly in two, realizing that Kanuga had taken perfect aim, purposely disabling the man by shooting his whip in half, so that he would have no control over his huskies.

She waited and watched for the huskies to come to a stop, and when they did, she glanced back at Kanuga. He was smiling smugly as he urged his own dogs onward.

She turned her gaze back to Kosko, hearing Kanuga laughing into the wind as the shaman jumped from his sled and began running along the banks of the river, yet surely smart enough to know that he could not outrun a trained set of huskies.

And soon they were just behind Kosko. Kanuga aimed and fired another deliberate shot over the shaman's head, causing Kosko to stop and turn with a start, pleading at Kanuga with his faded gray eyes as Kanuga stopped the sled and jumped from it.

Kosko took a few cautious steps backwards as Kanuga approached him. "I should have known you would follow," he said, his eyes narrowed with hate. He glared at Letitia as she stepped from the sled. "And you. You will be sorry that you did not stay with your people and return to America with them. Our ways are different. You will not adapt well enough."

He glared up at Kanuga again, still moving away from him. "And you," he said, his voice a low hiss. "Just like your brother, your powers were stronger than mine. In time, had I been given the chance, I would have removed your powers, as did I Atkuk's."

Kanuga's eyes became even more rage-filled at the mention of his brother. "And how did you do that?" he said, his teeth clenched. "What spell did you cast over him?"

"No spell was cast," Kosko said, his eyes gleaming into Kanuga's.

But Kosko didn't get the chance to go further with his confession. His feet began slipping on the snow, at the edge of the embankment, and soon he found himself toppling over, falling backwards onto the ice in the river.

Kanuga stood for a moment, watching the shaman's fear building as he tried to get back to his feet, only slipping back down, over and over again.

"Help me," Kosko cried, reaching out for Kanuga. "I feel the ice weakening beneath my weight."

Kanuga saw the true danger, then realized the full extent of it when the dull thud of breaking ice filled the serene spring air. He started to bend over, to grab Kosko's hand, but gasped and stared disbelievingly as the ice opened suddenly and the river seemingly swallowed the shaman whole as he plunged into its depths.

Letitia covered her mouth with her hand, watching, horrified, as Kosko was quickly sucked into the swift current and began floating away beneath the ice that had not cracked. A sickness grabbed her at the pit of her stomach as she watched Kosko, his eyes looking wildly up at her through the ice, his fingers clawing at the ice above him.

And then Kosko was gone. Letitia was numb, horrified at the thought of dying such a death as that. She welcomed Kanuga's strong arms as they engulfed her, drawing her against him.

"It's so horrible," she said, clinging to him. "Although he was an evil man, no one should have to die so horribly!"

"His life was ruled by demons," Kanuga said softly. "A violent death was to be expected."

He circled his arm around her waist and led her to the sled, helping her on to it. After attaching Kosko's dog team to his own, he made a wide circle in the snow and headed back to his village, filled with wonder over what Kosko had said about his brother. What had he meant?

He shook his head mournfully, realizing that now he would never know what Kosko had done to his brother.

Then his eyes widened and pain circled his heart, remembering the moment of his brother's death. With the knife protruding from his back, he had tried to tell Kanuga who had murdered him, but his breath had been sucked away by death much too quickly.

Kosko! He had killed his brother! Kanuga concluded.

But why?

Then it came to him—something else that Kosko had said. Something about Kanuga's and Atkuk's powers being greater than his....

He shook his head sadly, now realizing not only who had killed his brother, but why....

But knowing who had killed his brother did not make missing him any more bearable. In fact, it pained him even more.

Letitia was relieved when they were finally home. Arm in arm, they entered their house and were stunned to find Athas, the village's only remaining shaman, there, sitting beside the fire, waiting for them.

Kanuga stepped away from Letitia and went to Athas, looking at him questioningly. "Why have you come?" he asked, slipping out of his heavy fur garment.

Athas rose to his feet, facing Kanuga with a solemn face. "Kosko is dead," Athas said.

Letitia moved to Kanuga's side, as stunned as he that the shaman would know that Kosko was dead, when only she and Kanuga had been witness to the death.

"How do you know that he is?" Kanuga asked.

"The evil spell that he cast over me was broken a short while ago," Athas said. "It is because at the moment of his death, my soul was set free of the spell. I have come to tell you many things that Kosko has done. While under his spell, I was made not to speak freely of his evil ways."

Kanuga gestured toward the mats on the floor. "Sit," he said. "We will talk."

Letitia removed her coat and laid it aside, then sat down beside Kanuga, looking across the fire at the shaman as he sat down.

"Kosko cast a spell over you also, Kanuga," Athas continued. "But of course you know that now."

"Yes, I know that, and I have rectified the wrong that he tried to do," Kanuga said, folding his arms across his chest. "My wife sits by my side again."

"Your brother can never sit with you again, sharing in talk and laughter," Athas said. "That, too, is because of Kosko!"

Kanuga leaned forward, his eyes slowly filling with rage. "You knew that Kosko killed my brother?" he said, his jaw tightening.

Letitia looked suddenly at Kanuga, shocked. What did he mean? He had never told her that Kosko had killed Atkuk, and that was something that Kanuga would have told her. He did not keep secrets from her, especially those that had to do with his brother's death!

Then she recalled what Kosko had been saying just before he fell into the river. From that, Kanuga had assumed the worst.

Her eyes were drawn back to the shaman as he resumed talking.

"Yes, I knew that Kosko killed Atkuk," he said solemnly, his eyes wavering. "Also the son of the Russian colonel. And the warrior who was assigned to guard Iuril, to make it look as though he killed himself after killing Iuril!" He paused, then added sorrowfully, "He also set fire to your house. He wanted you and your wife to die in that fire, Kanuga."

In the face of such truths, Kanuga was momentarily stunned speechless. Then he said, "You knew all of this, yet you did not come forward?" he growled.

"The spell that Kosko cast on me was one of strong magic," Athas replied, again casting his eyes downward. "I knew everything that he did, as though his magic brought it to my mind's eye. I saw everything enacted before me as if I had been there, in person, seeing it."

Athas raised his eyes to meet the anger in Kanuga's. "But the evil forces behind Kosko's spells kept me from being able to tell about it," he said. "When he died, the spell was broken. I have come forth, to tell you the truth, even knowing that you might choose to banish me from the tribe for having held so much uglinesses from you."

Kanuga was still numb from these truths. He sympathized with Athas, who had been forced to live lies, because of Kosko's evil powers, because hadn't Kosko even cast one of them on him?

He had almost lost Letitia because of it!

"No matter what your plans are for me, you should also know that Kosko had persuaded me that Atkuk was the evil sorcerer in our village," Athas said. "Kosko and I had meetings. We plotted against your brother! But all along it was Kosko who was the sorcerer! And he knew the ways of sorcery well! I am shamed, my chief, that I had a part in any of it. Please believe that it was innocently done—that my mind was not mine at that time and my heart had been turned to stone because of Kosko's evil!"

Letitia watched as Kanuga rose slowly to his feet and went to Athas and placed his hand on his shoulder. Tears sprang to her eyes, seeing him again as such a compassionate, caring, understanding man, when he began talking to the man in a quiet voice.

"You will not be banished from our tribe," Kanuga said, now drawing Athas up and embracing him to prove that he had forgiven this thing that had not been of Athas' doing. "You are not at fault here. And none of our people will ever know that you were a part of Kosko's plan. As I could not tell, no one else of our village knew that you were anything but a caring shaman. And so it shall be from now on. Cast from your mind and heart this evil that was forced upon you. Go among our people and spread the love that you always have."

Athas looked up at Kanuga with admiration

and devotion in his eyes. "Thank you," he said humbly.

Athas placed a hand on Kanuga's arm. "I knew that Kosko was dead, because I was released from the spell at the moment of his departure from this earth," he said. "But I do not know *how* he died."

Kanuga's eyes got a faraway look in them, then his lips tugged into a slow, sure smile. "He is not traveling peacefully to the Land of the Hereafter," he said. "The river swallowed him, trapping him beneath the ice. I last saw him struggling beneath the ice as the current carried him away from me. At last, we are rid of him *and* his evil ways!"

Athas embraced Kanuga again, then to Letitia's delight, went to her and shared the same affection as he also gave her warm hugs.

And after he was gone, she went to Kanuga and framed his face between her hands.

"How are you feeling about things now?" she murmured.

"Torn," Kanuga said, looking down at her. "I do not understand what caused Kosko to do these things to us all. How could Kosko have been this evil?"

"Darling, if it is possible to cast evil spells, then don't you think that he was under some spell himself?" Letitia murmured. "Perhaps this demon claimed Kosko's soul while he was being carried in the womb of his mother."

Suddenly it came to her that she had felt nauseated while searching for Kosko in the sled. She started to break the news to Kanuga that she thought she might be pregnant, knowing that this news would make his other burdens less.

But just as she began to speak, she felt a hot wetness between her thighs and realized that no, she was not pregnant at all. Her monthly bleeding had just begun. The nausea had perhaps been brought on by all of the excitement of these past several days.

"Let us place all of this behind us," Kanuga said, his mind suddenly transported to how he had wrongly accused Colonel Golodoff of so much, thinking that he had done these things to avenge his own son's death. How could he have been wrong about so many things? It seemed that the only thing he had been right about lately was knowing that Letitia loved him as devotedly as he loved her.

He drew her into his gentle embrace. "I love you so much," he murmured. "So very, very much."

He kissed her gently, all of the wrongs in the world suddenly not as important to him as they had been only moments ago.

Letitia was there, his wonderful, sweet Letitia....

Chapter Twenty-six

A moment all will be life again
  —one moment more
The death cry drowning in the battle's roar.
                                    —BYRON

THREE MONTHS LATER

The snow was thick on the ground again; the bitter air rattled the trees outside. Stew was simmering over the hot coals of the fire, emitting a pleasant aroma in the longhouse.

Content to be Kanuga's wife, Letitia sat beside him, an astute student as he taught her many things that a Tlingit wife should know, to help the husband in his everyday life. She had already learned how to prepare many Tlingit meals, how to make traps and snares, and how to scrape and stretch pelts needed for clothing and for making bags and overshoes.

She watched attentively as Kanuga chewed the edges of a fox skin, then took it as he offered it to her.

"To soften the leather so that the bone needle will go through it, you must chew the skin as I have just shown you," Kanuga instructed.

Letitia placed the skin to her lips, shuddering as its strong aroma curled her nose. She couldn't tell exactly what the smell was, hoping it wasn't blood. She did not like to think of having to kill the tiny animals, but she knew that the Tlingits' survival depended on it.

She sank her teeth into the skin and began chewing the edges, in the same fashion that she had seen Kanuga chew, finding that this put her teeth on edge, and quickly dried her mouth out.

She couldn't help but think about the sharp needles that had always been in her mother's sewing basket in the parlor back home in New York. Even such conveniences as that had been taken for granted!

But she continued chewing along the full length of the skin, returning Kanuga an awkward smile as he smiled at her.

Then a commotion outside startled Letitia into dropping the skin, and looking at Kanuga with alarm. These past months things had been peaceful in the Tlingit village. The Russian ship had left, and Letitia's father's ship also had left Alaskan waters. It saddened her still, knowing that

Kanuga had not given her parents permission to stay.

Yet, she understood. He had already been forced to share too much with too many that were not of his skin coloring or heritage.

Kanuga rushed to his feet as a voice shouted his name outside the door. He flung on his beaver cloak, gave Letitia a troubled frown, then went outside, leaving her by the fire, her face white with worry.

Kanuga eyed his warriors warily when he found so many standing outside the door, their rifles clutched in their hands, their eyes filled with concern. "What is it?" he asked, looking from man to man. "What brings so many of you to my door? What is the need for weapons?"

One of his most trusted scouts stepped away from the others, eye to eye with Kanuga. "We bring troubling news, my chief," he said glumly. "It is something that we saw while searching for caribou. You will find the news quite distressing."

"What did you see?" Kanuga asked, glancing down at Letitia as she stepped to his side, clutching a cloak around her shoulders.

"A white man's ship," the scout said, looking slowly over at Letitia. "I do not know if it is Russian or American." Then he glared at Kanuga. "Not only did we discover a ship, but also a fort along our shores! The white man has returned! We must not allow it!"

Letitia issued a slight gasp and placed a hand to her throat, wondering if her father had returned—or had he never left at all?

Had he gone against Kanuga's orders so blatantly?

Had he done so just to be close to her, yet not let her know that he was?

Yet, it could be Colonel Golodoff.

It could be anyone!

Whoever it was, she was filled with dread, for she knew that Kanuga would not stand for it. There had been too much peace these past months to allow anyone to disturb it ever again!

The news had stunned Kanuga speechless. But the longer he stood there, going over and over again in his mind the possible repercussions of this discovery, the more his eyes became filled with rage.

And then he doubled a hand into a tight fist and thrust it into the air. "Prepare for war!" he shouted. "We will rid the land of the parasites again. But this time there will be no talking. There will be warring! I have had enough of being patient with these invaders of our land! I will see that they leave this time, once and for all!"

Loud, excited shouts filled the air as the warriors raced off to go to their houses, to dress themselves in warring attire.

Kanuga turned to Letitia and took her hands in his. "I know that you are thinking the ship could be your father's," he said. "No matter if it is, we must force him to leave. If he stayed, others would come after him. Then Alaska would become white man's territory, not Tlingit."

"I understand why you feel the need to do this,"

Letitia said, pleading with her eyes. "But, Kanuga, please reconsider. If it is my father, my mother will also be at the fort. If you attack them, you—you will more than likely kill them both. I could not bear losing them, especially knowing that I was partially the cause!"

"No one is at fault except those who went against my orders," Kanuga said, his voice a low growl. "And, my woman, as before, you will accompany me on this mission. If you must, you will pull the trigger that snuffs the life from the Americans." He paused, then added, "Even if it is your father who has raised a firearm against the Tlingit!"

Letitia paled and her body swayed as a lightheadedness swept through her. She steadied herself and shook her head slowly back and forth. "I cannot do this thing you ask of me today," she murmured. "You cannot expect me to! Before you, Kanuga, my family was my world!"

"I am now your family! I am now your world!" Kanuga said, gripping her hands more tightly. "And what must be done to preserve my people's future must be done, no matter who is forced to fight or die today. And so shall you fight. You are now Tlingit, for you are wed to a Tlingit chieftain!"

"But, Kanuga, this is different," Letitia persisted, not willing to lose this fight with Kanuga. It was true that her commitment was to Kanuga—even more so now than before. But there was another commitment that she must think about! She had only these past few days realized that she was finally with child!

She had planned to tell Kanuga today. Now the waiting would be delayed, for this was not the sort of atmosphere that she had planned for breaking the wonderful news to him!

"You cannot expect me to fight my own parents, if they are the ones at the fort," she said softly.

She paused and pleaded up at him with her eyes. "And must you kill them?" she blurted.

"You will fight at my side. And if they do not leave peacefully, yes, whoever fires against the Tlingit will be killed," Kanuga said, easing his hands from hers. "Now, my wife, come. It is time to prepare ourselves for warring."

The usual spring to Letitia's steps was gone as she went with Kanuga into their house.

"Sit beside the fire," Kanuga instructed her. "I must paint your face for warring."

Wide-eyed, Letitia gaped up at him. "I must even do that?" she said, her voice breaking.

"Yes, that also," Kanuga said, bringing to her a wooden case, from which he took three smaller wooden containers of paint that he had prepared from the plants available for the various colors.

Dispirited, Letitia eased down onto a mat and sat straight-backed and stiff-shouldered as Kanuga knelt before her. He thrust his fingers into one of the containers, then brought them out, highly colored with a brilliant blue paint. He placed his fingers to her face and slowly applied the paint in a streak across one cheek, and then the other. This was repeated until there were also yellow and red streaks on her cheeks.

Then Kanuga turned to her. "You will apply the same to my face," he said, leaning close to her.

Her fingers trembling, convinced that she must look hideous, Letitia painted Kanuga's face in long, jagged streaks, then wiped her hands on a cloth that he had used to cleanse his fingers.

"And now we must hurry and get into our battle gear," he said, rushing to his feet. "I hear the warriors assembling outside. We soon will return home again, victorious!"

Kanuga helped Letitia into her armor, the thick, wooden armor consisting of rows of slats laced together with rawhide. Then he placed her helmet on her head, with its protruding beak and gaping jaws.

He stepped away from her, smiling. "And now you are ready," he said. He hurried into his own battle gear, then went to his weapons and chose two of his most powerful rifles. Going to Letitia, he placed one in her hand.

Letitia looked through the slits in her helmet and felt sick inside when she realized that soon she would be expected to fire the weapon against another human being—perhaps even her parents!

For the first time since she had made the decision to become Kanuga's wife, she found herself wondering about her sanity for having done it! How could she be expected to do this thing that he asked of her today?

Yet, she knew that she must. She was committed to Kanuga.

And she loved him!

But just how far must her commitment and proof of her loving him go?

When it came right down to it, if she found herself face to face with the decision of firing upon *any* human being, could she? Even if Kanuga was at her side, watching to see if she performed as was expected of her?

Then the thought of the child that was just beginning to form in her womb entered her thoughts again, reminding her that it was not so much Kanuga that she must survive for. It was for their child!

She would do anything to make sure nothing happened to it.

"Kanuga, I have another reason why I should not join the fight with you," she blurted out, having only one more chance that he might exclude her from it.

"You are my wife," he said stubbornly. "You will fight at my side."

"And what of our unborn son?" she dared to say. "Do you wish that he also join the fight? Would you take the chance of losing this son before you ever see or hold him? Would you chance losing this son that is to be the future leader of your people?"

Kanuga clasped his fingers onto her shoulders. "What are you saying?" he said, his jaw tight.

"Kanuga, I was going to tell you tonight, while we were snuggled beside the fire, that I am with child," Letitia said, forcing back the urge to cry. "This child *could* be a son—the son that you so badly want. Please let us not do anything to chance my losing him. Please don't expect me to fight alongside you. I want this child as badly as you."

Kanuga dropped his hands to his sides. He had always envisioned this moment, when he was told that his wife was with child, as something beautiful!

And no!

Because of these intruders onto his land, he had to be told about his child while he and his wife both wore battle gear!

Somehow that made it ugly!

He looked away from her, then back at her again. "A child?" he said thickly. "We are going to have a child?"

"Yes, my darling," Letitia said, reaching for his hand and taking it into hers. "So you see why I feel it is not best for me to go into battle with you?"

"And you won't," Kanuga said flatly.

She wanted to lunge into his arms, to hug him while thanking him, but their armor kept them apart. "Oh, Kanuga, thank you," she said. "Now I can take off this dreaded battle gear."

"You must leave it on," he said flatly.

"Why must I, if I am staying here?" Letitia asked, fearing his answer.

"You will accompany me to the fort, but stay behind in the sled as I go into battle," he said. "I will not leave you behind at our village while foreigners are near. I will not take a chance that you will be abducted again." He paused, then added, "Nor our child."

Letitia sighed heavily, but did not fight this decision of his, at least glad that she was not going to have to take up arms—perhaps against her own father and mother.

The sled ride was a long and tedious one, the fort having been built much farther down the river than Fort Anecia. Weary from the long day, and cold from the never-ending blast of wind against her fur-wrapped body, Letitia tried to draw the furs more snugly around her.

Sighing heavily, she gazed at the other warriors leading their dog teams across the white sheet of snow. She shivered at the sight, thinking that with their slat armor and wolf and raven head helmets, they resembled a pack of gargoyles sprung to malevolent life!

Her gloved hand went to her own helmet, knowing that she did not look any less monstrous herself!

She gazed heavenward. The sky was becoming diffused with a pale, pink light as the sun crept lower and lower toward the horizon. Soon it would be dark. Soon the chill would be twofold.

"Oh, but if only this could soon be over with!" Letitia whispered to herself.

Her heart leapt fearfully into her throat when up ahead she saw the fort that had just come into sight. She became tense and looked over her shoulder when Kanuga stopped the huskies at the

Cassie Edwards

top of a hill, the warriors on all sides of him following his lead.

Kanuga went to Letitia and looked down at her through the slits in his helmet. "We warriors will go the rest of the way by foot. But I will return soon," he said. "And do not fret. After the battle is over, our child will still have a father, for only the Tlingit will be victorious today!"

Letitia so badly wanted to give him a hug and kiss, but the dreaded armor was in the way. "God speed," she murmured, choking back a sob when he left with his warriors.

She watched as they cascaded down the hill, gaining momentum with every bound. She craned her neck to see farther, but the helmet was in the way.

Without further thought, she jerked it off and lay it aside, then became tense as she watched as Kanuga and his men approached the fort. She was able to see right into the opened gate of the fort, which would give her a full view of the battle that would soon erupt.

She screamed when muskets suddenly flamed from the fort, but was relieved when the bullets bounced off the Indian armor. She chewed on her lower lip as she watched Kanuga and his warriors run through the wide gate before those at the fort were able to close it.

Numb, Letitia sat there and continued watching, feeling helpless. Daylight was still stubbornly clinging to the sky, allowing her to witness Kanuga and his warriors exchanging gunfire with the defenders of the fort. Cannons roared.

Muzzle flames danced through blossoms of smoke, the reports of the firing echoing across the land like roaring thunder.

Letitia did not want to lose sight of Kanuga, but she could not help but search around with her eyes, trying to see who the true occupants of the fort were.

Russians?

Or Americans?

At this distance it was impossible to tell, yet she did not see anyone she recognized, which made her have some hope that her father had not returned only to find himself battling the Tlingit to the death.

Letitia screamed when a man lunged for Kanuga from the door of the main building, then dropped to his feet when Kanuga shot him in the chest.

Wild-eyed, she watched as the occupants of the fort crumpled to the right and left of Kanuga and his warriors as they tried to rush from the building. She looked upward, at the second story of the building, where the men were replying to the Indians' gunfire as best they could, dividing this time between shooting and throwing the numerous flaming torches the Tlingit had thrown into their midst back out through the window.

But it seemed to Letitia that such efforts were too little and too late. The hungry flames greedily consumed the logs, until the whole upper story was a seething inferno.

Desperate, singed defenders jumped to the ground below, seemingly preferring a quick death from the Tlingit guns to the torment of roasting alive.

The main building's lower floor seemed to be the last pocket of the enemy's resistance. Then the licking flames, like a dragon's breath, sent those men outside, to be met by a swarm of howling Tlingit, Kanuga at the lead.

Suddenly another man appeared from the burning building, waving a white flag of surrender.

The firing ceased and the Tlingit surrounded all of those at the fort who had not yet been killed.

Unable to stand being away from Kanuga any longer, and having seen the white flag, which meant that the danger to her and her unborn child was over, Letitia left the sled in a bounce. She quickly placed her snowshoes on and hurried down the hill, then breathlessly reached the wide gate which led inside, where blood pooled along the ground.

Letitia kept her eyes directly ahead, not wanting to see the death strewn all around her. She was afraid that if she looked closely enough she might find some familiar faces.

Oh, Lord, she thought woefully, she might even find her father among the dead!

Perhaps even her mother!

Yet she took comfort from knowing that she had not seen any women among those who had fled the buildings.

She hurried to Kanuga's side, but he did not show any signs of being aware of her presence. He had removed his helmet and was staring at the man who still stood there with the flag of surrender, drawing Letitia's eyes to the man also. She raised an eyebrow, wondering who he was. He had most certainly captivated Kanuga!

"Colonel Golodoff," Kanuga said in a low growl. "You returned. And now you are a defeated man. Would it not have been better if you returned to your homeland a man who had not been stripped of all of his pride?"

Letitia's eyes widened, relief flooding her when she discovered that this man was the Russian colonel. It was wonderful to know that it had been the Russians defeated today—not the Americans. It brought joy to her heart to know that her parents were somewhere else, safe.

She glanced at Kanuga, so happy that he was safe! His valiant fighting had even assured a future of happinesses for them and their child!

Proud of her husband, she stood beside him, seeing how he further handled this situation— this confrontation with the Russian colonel— hopefully for the last time.

"I could not stay away," Colonel Golodoff said grimly. "And, Kanuga, we shared the land before. I could not see why it could not be possible again. I had planned not to set traps close to your village. I had ordered my men to kill only those animals that were necessary to meet our quota for trading."

"That would be one animal too many," Kanuga said, then took the flag from the colonel. "Leave. Take those that are still alive. Because of the friendship you shared with my father, I let you go today. And because I admire you as a man, I—"

A shot rang out suddenly. Colonel Golodoff grabbed at his chest, his eyes wildly looking at Kanuga. Blood curling around his clutching fingers, he crumpled to the ground. His body convulsed, then he lay still, his eyes locked in a death trance.

Kanuga and Letitia stared down at the colonel, stunned, then turned together as a voice spoke up behind them.

Broderick Bowman, carrying a smoking pistol and sporting a wide grin on his face, stepped forward through the silent Tlingit. "I have rid the earth of the Russian for you," he boasted. "I did this for you, Kanuga, to prove to you that I am a true friend of the Tlingit!"

Enraged over the cowardly act of shooting an unarmed man—a man who had just surrendered and who was an old friend of his father's—so needlessly, Kanuga raised his rifle and pulled the trigger.

Broderick's eyes widened in surprise as he grabbed at his chest, blood spurting from the wound. He fell to the ground, gasping for air.

Kanuga did not wait to see him die, yet he knew that he had rendered him a mortal wound. He walked Letitia back to the sled, his warriors obediently following. Soon they were headed home, singing victory songs.

Letitia rested her hand over her abdomen, thankful to be safe again.

Chater Twenty-seven

Our actions are our own;
Their consequences belong to Heaven.

—FRANCIS

NEW YORK

Barbara hung her head over the wash basin again, retching until she was weak.

Once she found some reprieve, she went to bed and stretched out on her back, holding a cold compress to her brow. She listened for the faint footsteps of her aunt as she came to the door and opened it. Her aunt and uncle had taken pity on her when they had been told that she was pregnant and not doing at all well under the circumstances. She was to have full bed rest for the next six months.

And she didn't know whose child it was.

She had been with two men.

Broderick Bowman and Kanuga.

"And how are you doing today, dear?" Kimberly asked, coming to stand over Barbara's bed. "My, but you are so pale. Can I get you some more chicken soup?"

Barbara looked up at Kimberly and groaned.

Chapter Twenty-eight

An assignation sweetly made,
With gentle whispers in the dark.

—FRANCIS

ALASKA

The fires were ablaze in all four firepits in the
feast house, filling the air not only with golden
light, but a pleasant warmth. Having joined the
dancers in the feast house, who were celebrating
the victory over the Russians, Letitia was laughing, feeling disjointed and awkward as she tried
to keep time with the beating of the drums. Kanuga, dressed in only a loincloth, leapt around
Letitia, his eyes gleaming into hers.

"I shall never learn the art of Tlingit dancing,"
Letitia said, breaking away from the circle of men

and women who were dressed in all assortments of interesting costumes.

Winded, she went back to the fur-piled settee and sat down, Kanuga soon there beside her.

Kanuga gazed down at Letitia's flushed cheeks, then lower still, at how her breasts strained against her white doeskin dress. Already he could see that being with child was changing her, making her even more desirable.

"My woman, you cannot rush into the learning," he said, pulling her into his arms. "In time, it will all come to you. For now, let us concentrate on our child. It is to be a magical time for us, experiencing your body changing from day to day."

"I will become ugly in my hugeness," Letitia said, snuggling close. "Will you still love me, even then?"

"How could I not love you, then as now?" he said seriously. "It will be a feast for my eyes, this larger woman who carries our child within her womb."

Letitia started to reply, but was stopped when a warrior came to Kanuga, smiling broadly. "It is time to challenge my chief to a wrestling match," the warrior said, reaching a hand to Kanuga. "Come. Join me. Let our people enjoy the challenge." His eyes danced as he looked over at Letitia, then back at Kanuga. "Should I win, your woman is mine!"

Mortified, Letitia's lips parted with a gasp as Kanuga accepted the challenge, not giving her even a glance as he slipped away from her arms and went to the center of the feast house, standing face to face with his challenger. The Tlingit people made a wide circle around them. The drums beat softly in the background, and the air filled with apprehension.

Numb and pale, Letitia watched Kanuga and the warrior begin wrestling. Kanuga soon had the warrior in a locked position against the floor, only then to be on the bottom, the warrior holding him down, smiling devilishly at him.

Over and over again they took turns overtaking the other, Letitia's breath catching every time it looked as though the warrior was going to be the winner.

She could not believe that Kanuga had accepted such a challenge, in which she was a pawn, the prize for the victor! Only a moment ago, Kanuga had been telling her that he would love her no matter if she got fat and ugly—yet he was so willing to give her away should he lose the wrestling match?

She now doubted his love for her if he could gamble her away so easily!

Aghast at the thought of being with another man for eternity, should Kanuga lose, she continued watching the match, and died a slow death inside when Kanuga came up the loser.

When the victor looked her way, smiling, Letitia scrambled to her feet and began running away, but when she reached the door, she jumped with alarm when the warrior appeared, blocking her way.

"You are now mine," he said, grabbing a cloak

from a peg on the wall and wrapping it around her. "You will now accompany me to my dwelling."

Letitia did not want to risk fighting him, fearing for her unborn child. She looked forlornly over her shoulder at Kanuga, who gave her a smile which she could not understand. She wanted to run to him and plead with him to explain, but she was soon ushered out into the cold of the night to the warrior's house.

Letitia moved quickly to the firepit and soaked up the warmth of the fire, yet even that could not help the cold she felt inside. Disillusioned, she eased herself onto a pallet of furs, clasping to the cloak around her as though it could protect her from what might transpire in the next moments. She would not even look the warrior's way, afraid that he might be disrobing. If she was forced to go to bed with him, she would soon find a knife and end it for herself—and her child!

"You will stay," the warrior said, bending down so that his face was directly before her eyes. "I must return to the challenge that is not yet over."

Letitia looked eagerly into his eyes. "What do you mean?" she asked, hope springing forth within her.

"Kanuga lost the first round," the warrior said, smiling smugly. "It is only fair that I give him a chance to win the second."

"Then you are saying that I am not solely yours?" Letitia asked, her voice rising in pitch. "This is . . . this is just another custom that I must get used to? If so, it is a cruel one!"

"Before the night is out, Kanuga can win you back many times," the warrior said. "But I can, also." He touched her face gently. "Do not fret. It is only a game. In the end, Kanuga will be the victor. He is the chief, is he not?"

"Why do this at all, if you already know who will be the victor in the end?" Letitia said, slapping his hand away from her face. "Why did you bring me to your house? Why wasn't I allowed to stay and watch until the end?"

"Because that is a part *of* the game we play for our people to enjoy," the warrior said, rising back to his full height. He gestured around him. "My house is yours until Kanuga comes for you. Rest. It should not be long."

Stunned that Kanuga could use her for his 'games', and that this Indian talked about it as though it were a normal thing to do, Letitia looked away from him, her jaw set. She waited for him to leave, then rose angrily, clutching her cloak snugly around her. In determined steps she left the house and, bracing herself against the icy wind, went on to her and Kanuga's longhouse.

Tossing her cloak aside, she sat down before the fire and folded her arms across her chest and waited . . . and waited . . . and waited.

Then when Kanuga finally came into the house and reached for her wrist and drew her up next to him, she glared into his eyes.

"I am not at all amused by the games you played today, using me as a pawn," she said.

His eyes dancing, his lips tugging into a smile,

Kanuga gazed down at her. "My woman is even more beautiful when she is angry," he said, chuckling low.

"How can you pretend that what you did was right?" Letitia said, her voice quavering. She jerked away from Kanuga and stamped back to the fur pallet and plopped back down on it. "I am not sure I can even forgive you, Kanuga. When the warrior took me to his house, I thought . . ."

She glared suddenly up at him. "I thought that you had honestly given me away to him, and that he was going to claim me!" she said, her voice rising in pitch with each spoken word. "Don't you understand how I felt? Never have I felt so humiliated—so used!"

Seeing how upset Letitia was, stunned by it, Kanuga once more took her by a wrist and brought her back up to stand before him. "The other wives always enjoy the games," he said. "How was I to know that you would take them so seriously?"

"You did not bother to explain beforehand how the games, as you call the ordeal, worked," Letitia fumed. "Kanuga, I know that I have much to learn about your people and their customs. But you must realize that I do not know them unless you teach me."

"Did you truly believe that I would ever allow anyone to take you away from me?" he said, stroking his fingers through her hair. "I would never have stopped wrestling until I *had* won you back, for keeps."

"I was filled with such doubts, so quickly," Letitia said softly. "Please never do such a thing to me again, Kanuga. I never want to doubt your love for me."

"I will never give you cause to, ever again," he said folding his arms around her. He held her close. He laughed softly. "Beautiful woman, I won and lost you seven times tonight."

Letitia looked up at him, awe-stricken by his confession. Then she saw the humor in it and began giggling. "My, but your muscles must be sore to have wrestled that hard to assure having your wife in your bed tonight," she teased.

"I look forward to another wrestling match tonight," Kanuga said, chuckling as Letitia looked apprehensively up at him.

"You are not here to stay?" she said fearfully. Suddenly, the humor that she had briefly seen in the custom was replaced by a sense of dread.

Kanuga lifted her gently up into his arms and began carrying her toward their bed. "Do you think I would leave?" he said, his eyes darkening with passion. "My beautiful woman, the wrestling I plan to do now is with you, the prize that I have won over and over again tonight."

Letitia sighed as he placed her on the bed and soon had her clothes removed. "My darling, you won me over the very first time our eyes made contact," she said, welcoming him at her side after he had quickly disposed of his brief loincloth. "No matter how many games you play, I will always be yours."

He rose over her and his mouth came down on

hers and she stopped thinking. She strained up at him as his hands roved over her body, her every secret place becoming his. Her insides seemed to be bubbling with happiness as the enticing feel of his fingers caused pleasure to spread through her body. Her body arched to his as he pressed his manhood into her, causing her heart to give a great leap. She gave herself up to the rapture and moved with him, their bodies sucking together as his lean, sinewy buttocks moved.

Kanuga buried his face next to Letitia's neck and groaned in whispers against her flesh as the fires within him flamed higher and higher, scorching in their intensity. He moved faster, in quick and sure movements, and then slowed his pace within her, the euphoria that was filling him almost more than he could bear.

Yet he wanted to postpone the final leap to passion. Tonight there were many things to celebrate. Being with Letitia was the grandest celebration of all!

And soon there would be another heartbeat and quiet breathing in their house.

A child!

A child who would be theirs to join in all of their future celebrations!

But now he and Letitia were the only two people on the universe. And he was so proud! So exceedingly happy; a man fulfilled!

If he did not know better, he would think that he was a part of an incredible, beautiful dream.

Letitia tremored with ecstasy and arched her throat backward as Kanuga buried his lips along its delicate, vulnerable line, then cried out with pleasure when his mouth slipped down and fastened gently on her breast.

Her body turned to liquid and she clung to him as his mouth seized her lips in a splendid, deep kiss, coming to her thrusting more deeply, until she could not hold back the rapture any longer. She abandoned herself to the ultimate of pleasure, as he, too, shuddered and quaked against her.

And then they lay quietly together, yet breathing hard. Letitia ran her hand down his wet, perspiration-laced back, then up again, and around, so that she was framing his face between her hands as he still lay atop her.

"My darling, I shall try harder to accept the customs of your people as I am faced with them," she promised. "Never do I want to disappoint you."

"Never shall you," he whispered against her cheek.

He rolled away from her and covered her with a blanket, then sat there, his arms locked around his upraised legs, gazing down at her. "Our future is bright, filled with so much promise," he said, smiling down at her. "And how do you feel about tomorrow? A tomorrow that does not include your parents?"

Letitia's eyes took on a faraway look. "One day I hope to see them again," she murmured. Her eyes locked with his. "Somehow, Kanuga. Somehow."

"I will never venture farther than Alaska's

shores," he said, his voice flat.

"Perhaps my parents will return just for a visit," Letitia said, envisioning such a grand moment as that. She would have a grandchild to show them.

Perhaps by then, two or more!

Ah, but wouldn't her mother and father idolize their grandchildren? They had been such perfect parents to her!

And also to Barbara, she thought bitterly to herself, remembering how Barbara had proved to be so uncaring, so ungrateful.

"I do hope the day will come when I can proudly show off our children to my parents," she confessed, erasing thoughts of Barbara from her consciousness. "My father is a world traveler. It would be nothing for him to come to Alaska again."

"If he does, it must be only in the capacity of father and grandfather," Kanuga warned. "Not as a builder of forts and hunter of pelts!"

Letitia smiled wanly up at him, knowing the seriousness with which Kanuga had made that last statement. She prayed silently to herself that her father did not return with plans of trying to establish a fort again.

But she knew that he was a stubborn man, and stubborn men did that which most would turn their backs on.

Letitia reached for Kanuga's hand and led him down beside her. "The only father I wish to talk about now is you," she murmured, giggling. "Oh, Kanuga, you will be such a wonderful, caring father. It will delight me so to see you with our children."

Kanuga smiled down at her, this talk of children also seeming to be a dream that surely belonged to someone else, not him. He had lost everyone that was important to him except for Letitia.

He had to be sure to guard her always—with his life!

Chapter Twenty-nine

Was I deceived, or did a sable cloud
turn forth her silver linings in the night?
—MILTON

NEW YORK

Barbara tossed fitfully on the bed, her body ravaged with fever. Kimberly sat on the bed beside her, washing down her heated body with cold compresses.

"Let me be!" Barbara cried. "Let me lose the baby! I don't want the baby!"

"You got yourself pregnant," Kimberly said in a determined tone that was not usual for her. "And so we shall do everything we can to see that you have the child. Your fever will soon break, and then both you and the child will be out of danger."

"I want to die," Barbara sobbed. "Just let me die."

"If I have anything to say about it, neither you nor the child is going to die," Kimberly said, looking cautiously up at Jerome as he stood over the bed, nervously kneading his chin.

Then she looked back down at Barbara. "You let yourself get a chill on purpose, hoping that a fever would cause you to lose the child," she accused her. "That was shameful, Barbara. And I will not allow your scheme to work!"

"Once the child is born, it can be yours if you are so determined that I have it!" Barbara screamed at Kimberly. "I don't want it. Do you understand? I hate children!"

"We shall see about that," Kimberly said, tsk-tsking as she looked pityingly down at Barbara.

Chapter Thirty

The dews of heaven fall thick in blessings on her.
— SHAKESPEARE

SEVEN MONTHS LATER
ALASKA

Thirteen hours had passed, and still Letitia had not given birth. Sweetwater sat at her bedside, smoothing cool compresses across her brow, as Letitia breathed hard, wondering if the child would ever come.

Kanuga came and stood over her, his brow furrowed with worry. "My wife," he said thickly. "Will your strength hold out? It has been so long since your pains first began." He knelt down beside the bed and took her hand in his. "Seeing you suffer so makes me think we should not have more than this one child. One child will be enough. Your welfare means more to me than my being able to boast of two or three children!"

Her hair wet with perspiration, her eyes weary, Letitia forced a smile and squeezed his hand affectionately. "I bear this pain with much love," she murmured. "And I shall bear it as often as it takes to give you a son."

"This child will be a son," Kanuga said, his jaw tightening. "I have willed it to be so! I have spoken to the Chief Above and came away from that silent meditation knowing that I will soon hold a son against my bosom."

"But should you be disappointed, remember that I will try again, my darling, to give that which is so important to you," she murmured. "The future chief of your people!"

A stabbing pain, spreading throughout her abdomen, and then a hard bearing-down pain caused Letitia to clench her teeth to keep from crying out. She rolled her eyes back into her head and grabbed at her tightening abdomen, Sweetwater soon there, spreading her legs apart, checking to see if there were any signs yet of the child's head.

Sweetwater came away, her eyes heavy with worry. She again stroked Letitia's brow with a cool, wet compress. "Soon," she reassured her. "Relax now, between your pains, for soon you will need all of your strength to give your child that one last push to release him from your body."

Relieved for the moment that the pain had subsided, yet even more exhausted than before, Letitia eased her hand from Kanuga's and touched his cheek gently. "Go and get a breath of fresh air," she whispered, her bosom heaving. "Perhaps when you return I will have a gift to place in your arms."

"I will not leave you," Kanuga said, leaning a soft kiss to her lips.

The house was quiet now, except for Letitia's heavy breathing. Sweetwater and Kanuga gazed intensely down at Letitia, both feeling her pain.

And then the silence was disturbed by a strange sort of scratching at the door. Kanuga turned questioning eyes toward it, then shrugged and turned his attention back to Letitia, thinking that he had been imagining things.

Again Letitia's body was wracked with pain. Kanuga clasped onto her hands tightly while Sweetwater took her place again between Letitia's spread legs, again coming away disappointed.

"The child is stubborn," Sweetwater said, dabbing Letitia's face gently with a cloth, removing the beads of perspiration. "But that is good. In life, the child will prove to be strong—a great leader!"

There again came the strange scratching at the door, momentarily drawing all of their attention away from the child. All eyes went to the door as the scratching became even more insistent.

Kanuga rose to his feet and went to the door. He opened it slowly, his gaze drawn quickly down to a ball of white fur standing there, with silver eyes peering up at him through the fur, as though it belonged there and was trying to relay a message to him.

"A wolf pup?" Kanuga said, startled by his discovery. He knelt and picked up the pup, having never before seen such a beautiful wolf. Its fur was thick and soft, and as white as snow.

As far as he could see, the pup had only one flaw. Even without its mouth being opened, Kanuga could see a tooth protruding from the gum and pushing out from between the lips, the way his brother's teeth had grown into his gums—two teeth fighting for one space, giving the one on top the appearance of a strange sort of fang!

"What are you holding, darling?" Letitia asked, since Kanuga's back was to her. "What was there? What did you pick up, into your arms?"

Holding the pup in his arms as it snuggled against his chest, Kanuga closed the door. "A wolf pup," he said, turning to show her.

As he walked toward the bed, he studied the pup again, his eyes always going to the fang tooth. He felt a strange sort of closeness to the pup, as though it had come to him for a purpose.

And then something grabbed him at the pit of his stomach, making his heart lurch. The way the pup looked up at him, so devoted, and the way he was now licking his face so lovingly, as though it were a kiss from the heavens, he could not help but believe that this—this was his brother, reincarnated!

Atkuk had returned in the form of a lovable pup!

A wolf pup that would never be set free to roam the wilds searching hungrily for food, for survival!

Letitia saw how Kanuga suddenly paled and faltered in his footsteps, and how he was looking so strangely down at the wolf pup. She managed to get up on one elbow to get a better look at the pup as Kanuga brought it to her bedside.

"Why, it is so beautiful," she said, still in awe of Kanuga's strange, silent reaction to it. "Kanuga, what is it? Why are you looking at the pup so strangely? And, darling, you are so pale, as though you have just seen a ghost."

Kanuga sat down on the edge of the bed. "I must see one more thing before telling you what I suspect is a most wondrous discovery," he said, turning the pup, so that he could see if it was a male or female. When he saw that it was a male, his face brightened into a smile.

He held the pup close to Letitia. "Touch him," he said, his voice breaking. "See how soft he is?"

Letitia petted the pup, for the moment forgetting the pain that was suddenly gripping her again. Her attention was drawn to the fang-like tooth protruding from between the pup's lips. "Why, look, darling," she said, breathing hard against the soaring pain. "He . . . he has a fang-like tooth, just like Atkuk. . . ."

Her eyes widened and she gasped, suddenly recalling how Kanuga had said that Atkuk would return to him, reincarnated into something gentle—something loving.

"It *is* Atkuk," Kanuga said, nodding. He placed

the pup's nose to his, then held him tightly against his bosom again. "He has returned to us. He has come to witness the birth of his nephew!" He stroked the fur. "But in his new life, he shall be called Fang."

"I never believed in reincarnation before," Letitia said, staring at the pup, instantly in love with it. "But, Lord, I do now. I . . . do . . ."

She eased back down onto the bed, another pain grabbing her, this one so bad that she felt as though she might faint. "Sweetwater, I feel . . . I feel as though it is time," she said, panting. "The bearing down is worse. The baby. It's . . . it's coming!"

Kanuga set the pup aside and went to Letitia to let her grip his hands. His heart pounding, already so joy-filled because of the arrival of the wolf pup, he gazed in a sort of wondrous bliss as Letitia gave a hard shove, and the baby was suddenly there, in Sweetwater's hands.

Letitia could hardly get her breath, bone-tired from the experience. But when she saw her child, everything was forgotten but the happiness that soared through her.

"It is a son!" Sweetwater said, cutting the umbilical cord. Then she held the child up so that its sex was revealed to its mother and father.

"A son," Letitia said, now breathing much more easily. Tears flowed across her cheeks as she looked up at Kanuga. "I did it, darling. I gave you a son."

While Sweetwater cleansed the child, Kanuga bent low over Letitia and enfolded her within his powerful arms. "Thank you," he whispered against her tear-soaked cheek. "You have made me very happy today, my wife."

Letitia stroked her hands through his thick, black hair. "I promised you, didn't I?" she murmured.

"Yes, you promised," Kanuga said, leaning away from her, looking adoringly down at her.

"And there will also be a daughter, and then more sons," she teased, her throat dry.

"We shall see," Kanuga chuckled, then was awe-struck by the loveliness and perfect features of his son as Sweetwater came and placed him in Letitia's waiting arms. Tears came to his eyes as he reached out and touched his son gently on the cheek, relishing the softness of his flesh—the color of copper, like his own.

"And what shall we call him?" Letitia asked, gazing rapturously down at their child.

"Atkuk," Kanuga said at once. "He will be called Atkuk." He looked down at her questionably. "Unless you have another name that you prefer."

"That is a lovely name," Letitia said. "And he will wear it proudly, as did his namesake."

The wolf pup came sniffing and whining at Kanuga's heels. Kanuga reached down and picked him up so that he could see the child. "Fang, is he not a wonderful child?" he said, stroking the pup's silken fur. "And did you hear what name we gave him?" He held the pup up, eye to eye with himself. "Atkuk. We named him

Atkuk. Do you approve?"

The pup barked, then licked Kanuga on the face.

Everyone laughed, so perfectly content.

Chapter Thirty-one

The best portion of a good man's life,
His little nameless, unremembered
Acts of kindness and of love.

—WORDSWORTH

NEW YORK
TWO MONTHS LATER

Jerome paced the floor, glancing over and over
again at the closed bedroom door. He jumped
with a start when the doctor came from the room,
closing his black satchel, his face shadowed
gloomily.

Jerome went to Doc Rose. He gazed down at
the white-haired, hefty doctor, afraid to ask how
Kimberly was faring today. Every day now she
weakened more and more. Always a frail person,

she had not been able to shake the consumption that had her in its grip.

"How is she, Doc?" Jerome asked anxiously, himself more white-haired and much thinner since having worried about his wife for these past several months.

Doc Rose set his satchel aside. "I could use a drink, Jerome," he said, settling heavily into a chair before a roaring fire in the fireplace. "We've got some talkin' to do."

Jerome went to the liquor cabinet and poured Doc Rose a glass of wine.

"Better pour yourself something stronger," Doc Rose said over his shoulder. "What I've got to say will require it, Jerome."

His hands trembling, his heart thudding, Jerome poured himself a glass of whiskey, then went to Doc Rose and gave him his wine, while clasping his own glass so hard he felt that he might break it. He settled down in a chair next to the doctor.

"Well, damn it, tell me," he said, glaring at the doctor.

Doc Rose's eyes wavered as he glanced over at Jerome. "Drink the whiskey first," he suggested softly.

"The news is that bad?" Jerome said, his voice almost failing him.

"It's that bad," Doc Rose said, then took a brisk drink of the wine.

Feeling that his world was falling apart, knowing that he was losing his beloved wife, Jerome placed the drink to his lips and swallowed several deep gulps of the whiskey. He slammed the glass down on a table beside the chair, clearing his throat as it burned from the whiskey.

Then he leaned closer to the doctor. "I've waited long enough," he said, his voice breaking. "Tell me. Tell me how my wife is."

Doc Rose set his glass down on the table. He gazed into the rolling flames of the fire. "You'd best make peace with your wife real soon," he said. "She won't make it through another night." He then looked over at Jerome. "Your daughter. Can you get in touch with her?"

Jerome buried his face in his hands, choking back a sob. "My daughter is in Alaska," he said shakily. "There's no way she can be at her mother's side to say . . . to say a final goodbye."

"That's too bad," Doc Rose said, nodding. He cleared his throat nervously. "And what about Barbara? Has she been in touch with you since she left you in charge of her baby daughter?"

"Nary a word," Jerome said in a growl. "It's as though she's disappeared from the face of the earth."

"What are you going to do with the baby once Kimberly is gone?" Doc Rose said, again looking away from Jerome, staring into the fire. "You can't raise her alone. I know of a family who would take her off your hands. They are childless. They would give her a good home. And she would have the best of education."

Jerome paled at the thought of giving up what he considered his granddaughter. Yet he was not all that well himself, and he did not see how he would be able to raise her properly.

And, there was the fact that she was part Indian! He was afraid that prejudices would set in once she reached school age.

"No," he said, shaking his head woefully. "I can't give her up. She has my wife's blood flowing through her veins."

"Well, give it some more thought," Doc Rose said, grunting as he shoved himself up out of the chair. "You'd best get her in a home that you can trust now, for later, if anything would happen to you suddenly, she'd be at the mercy of whoever'd take her."

Jerome nodded and pushed himself out of the chair, then walked Doc Rose to the door. "I've got a lot to think over," he said. "The world won't be the same without my Kimberly."

When they reached the door, Doc Rose turned and looked sadly into Jerome's eyes. "I wish there was more I could do," he said. He patted Jerome on the shoulder. "But there's only so much a doctor can do these days. Perhaps in the future someone will invent miracle drugs that can help rid the body of infections like those that have invaded your wife's lungs."

"Perhaps," Jerome said, nodding slowly.

They shook hands and Doc Rose left, leaving Jerome filled with an agonizing emptiness. He walked up the corridor and stared pensively at the closed bedroom door, then went to another bedroom and went quietly into it. The room was softly lit by one lone, flickering candle. Going to the cradle, he peered down at the five-month-old child, so peacefully asleep on her back.

Tears flooded Jerome's eyes as he watched the child's lips moving in her sleep, as though nursing, when in truth, she had never had a woman's breast to feed from. She had been fed milk from a bottle from the day she had been born, Barbara having refused to even look at her daughter, much less let it take nourishment from her.

"My little Indian princess," Jerome whispered, smoothing a raven-black lock back from the child's tiny brow. "Thank God you were born Indian. That gave us the truth of your birthright. You are Kanuga's daughter, Stephanie. Not that bastard Broderick Bowman, or whoever else Barbara slept with! There was only one Indian in her life. Kanuga!"

Bending over the bed, Jerome slipped his hands beneath Stephanie and slowly picked her up. When her lashes fluttered open, and her silver eyes smiled up into his, his heart melted with love for her. "My darling child," he said, drawing her close to his chest as he carried her from the room. "Never will I give you up to strangers! Never!"

Going to the room where Kimberly lay beneath a layer of blankets, making strangled, gurgling noises from the depths of her lungs, Jerome's heart cried out for her as she looked up at him and greeted him with a weak smile. Stepping up to the bed, gazing down at her, he could hardly keep from crying. She had always been thin and frail, but now she was gaunt. Her pale skin was stretched like parchment over the fragile bones, and there were deep, dark circles under her eyes. She was a mere skeleton of what she had once been.

"Thank you for bringing Stephanie to me," she said, easing her bony arms and hands from beneath the blankets. "Please let me hold her this one last time, darling. I'll be careful not to breathe on her. We wouldn't want our precious to get ill."

Jerome placed Stephanie in Kimberly's arms, and helped hold her there, fearing that Kimberly was too weak to hold the baby by herself. "Doc Rose told me about a family who wants to take Stephanie and raise her as their own," he said thickly. "I told him a flat no, Kimberly."

Kimberly stroked the baby's soft copper cheeks, then combed her fingers through her thick, dark hair. "Of course you would say no," she said, tears spilling from her eyes. She looked up at Jerome. "Jerome, you know what you must do with her, don't you? Immediately after I am laid to rest, you know where to take her, don't you?"

"Yes, we've agreed," he said, nodding. "And so it shall be done."

"Then I can go to God with a peaceful heart," Kimberly said, smiling lovingly up at Jerome.

Jerome bent low over her and the child, wrapping them both in his trembling embrace.

Chapter Thirty-two

Beauty is truth, truth beauty—that is all
Ye know on earth, and all ye need to know.

—KEATS

TEN MONTHS LATER
ALASKA

Kanuga had spied the ship out at sea long before
it swung around and headed toward shore. Although warning shots had been fired across its
bow, showing that it was not welcome, the ship's
captain had ignored the warning, persisting in
bringing his ship to shore. Its anchor had been
cranked down into the water.

His faithful Fang at his side on his sled, all
grown-up and powerful-appearing with his thick
mane and bold eyes, and with his warriors on
both sides of him in their sleds, their weapons

drawn, Kanuga waited for the gangplank to be dropped to the land. The intruders would not be allowed to set one foot on the land, unless they could convince Kanuga that they had come to trade with him and his people, then leave when the transactions were over.

He would have preferred, though, that the warning shots had discouraged them from stopping at all along the shores of his wonderful land. He was afraid that it would be like all of the other times before.

The white people would see the wonders of Alaska, and want to stay.

His eyes stony-cold, his hand clutched feverishly to his rifle, Kanuga watched the activity on the ship, seeing the crew actively preparing to lower the gangplank.

Then Kanuga's mouth opened with surprise, when at this distance, he saw someone familiar to him—somewhat more aged, but quite familiar!

"Letitia's father," he gasped to himself. Then he grew tense and stood taller, straining to see what Jerome held in his arms. A child? Was that a child whose arm was locked about Jerome's neck, bundled in fur, a hood framing a delicate copper face?

Kanuga's eyes wavered. "The child is Indian!" he said aloud, causing his warriors to look over at him. Whose child could it be? And why had Letitia's father brought the child to Alaska? Why had Letitia's father come at all, if not only to see his daughter?

Then Kanuga's eyes moved along the deck of the ship for Letitia's mother. She was not there.

He searched further for Barbara. He was relieved that she wasn't there, either.

Then his attention was drawn back to Jerome as he walked down the gangplank that had just been lowered.

Jerome's eyes met and locked with Kanuga's as Kanuga lay his rifle aside and left his sled to go to him.

Seeing the puzzled look in Kanuga's eyes, Jerome was the first to speak. "My daughter?" he asked, Stephanie still hugging him, yet closely studying Kanuga. "How is she?"

"She is happy and well," Kanuga said, staring down at the lovely child, now realizing that she was a girl. Her features were delicate. They were so pure! And there was something about her, besides the color of her eyes and skin that seemed to match his own. There seemed to be an instant bonding as their eyes locked and held.

Kanuga shook his head slightly to draw himself out of this spell that the child seemed to have cast over him. He forced himself to look up at Jerome. "Your grandson is also well and happy," he added.

Jerome's eyes lit up. "A grandson?" he said, his voice breaking. "I have—a grandson?"

"Yes," Kanuga said, nodding. "He is soon to be one winter of age." He gazed back down at the child. "And this one? How old is she? What is her name? And why do you bring her here?"

Jerome's eyes became uneasy, not knowing

how Kanuga would take knowing that he was not only a father to a son, but also to a daughter. But he had found, in his short time with Kanuga, that he was a man of heart. He would not turn his back on a daughter, anymore than he would a son!

"Stephanie is soon to be thirteen months old," Jerome said. "And why have I brought her with me to Alaska?" He stopped and cleared his throat nervously. "Kanuga, I have brought her to you, to ask if you and Letitia will care for her."

Jerome's eyes became haunted as he recalled the burial of his dear wife. Then he cleared his thoughts of everything but the welfare of Stephanie. Also he was eager to get this chore behind him! He was anxious to see Letitia! And his grandson!

"Whose child is she?" Kanuga said, his voice soft and low with wonder. "And why would you ask Letitia and me to take her in, as though she were our own?"

"She *is* your own, Kanuga," Jerome blurted out. "She is your child. Yours and Barbara's."

Kanuga took a quick step away from Jerome, stunned. In his mind's eye he was recalling the fateful night with Barbara, having always regretted it.

But now, how should he feel? That night had brought a child into the world! His child!

"Where is Barbara?" he asked, unable to take his eyes off Stephanie now, studying her every feature. His heart melted when Stephanie smiled at him, then held her arms out for him.

"Take her, Kanuga," Jerome encouraged. "Hold her. You will soon be in love with her. My wife and I have cared for her since Barbara's disappearance shortly after Stephanie was born." A lump formed in his throat. "My wife adored her. Adored her!"

"Your wife," Kanuga said. He hesitated to take the child, not sure yet how he felt about discovering how she had been born, and from whom. "She did not accompany you to Alaska?"

"She couldn't have," Jerome said, lowering his eyes. "She's dead."

Kanuga gasped and paled, knowing what this news would do to his wife. She would be devastated. Also, how would she feel to know that another woman had borne him a child? He knew how she felt about Barbara! She despised her! Could she love the child when she so disliked the child's mother?

Stephanie still held her arms out to him.

"Take her, Kanuga," Jerome encouraged, handing Stephanie toward him. "She will capture your heart right away. You will not be able to say no to keeping her."

Kanuga's heart thudded wildly within his chest as he finally took Stephanie into his arms. His hands trembled and his knees grew weak when she smiled up at him again, then lunged herself against him, wrapping her tiny arms around his neck. His heart melted into hers then, when she even kissed him on the cheek, her lips so soft, so sweet!

"My daughter," he said, snuggling her close.

"Now I would like to see *my* daughter," Jerome said, nodding at a driver who had unloaded a dog team and sled from the ship. "Take me to her."

After Jerome got settled in the sled, Kanuga handed him the child, then went to his own sled, and with a wild heartbeat, turned his huskies around and headed them back toward his village. He wasn't sure how he should feel, but he could not deny that having a daughter was exhilarating to him!

A son and a daughter. He felt suddenly blessed. Then he frowned, wondering if he was feeling too jubilant too soon, when he still had Letitia to face with the truth.

Letitia and Atkuk were sitting on the floor beside the fire, rolling a ball back and forth to each other.

"You're such a smart little boy," Letitia said, going to Atkuk and lifting him up on her lap. "You're going to be just like your daddy, aren't you?"

Atkuk giggled as he squirmed from her lap again, crawling to the ball. He turned around and flopped down again on his behind, looking adorable to Letitia in his small buckskin attire and moccasins. She caught the ball as he rolled it to her, then his eyes widened when he heard the arrival of the dogs outside.

"Da-da," Atkuk said, rising clumsily to his feet. He had learned to walk even before his first birthday. He toddled toward the door, then laughed against Letitia's chest when Letitia grabbed him up and swung him around and around, laughing along with him.

"I'm going to tell Da-da what a good boy you've been while he's been hunting," Letitia said, stopping to hold him over her head. He giggled, wriggling to be put down, then turned his attention to the door as Kanuga stepped inside, Fang devotedly at his side.

"Da-da!" Atkuk said, reaching his arms out for Kanuga as Kanuga slipped his cloak off his shoulders.

Kanuga went to him and took him from Letitia's arms, then looked guardedly down at her. "A ship has arrived in Alaska," he said, cuddling Atkuk close as he twined his tiny arms about Kanuga's neck.

"A ship?" Letitia said, her eyes widening. She placed a hand to her throat, peering past Kanuga at her father who was just entering, carrying a child.

"Papa?" Letitia gasped, feeling faint, seeing her father unexpectedly.

Then she broke into a run and went to him, sobbing. She found it difficult to hug him, with the child in the way, but she managed. "Papa, how wonderful it is that you have come!" she cried.

Then she stepped away from him, suddenly aware that her mother had not come into the house with him. She searched his face questioningly. "Mama?" she murmured, seeing a strange foreboding in her father's eyes. "Where's Mama?

Did she stay on the ship? Why? I'm dying to see her, also."

She glanced down at the child and raised an eyebrow. "Whose child is this?" she asked softly. "Why did you bring her with you?"

Kanuga placed Atkuk to the floor and went to Letitia. He took her hands and led her down on the mats beside the fire, then sat down beside her, while her father still stood, watching.

"What's wrong?" Letitia said, her voice rising in pitch. "Why did you make me sit down? What is it? Is it something you have to tell me that . . . that is going to upset me?" A coldness circled her heart. She paled. "Oh, no. Don't tell me it's about Mama. Don't tell me that she's dead."

Jerome placed Stephanie on the floor, taking time to remove her fur wrap, and then his own, before sitting down beside Letitia. Kanuga moved aside, giving her father room beside her.

"Honey, I buried your mother shortly before I boarded the ship for Alaska," Jerome said, taking Letitia's hands and gripping them tightly. "Darling, there was nothing the doctors could do for her. It was a lung disease. She just didn't have the strength to fight it." Tears splashed down his cheeks. "She went peacefully. She's with God now, honey."

Letitia sat still for a moment, staring at her father; then the realization finally sank in that she would never see her mother again. She lunged into her father's arms, crying. She clung to him, her body wracked with sobs. Then, when she heard Atkuk begin crying, her distress having transferred to him, she composed herself and wiped her tears away and took Atkuk into her arms, hugging and comforting him.

Jerome rose to his feet and went to Letitia and Atkuk. "And so this is my grandson?" he said, stroking Atkuk's thick black hair. "Letitia, he's such a beautiful child."

Letitia transferred Atkuk into her father's arms. "Atkuk, this is your granpa," she said, glad that Atkuk was receptive, the sort of child who made friends easily. "Can you give your granpa a kiss?"

Atkuk wiped the last trace of tears from his silver eyes, puckered his lips, and gave Jerome a wet kiss on the cheek.

Jerome gave out a pleasurable sigh, then hugged Atkuk tightly to him. "He's a wonderful boy," he said, relishing the feel of his grandson in his arms. "And so healthy."

"Yes, he is one who likes to eat," Kanuga said, stepping forth with Stephanie in his arms.

Letitia eyed the child questioningly, and an apprehensiveness enveloped her when she saw the resemblance of Stephanie to Atkuk, so much that it was as if someone had splashed cold water on her face.

"Papa, you haven't told me yet about this child," she murmured, confused by how Kanuga seemed so attentive to her—a stranger.

Jerome eyed Letitia warily, then blurted out the truth. "She's Barbara's child," he said, seeing the shock registering in his daughter's eyes. "Barbara abandoned her shortly after she was born.

Your mother and I have been raising her." He cleared his voice. "But now that your mother is gone, I don't see how I, alone, can take care of her." Again he cleared his voice. "And I didn't want to hire strangers to come into the house. That would last for only as long as I live. After that, she would be at the mercy of the courts."

"So you have brought her here for me and Kanuga to raise?" Letitia said, interrupting her father. Faintly, her heart sinking, already too aware of the answer to the question she was about to ask, she said, "And who is the father? Why can't he take the child to raise?"

"That is the true reason I have brought her here," Jerome said, his voice breaking. "I *have* brought her to her father to raise."

The world seemed suddenly to spin around Letitia. She bit her lower lip to keep from crying out, then steadied herself against Kanuga when he was suddenly there, beside her, the child on the floor, looking up at them—all of her features Tlingit!

"That one night with her?" she said, gazing forlornly over at Kanuga.

"Yes, it seems that way," Kanuga said, looking at her apologetically. "What can I say? It was most certainly not planned."

Letitia stared at him for a moment, then turned her eyes away, closing them in an effort to block out the thought of that night—a night when her cousin had stolen her man away, and then got pregnant by him!

"Letitia," Kanuga said, gripping her shoulders. "Look at me."

Letitia choked back a sob, then turned her eyes slowly to Kanuga.

"I know that everything you've been told today is a shock," he said softly. "But you are strong. What you must do is forget the past, and let us live for the future."

He glanced down at his daughter, a sudden rush of feeling soaring through him. He loved her, as though he had seen her take her first breath of life!

He then gazed into Letitia's eyes again. "This child did not ask to be born," he said. "But she is of my flesh. I am her father. And I wish to raise her as my child."

He drew Letitia close and placed a finger beneath her chin, causing their eyes to meet and hold. "She needs a mother," he said gently. "Her true mother deserted her. Be her mother now, Letitia. Let's give her the love all little girls deserve. And Atkuk won't lack any loving because of it. We have enough love to give to them both."

Letitia's eyes moved to Stephanie, seeing her sweet innocence as she gazed back at her with eyes the identical color of Kanuga's.

Then she looked over at Atkuk, who seemed oblivious to the tension in the air as Fang romped over to him, nudging his chest playfully with his nose, causing Atkuk to fall over on his back, giggling.

When Stephanie went to Fang and hugged him, giggling, then helped Atkuk up from the floor, treating him gently and sweetly, Letitia's heart melted. "Atkuk would love having a sister, wouldn't he?" she said, wiping tears from her eyes.

"They would be wonderful company for each other," Kanuga said, smiling as Atkuk and Stephanie began hugging each other, then cementing their friendship with a kiss.

"Then I approve of her staying," Letitia said, hearing more than one sigh of relief in the longhouse. She looked from Kanuga to her father.

She went to her father and moved into his embrace. "But what of you, Papa?" she murmured. "You'll be all alone in the world."

"I don't think so," Jerome said, chuckling as he slipped from her arms. He looked over at Kanuga. "Do you think you might have a spare longhouse for this old man to take residence in?"

Letitia's eyes lit up. "You want to stay in Alaska?" she asked. Then her smile faltered when she heard Kanuga's strained silence as he stood beside her.

"You want to stay in the capacity of father or trader?" he said, his voice low and emotionless.

"I want to stay in the capacity of father and grandfather," Jerome said, his eyes gleaming. "I've nothing else in my life now. I sold the business to the man who brought me to Alaska. It was a part of the business agreement—that he would bring me here before he took full possession of my ship."

"I think that's wonderful, Papa," Letitia said,

thrilled at the thought of having her father near, forever!

"Then it's all right for me to send for my things on the ship?" Jerome said, his face flushed with excitement. "The ship's captain is anxious to be on his way, I am sure."

"I would be happy to send my warriors to get your personal belongings," Kanuga said, knowing what having her father near would do for Letitia. Her world would now be complete.

A knock on the door drew Kanuga quickly to it. When he found Sweetwater standing there, her eyes filled with questions, he invited her in the house.

A smile sprang to Sweetwater's lips when she saw Jerome, then she went to him and hugged him fitfully. "It is so good to see you again," she said. Then she backed away from him, embarrassed for her show of emotion.

Jerome laughed softly, then went to Sweetwater and touched her cheek gently. "You're still as pretty as I remember you being," he said. "I couldn't have had a prettier nurse, you know."

Letitia watched her father and Sweetwater with an air of caution, seeing so much between them that she felt she could not accept. Her mother had been dead for such a short time. . . .

Chapter Thirty-three

A thing of beauty is a joy forever,
Its loveliness increases.
It will never pass into nothingness.

—KEATS

TWO MONTHS LATER

The morning was still, the sun casting its first golden glow through the smokehole in the ceiling. Letitia snuggled close to Kanuga, relishing the sound of his breathing as he slept soundly beside her. She slowed her own breathing for a moment, proudly listening to the sounds of her two children's breaths as they slept peacefully across the room in their separate, tiny beds. Stephanie had adjusted well to her new home, taking to her new family as though she had never been apart from them.

Letitia turned on her side, her thoughts now on Barbara, wondering where she was and what sort of a life she was leading. Without family, surely her life had to be empty!

And how could any mother turn her back on her own child?

A daughter, no less!

Then her thoughts went to her father, and a surge of bitterness crept around her heart. She could not help but think of her father in bed with Sweetwater, taking the place of the wife he had held within his arms for thirty long years.

How could her father forget her mother so quickly—so easily? He had taken Sweetwater to his house with him the very first night of his return to Alaska!

He had tried to explain to Letitia how lonesome he had been these past several months while her mother was so ill. He had told her that since Kimberly's death, he had felt only half alive. He had pleaded with Letitia to understand that Sweetwater had suddenly changed that for him! He now had a reason to wake up in the morning—and to go to bed at night!

Tears filled Letitia's eyes, wishing that she could accept her father's decision to take another woman to replace the one he had lost.

But she found it too hard. She doubted if she would ever be able to accept her father's new life.

A hand suddenly snaked around her, then encircled her breast, cupping it tenderly. Letitia sucked in a wild breath of pleasure, tingling all over as Kanuga moved up behind her, shaping his body to hers beneath the blankets.

"My wife awakens early today," Kanuga said, his hand moving slowly down her body to cup her triangle of curls between her thighs, gently thrusting a finger inside her. "Do your hungers awaken you?"

Letitia closed her eyes in rapture as Kanuga lifted her hair and kissed the nape of her neck. "Always," she murmured. "But only my hunger for you, darling."

"What were you thinking so hard about?" he whispered against her neck.

She knew that Kanuga would not want to know that she was worrying about her father again, for he did not approve of her worrying so much about anything. She was pregnant again. He did not want her to do anything to jeopardize the unborn child's life, or her own.

"I was thinking about Barbara, and where she might be," she said, not actually lying, since only moments ago she had also been thinking about Barbara.

"She is a woman lost," Kanuga said darkly. "She will never find herself. To give up a child is to give up one's soul."

"And what a beautiful child Stephanie is," Letitia said, sighing.

"We must give her a new name," Kanuga said, turning Letitia to face him.

"A new name?" she said, her eyes wide.

"Something more fitting with her skin coloring and heritage," Kanuga said, smiling down at Letitia.

"You have been thinking about this, haven't you, darling?" she said, smoothing her hand along his thick, raven-black hair. "You already have a name for her, don't you?"

"Yes," he said, chuckling.

"And what is it, darling?"

"Hope."

"Hope," Letitia said, testing the name on her lips.

"Yes, Hope," Kanuga said firmly. "It fits her well, don't you think?"

"It's perfect for a child whose mother turned her back on her," she murmured. "A child whose life is filled with much hope now that she has found parents who care."

"Didn't you say that you awakened this morning with much hunger?" Kanuga said, chuckling as his hand began moving down her body again, stopping at her throbbing center.

"Very," Letitia said breathlessly as his finger moved inside her.

"Then I must see that your hungers are fed," he said huskily, drawing her body against his.

Letitia twined her arms around his neck as his mouth covered hers in a frenzied kiss. She slung a leg over him, opening herself to him as his manhood probed, then found entrance into her. He thrust himself inside her, his fingers clasped to her buttocks, guiding her in her own quick movements, answering his.

Her mind soaring, Letitia clung to Kanuga, the joyous bliss that she always felt while with him building...building....

An anxious voice outside the longhouse, followed by a frantic knocking on the door, drew Letitia and Kanuga apart.

"It's Sweetwater," Letitia said, hurrying from the bed. She grabbed a robe as Kanuga slipped his fringed buckskin breeches on. "Perhaps it's Papa. What if something has happened to him?"

Kanuga went to the door and opened it, finding a wild-eyed Sweetwater clutching a fur cloak around her shoulders. She hurried into the house and grabbed Letitia by the hand.

"You must come," she said, her voice harried. "Your father. He has had some sort of spell. I am so worried for him!"

Alarm filled Letitia. She looked anxiously at Kanuga. "I must go to him," she said, glancing over at the children who had been awakened by the noise and were peeking over the tops of their beds. "The children. Will you stay with them?"

Kanuga gave her a quick kiss, then ushered her to the door. "Go to your father," he said. "If he requires a shaman, one will be sent to him."

Letitia blinked back tears, hoping her father wasn't so ill that he required a doctor. There were no doctors in Alaska. Only shaman!

With Sweetwater at her side, she left the house and trudged through ankle-deep snow to her father's longhouse, a short distance from her own. When she got there and hurried inside, she almost fainted from a quick, gripping fear that spread through her. Her father was lying in bed, as pale as the snow that covered the earth outside the house. His facial features had become strangely twisted, as though the muscles had been removed from the left side of his face. His eyes were wild as he pleaded silently up at her.

Falling to her knees beside the bed, Letitia touched her father's brow, wincing when she felt its clammy coldness. "Papa, what is it?" she murmured, trying to hold her fear at bay for her father's sake.

But she could see that something was terribly wrong. As he tried to move his lips, spittle rolled from the corners of his mouth in tiny streams. This made Letitia become weak all over as panic rose within her, yet she still had to keep her composure—for her father's sake.

She took a cloth from a basin on the table beside the bed, wrung the water from it, then gently dabbed the drool from his chin.

Jerome tried to lift his left arm, then began crying when he couldn't. "A stroke!" he finally managed to say. "I ... a ... stroke ... !"

A dizziness seized Letitia. She gripped the side of the bed for support, then again wiped spittle from her father's chin. "Yes," she murmured, fighting back her own tears. "It appears so, father. But you're going to be all right. In time, you will regain the muscles in your ... in the left side of your body. You're a fighter. I know that you can do it."

Sweetwater went to the other side of the bed and took Jerome's limp hand within hers. She clung to it as she leaned over Jerome and kissed his trembling lips. "You will be like new again," she whispered against his lips. "I will work with you. I will make it so!"

Letitia saw Sweetwater's devotion and the way her father turned his eyes to her, looking adoringly up at her. But she could not help but blame Sweetwater for her father's stroke. She was a young woman. He was an aging man, perhaps not able to keep up with the needs of his wife!

She looked at Sweetwater bitterly, then was stunned speechless when she heard what Sweetwater was telling her father.

"A child will make you well again," Sweetwater murmured. "Your child, darling. We are going to have a baby, Jerome."

Letitia rose shakily to her feet, staring disbelievingly down at Sweetwater, then at her father. Then she crumpled back down onto her knees, softening inside when she saw her father's reaction to the news. Never had she seen such a radiant expression in her father's eyes!

And the news seemed to have eliminated the frantic fear that had been consuming him. He now seemed happy, even accepting the fact that he could not speak without searching frantically within his brain for the words.

Letitia could not find it in her heart to blame Sweetwater any longer, not seeing the depths of her father's feelings for her and their unborn child. Somehow, she knew that this alone would make him well again—as well as one could get after suffering a debilitating stroke. His happiness seemed complete. How could she ever begrudge him that, or the woman that he now loved?

With a bundled-up child in each arm, Kanuga came into the house, Fang devotedly at his side. He stepped up beside Letitia, looking sadly down at Jerome.

"He's going to be fine," Letitia said, rising to stand beside Kanuga. She slipped an arm around his waist, smiling at Sweetwater. "And I think we'd better plan a wedding ceremony very soon."

Sweetwater smiled with much graciousness up at Letitia, then leaned over Jerome, gently hugging him.

Chapter Thirty-four

*Act well at the moment and you have performed
a good action to all eternity.*

—LOVATER

NEW YORK

The room was dreary and sparse of furniture. Her
hair drawn back into a tight bun atop her head,
dressed in a plain cotton dress, Barbara went to
look out a window onto a courtyard full of nuns
in their habits, strolling through a lush garden
of roses.

With the faint sound of organ music playing
outside her room, a gentle peace filled Barbara.
She was glad to have finally found her lot in life,
after having been found half-alive in a park, a
victim of rape and repeated stabbings by an unknown assailant. She had fought for her life for

several weeks, then after having been prayed over by Sister Jacqueline, both day and night through her long ordeal, she had awakened and had soon been catapulted into a new way of life, all safe and secure, working as a housemaid for both priest and nuns, a welcome part of their large family.

Humbly, she held her face in her hands, knowing that she had been so wrong to have chosen the life of a prostitute after leaving her aunt and uncle's house. But being alone, having to find ways to fend for herself, she had found prostitution to be the only way to survive—to eat and pay for her lodging in a hotel inhabited by others like herself. She had realized too late the mistakes she had made, the wrong roads she had chosen to travel.

But the worst of her crimes was the abandonment of her child!

"Oh, how I hunger to hold her," Barbara whispered to herself. The memory of how her daughter had so resembled her father flooded her memory, recalling the night that she had made love with Kanuga the whole night through, how he alone could have turned her life around—had he loved her.

"It was never meant to be," she said, choking back a sob. She went to the mirror and gazed at her reflection, running her fingers along the thin lines of her face. She did not see a resemblance to that woman she used to be. She felt that she was prettier, for in her face, she could now see peace!

Then she strolled to a chair and sat down, folding her hands on her lap and staring blankly ahead. She had only recently gone to her aunt and uncle's house, wanting to take one last look at her child and to apologize to her aunt and uncle for having treated them so callously, after they had been nothing but kind to her.

A sob lodged in her throat when she recalled having discovered someone else living there and hearing that her Aunt Kimberly was dead. When she had questioned the new occupants about her uncle's whereabouts, she had discovered that he had gone to Alaska with her little Stephanie.

"I am sure that Stephanie is now with Kanuga, her father," Barbara said, wiping tears from her eyes and suddenly smiling. "And that is the way it should be."

She rose from the chair and went back to the window, staring into the distance, where she could see the wide stretch of the ocean beyond the city. So often she was tempted to board a ship for Alaska, but each time she was tempted to go, she decided against it.

"It's best to let sleeping dogs lie," she whispered, nodding.

A faint knock on the door drew her from her reverie. She opened the door and found Sister Jacqueline there, smiling at her, a reminder always of the goodness of life, and how blessed she was to be a part of it.

"Are you ready to join the others for choir practice?" Jacqueline asked, placing a gentle hand on Barbara's arm.

Barbara stood there for a moment, motionless, then lunged into Jacqueline's arms. "Thank you so much for everything," she murmured. "Thank you, thank you, thank you...."

Chapter Thirty-five

Grace was in all her steps,
  heav'n in her eye,
In every gesture dignity and love.

—MILTON

TWO YEARS LATER
ALASKA

Sweetwater had miscarried their first child, but
now Letitia was thrilled to hold her new brother
as her father eased the little bundle of joy into
her arms. She smoothed a corner of the blanket
back from his face and looked down at the perfect
features, a face that revealed a mixture of his
mother's and father's heritage.

"He is so beautiful," Letitia sighed. "A brother.
How wonderful to have a brother."

She looked up at her father, so happy for him,

not only for having a wife and son whom he worshipped, but also for having regained most of his muscular control. He only partially limped, and sometimes his left arm did not want to obey his commands, but otherwise, he had become his old self again.

Kanuga came to Letitia's side. "You're needed at home," he said, slipping her cloak over her shoulders. "There's only so much a father can do for a crying baby. He wants his mother's comforting arms."

Letitia relinquished her brother back into her father's arms, then left the house with Kanuga, going to their own. When she entered, she questioned Kanuga with her eyes when she found all three of their children on the floor, playing.

She laid her cloak aside, then went to the children and fell to her knees among them.

"And what is this?" she said, smiling down at them. "What are you up to?"

"Adam can walk!" Hope said excitedly, clapping her hands. "That's why Daddy came for you. To show you that Adam can walk!"

Letitia looked radiantly at her youngest son, Adam, a name that he would carry with him only until he sought his vision, which would introduce him into manhood. "And so you can walk, huh?" she said, reaching her hands out toward him as he pushed himself shakily up from the floor, eyeing her with laughing blue eyes, his face as white as all Alaskan snows.

Kanuga got behind Adam and held him steady, then released him, watching proudly as he toddled toward Letitia, then lunged into her arms as he finally reached her.

Everyone joined in the laughter, Letitia hugging Adam while she gazed at her other children, hopelessly content—except for the moments when she would allow herself to worry about Barbara. She lived with the fear that Barbara might come for her daughter one day, and take her away. Yet she knew that fear came with raising another person's child, and she accepted it. She had no other choice.

Kanuga urged Letitia up from the floor. He eased Adam from her arms and placed him with the other children, then walked her away from them to stand over the warmth of the fire in the firepit. "A ship came to our shores today," he said, his voice drawn.

Letitia looked quickly up at him. "Oh, no," she said, placing a hand to her throat. "Will the trouble begin all over again? Was it an American ship? Or Russian?"

"It was Russian," Kanuga said, turning her to face him. He gripped her shoulders gently. "But it is already gone."

"It was Russian? And it is gone?" Letitia said, her eyes wide. "Why then did it come to Alaska?"

"Someone has gone to a lot of trouble, it seems, to bring you word about your cousin Barbara," Kanuga said, searching her eyes when he saw panic fill them.

"Oh, no," Letitia cried. "Barbara isn't coming to Alaska herself, is she?"

"Seems not," Kanuga said, his voice drawn.

"Then what?" Letitia persisted, her voice rising in pitch. "What is this all about?"

"There is a Sister Jacqueline, who is of Russian descent," Kanuga said softly. "This message brought to you today is from this Sister Jacqueline, whose Russian brother was in New York, transacting business. It seems that Sister Jacqueline took Barbara in many months ago and changed her life. Barbara lived with the nuns and she was quite content. She had completely changed. Then she became ill with a strange illness that sapped her strength and caused her to waste away to nothing before she died."

Letitia paled. She swayed from the shock, glad when Kanuga grabbed her and drew her into his embrace. "She's dead?" Letitia gasped. "Barbara is dead?"

"Yes," Kanuga said, caressing her back. "But before she died, she asked Sister Jacqueline to find a way to send you word of her death, so that you wouldn't worry forever about her coming for her daughter. She did not want you to spend a lifetime of worrying about something that would never be. And most of all she wanted your forgiveness. When Sister Jacqueline's brother came to New York for business, stopping in to visit her before returning to Russia, she asked him to stop at Alaska on his way back to Russia and find a way to get the message to you about Barbara. This was simply done. My warriors are always watching for ships, ready to send them away again as soon as they reach shore."

A calming peace settled over Letitia. She

slipped from Kanuga's arms and looked up at him. "She was a changed person," she murmured. "Never would she have cared about me worrying over anything nor would she have ever asked for my forgiveness. The Barbara I knew would have gone to extremes to give me cause to worry." She choked back a sob. "And I will never get a chance to thank her, Kanuga."

"There is no need," Kanuga said, enclosing her within his muscled arms again. "If ever there was cause for giving thanks, she owed you many."

Letitia gazed at the three children rolling and laughing on the floor with Fang, so innocent, so carefree. It was up to her and Kanuga to see that nothing ever changed for them. Their lives would never be filled with the sorrows that Letitia had been forced to face.

Then she looked up at Kanuga. "I am so lucky," she murmured. "So very, very lucky."

He lowered his mouth to hers. "I am the lucky one," he whispered against her lips.

Then he kissed her, a kiss filled with promise ...a savage promise....

Dear Reader:

I hope that you have enjoyed reading SAVAGE PROMISE. My next LEISURE book in the continuing SAVAGE series, in which it is my endeavor to write about every major Indian tribe in America, is SAVAGE MISTS. This romance will be about the Omaha Indians of Nebraska and their struggles to remain a proud people during the time when most Indians were being confined to reservations. SAVAGE MISTS promises to be filled with much passion and adventure!

I would like to hear from you all. For my newsletter, please send a legal-size self-addressed stamped envelope to:

CASSIE EDWARDS
R#3 Box 60
Mattoon, Il. 61938

My Warmest Regards,

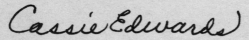

by STEF ANN HOLM

To lovely young immigrant Kristianna, the virgin Wisconsin land was the perfect place to carve a homestead. But arrogant trapper Stone Boucher disagreed violently. Stone wanted nothing to do with encroaching civilization, yet he couldn't resist Kristianna's passionate hunger. And once she was in his arms, she discovered that Stone was as exciting and untamed as the land itself.

_2983-9 $4.50 US/$5.50 CAN

by ELIZABETH CHADWICK

When Justin Harte looked into Anne McAuliffe's beguiling eyes, his troubles were only beginning. Anne could shoot better than most of his ranchhands, clean a gunshot wound as well as any doctor, and charm a rattlesnake out of striking. She was the perfect mate for him, and her soft woman's body tempted him beyond all reason. But a twist of fate had decreed she could never be his, no matter how he longed to caress her porcelain skin, or burned to taste her pleading lips...

_2976-6 $4.50 US/$5.50 CAN

SPEND YOUR LEISURE MOMENTS WITH US.

Hundreds of exciting titles to choose from—something for everyone's taste in fine books: breathtaking historical romance, chilling horror, spine-tingling suspense, taut medical thrillers, involving mysteries, action-packed men's adventure and wild Westerns.
